SLING SHOT

Also by Matthew Dunn

Sentinel
Spycatcher

SLING SHOT

MATTHEW DUNN

WILLIAM MORROW

An Imprint of HarperCollins*Publishers*

SLINGSHOT. Copyright © 2013 by Matthew Dunn. All rights reserved. Printed in the United States of America. No part of this book may be used or reproduced in any manner whatsoever without written permission except in the case of brief quotations embodied in critical articles and reviews. For information address HarperCollins Publishers, 10 East 53rd Street, New York, NY 10022.

HarperCollins books may be purchased for educational, business, or sales promotional use. For information please write: Special Markets Department, HarperCollins Publishers, 10 East 53rd Street, New York, NY 10022.

FIRST EDITION

Library of Congress Cataloging-in-Publication Data has been applied for.

ISBN 978-0-06-203802-9

13 14 15 16 17   OV/RRD   10 9 8 7 6 5 4 3 2 1

To my children and Margie, Bill and Jayne,
and to the men and women who risk their
lives operating in the secret world.

SLING SHOT

PART I

ONE

Berlin, 1995

Each step through the abandoned Soviet military barracks took the Russian intelligence officer closer to the room where men were planning genocide.

Nikolai Dmitriev hated being here.

And he loathed what he was about to do.

The barracks were a labyrinth of corridors and rooms. Icy water dripped over the stone walls, covered with paintings of Cold War–era troops and tanks; the air was rank with must; the officer's footsteps echoed as he strode onward, shivering despite his overcoat and fur hat. Previously, the complex would have housed thousands of troops. Now it resembled a decaying prison.

He turned into a corridor and was confronted by four men. Two Russians, two Americans, all wearing jeans, boots, and Windbreakers, carrying silenced handguns. The Special Forces men checked his ID and thoroughly searched him. It was the seventh time this had happened as he'd moved through the barracks. Two hundred Russian Spetsnaz operatives and an equal number of U.S. Delta, SEALs, and CIA SOG men were strategically positioned in the base to ensure that every route to his destination was defended. Their orders were clear: kill any unauthorized person who attempted to get near the men in the room.

The men motioned Nikolai forward.

Reaching the end of the corridor, he stopped opposite a door. Extending his hand to open it, he hesitated as he heard a high-pitched noise. Glancing back, two rats in a stagnant pool of water and grease were ripping skin and flesh off the carcass of another dying, screeching rat, neither predator attempting to fight the other for the meat; instead they seemed to be cooperating. He wondered if he should turn around and leave while there was still time. Everything about his presence here was wrong. But he was under orders.

He entered.

It was a large mess hall. Ten years ago, he would have seen long trestle tables and soldiers eating their meals. Now it was bare of any furnishings save a rectangular table and chairs in the center. Graffiti covered the walls, most of it crude, deriding the Soviet Union. Cigarette smoke hung motionless in the stagnant air. Rainwater poured from cracks in the high ceiling onto the concrete floor.

Sitting on one side of the rectangular table were a U.S. admiral, a U.S. general, and a CIA officer. Opposite them were two Russian generals. Between them were two files, and ashtrays. None of the men were in uniform; the presence in Germany of America's and Russia's most powerful military commanders was secret.

As was the presence of the intelligence officers. Nikolai himself was Head of Directorate S—the SVR's division with responsibility for illegal intelligence, including planting illegal agents abroad, conducting terror operations and sabotage in foreign countries, and recruiting Russians on Russian soil. The CIA officer at the table was Head of the Special Activities Division—responsible for overseas paramilitary activities and covert manipulation of target countries' political structures.

At the head of the table was a small, clean-shaven, middle-aged man with jet black hair. Dressed in an expensive black suit, a crisp, woven white silk shirt, and a blue tie that had been bound in a Windsor knot, the man removed his rimless circular glasses, polished them with one end of his tie, and smiled. "Always late for the party, Nikolai."

Nikolai did not smile. "A party requires salubrious surroundings. You've chosen unwisely, Kurt."

Kurt Schreiber nodded toward the vacant chair next to one of the Russian generals. "Sit, and shut up."

Nikolai said with contempt, "You've no authority over me, *civilian*."

Kurt chuckled. "When you and I were colonels in the KGB and Stasi, you'd have called me *comrade*."

Nikolai sat and nodded. "Different times, and I'd have been lying to your face."

Kurt's shrill, well-spoken words were rapid: "The Russian premier chose me to chair this meeting. Not you." He placed his manicured fingers together. "That is telling."

"I agree. It tells us how low we've stooped." Nikolai looked at the Americans. "Have the protocols been drawn up?"

"They have." Admiral Jack Dugan nodded toward the Russian generals. "It took us two days."

General Alexander Tatlin lit a cigarette. "It was worth the effort." The Russian exhaled smoke. "The results are precise."

"Seems to me," CIA officer Thomas Scott said, eyeing Nikolai with suspicion, "that you're not comfortable with this."

Nikolai laughed, his voice echoing in the bare hall. "How can any sane man be *comfortable* agreeing to this?"

"Kurt Schreiber's idea is brilliant."

"It's psychotic." Nikolai looked at Schreiber and repeated in a quieter voice, "Psychotic."

U.S. general Joe Ballinger pointed across the table. "Schreiber's right. The act has to shock the fuckers into submission. Man comes at you with a knife; you defend yourself with a gun. Trouble is—we haven't got anyone on our side of the fence who's got the balls to do another Hiroshima or Nagasaki. So we make the decision, and it's a sane one—as uncomfortable as it may make us."

Nikolai frowned. "You haven't reported the true meaning of the protocols to your president?"

The U.S. commander shook his head. "Nope, and we're never going to. Nor are subsequent presidents going to find out." He gestured toward his two American colleagues. "We're the only Americans who'll know the secret. No one else stateside would ever agree to this plan."

"And that's because they lack my . . . *imagination*." Kurt withdrew two ink pens, handed one to General Leon Michurin and the other to Admiral Dugan. "Signatures, please."

The Americans signed a sheet of paper inside one of the files; the Russian generals did the same in their files; they exchanged documents, countersigned, and moved both files in front of Nikolai.

The SVR officer stared at the two files. All that was needed to make this official was his signature on both documents.

"Nikolai, we're waiting." Kurt's tone was hard, impatient.

Nikolai looked at the men opposite him; ordinarily they were his enemies. He pictured the two large rats, feasting at opposite ends of the third rodent.

"Nikolai!"

The Russian intelligence officer shook his head. "This is wrong."

"And yet the alternative isn't right."

"If I sign this, millions of people could die."

"Not *millions*, you fool." Schreiber smiled. "*Hundreds* of millions."

Nikolai couldn't believe this was happening. He'd always hated Kurt Schreiber. The man was undoubtedly highly intelligent, but also untrustworthy, manipulative, and cruel, and since the collapse of East

Germany he had made millions through illegal business ventures. Now he had the ear of the Russian president, and that made him more dangerous than when he'd been a Stasi officer. "How can you live with yourself?"

Schreiber shrugged. "I view the deaths as necessary statistics. I suggest you do the same."

Nikolai was tempted to respond but knew there was no point.

Schreiber would not listen to reason.

Pure evil never did.

Nikolai gripped the pen, momentarily closed his eyes, muttered, "Forgive me," and signed both documents.

"Excellent." Kurt reached across, grabbed both files, shoved one at the Russian generals, the other at the Americans. The former Stasi colonel smiled. "The protocols for Slingshot are now in place, ready for use should ever the need arise."

"Great." General Tatlin stubbed his cigarette out. "So now we can get out of this shithole."

"Not yet." Kurt placed his hands flat on the table. "How can we ensure that no one in this room ever reveals the secret of what's missing in the files?"

Thomas Scott huffed. "Slingshot won't work if one of us talks. We agreed on that."

Kurt stared at nothing. "We did, but we need more than agreement."

"What are you proposing?"

"Insurance." Kurt looked at the men before resting his cold gaze on Nikolai. "Time can erode a man's resolve. But fear can keep him resolute."

"Speak plainly."

Kurt nodded. "One day, one of you may wake up with a crisis of conscience and decide that he can no longer carry the burden of this secret. That can't happen. So, my solution is simple and effective. The Russian president has authorized me to activate an assassin. He will be deployed as a deep-cover sleeper agent, and his orders are to kill any of you"—he looked at the CIA officer and smiled—"who *talks.*"

General Tatlin lit another cigarette and jabbed its glowing tip in the direction of Schreiber. "You expect us to live our lives with a potential death sentence hanging over us?"

Schreiber interlaced his fingers. "Yes."

Dugan laughed. "Take a look around this base, Schreiber. We're the kind of men who like to have impenetrable security wherever we go."

"Impenetrable?"

"Damn right." The admiral's tone was now angry. "Send out your assassin, for all we care. But you're going to need better insurance than that."

"There is no better insurance."

Nikolai wondered why Schreiber looked so smug. "Who's the assassin?"

The sound of rainwater striking the concrete floor seemed to intensify as Schreiber momentarily closed his eyes. "You know of him by the code name Kronos."

"Kronos!" Nikolai's stomach muscles knotted. "Why was he selected for this task?"

Before Schreiber could answer, General Ballinger asked, "Who the hell is Kronos?"

Nikolai looked at the American commanders as he began to sweat. "He was a Stasi officer, tasked on East Germany's most complex and strategic assassinations. Since the collapse of communism, he's been on the payroll of Russia. He's . . . he's our most effective killer. One hundred and eighty three kills under his belt. Always successful." As he returned his attention to Schreiber, he felt overwhelming unease. "Why was he selected?"

Schreiber opened his eyes. "Because the Slingshot secret is so vital. We needed our very best assassin to ensure that"—he swept his arm through air—"no amount of *impenetrable* security can protect a man who might betray us." Schreiber checked his watch and looked toward one of the far corners of the mess hall. In a loud, clipped tone, he called out, "Show them."

Nikolai and the others immediately followed Schreiber's gaze. At first nothing happened. Then, movement from within the shadows at the corner of the room.

A big man stepped into the light.

Standing directly underneath one of the streams of water pouring down from the ceiling.

Was motionless as he allowed the icy rain to wash over his head.

His handgun held high and trained on them.

Kronos.

Schreiber smiled and looked at the others. "Not only did Kronos get past all of your men, he did so with very precise timing. I ordered him not to enter this room until one minute ago, so that the contents of our discussion would remain confidential to only the men around this table. Since then, he's been pointing his weapon at you."

• General Michurin slammed a fist down onto the table. "How dare you make fools of us!"

Schreiber responded calmly, "It wasn't my intention to make fools of you. Rather, to demonstrate to you that you do indeed have a potential death sentence hanging over you." He darted a look at Kronos. "Give them what they need."

Nikolai felt fear course through him as he watched the German assassin take measured steps toward the table, his gun still held high. Though Nikolai was one of only a handful of SVR officers who was cleared to know all about the Kronos operations, he didn't know the assassin's real name. Moreover, this was the first time that he'd been in the presence of the man. Kronos was well over six feet tall, muscular, had black hair, and was wearing clothes identical to those Nikolai had seen worn by the base's protection detail.

Kronos lowered his weapon, withdrew a piece of paper from his jacket, tore it in half, and slapped one piece of paper on Admiral

Dugan's chest before moving to the other side of the table and doing the same with the other bit of paper on General Michurin.

Schreiber spoke to the Americans. "I suggest you bury your paper deep in the vaults of the CIA." Then to the Russians, "Put yours in the SVR vaults." He cupped his hands together. "*Never* combine them, unless there is reason to do so."

"Reason?"

"One of you needs Kronos to put a bullet in your head."

"You . . ."

"Enough, admiral!" Schreiber composed himself. "The relevance of the two pieces of paper will be made known to you if the need arises. Until that time, Kronos will vanish. No one, not even me, will know of his location. He'll wait for years, decades if necessary, until he is . . . needed."

Thomas Scott shook his head. "Our men have been here for three days." The CIA officer felt disbelief. "And when they arrived, they searched the entire base."

General Ballinger shrugged. "There's no way he could've penetrated the base today. He must have entered the complex before our men arrived and hid in a place they failed to search."

"That's the only possible explanation." Admiral Dugan pointed at Schreiber. "Next time we'll be more thorough."

Schreiber grinned, though his expression remained cold. "Kronos— show them where you were two and three days ago."

The German moved around the table, placing a photograph each in front of the Russians and Americans. Incredulity was on all of the men's faces as they stared at the shots.

Each showed the inside of their homes in America or Russia.

A local newspaper clearly showing the day's date.

And Kronos pointing the tip of a long knife toward family photos. "Bastard!"

Kronos retrieved each photo, placed them in a pile in the center of the table, and lit them with a match.

Schreiber watched the flames rise high. "Our meeting is concluded. You will take the Slingshot protocols back to your respective head-quarters. You will secrete the torn papers as instructed. You will keep your mouths shut. Otherwise, my assassin *will* find and kill you."

Kronos stepped away from the men, hesitated, then turned to face them. In a deep voice, he said, "Gentlemen, I left all of your men alive, though I must apologize for the harm I had to cause some of them."

Then he disappeared into the shadows.

TWO

Gdansk, Poland, Present Day

Will Cochrane looked toward the end of the cobbled street. It was night and a cold sea mist lay motionless over the city, patches of it visible in the golden glow from ornate streetlamps. The city's Old Town seemed deserted, though Will knew that close to his position in a café's doorway there were twenty armed and dangerous men. Some of them were his allies, some not.

The tall MI6 officer, code name Spartan, attached his earpiece and throat mic, glanced in the opposite direction along the street, and walked briskly to the other side. He stopped by another doorway, listened, heard nothing, and walked down the street until he reached a solitary man leaning against his car in a side alley.

He whispered, "The Russian defector should be here in less than one hour."

The man stared at Will, his eyes cold, anger in his hushed voice. "You're making a grave mistake going ahead with this operation. If we get this wrong, the repercussions will be catastrophic."

Will looked up and down the street again. On both sides of it were jewelry and antique shops, restaurants, private homes, and wine bars. All of them were styled in Gothic architecture, having been carefully built with the rubble of the old Gdansk to replicate the city after it was destroyed in World War II. Every business was shut up for the night. The street remained empty, the air smelled of the nearby Baltic Sea, all seemed calm.

He glanced at the man. "Luke, nothing will go wrong if you follow my orders."

Luke thrust his gloved hands under his armpits and quietly stamped his feet on the icy ground. "Your orders?" Though barely audible, his tone was unmistakably sarcastic. "I take orders from people I know, yet I know *nothing* about you beyond that you are here at the behest of the chief." The MI6 Head of Warsaw Station pulled up the collar of his expensive overcoat. "Poland's my patch. I resent your presence here and I resent your intended course of action."

Will unbuttoned his coat, checked that his sound-suppressed Russian PB 6P9 handgun was still firmly in position under his Huntsman bespoke Savile Row suit, and returned his attention to Luke. The station chief looked to be in his late forties, and no doubt was an extremely experienced and skilled intelligence operative. "I'm here to do my job. Nothing gets in the way of that."

Luke frowned. "Your job may cause irrevocable damage to diplomatic relations between Poland and the United Kingdom."

Will shook his head. "It won't come to that. Even if things go wrong, no Poles will be killed tonight."

Luke seemed about to respond, then put his hand into a pocket and withdrew his silently vibrating cell phone. Its screen was flashing to show he had an incoming call. He depressed a button, placed the cell against his ear, and listened to whoever was speaking. Ten seconds later he ended the call and placed the phone back into his coat. "Still nothing out of the ordinary at the embassy."

Luke's MI6 officers had been observing the Russian embassy in

Warsaw for three days, looking for any indication that the embassy's SVR Polish station had changed its alert status, meaning they could be aware that one of their own was about to defect.

Will felt uncertain and tense. Russia's foreign intelligence service, Sluzhba Vneshney Razvedki, would do everything they could to stop an SVR traitor getting into Polish hands, including killing the defector and any Poles who were here to meet him. He checked his watch and exhaled slowly, his breath steaming in the icy air. It was nearly 2:00 A.M. In the distance, a port foghorn droned, its noise echoing off the nearby buildings. As the sound abated, he asked, "Do you know anything about the Polish operatives who are out to play tonight?"

"All I know is that six men are from the state security service"— Agencja Bezpieczeństwa Wewnętrznego—"and two from its foreign operations service"—Agencja Wywiadu. Luke's expression seemed bitter. "In all probability, I've worked with some of the men you're planning to render unconscious tonight."

"One of the two AW men will be the defector's handler." Will rubbed fingers through his short, dark hair. "You're certain your team's hidden from them?"

Luke shrugged. "I can't be certain of anything. But I got all twelve of them from London. They arrived this morning. They're MI6 Q operatives."

Men who knew how to stay hidden. Q operatives were all former British Special Forces.

Will asked, "What are the Poles wearing?"

"Windbreaker jackets, jeans, and combat boots."

"And our men?"

"Similar, but just before the green light's given they'll don black baseball caps so that they're distinguishable from the Poles."

"What weapons do the Q men have?"

Luke muttered, "Silenced pistols and tranquilizer guns."

"That's all? I asked for them to be armed with suppressed semiautomatics."

"And I decided to ignore your request." Luke shook his head. "We shouldn't be doing this to the Polish operatives. This is their country, and the defector's coming to them. Bloody hell, I liaise with the Polish intelligence services every day. The moment we got the tip-off, I should have been tasked to use my influence with the Poles to see if they could share the defector's intelligence with us."

"Impossible. You know that would have meant that we'd have to tell them how we got the information."

Luke sighed. "So you decided to turn everything on its head, overrule my authority, and construct a kidnap operation."

"Not kidnap, a sleight of hand."

Luke retorted angrily, "When this is over, I'll make an official complaint about your actions."

Will grabbed Luke's jaw. "I've had enough of your crap!"

The shock on Luke's face was vivid.

Will held him firm. "We're not here to snatch the defector from the Poles. We're here because you told the Russians about the defector. And because of that, we had no choice other than to come here to protect the Poles and ensure they got their man."

Luke's eyes were wide with fear. He tried to speak.

But Will squeezed harder. "Save your breath. You've been under investigation for weeks, your burst transmissions monitored by GCHQ. But rather than have you lifted, we wanted to let you continue speaking to the Russians, with information that we fed you. False information, of course. But when you told the SVR about the defector's use of the exfiltration route, matters had to be accelerated." He pulled Luke's head close to his. "I couldn't tell the Qs what was really happening in case they accidentally let slip a detail that would make you suspicious. It's a *real shame* that you underequipped them." He smiled, though he felt nothing but anger. "I'm told that money was the reason behind your treachery. Pity really. I'd have had more respect for you if you betrayed us for other reasons. Still, doesn't matter now because you're fucked and we're fucked."

Will thrust Luke's head back.

Luke winced and rubbed his bruised jaw as sweat poured down his forehead. "I . . ."

"Shut up!" Will pulled out his Russian handgun and placed its nozzle against Luke's head. "Is there anything you want to say to me?"

"My family . . ." His voice trailed.

"I'll make sure they're comfortable, are looked after, and are told that you were killed in the line of duty. No one needs to know."

Luke closed his eyes and quietly said, "That's kind of you." He bowed his head. "Pull the trigger."

Will hesitated.

"Pull the trigger!"

Still, Will did nothing.

"Please! I can't face the disgrace."

"You're already disgraced." Will gripped his gun tight, but his trigger finger was motionless. Even though he was under orders to kill the traitor, something was holding him back.

Luke opened his eyes, raised his head, and looked at him with wet eyes. "Do you pity me?"

Will felt confused, no longer angry. "Perhaps."

Luke nodded slowly. "I don't deserve your pity." His tone strengthened. "Men are going to die tonight because of me. Do your duty! Pull the trigger!"

Will sighed, knowing Luke was right, and spoke with a genuinely bemused tone. "Why did you do this?"

Luke shrugged. "The world's full of self-seeking charlatans. I'm just one of many."

Will frowned. "And men like me have to clean up your mess?"

"It appears that must be the case."

"I wish I didn't have to keep doing that."

He shot Luke in the head.

• • •

Will stood alone, facing the fog-covered Baltic Sea. Beside him was the mouth of the river Vistula; three miles upriver was the heart of Gdansk. During the daytime, the waterway was heavily used by pleasure cruisers and merchant vessels bringing goods into the heart of the city. Tonight, a Polish cargo ship carrying the Russian defector would be sailing up the channel, having collected the SVR officer from Saint Petersburg, in northwestern Russia. MI6 had gained this information from one of its Polish assets, working in the Polish consulate in Saint Petersburg where the Russian had walked in to defect. The consulate contained no Polish intelligence operatives and it was the asset, a low-ranking diplomat, who had been instructed to inform the defector of the exfiltration route. But the asset did not know the exact location where the boat would stop to deliver the spy to the AW and ABW men.

He adjusted his radio throat mic and spoke quietly. "This is Zulu. I'm in position, but this sea mist is making visibility diabolical."

The Q team leader responded in a deep voice. "Delta 1. We've not moved. Nor have the locals. Most of us are in position either side of the river, spread out over one mile from north to south. What's your local doing?"

Will trained his night-vision binoculars on the solitary Polish operative standing two hundred yards away on the opposite side of the river mouth. "Just waiting. Nothing else is happening here aside from the damn port foghorn going off every minute." He checked his watch. It was nearly 3:00 A.M. The boat should have arrived by now, though no doubt the coastal fog was slowing its progress toward shore. His body tensed. "I've got lights out at sea. They're moving parallel to the coast, east to west."

"Delta 1: heard. It might be the target vessel. Perhaps it's following a deep channel until it can turn toward you. Any reaction from your local?"

"Nothing yet. The boat's changing direction. Looks like it could

be turning toward shore. Hold." Silence. "The local's pulled something out of his jacket."

More silence.

Then, "He's looking through binoculars. He's standing very still,
just watching." Will's chest muscles tightened. "Okay, he's put the
binos away. He's lighting a cigarette. He's not doing anything else.
Wait. I can see it now. It's not the target. Repeat, not the target. Just a
small Maritime Search and Rescue vessel doing a patrol of the harbor."

"Delta 1: okay."

Will glanced at the Pole. "Local's binos are back out. He's looking
out to sea. Moving his head slightly, meaning he hasn't seen anything
yet."

The foghorn blared.

"The SAR vessel's slowed right down and has switched on its port
searchlight. The local's motionless. He's got a cell phone by his head,
still looking through his binos. I'd say he's spotted something."

"Delta 1. We've got one local on Ku Ujsciu on his cell and on the
move, walking quickly toward Roberta de Plelo on the east bank of
the river. Plus another now moving down Oliwska toward the river's
west bank."

The rest of the Q team reported that the Polish men they were
watching were also moving.

Will's heart rate increased. "Okay. The locals have been alerted and
are taking up formation. All Delta: baseball caps on." His hand moved
to his pistol. "I've got different lights out at sea. The SAR's turning
toward them. Its searchlight should pick up something any moment..."
Will saw several more lights, some electric blue, others red. They were
spread out, the highest about ten yards above sea level. Then he heard
the distinct sound of engines. He waited. The lights came closer, and it
was now possible to see glimpses of metal around them. Gradually the
ship emerged out of the darkness and fog. "Got it! Cargo ship."

Delta 1 shot back, "Ship's name?"

"Hold."

Nobody else spoke as they waited for Will.

"Searchlight's fully covering the vessel. The name's clear. It's the *Paderewski*. Repeat, it's the target!" Will watched the Polish operative. "My guy's holding something in his hand. He's walking right up to the seawall. Now he's leaning against it. He grips the object in two hands."

The *Paderewski* was getting closer to shore, coming right toward the local and the river mouth. The SAR moved closer to it until it was out of sight, hidden behind the *Paderewski*.

Will could feel his pulse throbbing in his temples. "The local's holding a torch, pointing it toward the target. He gives one, two, three, four, five . . . yes, five flashes . . ." He looked at the *Paderewski*. "Nothing yet from the target . . . nothing . . . now! One, two, three . . . four, five, six, seven flashes from the deck."

"Is the boat slowing down or changing course?" Delta 1 spoke rapidly.

"No, it's still heading right for the river mouth."

"Do you think the all-clear signal's been given?"

"Yes. The *Paderewski*'s committed to the river entrance. It hasn't got a turning circle to change course."

"In that case we're ready."

"Hold on, Delta 1." Will broke into a sprint, moving west to get a line of sight on the SAR. "The SAR vessel's following the *Paderewski*."

Delta 1 responded immediately. "Is it making any attempt to stop the target?"

"No."

"Is the target aware of the SAR vessel?"

"Must be. The SAR's barely ten yards behind it. Its searchlight is illuminating the rear half of the boat."

"This is odd."

"Agreed!" Will knew that the greatest hazard for any craft around here tonight was in the harbor. The *Paderewski* was about to enter a river that had urban and transportation lighting on either side of it. It would be safe and of no concern to the SAR vessel. Plus, if it was a routine escort, the SAR would be in front. He felt his stomach churn as he scrutinized the SAR. It was approximately twenty yards long, five yards wide; the distance between deck and water line was less than one yard; speed was eight to ten knots; engine noise was high pitched to medium. "I can't be certain, but I'd say the SAR vessel is heavy laden."

"Could that cargo be men?"

"How the hell would I know? But if it is, I'd hazard a guess there are at least ten men in there."

"Looks like more of our ABW and AW friends are out to play tonight, on board the SAR vessel, making sure that their prize is not attacked from behind."

"I know that!"

"Do we abort?"

Will's mind raced fast. "No."

The *Paderewski* was now in the river, heading toward Gdansk.

"Delta 1: We've got locals bolting northwest toward the oncoming *Paderewski*, handguns out. Something's wrong."

Will watched his local sprinting away from the coast, paralleling the *Paderewski*. "It's the SAR vessel that's wrong. That's what's spooked our Polish friends. It's not carrying ABW or AW men. It must be a team of SVR. They've come to assassinate the defector." Will began running. "All Delta: do not touch the locals. You have a new target and objective. Converge on the SAR vessel and get ready to kill anything inside it. Our priority now is to ensure the ABW and AW men get their defector."

"Delta 1. The Poles will think we're hostiles."

"Damn right." Will sprinted alongside the river. "But you mustn't kill any of them." After two minutes of passing cranes and warehouses adjacent to the river, he called out, "I'm about six hundred yards inland from the river mouth, following the target. The SAR's right on its tail. I can see the driver in the cabin, no one else."

"Reckon the SVR's going to do a hit and run the moment the *Paderewski* docks and the defector steps off the boat."

"Where are you?"

"I'm on the west bank of the river. The *Paderewski*'s just coming into my view, heading toward my position."

"Is there anywhere around you that the boat could dock?"

"No. I think it's going to head farther south toward the city, where most of the tourist vessel berths and cargo unloading bays are. But we still can't discount the possibility that the *Paderewski* may simply slow down, pull alongside an area of flat land, and allow the defector to jump off."

"Okay. Move south, ahead of the target. I'll stay on the boats."

"Be careful. I've got visual of two locals about seven hundred yards south of your position and on the same side of the river as you."

Will continued running. Ahead of him, the river forked. Between the forks was an island that was one mile long and half a mile wide. "Both vessels are taking the left fork into the Kanal Kaszubski." Will ran even faster. "Delta 1: that canal travels for one mile before it rejoins the main river. Half your team and I are now completely blind to the target vessels. There are only two bridges to that island: the crossing in the west and the one in the south. Move to the southern road crossing. From there you'll be able to pick up sight of the *Paderewski* and SAR and continue to tail them if they keep moving beyond the island, or enter the island if they stop at that location. I'll take the western crossing onto the island."

Two Polish operatives ran across Will's path and pursued the SAR and the *Paderewski*. Will ducked for cover before they could see him, waited five seconds, and ran east along Na Ostrowiu. Within five seconds, he was crossing the river. Within ten seconds he was on the large island. The place was silent; sea mist hung thickly over the security lit warehouses, moored cargo ships, jetties, cranes, small factory units, roads, and the waterways around the island. He slowed to a jog and began moving across the island toward the canal containing the target vessels. He saw no movement of any sort and heard nothing beyond the distant foghorn. The whole island seemed deserted.

"Delta 1. The *Paderewski*'s slowing down." The Q operative's voice was a near whisper. "It's about two-thirds of the way along the canal. Speed now about five knots. Four locals near us, all of them holding handguns."

"Received." Will dashed along a narrow gap between two warehouses, gripping his handgun tightly with one hand, searching for glimpses of the canal. But so far all he could see were more industrial shipping units. The air was even colder here; the whole place felt eerie. He ran alongside a stack of big freight containers before reaching a small road. On the other side of it were two large warehouses, between them an alleyway. Lights were visible at the far end of the gap. He entered the gap, nearly fell as his feet struck loose girders on the ground, staggered to stay upright, and continued sprinting. The lights belonged to lamps straddling the broad canal.

"Delta 1. The *Paderewski*'s now at a crawl and so is the SAR."

Will slowed to a walk. Sweat from his exertions felt cold against his skin. He held his gun high with both hands, searching for sight of Russians or the local intelligence operatives. Reaching a road by the side of the canal, he stood still and looked left. Cargo boats were moored on either side of the waterway, derrick cranes beside them; a row of warehouses was adjacent to the road, larger ones on the other side of the canal. But here the icy mist seemed thicker and was moving slowly along the canal toward him. He was blind to anything beyond a forty-yard radius of his location. "I'm in position."

"There's a man who's emerged onto the deck of the SAR vessel." Delta 1's voice was still a whisper, but urgent. "Tall, athletic, dressed in overcoat and suit, hand inside his jacket."

Will saw lights draw closer along the canal.

The *Paderewski*.

"The tall man moves across the SAR's deck, he faces the island bank, he looks at the *Paderewski*, he looks back at the bank, he runs forward, jumps, and lands on the island. He pulls his hand out of his jacket. He's holding a pistol."

Will looked sharply away from the encroaching *Paderewski* toward the road he was on. The big Russian was somewhere in the darkness ahead of him.

"The *Paderewski*'s pulling alongside the island. Four Polish sailors are on deck."

Will watched the ship. "What's the SAR doing?"

"It's still right on the ass of the *Paderewski*. No sign of any other men coming out of it though."

"They're waiting. Everyone: stand by."

"Delta 1. We've got two locals moving across the southern crossing onto the island. Their handguns are out. My men are following them." Silence. "The *Paderewski*'s stationary. Two of the sailors are on the island, roping the ship to the berth. Four Delta and four locals are now on the east bank of the canal, close to the two vessels. Our locals have still got their guns trained on the SAR. Another man on the deck of the *Paderewski*. He's not dressed like the sailors."

Will took five quick paces toward the ship, but could not distinguish anything beyond the bow of the vessel. "That could be our defector."

"Men emerging on the SAR's deck! Four of them, now six, now . . . now eleven! All armed with assault rifles."

Pistol shots rang out.

"The Poles have opened fire!"

The sound of machine gun fire was deafening. "Russians are returning fire. Some of them are jumping onto the island."

"Take them down!" Will ran along the road toward the gunfight.

Four shots came from his left. One of the bullets ripped through the front of Will's overcoat, narrowly missing his body. He spun to face the direction of the shots, saw two Poles emerge from the darkness pointing their handguns at him, dived to the ground as they fired again, rolled, got to his feet, and sprinted as they kept shooting. The noise of a different handgun came from behind the Polish operatives. Will looked in that direction while continuing to run, caught a brief glimpse of a man wearing a baseball cap and pointing his gun at the sky, knew that man had to be a Delta operative, saw the Poles spin around to face the Q man, and then saw him dash away into the fog. The Poles spun back to face Will, but the Delta operative's distraction had enabled Will to get farther away from them and out of their sight.

He reached the side of the *Paderewski*. Two sailors were lying on the ground, immobile and moaning in pain. He was about to move to them when he felt a tremendous force on his shoulder blade. He collapsed to his knees in agony. A man emerged from behind him. He was tall and dressed in an overcoat and suit—he had to be the SVR officer. Will tried to raise his arm to shoot him, but winced in pain from the movement and involuntarily lowered it. The Russian ignored him, walking quickly to the sailors. He grabbed one of them, hauled him onto his shoulder, carried him twenty yards away from the boat, lowered him onto the ground, and then did the same with the other sailor.

Over the sound of near continuous gunfire, Delta 1 screamed, "The defector's jumped onto the island. He's somewhere close to you."

Gritting his teeth, Will forced himself onto his feet, this time managing to keep his arm moving upward. Pointing his gun at the Russian, he saw the man turn to face him. He was holding something in his hand.

A detonator.

Four explosions happened in quick succession to his right, causing Will to twist and fall back to the ground. Shards of metal flew through the air; smoke and fire seemed to cover everything. Will covered his head and lay flat on the ground, feeling small pieces of debris fall over him. He turned his head, his ears ringing from the explosions, and saw that the *Paderewski* was ablaze and beginning to sink.

He looked at the Russian. The man was facing Will and firing, but not at him. The SVR officer began running and by the time he passed Will's prone body he was at full sprint while still shooting. Will rolled onto his side, ignored the intense heat from the fire in the canal, saw an unarmed man disappear down the road and saw the

Russian chasing him. He looked back and frowned as he saw that the two sailors had not been hurt by the explosion because the man who had blown up the boat had moved them out of harm's way.

Getting to his feet, he began running after the Russian, but after a few paces he heard a hail of machine gun fire. He threw himself sideways onto the ground and rolled away until he was behind the cover of a warehouse. More bullets hit the wall by his side, causing chunks of brick to fly off it.

Will clutched his mic against his throat. "Delta 1: I'm going after the big SVR guy. He's pursuing an unarmed man who is almost certainly the defector."

"Delta 1." The Q man was screaming over the sound of gunfire. "Men have just taken out my two Poles. There're six of them, and they're firing at us as well. But they're not the Russian SVR men."

"What?"

Delta 1 did not answer, and before Will could speak again, another voice shouted in his earpiece. "Delta 9. My two locals have just engaged four SVR men on the island. I'm going to get on their flank and assist the Poles with . . . What the hell?"

Will shouted, "Delta 9? What's happening?"

The noise of automatic gunfire was continuous.

"Delta 9: my locals and the SVR men are dead. Killed by the other team. I can see you, Zulu. I'm thirty yards behind you."

Will got to his feet just as the Q operative got alongside him. Both men began running east, in the direction of the big SVR officer and the defector, their guns pointing at the darkness and fog ahead of them. Muzzle flashes were visible coming from the other side of the canal on their left.

"No, no!"

Will grabbed his throat mic. "Delta 1?"

Nothing.

"Delta 1?"

"Delta 1: They're . . . they're dead."

"Who?"

"The Russians, the Poles, my men. Fucking everyone!"

Incredulity struck Will. "Get onto the island! Head west. We're pursuing the defector."

Will and Delta 9 suddenly stopped. In the distance ahead of them they could see the long road that led over the western bridge. Lights straddled it, and easily visible were three men running at full speed toward the crossing. The defector, the SVR officer, and the last remaining Polish operative.

Will raised his gun and moved its muzzle so that it was pointing slightly in front of the Russian's body. Tensing, he pulled back the trigger. But the moment his gun fired, the SVR officer stopped. Will's bullet passed in front of him. Will looked beyond the officer to the far side of the bridge. A van was heading fast toward the defector. The Polish operative and the SVR officer began firing at the oncoming van.

Will and Delta 9 sprinted and fired at the front windows of the vehicle. As they did so, they saw the SVR officer raise his gun and fire one bullet. The defector stumbled, then carried on moving toward the van, one of his legs limping. Nine men poured out of the van. They were dressed in fire-resistant black combat overalls, upper body and head armor, and night-vision goggles, and were carrying submachine guns.

Some of them fired at the SVR officer and the Polish operative behind him; others fired toward Will and Delta 9. Whatever handgun the SVR officer was carrying, it was obviously much more powerful than those being carried by Will and his team. The officer fired two rounds at two of the hostiles and dropped them both. Will dodged left and right, fired three times at three of the hostiles, and saw his bullets simply glance off their body armor.

"Delta 1: I'm pinned down! Center of the island."

Will looked toward the end of the bridge. Three of the hostiles ran along the crossing, passed the defector, and fired their automatic weapons at the Russian and Polish operatives. Both men remained stock still, firing their handguns at the hostiles. Two other men ran to the defector, grabbed him, pulled him toward the van, and bundled him into the vehicle. Then five of the hostiles started slowly walking along the bridge, firing their weapons continuously. Will stopped. He felt useless. The hostiles knew that they controlled the ground. The Polish operative fell down as one bullet struck him in the face. The Russian's powerful handgun boomed, flipping one of the hostiles off his feet and backward. The Russian then turned, looked at the prone Polish officer, looked back at the encroaching force, fired a couple more shots toward them, and ran to the stricken Pole.

Will watched the hostiles move back to the van and enter the vehicle. The van quickly reversed. Within seven seconds it was off the bridge, out of sight, and heading west away from Gdansk.

The defector had been kidnapped.

Though they all had different objectives, Will and his team had failed, the SVR team had failed, and the Polish AW and ABW men had failed.

Will watched the SVR officer. He had a clear line of sight and could easily shoot the man. But Will lowered his gun as he saw the Russian lift the Polish operative, carry him off the bridge back onto the island, gently lower him to the ground, lean down, pat his hand on the Pole's shoulder, and stand before him for a few seconds before running away into the fog.

Will glanced at Delta 9. "Help the Pole!"

He turned east, ran across open ground toward the central road, sprinted harder when he was on it, tucked his handgun into his waistband, dashed between buildings, ran across more open ground, and barely slowed as he saw three men.

One of them was a dead hostile, lying still and awkwardly on the ground. His neck or back had been broken. Another man was next to him on the ground. He was Delta 1. Standing over him was the last hostile. He was very big, and his physique was made all the more imposing by the body and head armor. The man was grappling with the Q team leader, but clearly was on the verge of overpowering him.

Will slowed to a brisk walking pace. He felt overwhelming anger and frustration that everything tonight had gone wrong. Reaching the large hostile, he saw the man turn to face him. Will kicked his armored chest with such tremendous force the hostile was lifted off his feet. He looked at Delta 1. "Are you injured?"

Delta 1 shook his head and started to push himself off the ground. Will walked over to the prone hostile, stamped his foot on the man's unprotected throat and pressed hard. He looked at Delta 1 again. "This has been a bloody mess." He pressed harder with his foot and kept it firmly in place as the hostile grabbed his ankle with two hands and tried to wrench his leg away. Shaking his head, he muttered, "The defector's as good as dead." He looked down at the hostile. "Who sent you?"

The man tried to speak but was choking.

Will lifted his foot a fraction.

"We're "—the hostile coughed—"private contractors."

"Who sent you?"

"Don't . . . know. My boss did, but"—his eyes glanced sideways toward his dead colleague—"he can't talk anymore."

Delta 1 moved to the dead body, expertly searched the man's clothing, looked at Will, and shook his head.

"You're British?"

"Me and a couple of others. The rest of the team came from all over."

Will nodded and stamped his foot down. The hostile arched his back, and his limbs thrashed for thirty seconds before he became motionless. Will looked away from Delta 1 toward the bridge. "Come with me."

Will jogged back toward the western bridge, Delta 1 by his side. They reached the beginning of the bridge and saw the Polish operative sitting against a wall, his face covered in his blood. Delta 9 was by him, attending to his wounds with a battlefield medical kit.

Will crouched down in front of the Pole. "Do you speak English?"

The operative opened his mouth, winced in pain, and nodded.

"Okay. We're British intelligence officers. We came here tonight to protect you from the SVR unit, but I let you and your men down. I'm sorry that you didn't get the Russian defector." He glanced at Delta 9. "How bad is he?"

"He's only got flesh wounds, but they're pretty nasty and he'll need medical attention."

Will returned his attention to the Pole. "We going to take you to a hospital."

Police sirens rang out in the distance.

"Help is on its way." The Polish operative grimaced as he adjusted position. "I'll be looked after. But you need to get out of here. If they find you, the police and security services will arrest you for operating illegally in Poland." He breathed in deeply and added, "I'll not say anything to my colleagues about you three. That will buy you some hours to get out of Poland. But they'll conduct a forensic analysis of this gun battle and in all probability will soon realize that there are men unaccounted for."

Will shook his head. "Thank you. But I can't ask you to cover for us and jeopardize your career."

The Pole shrugged. "It's dark, weather is bad, I'm injured. I could easily have failed to see three men escape this place."

Will nodded.

The AW officer spat blood onto the ground. "The whole thing was a setup."

Will frowned. "What do you mean?"

The operative looked at him. "After he carried me away from danger, the big SVR officer briefly spoke to me. He said that the defector had used my Agencja Wywiadu exfiltration route and resources to simply get out of Russia, but once in Poland it was never his intention to hand himself over to us. Instead, he'd come to Gdansk to be taken away by the team that showed up here tonight. The SVR man knew that and was here to try to stop it from happening. He said the defector was carrying something that must not get in the wrong hands."

Will felt his stomach tighten. "What?"

The Pole looked along the bridge toward the direction where the van had disappeared with its prize. "He's carrying a single piece of paper. The SVR officer told me that it's imperative the paper's retrieved, that my country's security service must do everything to stop the defector and his friends from escaping Poland. He said that he would hunt them down and that we should not attempt to stand in his way." He looked back at Will. "He told me that the paper is lethal."

THREE

The four senior CIA officers sat in silence within a windowless room in the agency's Langley headquarters. Save a table and chairs, the room was empty of anything else including telephones or any other electronic equipment. On the oak boardroom table between the men was a jug of ice water, four glasses, nothing else.

Tibor, the oldest of the men, was in his mid-forties and had twenty years of intelligence service under his belt. Wearing a bespoke blue striped Adrian Jules suit, a pink French-cuff shirt with cutaway collar, a silk tie, and handcrafted black leather brogues, and with his dark hair styled and held in place by cream, the Bostonian looked like a Wall Street investment banker rather than a government employee. "I asked you here because we've got a problem. Lenka Yevtushenko has momentarily reappeared on the radar before disappearing just as quickly."

"Where?"

"When?"

"How?"

Tibor took a swig of his water and winced as the cold liquid produced a few seconds of pain inside his head. "Gdansk. Yesterday." He paused. "How? Well, that's a bit more complex."

Damien, the blond man to his right, snapped, "But no matter how complex, we still know why he reappeared. Right?"

"Wrong." This came from a Texan named Marcus. "I'm betting Tibor's a little confused. *Right,* Tibor?"

Tibor nodded. "Right. But so would you be."

Lawrence, the youngest of the four, spoke, "Blow by blow, Tibor."

Tibor rubbed his temples. "Yevtushenko did a walk-in to the Polish consulate in Saint Petersburg saying he wanted to make the transition to the other side. And he said he had some major coin for the ferryman."

"Defection on Russian soil?"

"Stupid."

"More likely calculated." The pain in Tibor's head receded. "Looks like it was a setup."

"Exploiting the Polish exfiltration route?"

"Seems that way."

Damien shook his head. "Yevtushenko isn't clever enough to have thought this up himself. Someone gave him instructions."

Tibor agreed. "But that someone met some unexpected resistance. The Russians tailed Yevtushenko to Gdansk and most likely would have grabbed him there had it not been for the fact that an MI6 team was also on the ground."

"They were the ones who orchestrated the ruse?"

"No. The Brits were there because they had a tip-off about the defection from one of their assets in the consulate. They were deployed to shadow and protect the Poles, and to help them get Yevtushenko. MI6 didn't set this up. Someone else did. And Yevtushenko managed to get to that person."

The men were silent for a moment.

Damien muttered, "It has to be the Israelis, and yet . . ."

"And yet I agree with what you were about to say. It would have been a sledgehammer approach to grab such an unremarkable SVR target." Lawrence drummed his fingers on the table. "What's MI6's take?"

Tibor answered, "They think he's in the hands of private individuals, not a state intelligence service."

"And how do you know about the Gdansk operation?"

"Our golden source." Tibor was deep in thought. "Gentlemen. Perhaps we should agree with MI6 that Yevtushenko was extracted by private individuals, and if that is the case, perhaps we should conclude that he was extracted from Russia for other reasons."

"Reasons that won't trouble us?"

"Possibly." Tibor studied his three colleagues. Though he was older than them, everyone in the room was of equal rank. They trusted each other completely, and while technically they answered to the director of the CIA, in practice the team answered only to themselves. "There's no doubt that we were right in our assessment of Yevtushenko. He wasn't the big fish we initially thought he was, but he clearly has immense value to someone. And whatever that value is, I think it has nothing to do with our mistake in giving Yevtushenko's name to the Israelis."

"Mistake?" Damien snorted. "What we did was damn right illegal!"

"A tactical error, my friend. Nothing more, nothing less. And it was done with the best of intentions."

"Tactical error or not, it has serious jail time written all over it if the truth is ever discovered. I'd dearly like to track down Simon Rübner and grab him by the throat."

Tibor smiled. "Why? Because we fell for the Mossad officer's trick and failed to realize that he was an Israeli double agent? Come on, we must move on from that. We've got other priorities now."

"We're lucky the Brits didn't get their hands on Yevtushenko." Marcus frowned. "You think it's case closed for them?"

Tibor shrugged. "I can't be sure. Not yet. But I do know that the field officer who was in charge of the Brits' team in Gdansk is MI6's best operative."

Lawrence muttered, "Shit. He'll have the bit between his teeth. It's highly unlikely to be *case closed*."

Tibor placed his hands flat on the table and studied his three colleagues. He hesitated before saying, "I have information that could allow us to obtain an unorthodox solution."

"We're listening."

The officer paused for thought. "I have the field officer's name and home address."

"From the golden source?"

"Of course."

They sat in silence for a while. Lawrence was the first to speak. "We can't do anything with that information. It's too risky."

Tibor disagreed. "The information *can* be used without us getting our hands dirty."

Lawrence narrowed his eyes. "Give the name and address to someone who'll do the work for us?"

"That's what I'm thinking."

Damien clapped his hands. "We give it to Yevtushenko . . ."

"Who relays this data to whoever masterminded his exit from Russia . . ."

"A man who's not going to sit around and wait for MI6's finest to come knocking on his door."

Lawrence said, "Yevtushenko will have destroyed his cell phone. We've got no way of sending him a message."

Tibor grinned. "You're forgetting about his squeeze. I reckon that if we send the message to her, she'll find a way to get in touch with him: another cell number that no one knows about, a safe-deposit box, a third party. Who knows how she'll do it, but we do know that Yevtushenko's biggest weakness is his devotion to her. He'll have cut all other ties, but I suspect he'll have kept lines open with his woman. We gotta hope they have some private communication system in place."

"It's a long shot."

"We've got nothing to lose by trying it. Trouble is, Rübner must have told him we're Agency." Tibor drummed his fingers on the table. "Though, does that matter? He'll be confused about our motives, but he can't ignore the message. We tell him that we're sorry we misled him a year ago, that we still care about him, are looking out for him, have learned that he's got himself caught up in something big, that the Brit is coming after him." He smiled. "This should bury the Yevtush-enko issue once and for all. We encourage the private contractors to take the MI6 officer out of the equation. Are we all in agreement?"

The others nodded.

"Excellent." Tibor glanced at the door. Beyond it, thousands of CIA officers would be hard at work. Few of them knew about the existence of the four-man team in the room.

A team that carried the code name Flintlock.

And the CIA director's nickname, The Chosen Ones.

"Then let's set things in motion." Tibor nodded toward the exit. "But, as ever, not a word to the children."

FOUR

William Cochrane pulled up the collar of his overcoat, thrust his hands into pockets, and walked through London's Pimlico district. Rain lashed his face as he moved along quiet residential streets, apparently unaware of the white Regency houses, expensive parked automobiles, and the occasional umbrella-carrying pedestrian.

Turning a corner, he stopped for a moment and looked around, more out of habit than concern. He could perceive no security threat to the safe house. He saw nothing unusual, so he crossed the street and moved farther down the route before ringing a doorbell.

An elderly lady, immaculately dressed and with a streak of blonde in her otherwise silver hair, opened the door, barely glanced at Will, and beckoned him to enter. Stamping his feet on the doormat, he removed his overcoat and chucked it onto a side table before striding along the corridor toward a large living room.

Three men were in the room.

One of them was Delta 1.

One was Delta 9.

They'd both arrived back in the United Kingdom yesterday.

The third man was Will's MI6 Controller, Alistair, the Cohead of the Spartan Section, a joint MI6/CIA task force that was top secret and reported directly to the British prime minister and the U.S. president.

The tall, athletic Q operatives, dressed in jeans and sweaters, were sitting in sumptuous armchairs, their heads bowed over steaming mugs of tea. Alistair was standing with his back to Will, staring out of the window.

"Morning, all." Will rubbed his hands to aid circulation.

Alistair turned to face him, withdrawing a pocket watch from the waistcoat of his Royal Navy three-piece suit. He sighed. "It's nearer to afternoon. Did you get . . . *delayed*?"

Will shook his head. "I had to route via three different airports to get back. It took some time."

"*My* time." Alistair replaced the timepiece into his pocket. The slender, blond-haired, middle-aged man looked uncharacteristically weary.

Will slumped into a sofa and looked around. The safe house was like many others he'd been to in London—tastefully furnished, immaculate, homely yet unlived-in. The woman he'd met at the door would have been the housekeeper, on MI6's payroll and only visiting the property to clean it, forward mail, and ensure the kitchen was stocked with food and drink for meetings like these. "I could do with a cup of tea."

Alistair nodded toward the teapot and mugs, and asked sarcastically, "Would you like me to make you one?"

"No. You'll put milk and all sorts of other nonsense in it." Will sprung up to make it himself.

"Tell me"—Alistair's tone was once again sharp—"what went wrong in Poland."

Will removed the lid to the teapot, shaking his head as he saw that the brew had stewed. "The unexpected happened."

"Resulting in ten dead Q operatives."

Will raised a jar of fresh tea to his nose, recognized the leaves as Assam breakfast tea, and carefully placed two spoonfuls into a cup.

"And all but one man from the AW and one man from the SVR teams killed."

Will poured boiling water over the leaves.

"A bloody massacre. The Polish government wants answers."

"Our men were deniable. No links to HMG." Will placed a tea strainer over another mug and slowly poured the tea into it. "Sure, they'll be asking around—other European countries, the Americans— and we'll all plead ignorance."

"Not all of your men were deniable."

Alistair was referring to Luke. Despite his alias documentation, it would only be a matter of time before the Polish police matched Luke's dead body to the fully declared post of Head of Warsaw Station.

"Your mission was an utter failure!"

Will took a sip of the tea and momentarily closed his eyes in appreciation. Turning, he stared at Alistair. "It was a failure." He looked at Delta 1. "I'm truly sorry for what happened to your men."

The Q operative stared at him and asked with a deep south London accent, "Did you know the Russians were coming?"

"That's none of your—"

Will held a hand up to interrupt Alistair. "Yes, but I didn't know about the private contractor team. That was the unexpected part."

Delta 1 considered this. "Then you've got nothing to be sorry about. If the contractors hadn't turned up, together with the Poles we'd have held the Russians off."

"Aye." Delta 9 spoke with a strong Scottish lilt. "But even so, we were underequipped."

"You were." Will gave a slight shake of his head to Alistair to indicate that he wasn't going to mention Luke's treachery. "That was due to a breakdown in communication. We're looking into it right now."

Delta 1 carefully placed his mug down before looking up at Will.

"Whoever's responsible for the breakdown in communication needs to be strung up. I've lost most of my team."

Will recalled the frozen look of terror on Luke's face as he'd dumped his dead body in the trunk of the Head of Warsaw Station's car. "What are your names and backgrounds?"

Delta 1 answered first. "Mark Oates. Nine years in the Qs, two as team leader. Prior to that, twelve years in the Royal Marines, eight of which SBS."

Will looked at Delta 9.

"Adam Tark. Five years in the Qs. Before that seven years in the SAS."

Will frowned. "I once knew a Scot called Ross Tark who was also SAS."

"Aye, he was my younger brother." Adam smiled. "Always followed me around." His smile vanished. "Were you there when he died?"

Will answered, "No," as he recalled gathering up Ross's entrails and inserting them back into his stomach. The SAS soldier had been gutted by a Russian Spetsnaz commander during Will's last mission. That operation was so sensitive that everyone involved in it was instructed to never speak to anyone else about what happened, anyone including security-cleared relatives of those who'd died in the mission.

"And who are you?" Mark flexed his muscular hands.

"That"—Alistair held up a hand toward Will—"really *is* none of your business."

Will studied the Q men. Adam looked nothing like his deceased brother. Though probably in his early thirties, he was prematurely balding with graying hair, and clearly had undergone emergency reconstructive surgery on what would have once been a handsome face. Mark was older, probably early forties, with cropped brown hair. His face was weathered, tanned, and partially covered with stubble. Aside from their physique, both men shared one trait. Their eyes looked dead.

Will asked Mark, "What's your brief right now?"

"Fuck knows. Vauxhall Cross"—MI6 HQ—"wants us to report in tomorrow. I suspect we're going to be put before the Inquisition. Seen it happen to other Qs before. Our bollocks will be squeezed until we're without a job and a hair's breadth away from prison."

"But you've done nothing wrong!"

"On paper, I did nothing right."

Will looked at Alistair. "We can't let that happen. We owe these men, plus they performed impeccably."

Alistair frowned. "And what would you have me do?"

"We're light by two men on the paramilitary front. Make them part of the section. If you do that, you'll save them from the bureaucrats."

Alistair looked affronted. "Selection to the unit is rigorous . . ."

"It is. And Mark and Adam passed the test in Gdansk."

Alistair darted a look at the Q men. "Gentlemen, would you be kind enough to leave the room for a moment?"

"Let them stay. After what they've been through, I believe we can talk openly in front of them." Will nodded at Mark. "My name's Will. There *are* real sensitivities around what I do, but don't take it as a slight against you that we can't go into what they are."

Mark shrugged. "Fine by us."

Alistair moved up to Will and whispered, "What would Roger and Laith think?"

Roger Koenig and Laith Dia. The two CIA SOG paramilitary officers who were permanently seconded to the Spartan Section.

"They'll want to know they're working alongside professionals of equal caliber. Once they've ascertained that's the case, their respect for you will grow exponentially. They'll have seen that you've put your powerful wings around two men just like them, and that will make you stand out from the pencil pushers."

"I don't need faux flattery."

"I know. But you need a team."

Alistair seemed unsure. "If I requisition them, I'll upset quite a few people."

"Since when do you care about pissing off senior management? In any case, if you requisition them for the section, nobody can do anything about it."

Alistair nodded slowly, deep in thought. "It would, I concede, complete the team." He turned toward the Q men and studied them for a moment before speaking in a commanding voice. "Gentlemen, in days gone by, condemned men were sometimes given a choice between the rope or a lifetime of serving on the very worst battlefronts. I'm giving you a similar choice."

Mark smiled. "Nobody's going to put me in a rope."

Adam nodded. "My sentiments, exactly. But what is this section?"

Alistair wagged a finger. "You'll need to sign some nondisclosure documents before I get into that." He glanced at Will. "Then, things will become clearer."

Will looked at Mark and Adam. "Once you've signed the papers, you'll be outside of all other chains of command. Trust Alistair, trust me, trust everyone else in the section, but no one else." He guided Alistair away from the Q men and asked quietly, "Patrick?"

The CIA cohead of the section.

Alistair frowned. "What about him?"

"He needs to be here, together with Roger and Laith. When are they flying over?"

"For what?"

Will felt exasperated. "You know *what* the AW operative told us. We can't allow that piece of paper to remain in the wrong hands. The mission is clear . . ."

"It's not! We don't know anything about the paper."

"We know its value. What happened in Gdansk proved that."

Alistair spoke with deliberation. "You can't expect me to deploy the section on something so intangible. And I'm certainly not going to do so just to allow you to make up for the fiasco in Poland."

Will snapped furiously, "It's got nothing to do with that. The Russians deployed a whole SVR team to retrieve the paper."

"Then let them find it."

"What happens if they can't? There's only one of them left."

"They'll send him more bodies." Alistair shook his head. "You can't expect Patrick and me to take this to our premiers to get them to sign off on the section's deployment."

"I can."

"This is wrong."

"Have I ever been wrong in the past?"

"Yes, lots of bloody times."

"I mean in terms of the results of the operations I've conducted?"

Alistair hesitated before saying, "You've got nothing more than a hunch that this is worth pursuing."

"Perhaps, but every operational instinct in me says it's vital we get involved."

Alistair sighed. "We'd have to tell the premiers that we're recommending this course of action purely based on your *instincts*."

"Tell them what you like. Just make sure they sign off."

"And what if we do deploy and you're wrong, William?" His expression changed to one that looked like sympathy. "The premiers' patience with you is already stretched to near breaking point."

Will shrugged. "What are they going to do? Find someone to replace me? I wish them luck, because I doubt anyone else is able to complete the Program."

"They know that!" As did Alistair. Eight elite MI6 officers had not only failed the Spartan Program before Will had gone through it to earn the code name Spartan, they'd been left psychologically and physically damaged and had needed to leave the service. "But things are changing. There are cries for transparency from the intelligence community, demands to do away with so-called *shadowy* task forces and the like. This is not just about you. If we get this wrong, some might grab this as an opportunity to shut us down."

Will nodded slowly. "I see."

"I'm so glad that you do."

"But conversely, if we get this right we might turn some of those detractors into supporters."

"That's a damn big risk."

"Worth it though, don't you think?"

Alistair was motionless. "I concede, you have always been *right* about the things that matter. But there is a first time for everything. This would be an almighty gamble."

"Please, Alistair. Say what you like to the premiers. Position it however you think is best. Just get them to sign off on this."

Alistair lowered his head. "If you're wrong and they shut down the section because of that, all of the section members, me included, would be given other jobs in the service or the Agency." He lifted his head. "But you've been operating on your own for too long. No one would want someone with your kind of skill set. It would be over for you."

Will smiled, patted Alistair gently on the arm, and said, "I know."

FIVE

Kurt Schreiber was motionless as he heard vehicles drive close to the main farmstead building. His back to the windows, he placed his manicured hands flat on the large cowhide writing desk and remained seated in the leather chair. Every wall in his big study was covered with bookshelves containing works on philosophy, mathematics, politics, economics, and history. Positioned over carpet and Oriental rugs were a three-piece suite and coffee table; straight-backed chairs; a rare nineteenth-century Thomas Malby globe that had cost nearly one million dollars; a beautiful burr walnut occasional table covered with antique maps and charts, and maritime navigation and timekeeping equipment; and a locked steamer trunk containing files on men and women he'd had cause to hurt or kill.

The old man ignored his surroundings and focused only on the noise of the vehicles. He knew there'd be four of them, two of which were SUVs, the other two performance sedan cars. A total of sixteen men were in the convoy; fifteen of them had worked for him for years; the sixteenth was a Russian who'd only just joined his payroll, although his employment would be short lived.

Having taken possession of its prize from the deniable private contractors, the group had taken nearly thirty-six hours to drive from Gdansk, covertly cross Poland's border with Germany, continue on to the country's northwestern state of Lower Saxony and head to the isolated farmstead, deep within the vast Lüneburg Heath.

The vehicles stopped. Doors opened and closed. A man shouted an instruction. Fast movement. More noise, this time from within the large building. Then silence.

The retired Stasi colonel smiled, removed his rimless glasses, breathed onto the lenses, and wiped them clean with a silk handkerchief. Fixing the glasses back in place, he interlaced his fingers and stared at the oak-paneled entrance. His breathing was slow; he felt very calm.

The door opened, and Simon Rübner entered. The forty-five-year-old Israeli walked up to the desk and stood before Kurt. Blond-haired, with a short groomed beard, an athletic build, and a penchant for wearing turtleneck sweaters, Simon looked more like a German U-boat commander than a former Mossad intelligence operative, which had always amused Kurt.

Simon's eyes twinkled, the slightest smile emerged, and he nodded. "We got it, Mr. Schreiber." He held out a folded piece of paper.

Kurt stared at the paper but remained motionless. "Were there any complications that I should be aware of?"

"The team had to fight their way through Gdansk. They met greater resistance than—"

Kurt held up one of his frail hands. "I'm not interested in the minutiae of who did what violent act to whom."

Simon grinned. "No complications."

Kurt nodded. "Excellent work, Simon." He glanced at the door. "Where is the Russian?"

"Yevtushenko's in the basement, with a hood over his head."

"His demeanor?"

Simon shrugged. "He's petrified. Once we got him over the

border, we put him in shackles. I think he expected a hero's welcome."

"That's what I told him to expect." He took the folded paper and placed it on his desk.

"What shall we do with him?"

Kurt waved a hand dismissively. "He's served his purpose. You've searched him?"

"Of course. No tracking devices. He brought one small bag containing clothes, his passport, cash"—he reached into his pocket—"and this."

Kurt looked at the cell phone with an expression of contempt. He hated modern communications technology because it was insecure and, in his view, made people stupid. "Is there data that's relevant?"

Simon put the phone on the desk. "It's the lack of data that's relevant. There's only one number stored, no name attached to it, and a check of his call records shows that number is the only one that's ever been used."

"Interesting." Kurt was deep in thought. "Keep him alive for now. He might be useful."

After Simon left the room, Kurt waited a few minutes before opening a small velvet-covered stationery box and withdrawing another piece of paper. He unfolded it and placed it flat on the desk. It was a copy of the paper the German assassin had handed to the Americans in 1995. In the center of the paper were ten numbers. He looked at the other paper. He hadn't seen it for nearly two decades. During that time he'd built a business empire that was highly lucrative, invisible, and illegal. Constructed on the principals of a global intelligence organization, it spanned four continents and employed over five hundred assets, most of whom were former intelligence or security service operatives. Its expertise consistently wrong-footed its competitors, though in truth it had none that were comparable or as powerful.

He unfolded the paper.

Four letters, written by Kronos. At the top of the paper, in red

Cyrillic script, were the words *Top Secret, Director, First Deputy Director, Head Directorate S, SVR Only.*

Handwritten under the code were the words, *These letters pertain to KRONOS. Access to this document is restricted to above individuals and Generals Leon Michurin and Alexander Tatlin. 7th December 1995. Head Directorate S.*

Kurt smiled and said quietly, "All that effort to get four letters."

He slid Nikolai's paper next to his paper. The four letters were now alongside the ten numbers. Combined, they revealed a global military grid reference that pinpointed one square meter in Germany's vast Black Forest. Underneath soil on that spot was an empty metal box, placed there by Kronos. The dead-letter box was the only means to contact the German assassin. Now that Schreiber had the full code, he could deposit a message in the DLB instructing Kronos that he wanted to meet him.

At that meeting, he would order the assassin to kill the traitor who wanted to betray the secret of Slingshot.

SIX

Will walked up the stairs to his third-floor apartment, unlocked the door, opened it as far as he could until it hit a large packing box, squeezed through the gap, and shut the door behind him. More packing boxes lined the corridor leading to a tiny kitchen, two bedrooms, a bathroom, and a living room. He switched on the light and moved between the boxes, careful not to hit them with the two bags he was carrying. He dropped one of the bags in the kitchen and entered the living room. Unlike the other rooms in the property, the living room was quite large and contained an Edwardian mahogany three-piece suite and chaise longue; antique rugs that he'd bought in Mongolia; free-standing shelf units containing vinyl LPs and rare secondhand books; a gilt-framed oil reproduction of J. M. W. Turner's *Fighting Temeraire;* a side table containing a Garrard 501 turntable, a stereo amplifier, and a German chinoiserie clock; and a dining table that could seat six but had never done so since he'd bought it. The place was also cluttered with more packing boxes that he'd yet to open because he hadn't had time to do so, despite having moved in a month ago.

Located in the London Borough of Southwark's two-hundred-year-old West Square, his home was in a converted house that contained four apartments. It was nothing like his previous home, a Thames-facing penthouse, and that was precisely why he'd sold and moved here.

He turned on a wall lamp, removed his overcoat, and withdrew the item from the bag. It was an LP he'd bought from his favorite record store in Soho, and he smiled as he looked at the cover. Andrés Segovia's guitar recital including Bach's "Chaconne." The rare vinyl had cost him £180, but he didn't care because he'd been searching for it for years. Reverently, he placed the disc onto the turntable and turned it on. A few seconds after the stylus had settled, the Spanish maestro's music drowned out the sound of rain lashing against the windows.

He placed kindling, coal, and a log in the fireplace, and after lighting the fuel he rubbed his cold hands close to the flames, then entered the kitchen and emptied the contents of the bag onto a tiny breakfast table. A pheasant, bacon lardons, sprigs of sage, celery, shallots, and hedgehog mushrooms, all purchased at Borough Market. He expertly deboned and panfried the meat, chopped and sautéed the vegetables, then transferred the food to a casserole pot, added cream and calvados, and put the dish into the oven.

The food was more than he needed, but that didn't matter. What mattered to Will was that he was trying to make his life different.

Alistair was right. As an adult, Will had always been alone—during his five years as a special operator within the French Foreign Legion's elite Groupement des Commandos Parachutistes, in which time he'd been frequently requisitioned by the DGSE for black operations; during his undergraduate degree at Cambridge University; during the brutal twelve-month MI6 Spartan Program, and during the subsequent eight years of near-constant deployment as an intelligence officer within the Spartan Section. He had no woman in his life and, for the most part, his encounters with women had always been brief because he was constantly terrified that his work would endanger them. Three women who had meant something to him had proven his fear correct, because they had been killed. One of them was his mother; two of them were women he believed he could have married. Friendships also eluded him, because he felt dislocated from the normal world and didn't know how to act with ordinary people. Roger Koenig was the only person who came close to being a friend, but even he was more a brother-in-arms.

Will wasn't stupid. On the contrary, he was highly intelligent and knew that his isolated existence was a result of the work that he did and the man that he'd become. A man who hated seeing innocents in danger, a man who had spent his entire adult life sacrificing himself to protect others, a man whose humanity had somehow remained completely intact yet was hidden beneath a battered, armored shell.

However, despite his fear of the potential consequences, he still fantasized about finding someone he could love and who could make him smile.

But he doubted that could happen. Not anymore. So he'd made a decision to change what he did have some control over. A new home filled with things that he'd collected over the years but had never displayed, cooking a good meal, listening to music he loved, doing anything to take his mind off the one thing he hated.

The loneliness.

He ran a bath, stripped out of his clothes, poured the remainder of the calvados into a tumbler, and eased his muscular and scarred body into the hot water. Taking a sip of the liquor, he closed his eyes.

Segovia's music was easily audible in the bathroom, but it no longer registered with Will.

What did register was that brave men had died in Gdansk because he had failed.

SEVEN

All of the Spartan Section was present in the large, damp basement of a residential house in Vienna's old town. The Austrian safe house was officially the property of MI6, though there were no records of it in any of the service's files. Its rent was paid for in cash out of Alistair's budget and only the section knew of its existence.

During the daytime, the area around the property would draw tourists wishing to walk along the narrow cobbled streets and through the hidden courtyards to see the Gothic architecture of Saint Stephen's Cathedral, the imposing Hofburg Palace, and the stables for the renowned Lipizzaner stallions; to buy confectionery, watches, perfumes, and tobacco in the Kohlmarkt; to watch pleasure cruisers and cargo boats sail along the Danube, and to stand in Heroes Square and be told by guides that this is where Adolf Hitler announced that Austria would be annexed to Nazi Germany.

But there were no tourists around the safe house now. It was 2:00 A.M., minus eight degrees Celsius, the ground thick with snow, with more of it pouring out of the sky.

The poorly lit basement gained extra light from a couple of oil lamps and a camping stove that was busy brewing a pot of coffee. Will Cochrane was leaning against the rear corner of the room, his arms folded. Beside him was the section, listening to Alistair and Patrick. The coheads were talking fast. Will was not listening to them. He was studying the team.

Roger Koenig. The CIA SOG team leader of the section's paramilitary unit. He'd worked with Will on two missions and had proven to be an excellent operator and leader. The former DEVGRU SEAL's tall and sinewy frame was motionless, his face totally focused, his professionalism evident in his posture. Roger's forefathers had all been warriors: a grandfather who'd earned the Iron Cross as a paratrooper in Germany's elite First Fallschirmjäger Division during World War II, and a father and uncles who'd served in Vietnam with the Australian SAS and the top-secret U.S. MACV-SOG. Roger had killed hundreds of men and had done none of it for God or country. He believed in duty to the man by your side. But he was also an occasional languages teacher at his children's school, liked to think of himself as a gardener even though he was lousy at it, was devoted to his wife, a silly and fabulous father, and had a mischievous streak. Will could see that the family man's eyes were twinkling and he wondered what Roger was secretly thinking as he listened to the senior CIA and MI6 officers give their briefing.

Laith Dia. The other CIA SOG officer. The black man sat on the floor, leaning against a wall, smoking a cigarette, and looked totally disinterested, though Will knew that he would be digesting every word spoken and would be thinking very fast. Laith was the size of a high school quarterback, though Will preferred to think of him as the ideal lead for Shakespeare's *Othello*. Which was not wholly inappropriate, because Laith had never played football and instead had excelled in school plays. He had been alongside Roger and Will during their last two missions and had suffered agonizing injuries during both. The jet-haired former Delta Force operative was divorced and had two children whom he adored, was one of the fittest men Will had ever met despite smoking two packs a day, was fearless, smart, irreverent, gentle, and a very effective killer.

Mark Oates and Adam Tark were here. The men were no longer part of the Qs, having signed the papers and been officially transferred to the section.

Mark was sitting with one leg resting on the other, flexing his fingers. No doubt he'd been to hundreds of briefings given by senior intelligence and Special Forces commanders, though Will wondered if he'd ever been briefed in a place like this. Will had read his file. Mark had served all over the world with the SBS, typically deep behind enemy lines, in most covert and overt theaters of war that had involved the West during his service in Special Forces. His time in the Qs had given him enhanced training in espionage tradecraft, including surveillance and business cover deployments, and he had achieved several notable citations for the complex and highly risky operations he'd led and supported. He was a widower, his wife having died of pneumonia a year ago, and saved every spare penny from his government salary to send his two daughters through university.

Adam was leaning forward, one hand gripping his mug of black coffee, the other rubbing his disfigured face. Will had read in the files that Adam had received the injury in Afghanistan while protecting a village from a Taliban attack. The village's men were all away, helping a U.S. Marine unit do a reconnaissance in the mountains, and the only people left to protect the women, children, and elders in the settlement were five inexperienced young marines. Adam and three other SAS men were four miles away when the attack on the village commenced. The SAS patrol was itself engaged in a fierce firefight with another Taliban group, but when they received news of the attack on the village, Adam broke away, ran on foot to the village, took command of the marines, told the women to fetch them any remaining rifles, lined the weapons up along a waist-high wall on the roof of the biggest building in the village, and told the marines that they had to make the Taliban think they were facing one hundred men. For two hours, Adam sprinted back and forth along the wall, picking up rifles and firing them before moving to a new position and repeating the same drill. He carried on doing this even after a mortar shell exploded near him and ripped half his face off. It was only after the Taliban were defeated that he collapsed and had to receive emergency treatment from the marines.

Will looked at the only woman in the room.

Suzy Parks. CIA analyst. Like most of the men around her, she was wearing a thick sweater, jeans, and hiking boots. She was in her late thirties, had short black hair, was married to a rocket scientist who she'd met at a ballroom dancing class, and was four months pregnant with their first child. Patrick had talent-spotted her for the section from another Agency team one year before. He was drawn not only to her photographic memory and brilliant analytical brain, a brain that had been used on some of the Agency's most complex cases during her thirteen years as a desk officer, but also to a peculiar talent: she could go without sleep for days while continuing to function at optimum levels.

Will looked at the last person listening to the briefing.

Peter Rhodes. An MI6 intelligence officer whose role was to provide risk assessments of the section's operations, and to act as Alistair and Patrick's aide de camp when they liaised with Capitol Hill and Whitehall. Though no longer operational, most of Peter's career had been in the field. He'd spent four years in Shanghai as a NOC, operating under cover as an advisor to a wealthy and powerful Chinese mogul, before undergoing operational tours as a case officer within MI6's Russia and China teams and postings to the U.K.'s embassies in Jakarta, Abu Dhabi, Tokyo, and Washington. In his early forties, Peter was slender and had a youthful appearance, a razor-sharp intellect, and a strong sense of humor. Alistair had identified him as a potential applicant for the section one month ago, and Will had backed the appointment because he not only admired Peter's operational experience but also liked the man.

He turned his attention to the coheads of the section. Aside from the fact that Patrick's hair was silver, Alistair's blond, both men looked physically similar; they were in their mid-fifties but looked ten years younger. Alistair had always been Will's Controller, but Will had worked with both men only on his last two missions, one to hunt down a senior Iranian general, the other to prevent war between Russia and the United States, and during that time he'd discovered that they had a deep and dark history of collaboration that started when they were junior field officers and had witnessed the capture of Will's CIA officer father in Iran. It was only recently that Will had learned that both men had been secret benefactors to Will's family. After his father had been tortured and executed, Alistair and Patrick had sent their own cash to Will's mother. When she had been murdered by criminals in front of a teenage Will, they funded university scholarships for Will and his sister, Sarah. They were honorable men, very experienced operators, disliked by their peers within the CIA and MI6 because of their autonomy and power, fearless, and totally dedicated to the section, its members, and the extreme nature of its work. Will respected and trusted them wholeheartedly, even though they'd repeatedly made it clear to him that they thought he was impulsive, insubordinate, uncontrollable, and a danger to himself.

"Do we have your attention, Mr. Cochrane?" Patrick was staring at Will, his expression stern.

Will nodded at the CIA officer. "Partially."

Roger laughed.

Patrick did not. "We're here because of you. Some of us think this is a nonstarter."

"But some of us think differently." Peter winked at Will. "Mind you, searching the world for a single piece of paper is a bit of a tall order."

Will moved until he was facing the team. "It *is* a tall order."

"And that's why we're involved." Laith grinned and said in his deep southern voice, "The *best of the best of the best.*" He held his fist to his mouth and mimicked the sound of a cavalry trumpet.

"Please stop that." Alistair turned away from the American, his disapproving schoolmasterly expression changing to one of coldness as he locked his attention on Will. "We have *no* starting point for this operation."

Will ignored the comment and looked at Suzy. "What have we got on the defector?"

The CIA analyst leaned forward, cupping her hands and placing her elbows on her thighs. "Lenka Yevtushenko. Fourteen years in the SVR but not on the fast track."

"Remit?"

"For the most part, eastern Europe."

"Postings?"

"One, to Belarus, returned six months ago."

"Home address?"

"We don't know."

"Extracurricular activities on his Belarus posting?"

"No interests, no foibles. He was a quiet man."

"Wife, kids?"

"None."

Will frowned. "Lovers?"

Suzy smiled. "I wondered how long it would take you to ask. Yes, one woman. A Belarusian, based in her home country."

"Poor?"

"Yes."

"A looker?"

"Well above average."

"Entrapment?"

"Unlikely. Belarusians really don't do that, plus Yevtushenko wouldn't have been worth the risk."

"Did he give her cash?"

Suzy shrugged. "We don't know."

"Loved her?"

"Don't know."

"Did she carry his child?"

Suzy rubbed her stomach. "I don't know."

"What's your source?"

"The Agency looked at Yevtushenko a couple of years ago. He was a potential target but was soon dropped because he was deemed as too low level. We have a file on him, but it's as slim as the data you now have."

"Do you have his lover's name, address?"

"Of course."

Will nodded. "Russian movement in Europe in the last three days?"

Suzy held Will's gaze. "Take your pick. A First Secretary Political who's been shunted in at short notice to France after the last incumbent was in danger of enjoying Parisian life too much; a Russian front consultancy company opening up in Belgrade; a defense attaché who's moved to Berne to hill-walk in the Alps with his counterpart in the Iranian embassy. All of them SVR."

Will shook his head. "None of them are right. What else have you got?"

The CIA analyst frowned. "That's all I have on SVR movement."

"Forget information we have on known SVR personnel. Think Russian military or police, past or present, business covers that would match a paramilitary IO."

"We've had nearly a hundred standard Russia-related trace requests from foreign security services over the last seventy-two hours."

"Have you seen them all?"

"I've made it my business to do so."

"One of them could be our Russian team."

Suzy was still, though her eyes were darting left and right, her mind racing.

The room was silent for ten minutes.

Then Suzy nodded. "Yesterday the BfV requested a trace on four Russian males who'd entered Frankfurt. They work for a company called Vitus."

"Is the company legitimate?"

"Yes, it specializes in close protection and antikidnapping training programs for corporations and the media."

"Employees listed on the website?"

"No."

"That would be normal for this kind of firm. Why are they in Germany?"

"They're attending a conference in Munich. A two-day event focusing on corporate risk within emerging markets."

"Why did the German security service request the trace on them?"

"Because they bought tickets for the event two days ago."

"That's all?"

Suzy shook her head. "They've checked into the Grand Hyatt in Berlin. Seems they've no desire to head south."

"Odd, but not necessarily suspicious. They might have used the conference as a pretext to enter Germany but are instead having a meeting with a client whose details they'd rather not share with the border police. Ages?"

"All in their thirties."

"Have the traces been done?"

"Yes. We can't find anything on them."

"Nothing?"

Suzy shook her head. "We could put their names out to some of our Russian sources, see what they say."

"No. We don't have the time to do that—plus, if they're the team, we've got to say nothing to anyone about them. Anything else in the German report?"

Suzy rubbed her temples, clearly trying to mentally wade through the vast amount of data she'd read yesterday. "Something that stood out . . . but not anything that would prick up our ears . . ." She paused. "Yes, one of the men went through customs with goods to declare. He's epileptic and has a license to carry Clonazepam."

"Epileptic?"

"The paperwork all checked out and the dosage he was carrying was correct for the duration of his stay in Germany. There was nothing else in the report."

"Has any reply been supplied to the BfV?"

"Not yet. The request was marked Routine."

"Okay. Make sure we tell the Germans that we've got nothing on the men and don't believe them to be suspicious." He looked at Alistair and Patrick. "I could be wrong, but there are too many coincidences here. A four-man Russian group enters Europe so quickly after the Gdansk incident, most likely military backgrounds given their alleged employer, no obvious intention of doing business, no history to their identities. Plus they're the right age to be experienced operators."

Patrick said, "Possibly, but one of them needs his pills to stop him from going into a seizure. Doesn't sound like an operative to me."

Will shook his head. "The Clonazepam can be taken in higher doses to sedate. It's possible the team's brought it into Germany to drug Yevtushenko after they capture him. They must have a different route out of the country and they're going to use that route to get Yevtushenko back into Russia while he's unconscious." He looked at Roger. "You, Laith, Mark, and Adam need to be all over those men." He turned to face Patrick and Alistair. "If I'm right, the Russian men are SVR. They've been deployed to Germany under business cover to link up with and support the big Russian who survived the Gdansk fight. The Russians know considerably more about the paper and possibly where it's gone than we do. If we stick to them, we'll be close to the paper. Meanwhile, I need to work this from the other end of the spectrum, and that means understanding Yevtushenko's role in the theft of the paper. Miss Belarus might be able to help me with that. If I can get her to talk, I might be on a path to establishing the identity of Yevtushenko's master." He smiled. "That gives us *two* starting points to this operation."

EIGHT

Will stood at the end of the long residential street and analyzed everything on it. A few people were on foot, walking as
quickly as they could through the thick snow, all of them dressed in
thick overcoats and hats. Stationary vehicles, caked in ice and snow,
lined the street. Adjacent to them were streetlamps that were starting
to come on as dusk descended on the Belarusian capital of Minsk. The
1980s Soviet-designed buildings that straddled the road looked functional and drab, a combination of row houses and apartment blocks.
One of them would contain the woman.

He waited, his hands deep inside the pockets of his stylish overcoat, his leather shoes offering little protection from the cold ground.
The pedestrians kept moving, some coming toward him, others
going in the opposite direction. None of them looked suspicious.
They had the appearance and postures of people who just wanted to
get to the shelter of their homes before nightfall. Turning his attention
to the vehicles, he methodically moved his gaze from one to the next.
Those nearest to him were certainly unoccupied and in darkness, but

the street was over three hundred yards long and he couldn't be certain that at least one of the cars farther down the road wasn't occupied by a local security service or Russian SVR surveillance team.

He wished he could have dressed in attire that matched the few poorly paid workers who were heading home. That way he could have walked the full length of the street and made an assessment as to whether the woman's house was being watched. But the suit he was wearing was necessary for what he needed to achieve. He needed her to know who he really was.

He glanced at the building opposite hers. It was in darkness. He wondered if the people who owned the place were still at work, were perhaps out for dinner, or whether the place was instead occupied by men and women with binoculars, military communications systems, and night-vision equipment. If he'd had Roger's team and more time, he could have ensured that a full reconnaissance was made of the area around him. Having the luxury of neither, he was going to have to take a risk.

He moved forward, his hands in his pockets, his head still, his eyes flickering left and right to look for sudden movement. After seventy yards, he stopped at an apartment block, made no attempt to look around, and quickly pressed one of the buzzers adjacent to the door. A woman's voice spoke in the intercom. Will said in Russian, the second language of Belarus, "I need to speak to Miss Alina Petrova."

The woman hesitated before answering in the same tongue, *"Da,* that's me."

"Can you let me in? This is official business."

The intercom was silent for ten seconds. Then, "What business?"

"Business that concerns you. Please, let me in."

"Are you police?"

"No."

"A government man?"

"No."

"Then there is no *official* business to be conducted."

Will stamped his feet and silently cursed. "This matter concerns someone you know. He's done something stupid and is in trouble. You might be able to help him. But I can't talk to you over the intercom."

He didn't know what else to say, couldn't stay out here for more than a few seconds longer, and decided that if she didn't let him in he'd have to come back in the morning and approach her as she was going to work.

But the door buzzed and its lock was released.

He entered the building, allowing the door to swing shut behind him and automatically relock. Ahead of him was a flight of stairs and adjacent to it a graffiti-covered, dilapidated elevator. Taking the stairs, he walked quickly up six flights to Alina's apartment. He knocked on the door, heard a bolt being snapped open, and watched the entrance open a few inches until a security chain went taught. A young, dark-haired woman was partially visible in the crack between the door and its frame.

"Alina?"

She stared at him, her expression suspicious. "Who are you?"

"Someone who's here to help."

"You could be here to hurt me."

Will shook his head. "If that were true, the door would be off its hinges by now."

Her suspicion remained. "Can I see your ID?"

"I don't have any that's relevant to this meeting."

Alina looked taken aback. "And yet you seriously expect me to let you in?"

"I'm here about Yevtushenko."

"Who?"

"Oh, come on Miss. Petrova. You were his lover, maybe still are."

"It's not illegal to love someone."

"Legalities don't matter to me. I need to know if he's been in touch with you during the last few days."

From somewhere within the apartment, a baby started crying.

Alina glanced over her shoulder, looked back at Will, and seemed uncertain what to do.

Will repeated, "I'm not here to hurt you."

The baby's crying grew louder.

"Nor am I here to give you any trouble. I just want to talk. Then I'll go."

Alina asked, "Who do you work for?"

"Myself."

"Nationality?"

"British."

Alina's eyes narrowed. The baby's cries were now echoing down the stairwell. Quickly, she released the chain, opened the door, turned, and hurried off toward the sound of the baby. Will entered the apartment, shut the door, and followed her into a small bedroom containing a cot. Alina lifted the baby, placed a hand underneath the swaddling and patted it against the girl's diapers, then rocked the baby until her sobbing began to recede. "Men's voices upset her. Probably she heard you."

Will nodded and withdrew into a tiny living room containing a worn sofa, one dining chair, a side table, an old television set, and a carpet that was threadbare in places but immaculately clean. He sat on the chair and waited.

A few minutes later Alina reappeared alone. The baby was still crying. "I can only hope she sleeps soon." She looked at him. "Would you like a hot drink?"

Will shook his head and said quietly, "That's very kind, but I'm not staying long."

Keeping her eyes on him, she moved to the sofa and sat. "What's your interest in Lenka?"

"I'm a private investigator and have been instructed by a client to check on the welfare of Mr. Yevtushenko. My client's concerned that he's done something stupid and is in danger. He's run away from his work and Russia."

"Who's your client?"

"I'm not allowed to say. It's sensitive."

"A British private investigator in Minsk, looking for a Russian diplomat, and with a client who can't be named?" Alina smiled. "I'm not stupid."

"I'm sure you're not and will therefore realize that some things are best left unsaid."

Alina shook her head. "Perhaps, but I have no reason to help you or the people you represent."

Will studied her. Suzy was right. Alina certainly had above-average looks. She was tall for a woman and wore delicately applied makeup, beige cords, and an elegant V-neck sweater that looked nothing like the dowdy clothing he'd expected her to be in. "You and your child live here alone?"

"Just us."

"Do you work?"

"I teach poetry, part time at one of the local universities. The campus has a nursery so it suits me." She looked around, then locked her gaze on Will, her expression now hostile. "If you're thinking of offering me British money, forget it. I might not live in the nicest place, but we manage just fine."

"You're sure about that?" Will held her gaze, then sighed. "I'm not here to offer you money. Honestly, I think Lenka might be out of his depth. I'm here to help him."

"The British are here to help a Russian man? Are *you* sure about that?"

Will leaned forward. "Has anyone else been here to speak to you?"

Alina shrugged and looked away.

"Belarusians? Perhaps the Russians?" He lowered his voice. "Yes, I'm sure the Russians have been here, haven't they?"

She returned her attention to him. "You're not worried about my Yevtushenko. He's done something or got something that you want."

"Do you know what that might be?"

"He never spoke to me about his work."

"Did the Russians tell you what it might be?"

"I didn't say they were here."

"Nor did you deny it."

A clock chimed. Will looked at it—a small silver antique carriage clock with beautiful engravings. He frowned, then said, "We *are* looking for something. And if we can get that something, there is every hope that we can extract Lenka from men who he shouldn't be mixing with."

"And then what? Put him in a cell and beat him?"

"No. Bring him to you."

Alina waved her hand dismissively before placing it against a necklace that matched her earrings. It had to be a replica, but could easily have been mistaken for a genuine diamond pendant.

"You don't love him anymore?"

"I didn't say that."

"Then why wouldn't you want to see him again?"

"When did I say . . . ?" Her expression became hostile again. "I don't know where he is, I haven't heard from him, and I've no desire to help a British stranger." She spat, "You haven't even told me your name."

"Even if I did, would it be of any value to you?"

"It would be a lie."

"Exactly."

She breathed deeply while staring at him, her hand falling to the tatty sofa arm. "You've wasted your time."

Will looked at the clock again and saw that next to it were three books containing the works of the Russian poets Nikolay Gumilyov, Osip Mandelstam, and Ivan Krylov. Clad in leather binding, they looked as though they'd been professionally restored. They were wrapped with silk ties that had been knotted in bows. He smiled. "He bought you things, didn't he?"

Alina frowned.

"Expensive things."

She said nothing.

"Clothes, French makeup, real diamond jewelry, a timepiece, books, no doubt other things." His smile vanished as he looked at her. "I wonder how he got the money to pay for them."

Silence.

"Because I can't imagine that his government salary was that good." He nodded toward the little bedroom. "Is she his?"

Alina's face flushed, her eyes looked venomous. "None of your damn business."

"Or is *your* Yevtushenko but one of many lovers and she is the result?"

"How dare you!" Alina rose quickly. "Get out!"

But Will remained seated. "Perhaps I was wrong. Perhaps the gifts have come from many men."

"I am *not* that type of woman!"

"Then what type of woman are you?"

Alina's breathing was fast, her anger vivid.

"Sit down."

She did not do so.

"Sit down!" Will kept his voice quiet though his tone was now stern. "I came here to help you and your man. I *know* the Russians have been here. It would have been one of the first things they did after Lenka's disappearing act. Do you think they have your interests at heart? If they get their hands on him, they'll throw him in prison. And the men he's with now—once his value to them is over, they'll do far worse. Almost certainly, they'll butcher him."

Alina's eyes widened.

"There are three organizations who want what Yevtushenko's got. None of us are friends."

"Good! Then you'll tear yourselves apart."

Will nodded. "That's a possibility." He looked at one of the books, thought for a moment, and said:

Whene'er companions don't agree,
They work without accord;
And naught but trouble doth result,
Although they all work hard.
One day a Swan, a Pike, a Crab,
Resolved a load to haul.
All three were harnessed to the cart,
And pulled together all.
But though they pulled with all their might,
That cart-load on the bank stuck tight.
The Swan pulled upward to the skies,
The Crab did backward crawl,
The Pike made for the water straight:
This proved no use at all.
Now, which of them was most to blame,
'Tis not for me to say,
But this I know—the load is there,
Unto this very day.

Alina stared at him, her expression different. Her baby's crying grew softer. "Ivan Krylov's 'A Swan, a Pike, and a Crab.'" She turned toward the books and frowned. "I'm surprised you . . ." She smiled, though when she spoke there was not attempt to hide the sarcasm in her tone. "You think I'll help you just because you can recite some poetry?"

"No. But you know that Yevtushenko's the load. A *dead* load if nothing is done to help him. You choose: swan, pike, or crab?"

She stared at him, for the first time the tiniest hint of confusion on her face.

"*Please.* Do sit down Miss Petrova."

She sat. "Which are you?"

"It's irrelevant. We're all stupid without cohesive direction. *Your* direction."

"My direction?"

"Yes. I want you to choose to work with one of us and tell us what to do." Will wondered how Alina was going to respond.

She said nothing for ten seconds. Then, "How can I trust you?"

"I can't persuade you to trust me. Use your judgment. Judge me alongside the Russians you met, and the men who now have Lenka."

"Who are those men?"

"I don't know."

"Do the Russians know?"

"I'm not sure, but I think they might."

"Then the choice is clear. I should work with the Russians!"

"Perhaps you should. Providing you trust them."

Alina's eyes narrowed as she looked him up and down. She seemed to make some kind of decision. "Our child is called Maria. We named her after Lenka's grandmother." She leaned forward, her expression stern. "Lenka was delighted when I told him that I was bearing his child. I've *never* been with another man since I've known him."

Will nodded, and for the briefest of moments wondered how it would feel to hear a woman declare that she was pregnant with his child. "Tell me about the Russians who came here."

Alina drummed fingers on the sofa, seemed deep in thought, and also looked scared.

"It's vital that you tell me everything."

She stopped drumming. "There was only one of them."

"Man or woman?"

"A man."

"Name? Appearance?"

"Mikhail. He didn't give me a surname." She smiled, though her fear remained evident. "Mid-thirties, I'd guess. Tall, short hair, muscular build. Immaculately dressed. Other than the fact that his hair was blond, he looked a lot like you."

And a lot like the man Will had seen firing a big handgun on the bridge in Gdansk.

Will felt a moment of unease. "What did he say to you?"

Her smile vanished. "He asked me if I knew the identity of the man who'd told Lenka to abscond. I told him the truth: that I didn't."

"Was that the truth?"

"Yes." Alina frowned. "Lenka was always a private man. Whenever he was with me, he'd prefer to talk about anything other than his work. I think his job sometimes embarrassed him."

"You knew he was an intelligence officer?"

She answered in a whisper, "He wasn't supposed to tell me, but he said he didn't want there to be secrets between us."

"Do you think he was cut out for the job?"

"I don't think so." She exhaled slowly. "We made plans. He was going to leave and come here to live with us. He said he'd apply for a job at the university."

"What else did Mikhail say?"

Alina lowered her head. "He asked me the same thing you did—if I'd been in contact with Lenka during the last few days. I told him that I hadn't."

"And was *that* the truth?"

She was motionless, silent.

"What else?"

"He noticed the things you'd observed; the things Lenka had bought for me. He said that Lenka must have had another source of income, that no doubt he was being paid by the man who'd got him out of Russia." She shook her head, and a tear ran down her cheek. "I just don't understand what's happening. Mikhail said that Lenka willingly absconded from Russia. Is that true?"

"Yes."

She was now visibly upset. "But why? It's so unlike him to do something like that. And he's left a mess." She swept an arm through the air. "As well as buying me things, during the last few years he's also been contributing to the rent on this place and to the upbringing of Maria. He's always been a good man. Always putting himself second, us first. But now he's gone, and there's no money." She shook her head, her posture and expression strengthening. "Don't misinterpret what I've just said. I'd rather have him back with no money than the opposite."

Will leaned closer to her, and spoke with genuine sympathy. "I don't doubt that. It's obvious to me that you love him. Don't be hard on him. He's done something stupid, and though I don't know why he's done that, I'm sure it was for honorable reasons. Reasons to do with you and Maria."

Alina seemed to be digesting Will's observation. "I believe you're right." She glanced in the direction of Maria's bedroom. The child was no longer crying and instead was emitting unintelligible words in between giggles. "She's not frightened of you anymore." Returning her attention to Will, she said, "The swan, the pike, or the crab."

Will was silent. He had to let her come to her own conclusions.

"The Russian man. He scared me at first. But then I saw kindness. And you're right. When I asked him what the Russians would do to Lenka if they found him, Mikhail said that he couldn't lie to me, that Lenka would face imprisonment, but that incarceration would be a better fate than death by the hands of the men he's with." She nodded. "He seemed a good man. What differentiates the two of you is that he has no choice other than to deliver Lenka to jail, but you seem to have no such ambitions." She frowned. "What has Lenka done?"

"He's stolen a piece of paper from the SVR. I don't know anything about the paper, other than it is of immense value and is extremely dangerous. Does that mean anything to you?"

Quietly, she answered, "No. Nothing." She suddenly placed her head in her hands, rocked back and forth, and muttered, "Shit, shit."

Will frowned.

"I wish you'd come earlier."

She continued rocking, then removed her hands and looked up with an expression of exasperation. "There's not just three of you involved."

"What?"

Placing her nails to her teeth, she said, "Yesterday, I was approached on the street by a man. He gave me a note and asked me to read it and relay its message to Lenka. I took the note home and did precisely what the man asked me to do."

Will's mind raced. "Nationality of the man?"

"I could tell from his accent that he was foreign, but other than that I don't know. He spoke to me in Belarusian. Looked European."

"How did you communicate the message to Lenka?"

More tears rolled down Alina's face. "He has a cell phone that only I know about. I sent an SMS to it."

"Has he replied?"

"No."

"Are you convinced he has the phone with him?"

"Yes. He told me that if he called me or messaged me from that number, then I could be sure that no one was listening or intercepting the message. He called it his 'safe phone.' It was his lifeline to me. He'll have it."

"And the note?"

Alina momentarily closed her eyes. "Does the name Will Cochrane mean anything to you?"

Will's stomach knotted.

She opened her eyes. "Are you Will Cochrane?"

Will was motionless, determined not to betray any emotion, though confusion overwhelmed him.

"If you want to see the note, I have to know."

Still, Will said nothing.

"I think I have made my decision, based on my judgment of you. But I can't be sure unless you answer me."

Oh dear God. Will had no idea what to say or do.

"It's time for *you* to make a judgment about me and to choose."

He stared at Alina. She seemed imploring, earnest, scared, confused. She seemed to be speaking honestly.

Finally, he answered, "Very few people call me by that name."

She held his gaze for several seconds, nodded once, and said, "But some people do." She stood up, disappeared out of the room, and reemerged a minute later holding a small piece of paper. She hesitated before handing it to Will.

Will examined both sides of the paper. It had been folded into quarters. One side was plain, the other contained printed black lines of text that looked as though they'd been written on a typewriter rather than anything more modern.

As Will read the note, he fought back every instinct to vomit.

To Miss Alina Petrova

Please forgive the rather crude manner in which this note was passed to you. The man who delivered it does not represent us, though we paid him to place it in your hands. We are desperate to reach out to our mutual acquaintance, Mr. Lenka Yevtushenko, because we believe he is in danger. Perhaps you have a means to forward the contents of this communication to him? We hope you do, and if so we implore you to get in touch with him with the greatest haste. The message you must relay to Mr. Yevtushenko is as follows:

We are sorry that in our business dealings with you, we misled you as to our real identities. We did that to protect you and when the time was right it was our intention to tell you the truth. That time never came due to unforeseen circumstances. No doubt you have since been told who we really are. That matters not. What does matter is that we continue to look out for your welfare and are concerned that you may now be in a vulnerable position. Be very careful because men are coming for you. The most dangerous of them is a British intelligence officer. He lives in West Square, Southwark, London.

His name is Will Cochrane.

NINE

The Lufthansa A321 Airbus touched down at Berlin's Tegel Airport at 0920 hours. Will was sitting in business class, staring out the window at the dark clouds hanging over the airport and the rain that was pouring down from them. The men and women around him—Austrians, Germans, a Czech, two Englishmen, a Ukrainian, and three Italians—were all dressed in suits and were looking not at the airport but at the seat belt sign, waiting for it to switch off so they could stand, grab their cases, and make a dash toward whatever business beckoned them to the city.

Will had flown from Minsk to Frankfurt during the early hours. During the seventy-minute journey from Frankfurt to Berlin, he'd briefly analyzed every passenger around him. None of them were operatives. Will was glad of that because he'd needed to be alone, and he was never more alone than when he was surrounded by normal people.

As the plane taxied along the runway, he rubbed his temples. The note to Alina had confused and deeply unsettled him and had bolstered Alistair's view that Will had too little to go on and was out of his depth. He wondered if he was doing the right thing by continuing to pursue the operation, whether the stolen SVR paper was less important than he'd thought, whether it was the right thing to do to follow his instincts and at the same time jeopardize the existence of the Spartan Section, whether he'd offered false hope to Alina, and whether the message to Alina meant he would be killed before he had a chance to get an inch closer to the truth of what was happening.

But these emotions and thoughts were also matched by anger. Knowledge of his existence within MI6 was limited to a small number of people. His home address was known to even fewer.

Someone had betrayed him.

That afternoon, Will was leaning against the wall of a short, stone-covered tunnel. Parkland was visible at either end of the tunnel, though he could see no one within the place. The heavy rainfall had driven every sensible person inside.

After checking into the five-star Steigenberger Hotel, Will had walked here, arriving nearly thirty minutes ahead of schedule, and waited.

A tall man came into view at one end of the tunnel. He stopped for six seconds, then strode quickly up to Will.

Roger Koenig was wearing a waterproof jacket, jeans, hiking boots, and a skin-colored earpiece and cord that was barely visible on one side of his face. Leaning against the wall opposite to Will, he ran fingers through his sodden hair, rubbed his hands to aid circulation, and asked, "How was Belarus?"

"Bloody freezing." Will forced a smile.

"Did Alina talk?"

"Yes."

"Anything of substance?"

"Difficult to know."

Roger produced a mock frown. "Let me help. Was she a bit more effusive than you're being right now?"

Will laughed. "Much more." His expression became neutral. "Tell me about the Russian team."

Roger drummed his hands against the wall. "They're in the Grand Hyatt and they ain't moving."

"Sightings?"

"We've seen two of them but only briefly. They're ordering room service and the two we spotted have only been down to the lobby twice."

"Who saw them?"

"Laith and Mark."

"What do they think?"

"They're sure we're looking at a team. Doesn't mean they're the right team though."

"I know."

Roger was silent for a moment before saying, "Mark has the same level of team leader experience as me. Did you put him in the section so that he could learn the ropes and then take over if I get shot?"

Will smiled, and this time it was genuine. "Exactly. I'm just waiting for you to take a bullet. Trouble is, every time you do, you recover."

"Yeah. I'm odd like that."

"You are." Will became serious. "I put him and Adam in because they fit. Do you foresee a problem?"

Roger seemed to consider this. "No. Mark doesn't seem concerned about status. He just wants to get on with the job. He'll be fine. Plus, since when did we have any hierarchy in the section?"

"We don't. It's better that way."

Roger nodded. "How long do you want us to stay on the Russian team?"

"As long as it takes. Do you mind?"

"Not in the slightest." Roger swept an arm through the air. "Germany's home from home for me."

"Your *fatherland* . . ."

Roger chuckled. "Stop that." His expression changed. "Base of operation's the Auguststrasse apartment."

A modern, luxury vacation home located in Mitte, the heart of Berlin's old city. Capable of sleeping six, more if the couches were used as beds. Peter had paid for the apartment in cash and told the owner that he and his business colleagues would need the place for at least three weeks while they were in town to close a major financial deal.

"Suzy and Peter have made it all quite homey. They've looked like newlyweds moving into their first home."

Will grinned. "I can't imagine two people more unsuited to marrying each other than Suzy and Peter."

"Yeah, and Suzy's real husband might have something to say about it." Roger frowned. "You think Suzy should be on the case given she's pregnant?"

"She's not going to be in the field."

"Even so . . ."

"Do you want to be the one to tell her that she should go home and rest?"

"No thanks."

"I thought not. Still, we're responsible for her." He looked at one end of the tunnel. Rain was pounding the walkway beyond the exit. "Alistair and Patrick?"

"Back at Vauxhall Cross to ensure that the Gdansk operation hasn't left an uncomfortable audit trail."

"Okay. How are you operating your team?"

"While the Russians are static, it's been easy. Two on at all times—one in the lobby; one making circuits outside."

"Cover?"

Roger told him that he'd introduced himself to the hotel's head of security, gave him false but verifiable credentials, said that he was responsible for the security of one of his guests, and that the identity of that VIP had to remain confidential, even from hotel staff. He'd further advised the hotel manager that there was no direct threat to the client, that Roger and three of his employees would be taking turns keeping an eye on the place, that they were unarmed, and that they would be grateful for the hotel's cooperation in allowing them to sit in the lobby and other parts of the hotel, day or night. After checking Roger's identity, the head of security had agreed.

Will nodded. "Diplomatic boxes?"

"They're at Auguststrasse, arrived yesterday."

Boxes that were sent from London and contained guns, ammunition, cash, alias passports and bank cards, tactical binoculars, night-vision scopes, and military communications equipment.

Will hoped that most of the equipment would remain unused. "Alina told me that she was visited by an SVR man. Based on her description of him and the circumstances of his visit, I'm convinced it was the big guy I spotted in Gdansk. He gave her the name Mikhail. No surname. It will be an alias, but give the name to Suzy so that she can do some digging."

"That's a hell of a dig."

"It is, but I've seen her do more with less in the past." Will lowered his head and was silent.

"Something's on your mind."

Will didn't respond.

"I reckon your lady *did* give you something of substance, something that's troubling you."

Will raised his head. "I've got a problem."

Roger smiled. "You always do." His smile vanished. "Tell me."

Will studied the former DEVGRU SEAL. He completely trusted Roger and yet he was still unsure whether to tell him about the note because he knew what Roger would say if Will told him what he was planning. "You've got your work cut out on the Russian team. Focus on that."

"You're not going to fob me off that easily, Cochrane."

Will sighed, hesitated, then said, "Someone knows my name and address and has given that to Alina, who in turn has relayed it to Yevtushenko."

"What!"

Will told him everything he knew.

"That's a *massive* breach of security. Alistair and Patrick need to get on it right away. They'll task Peter—he'll find the bastard who leaked this."

Will shook his head. "I'm not going to do that."

Roger's expression turned to one of exasperation. "Why, oh why, doesn't that surprise me? You *need* . . ."

Will held up a hand. "The note used the word 'we' ten times, 'our' twice, and 'us' once. It could have been done deliberately to hide the hand of one man, but I don't think so. Whoever wrote the note is not in direct contact with Yevtushenko, but they wanted him to know exactly who they were. Plus, they didn't expect the note to be read by anyone other than Alina. I'm certain we're dealing with a team, and that the team is wholly independent of the men who have Lenka or the Russians. The other thing that leapt out at me was the reference to their business dealings with Yevtushenko and the fact they misled him as to their true identities. What does that say to you?"

Roger answered immediately, "Business cover operation."

"Precisely."

"There are other possibilities."

"There are." Will had thought of fourteen other possible explanations for the reference. "But none of them are as convincing."

"Hostile intelligence agency trying to string a Russian SVR officer along by pretending to be a company?"

"It's the most likely hypothesis at present."

When he spoke, Roger's tone was solemn. "You *need* a witch hunt. Find out who leaked your name and we'll know which intelligence agency we're dealing with."

Will shook his head. "What's the most vulnerable time in a witch hunt?"

Roger considered the question. "When the number of suspects falls to a handful of people. At that point, the investigation may be visible to the culprit and he or she may bolt."

Will agreed. "Our problem is that the number of suspects is already small. The culprit knows that and yet has still leaked the information. I think he's covered his tracks and betrayed me knowing that if I became aware of the leak, he'd find out very quickly. Going after the man or woman who did this is too risky. Yevtushenko remains the key. If I can find him, I stand a chance of finding out who's got him, the location and significance of the paper, and who's trying to get the men he's with to take me out of the equation."

"Please don't say what I think you're going to say."

"I'm going to disappoint you."

"Then *I'm* going to come with you."

"No, you're not. I'm dealing with multiple assumptions and intangibles, but you've got four very tangible men holed up in the Grand Hyatt who remain our best hope of leading us to the paper. I can't afford for you to have your eye off the ball for even a moment."

When Roger spoke, his voice was measured, but tense. "Springing a trap sounds all good in principle. But you of all people know that it rarely works out that way. *Don't* go back to London."

TEN

"Not far now, sir." The London cabbie drove his vehicle onto Vauxhall Bridge. "Was it a long flight?"

From the rear passenger seat, Will answered, "Not too long." He looked along the Thames. It was evening, and the walkways on either side of the river were tastefully illuminated by old-fashioned streetlamps. On the north side of the river, lights within Thames House, a landmark building that was the headquarters of Britain's Security Service, otherwise known as MI5, were beginning to go out as employees were packing up for the day. Beyond the building, the Houses of Parliament were bathed in the golden glow of carefully positioned halogen lamps. He looked ahead. On the south side of the river, adjacent to the end of the bridge, was the headquarters of the Secret Intelligence Service, popularly known as MI6. Despite being prominent, imposing, and palatial in design, it had always amused Will that the MI6 HQ had been positioned at arm's length from London's political district. It also amused him that he'd only been allowed into the building twice—as a new recruit before he'd been selected for the Spartan Program, and years later when he'd been guided to a secure part of the building by men after they'd placed a hood and shackles onto him.

The cabbie increased the speed of his windshield wipers. "Still, bet you can't wait to get home though. Long flights, short flights, it's still bloody travel, ain't it? And those blinkin' queues at the airport . . . drives you crazy, don't it?" He reached the end of the bridge, drove alongside MI6, and pointed at the building. "I blame those boys. Seven P.M. and the place is all shut up. They should be out catching Al Qaeda and the Taliban and all of the other nutters who've made it impossible to take a bottle of aftershave through airport customs. But no, looks like the spooks have gone home for the night." He drove south. "Just a minute or so now. Business in Europe, was it, sir?"

Will yawned. "Yes, Germany. My company's setting up a new factory there. I had to go to sign off the paperwork."

"Long way to go just to give a few signatures."

"True."

The cabbie chuckled. "You know, in my business I have to put up with all sorts of crap—yobs, drunks, tight-arse tourists, City boys who talk to me like I'm some lowlife. But it ain't all bad. I reckon the best part of the job is getting travelers like you"—he pulled into West Square and stopped adjacent to Will's house—"home safe."

Will walked slowly up the flight of stairs, avoiding three steps that he knew creaked. Reaching his front door, he put down his bag, moved to the side, listened, heard nothing, placed a hand flat against the entrance, and pushed. The door remained firmly shut. Withdrawing his keys, he eased one of them into the lock, waited, then gradually began turning it until he felt the lock spring open. He placed the keys back into a pocket, put a hand onto the door handle, tried to calm his breathing, and began easing the handle downward.

His heart was beating fast.

He wondered if there was a man on the other side of the door, waiting with a heavy-gauge shotgun.

When the handle was fully depressed, he pushed the door open and simultaneously moved away from the entrance.

Nothing happened.

Out of habit, his hand moved toward the place where he would often keep a handgun on his person. His hand stopped midair. Because he had no handgun, no weapon at all.

Lifting his travel bag, he held it before him. Inside the soft canvas carrier were clothes and toiletries. The case wouldn't stop a .22 target round, let alone a high-velocity pistol bullet, but he held it anyway, ready to hurl it into the face of an intruder. He took a deep breath and swung into the doorway.

Everything before him was as he'd left it—a hallway full of packing cases and little else. Placing the bag on top of one of the cases, he pulled the door shut behind him and locked it. If there was a man inside his home, he had to make sure that person didn't escape.

Moving through the pitch dark, he reached the kitchen, stopped, and placed fingers over the hallway light. He hesitated, knowing that the moment he turned the light on would be a likely opportunity for him to be attacked.

He switched the light on and braced himself.

But nobody came at him.

The light illuminated the kitchen and one of the bedrooms. Both looked empty. He moved back down the hallway and crouched beside the entrance to the second bedroom. Reaching into the room, he flicked on its light, instantly withdrew his arm, waited for two seconds, glanced into the room, and pulled his head back out.

The room was unoccupied.

He stood, walked slowly to the bathroom, repeated the same drill, and saw that it was empty.

One more room. The living room.

Pausing by the entrance to the kitchen, he saw the pans, plate, and cutlery he'd washed after cooking the pheasant dish four nights ago. Lying next to them on the draining board was the razor-sharp chef's knife he'd used to prepare the meal. He grabbed the knife and held it close to his waist.

Beads of sweat trickled down the back of his neck as he inched closer to the living room door. It was shut, just as he'd left it before departing for Austria. He imagined where he would be in the room if he'd come here to kill the apartment's occupant. Probably waiting flush against the wall, to one side of the door, with a handgun pointing at the height of a man's upper body. One shot into the side of the rib cage, followed a split second later by another into the temple. Or perhaps he'd be on one knee at the far end of the room, positioned behind a sturdy piece of furniture, his gun pointing at the door, ready to put rapid two-round bursts into whoever came into view.

Or maybe he was dealing with a tough amateur. He hoped not, because their lack of training made them unpredictable.

He placed a hand on the doorknob, turned it, and pushed the door open while keeping his body away from the doorframe and his knife low.

The room was silent.

Though that meant nothing.

More sweat ran down his back. He had to go in the room, had to decide where the man was waiting for him. If there was only one of them.

Placing his free hand against the frame, he readied himself, sucked in a lungful of air, held his breath, rocked back on his heels, and lunged through the entrance while simultaneously spinning and thrusting the knife toward the wall opposite his hand. It sliced into wood paneling. No one was there.

Yanking the knife out, he turned to face the rest of the room, expecting a bullet to strike his head as he did so.

But the room was empty.

He spent the next ten minutes making a more thorough search of his home—in wardrobes, under beds, in cupboards, as well as kicking all of the packing cases to see if any of them had increased in weight. Satisfied that there was no intruder in his home, he moved back to the living room and stared at the two windows. Outside, there were at least nine places where a man could comfortably position himself with a rifle and remove a large chunk of Will's head—many more places farther afield, if the weapon was a military-spec sniper rifle and its owner was highly trained.

Lowering himself to the ground, he leopard-crawled along the floor, pulled both windows' curtains shut from his prone position, crawled back along the floor, and stood. Grabbing one of the dining chairs, he positioned it in the hallway so that it was facing the front door at the other end, placed one hand on the living room light switch, the other on the room's door handle, switched the light on, and immediately slammed the door shut.

If a man was observing the living room through binoculars or a telescopic sight, he'd know Will was home.

But Will was now in the windowless corridor, out of anyone's sight.

He sat on the chair, stabbed the tip of the knife into its wooden arm, and stared at the front door. In the absence of complete privacy and professional assault gear, no one would be able to enter the property through the barred windows. They'd come for him through the main entrance.

He stayed like this for two hours before checking his watch. It was 9:30 P.M. He felt hungry and tired but dared not move.

He tried to keep his mind active by recalling memories—any that came to him, it didn't matter.

He remembered a teacher announcing Will's high school grades to the rest of his class and saying that they were good enough to take Will to England and Cambridge University; going home later that day to find four criminals holding his mother and sister hostage while they looked for cash; feeling utter fear and confusion after he'd killed the men with a knife similar to the one by his side; his older sister telling him that he had to run away; and flying to France the next morning to enlist in the Foreign Legion.

He recalled the brutal training, the feeling that his transition from boy to man was not supposed to be like this. But over time he became numb to most emotions.

Other images raced through his mind: the day he received his *képi blanc,* placed it on his head, and was officially a legionnaire; earning his wings and being deployed to the Second REP; the mental and physical agony he'd felt as he underwent selection for the GCP; being given instructions by a DGSE officer and two days later placing a bomb underneath a car in Tripoli; and calling his sister from a pay phone in Marseille on the day his tour with the Legion had come to an end and her saying that she'd been wrong to tell him to run away after he killed his mother's murderers.

Years later, he'd found out that Alistair and Patrick had covered up what he'd done.

He briefly took his eyes off the door to check the time. Nearly midnight. Outside, London was almost silent.

He remembered his four years at university and the sensation that the GCP legionnaire and DGSE hit man was gradually being turned back into someone more decent, more human. He saw himself, in his final year of studies, walking through the university's Darwin College, clutching politics and philosophy books, and remembered the euphoric moment of feeling truly normal again.

It was the greatest feeling, and it lasted twenty-three minutes.

Up to the moment he was walking through Cambridge's shopping district, saw a man try to grab a young woman's handbag, watched the woman resist, saw a knife, and heard the victim yelp as she fell to the ground clutching her blood-covered tummy. He'd dropped his books, chased the man, grabbed him, and slammed him into a wall with sufficient force to not only make him unconscious but also fracture his skull.

At the moment the man's head caved in, the euphoria had vanished.

Now, as he sat waiting for a killer to enter his home, he doubted it would ever return.

No other memories came to him. He tried to think about the operation, about what could possibly be happening, but he couldn't concentrate. Time dragged.

Two A.M. He couldn't hear anything now. No passing cars, nothing.

Three A.M. His body craved sleep, but he kept staring at the door, knowing that it would be in the early hours that the man would most likely come for him.

Four A.M. He heard a scream, flinched, grabbed the hilt of his knife, then released it as he realized the cry had come from an urban fox.

Five A.M. His back and shoulder muscles throbbed from lack of activity.

Six A.M. A door opened somewhere in the building, followed by rapid footsteps. Then the downstairs front door opened and closed. Will knew that it was one of his neighbors going to work—David, a recently divorced mortician who usually left at this hour and always did so in a manner that suggested he was late. Three weeks ago the chubby man, who had taken to rolling his own cigarettes and cooking his way through a famous French chef's book, had met Will in the lobby, introduced himself, and given Will his business card "in case of need."

Six forty. Another door opening and closing. A woman in heels. That would be Phoebe, a thirty-something art dealer who loved champagne, middleweight boxing matches, and Chinese food, and who rarely went to work without a hangover. She'd met Will in the rather embarrassing circumstances of kneeling by the letter slot in his front door one evening and screaming in a drunken voice, "I know you're in there, you bastard! You can't fuck me and leave me!" It was only when Will had opened the door that Phoebe had realized that Will wasn't the previous occupant, a cad called Jim who'd sold Will the apartment in a hurry.

Six fifty. Retired major Dickie Mountjoy, former Coldstream Guards officer and now retiree, was leaving his home at exactly the same time as he did each morning. Dressed in a suit and mole- skin overcoat, and always carrying an immaculately rolled umbrella regardless of conditions, he would be taking a ten-minute walk to his local newsagents, which opened at seven A.M., would purchase a copy of *The Daily Telegraph,* and would then march on to the Imperial War Museum, formerly Bedlam Asylum. There, he would sit on one of the grounds' benches and read the paper cover to cover, before walking four miles to West Norwood cemetery, standing in front of his wife's grave, and giving her headstone a briefing on the latest news from around the world.

Major Mountjoy believed that Will was a life insurance salesman and had made it clear on their first encounter that Will's profes- sion was inhabited by the scum of the earth. Will had agreed and told him that he wished he'd had the discipline and courage to be a guardsman.

The West Square converted house was now empty of all, save Will.

He placed his hand over the knife's handle and scrutinized the front door.

He heard a man whistling, a stair ledge creak. He frowned.

The whistling grew louder, as did the footsteps.

Will pulled out the knife and stood. He estimated it would take him one second to reach the door to plunge his knife into the man's gut.

Though he wouldn't get halfway down the hall if the man was a professional and had a gun.

The whistling stopped. Right outside his front door.

Will dared not move, had to remain silent.

The man noisily stamped, scuffed his boots on wooden floor- boards, made a rustling noise, and began whistling again.

Then there was a bang that caused Will to leap sideways.

But the bang was caused by a cluster of letters being forced through the metal mail slot.

The man walked away from the entrance, still whistling as he exited the communal downstairs doorway.

A postman.

Will breathed shallowly and noisily through his nose as adrenaline pumped through his body. He pushed himself away from the wall and muttered, "Shit."

Because his all-night vigil had been a waste of time. Providing the Russian team remained in their Berlin hotel, he reckoned he had time to spend one more night in his home, meaning he'd have to do the same routine for another twenty-four hours.

He sighed, decided he could risk making coffee, and grabbed the pile of mail. Taking it into the kitchen, he flicked on the kettle and began leafing through the letters.

Junk.

His hand became motionless.

One of the letters wasn't junk. Handwritten on a cream envelope was his name and address. The postal stamp showed that it had been mailed from London.

Nobody sent Will handwritten letters.

Carefully he lifted the letter between forefinger and thumb and held it in midair. It felt light, though Will knew how to make letters of similar weight that could blind or poison when opened. He rotated it, and as he did so he caught the hint of a fragrant scent. Holding the envelope close to his nose, he frowned once he recognized the smell. His frown remained as the saw a water seal on the rear flap bearing the name of the stationer.

The Letter Press of Cirencester

A thought suddenly occurred to him, and it was coupled with panic. He dashed to the bathroom, opened the cabinet, and pulled aside deodorants, toothpaste, shaving gear, mouthwash, and a hairbrush. His bottle of Chanel Platinum Égoïste eau de toilette was missing. He ran into the living room, placed the letter on the dining table, and moved to his leather-covered writing desk. Inside its drawer he kept his gold fountain pen, given to him two years ago on the grounds of Versailles Palace by a Czech intelligence officer who'd placed a note inside it telling him how a terrorist unit was planning to kill the Chief of MI6. Alongside the pen would be a bottle of blue ink, a pad of high-quality writing paper, and matching envelopes.

He used the stationery to write to his sister, though she never replied.

The paper and envelopes had been purchased from the Letter Press of Cirencester.

He yanked open the drawers.

They were empty.

Turning, he stared at the letter on the table.

A letter that had been written with *his* pen on *his* stationery, and had been squirted with *his* eau de toilette in order to get him to do what he had just done. The message was clear.

You can't trace me via this letter.

Knowing that someone had been into his home, anger coursed through him. He strode up to the table, grabbed the letter, briefly wondered if he should get it analyzed by a team of forensic experts at Vauxhall Cross, then said, "Fuck it," and tore open the seal. Inside was a single sheet of paper, nothing else. He eased it out, sat at the table, and held it with two shaking hands.

Dear Mr. Cochrane

   I have learned from an unexpected quarter that you have made it your business to meddle in my affairs. You seek a man called Lenka Yevtushenko. You have no interest in him per se, but you are most interested in the sheet of paper that he has delivered to me—a paper comparable in size to the one you are now holding.

The paper belongs to me, you have no rights over it, and I will severely punish anyone who tries to steal it from me.

I did consider speaking to you in person about this matter, in a place of my choosing, and under circumstances that perhaps would be rather more conducive to me than you. But I'm told that you are not a man to hunt. Rather than fail in an attempt to capture you and thereby drive you out of contact, I concluded that a letter to you would be a far more efficient and civilized course of action. I'm sure you agree.

I'm also sure that a man of your intellect will understand that not all of our dealings can be civilized. If I told you to back down or face the consequences, I'm convinced you'd eschew the former in favor of the latter. That inevitable decision has placed me into a rather brutish tactical stance. I don't like that stance, but you put me there, and here I am.

You won't back down because you are not afraid. But you might for something else.

I'm going to give you a name for you to refer to me by. It is not connected to me and no one else has this name. But it's a label, eases our introduction to each other, and has been carefully chosen in order to remind you of the consequences of your actions.

Before I do so, know this:

If you don't stop, I will find the name and location of someone you care about.

And I will savage that person.

Yours,
William

PART II

ELEVEN

Stefan stopped and looked back down the mountain. In German, he said, "Come on, you two. We're nearly there."

His ten-year-old twin sons were several yards below him and were struggling with the walk.

"We're tired, Daddy."

"Can we stop for a rest?"

"Not yet." Stefan waited for them to catch up while looking at the view. No matter how many times he'd made this journey, the splendor of the Black Forest mountain range always captivated him. Today there was a clear blue sky and snow was only present on the very highest peaks. At the base of the mountain, his car was now a red dot, stationary next to a glistening, tranquil lake. "Another two hundred yards, then we can rest, eat, and play."

Mathias reached him first and asked, "If we keep doing this, will we be as strong as you, Daddy?"

Stefan smiled. "Maybe stronger."

Panting and red faced, Wendell drew closer and said, "I don't know anymore if I want to be strong like Daddy."

Stefan put his arms around his boys. "You've both done well today. Just you wait until I tell Mummy how far you walked. She'll be so proud of you."

"Are *you* proud of us?"

Stefan beamed. "I'm the proudest daddy in the world." He lifted both boys so that they were snug against his waist and said, "I think you've walked far enough. Next time we'll see if you can make it all the way to the top."

Carrying them in one arm each, the big schoolteacher strode onward up the mountain. His breathing was relaxed, and the cool air felt good against his smooth face.

Wendell giggled. "It's like being on a camel."

Mathias laughed and chanted, "Daddy's a camel. Daddy's a camel."

Stefan grinned. "Camels don't like mountains and they can't do this."

To the children's delight, Stefan broke into a run, leaping over uneven ground, sprinting fast despite the incline of the mountain and the weight of his burden. Reaching the summit, he placed them down, breathed in deeply, and said, "I think I was more like a horse. What do you think?"

Mathias frowned. "Maybe a donkey."

Wendell shook his head. "Donkeys don't run."

"Yes they do, stupid."

"No they don't. Not uphill anyway."

Stefan looked around. The peak wasn't high enough for snow, and the area was covered with grass and a few boulders. Removing his knapsack, he pointed at a spot of open ground and said, "This will do us nicely." They sat together and Stefan stretched out his legs as he began rummaging in the sack. He withdrew a Tupperware box, a bottle of water, and a metal flask. "Let's see what Mummy has made us for lunch." From the box, he took out cold meat sandwiches that had been wrapped in waxed paper, a salt-cured sausage, a small jar of homemade pickle relish, a hunk of Bierkaese cheese, and three slices of the stollen cake that his wife had baked for Christmas. Laying the spread on top of the sack, he stated, "Food fit for mountain kings!"

The boys grabbed the sandwiches and began devouring them. Stefan withdrew a penknife from his fleece jacket, opened the blade, and sliced into the sausage. After unscrewing the jar of relish, he dipped his knife into it, coated a piece of the meat, and tossed the food into his mouth. It tasted very good. "Okay, so what do we know about the Black Forest?"

Both boys instantly raised their hands.

Stefan nodded at Wendell.

In between chewing his food, the child said, "The Romans called it 'Black Forest' because the trees are so close together that there's no light inside the forest."

"That's good, Wendell. Mathias?"

"The highest mountain is the Feldberg."

"How tall is it?"

Mathias hesitated. "Four thousand six hundred . . . no . . ."

Wendell interrupted. "I know! I know!"

Mathias darted an angry look at his brother. "It's my turn to answer." He held his fingers in front of his face. "Four thousand *eight* hundred . . . and ninety-eight feet."

Stefan rubbed the boy's shoulder. "Excellent. Now, Wendell. What's the name of the state that administers the forest?"

Wendell narrowed his eyes. "Don't tell me the answer . . ." He lowered his head, then looked up quickly. "Baden-Württemberg."

"Correct." Stefan cut himself another slice of sausage. "The state has a big responsibility."

"But why, Daddy? Nobody comes here. We never see anyone when we do our walks."

"That's because we're not in a tourist area. And a place can be important even if people don't visit it." He smiled. "Anyway, we like being on our own, don't we?"

The boys grinned as they took more mouthfuls of their sandwiches.

Stefan placed his knife down and began unscrewing the flask's cap. "Last question. Who can tell me if there are any dangerous animals in the forest?"

The boys nudged each other, clearly excited by the question. "Are there wolves here?"

Stefan poured tea into a cup. "There used to be lots of them. Not so many these days."

"Are they *very* dangerous?"

Stefan smiled. "Only if you get close to them. They don't like that."

The boys turned to each other and broke into a private conversation.

"Even if they are really dangerous, they're not as strong as Daddy."

"Yes, Daddy would be able to defeat a whole pack of them."

"He'd probably kill the wolf leader first."

"Then the others would run away."

"Or maybe they'd make Daddy the *new* wolf leader."

Stefan took a sip of his tea and marveled at the way his sons worshipped him. He knew it wouldn't last. In three or four years they'd be disagreeing with everything he said and stood for. That wouldn't matter because he loved his boys unconditionally, though he had to admit that it did make him feel good when they talked about him in such admiring terms. Part of him wished they could stay as children forever. "You've both forgotten about a creature in the forest that is far more dangerous than a wolf."

The boys' eyes widened, their expressions expectant. "Tell us!"

"*Lumbricus badensis.* The giant earthworm."

"It lives here?"

Stefan nodded. "Only in the Black Forest."

"How big is it?"

In truth, the worms could grow to two feet, but Stefan liked to enrich his sons' imaginations. "Fifteen feet long, and three feet wide."

"Wow! Does it have teeth?"

"It has fangs. Five rows of them, all razor sharp and as long as your arms."

"Where's its home?"

"It hides under the ground, making huge tunnels in the mountains and in the valleys. It only breaks through the surface to feed."

"What does it eat?"

Stefan shrugged. "Deer, cattle, sheep. It drags them underground while they're still alive and takes them to a cavern that is littered with the bones of other creatures. That's where it kills them, devours them, and drinks their blood." He stared at them and pretended to look serious. "But, do you know what it *really* likes to eat?"

The boys shook their heads fast. They were hanging on his every word.

"Its favorite meal is little boys."

The twins' mouths opened wide.

Stefan laughed, and ruffled their hair. "Don't worry. He sleeps during the day. And anyway, you're right—nothing in the forest is as strong as Daddy, and that makes me the most dangerous creature here."

The boys broke into smiles and started talking to each other with hushed, rapid words, embellishing the size and prowess of the giant earthworm, creating stories about it, their imaginations fully fired up.

Stefan reached into the sack and withdrew two folded kites, which he assembled and handed to his sons. "Okay, time to have some fun. But remember, no running and try not to get them tangled this time."

The boys moved to the place they always stood to fly their kites and spent several minutes attempting to get them airborne. Eventually they succeeded, unspooling their lines all the way until the bright red kites were flying high over the valley.

Stefan watched his boys and felt utter contentment and peace. Nothing gave him greater joy than seeing his sons happy and carefree. He took another sip of his tea, withdrew an old briar pipe, filled it with his favorite Ottoman blend, and lit the tobacco. The boys were totally absorbed in their activity, staring at their kites, trying to ascertain whose kite was flying the highest.

They were not looking at him.

He grabbed the penknife, looked to his left, and jabbed the blade into the ground. For one minute, he cut through the surface until he found what he was looking for. Placing the knife down, he reached into the ground and pulled out a small metal box. He opened it, saw that it was empty, shut it, replaced it in the ground, covered it with the loose soil, and punched the soil until it was compacted.

He placed one hiking boot over the other, lay back, and relaxed while continuing to puff on his pipe and watch his darling sons. He'd let them play for another thirty minutes or so before they needed to make the descent to the car. After a sixty-minute drive, they'd be home, the children could rest, and he could prepare history lessons for the classes he had to teach the next day.

He stared across the Black Forest. This had been his home for nearly two decades, first as a single man and now as a husband and father. Every week during that time, he'd come here. But if one day he opened the box and found that it wasn't empty, then everything would change.

As he glanced back at his children, Kronos hoped that day would never come.

TWELVE

Will called Roger from his cell phone. "He's not going after me. Unless I back down, he's going to identify someone I care about and kill that person." He told him about what had happened two hours earlier. "What's your status?"

"The team remains static, though yesterday one of them left in a vehicle for three hours."

"Did you follow him?"

"I made the decision that we stay focused on the bulk of the team."

"Was he carrying anything when he returned?"

"No. But if his trip was to meet an asset and get weapons from him, the stuff could have been left in the car. You want us to take a peek?"

"Not yet. We can't risk them finding out we've tampered with their vehicles. How many cars do they have?"

"Two. Both SUVs, parked in the hotel garage. Accessible within two minutes of them leaving their rooms."

"Any sightings of someone who fits Mikhail's description?"

"Don't think so, but we can't be certain. Hotel's got too many damn entrances for us to cover all bases."

"Assessment?"

"I reckon they're still waiting."

Will said, more to himself, "What for?"

"That's the million-dollar question."

"I might be able to get back tonight. I've got a couple of things to sort out first."

The line was silent for five seconds.

"Your world ain't exactly brimming over with people who care about you. There's only one person who fits that description."

"I agree."

Sarah Goldsmith, née Cochrane, Will's sister.

"You think that person's been identified?"

"I don't know! Probably not, but it's only a matter of time."

"What are you going to do?"

"Get the person to a safe place."

"Police?"

"Not a chance." Will had to entrust his sister's safety to individuals he knew and who had proven themselves to him. "I've got people."

"Okay." Roger sighed. "I think you're right about the witch hunt. But this is getting out of control. The risks are—"

"Bloody obvious!" Will regretted snapping. In a calmer voice he said, "Not a word to anyone about all of this."

"Sure. When are you seeing her?"

"Today."

"Good luck, because it's going to be a fucking difficult conversation."

"That's putting it mildly."

Will sat on a bench in London's St. James's Park and waited. In front of him was a waterway containing ducks, pelicans, and other wildlife.

Visible to his left was Whitehall's Horse Guards Parade. Red-coated mounted Life Guards soldiers were moving in formation across the square, passing in front of the Old Admiralty's regal buildings and the Foreign and Commonwealth Office. Will wondered if Major Dickie Mountjoy came here during his daily trips down memory lane. He decided he would because Dickie's raison d'être was pomp, ceremony, and the celebration of bygone ages, and Whitehall had that in abundance.

A woman navigated her way across the parade ground, grimacing as one of the army horses defecated close to her. In her early sixties, she was slightly dumpy, wearing a winter anorak, tweed skirt, purple hat, and flat shoes, and holding a carrier bag. Will kept his eyes on her as she moved into the park, walked along the footpath adjacent to the waterway, and sat down next to him.

Placing a hand over Will's hand, she patted it, smiled, and said in a well-spoken voice, "It's been a while, my dear."

Will gave her hand a gentle squeeze. "It's great to see you again. Thanks for coming at such short notice, Betty."

Betty Mayne shrugged. "That's what I'm here for." She reached into the bag and withdrew a loaf of sliced bread. "Make yourself useful." She handed Will several slices of the bread. "But don't let the greedy ducks take it all." She began tearing a slice into pieces and tossing bits of bread into the water.

Will looked at the bread he was holding, felt unsure what to do, then began feeding the birds.

"Not done this before, have you?"

"I can't remember."

"That's no surprise."

Will tossed a larger piece of bread into the water and watched ducks noisily race toward it. "I need you and Alfie."

Betty's husband.

"And Robert and Joanna."

A retired married couple.

Betty nodded. "What for?"

"Two of you need to camp in my house. The other two need to take a holiday—Scottish Highlands, North Wales, one of the coastal islands, anywhere remote."

"Babysitting?"

"Yes."

"Threat to target?"

"Severe."

"Target's name?"

Will tore off another piece of bread, held his hand still, and said quietly, "It's my sister."

Betty turned toward him, her expression one of total sympathy. "Oh no. You poor thing."

Emotion welled up inside him. He tried to keep it in check. "I need you to start today. I'm so sorry I couldn't give you more warning."

"Nonsense." Betty's tone was now authoritative, her posture strong. "We'll get this sorted. Don't you worry about a thing. And the whole point of us is that despite our age, we can move quicker than your other assets. That was your idea, remember?"

Betty was right. He'd chosen the two husband-and-wife teams because they were retirees, therefore were not tied to an employer, and could support him at a moment's notice. It also helped that Betty was a former undercover operative with Fourteenth Intelligence Company that her husband Alfie had been a sergeant in the SAS, that Robert had been Alfie's captain, and that Joanna had been an MI5 case officer. The four operatives had first met in the mid-seventies in a farmhouse in a remote part of the United Kingdom. Joanna was there to debrief a source, the others there to ensure the agent and handler were protected. The agent never showed up; instead armed IRA men did.

Betty asked, "What's the threat to your home?"

"It's unlikely there's a direct threat. I need someone in there, as it's probable that I'm going to receive some very important letters, letters that will be trying to warn me off an operation. I'm going to be overseas. If a letter comes, its contents must be relayed to me straight away. But I need two of you in there just in case."

Betty seemed to consider this. "When do we collect your sister?"

"Today. She should be home around six. And it won't be just her, we need her husband as well."

"Are they expecting us?"

"No."

"In that case, you're going to have to do some pretty smooth talking to her, because"—she rubbed her legs—"the days of me being able to take part in a snatch operation are long gone."

Will smiled. Betty had always reminded him of the no-nonsense, get-on-with-it women who'd built Lancaster bomber planes, nursed air raid casualties, or parachuted into German-occupied France during World War II. "I will be talking to her. But I could do with your help to keep her calm."

With pinpoint accuracy, Betty threw the last of her bread into the gullet of a pelican. "Then that's settled. Alfie and I will pack our walking sticks and thermal undies; Robert and Joanna can play mum and dad spending a few days visiting their son's London pad."

As Will kept his eyes on Betty, he felt safe and secure. Betty was a remarkable woman, had a backbone of steel, and was a highly experienced operative. But what set her apart from others in Will's life was that she had always displayed an unconditional compassion toward him. He suspected she viewed him as the son she'd never had. He didn't mind, because to him she felt like family. "Is there anything you need?"

Betty patted his hand again. "Silly boy. You leave everything to us. We know what we're doing."

From the backseat of the vehicle, Will checked his watch. It was ten minutes past six. The three-bedroom row house in Richmond's Manor Grove was still in darkness, as were most of the other houses in the street. Will's sister and her husband were both partners in a law firm; Will imagined that the rest of the street's occupants were also white-collar professionals and were either still working or on their way home.

From the front passenger seat, Alfie glanced over his shoulder at Will and said in a south London accent, "Bit of money around here these days, ain't there, sunshine. Make you wish you were in the private sector?"

Will smiled, though felt uneasy. "I don't think the private sector would have me."

Alfie pulled out a filterless cigarette, stuck it in the corner of his mouth, lit it with a match, and partially rolled down his window. The sixty-five-year-old ex-SAS man was short and had a stocky frame that was clearly once very powerful, but now moved a little more slowly and more awkwardly. He was dressed in an ill-fitting suit, shirt, and tie, and Will knew that Betty had made him dress up for the occasion. "Look at 'em. Just ordinary terraced houses like my old folk used to live in. Couldn't afford it now. Bet these places cost a quarter of a million."

Beside him, Betty gave a disapproving sigh. "You're so out of touch with London prices, angel. A place like this would be at least half a million."

"Blimey, petal." Alfie looked out of the window, blowing a long stream of smoke into the cold exterior air. "Where did we go wrong?"

"We joined the army."

"Oh yeah, that was it."

Will looked over his shoulder in the direction from which he thought Sarah and her husband would be entering the street. He saw nothing, but wondered if there were armed men hiding somewhere on the route in an unlit vehicle, waiting to ram Sarah's car when she arrived and gun her down. "I'm going farther up the street."

Betty said, "Off you pop then, my dear . . ."

Will opened the door and put one foot out onto the street.

" . . . But I hope you're wearing a warm vest underneath that thin suit."

"I . . . I'll see you in a minute." He shut the car door and walked fast up the road until he reached another vehicle that was facing him.

The sedan car was at least twenty years old. Robert and Joanna were inside, and as he moved to the side of the vehicle Joanna rolled down her window and beamed at him. "It's lovely to see you again, William." Her formerly blonde, now gray hair was tied back in the severe style that she'd always had it in since attending the Chelten-ham Ladies' College as a teenager. It was at odds with the almost per-manent smile that she wore. At sixty-one years of age, she was the youngest in the team, though a recent onset of arthritis in her hips had aged her once pretty face and her physique. "I was sooo excited when Betty told me we could come out to play with you."

Will nodded, unsure how to respond.

"Hello, Willy old boy." This came from Robert, who was leaning across his wife from the passenger seat.

Will had always hated it when the ex-SAS captain called him Willy. Or old boy, for that matter. Will leaned forward so that his face was by the window. "Hello, Robbie."

Robert made the tiniest grimace at being called Robbie. His expression changed, and when he spoke it was in a clipped tone favored by army officers. "Hunkered down in a car"—he patted Joan-na's thigh—"bit of stuff by your side, watching a place and knowing it could all go to rat shit at any moment." He grinned. "Just like the good old days, eh Willy?"

Will smiled. "Your days, not mine."

Joanna asked, "Is there anything you'd like us to do with your place while we're there?"

Robert huffed, "Stop mothering the boy."

Will thought for a while. "Actually, I've got some boxes that need unpacking. Don't feel obliged, but it would be a big help."

Robert was about to say something, but Joanna held a finger to his lips and said, "We'd absolutely *love* to." She looked mischievous. "But have you got any naughty boy things you'd rather this shrinking violet didn't see?"

"Hardly." Will laughed.

As did Robert. "Shrinking violet?"

Joanna looked sharply at her husband while opening the glove compartment, withdrawing a Heckler & Koch MK23 handgun, expertly checking its workings, and saying, "No chance of being a shrinking violet when married to you. Is there?"

Robert shrugged. "Never said I was a saint."

Joanna held his hand, looked at him with adoring eyes, and said, "My man." She glanced back at Will. "When she arrives, make it fast. Speed confuses most people. Betty and Alfie will deal with the fallout en route to destination."

Will nodded.

Robert dropped his hand into his door's compartment and placed his hand over the hilt of a Remington 870 shotgun. His demeanor was now completely different. "*Very* fast, Mr. Cochrane."

"Will." Joanna was staring straight ahead.

Will turned and saw a vehicle's headlights in the distance. He stepped away from Joanna's car and moved into darkness. The vehicle passed Betty and Alfie's car, passed Sarah's house, passed Will, and continued on up the street. Will checked his watch again. Six twenty-five. He silently cursed, and wondered if Sarah and her husband were delayed at work or had gone out for an early dinner. The last direct flight to Germany tonight was an 8:00 P.M. Lufthansa flight to Frankfurt, but he doubted he'd make it, meaning he'd have to route to Germany via another European capital.

Another set of headlights emerged at the far end of the street. They grew closer, and the car's engine noise changed as gears shifted and the car slowed. It stopped right outside Sarah's house, and its ignition was turned off. Doors opened. A woman and man exited the vehicle.

Both were dressed in business suits and were clutching leather attaché cases. They were Sarah and her husband, James.

They moved to their front door, entered the house, and shut the door behind them, and within seconds all of the downstairs lights were illuminated. Will jogged back down the street until he was by Betty's car. She lowered her window but wasn't looking at him, instead had her eyes fixed on the property.

Will muttered, "It's imperative I have no idea where you'll take her. But if you get spooked by anything, *anything* at all, then move to somewhere else. Money's no object. I'll cover all costs."

While keeping her head motionless, Betty replied, "Just get her and her husband in the car. We'll take it from there."

He glanced at Joanna and Robert's car, then back at Betty and Alfie. The old operatives were well past their prime, but they had something that a younger and more agile team couldn't have: wisdom, and a been-there and seen-it-all wealth of experience. As well as all of that, they were incredible shots. One year ago, Will had watched them assemble at one end of the shooting range at one of MI6's training facilities. They'd looked like a group of retirees who'd taken a bus trip out of London's suburbs to catch a bit of fresh country air. The bemused range instructor had given them training on how to hold a Browning 9 mm at eye level and the stance required to compensate for the powerful handgun's recoil. Betty had been up first. With a grin on her face, she'd ignored the instructor's advice and, to Will's amusement, had held the gun with two hands close to her tummy and fired ten shots in eight seconds across the twenty-meter range and had placed all bullets within a three-centimeter spread of the bull's-eye. The instructor's jaw had dropped, and he'd said, "You look like me granny. How on Earth did you do that?"

Will knew his sister couldn't be in better hands.

He walked across the street, strode up to the entrance, hesitated for a moment, then rang the doorbell. As he waited, his stomach was in knots.

James answered the door. The diminutive lawyer had removed his tie and was holding a glass of red wine. As soon as he recognized Will, his expression was hostile and surprised. "What the hell do you want?"

Will looked over the man's shoulder, down the hallway. "I need to speak to Sarah."

James' face turned red. "You've got no right to be here."

From somewhere in the house, Sarah called out, "Who is it, darling?"

James ignored her, lowered his voice, but kept it full of anger. "Leave right now."

Will shook his head. "I can't do that, James. Please. It's vital I speak to her."

James took a step toward Will. "She doesn't need you in her life. Not since you got blood on your hands."

Will recalled Betty imploring him to be civil to his sister and James. He wondered what to say, but before he could stop himself, he blurted, "God, you've always been a self-righteous ass." He pushed past James, spilling the man's drink over his white shirt, and walked quickly into the house. "Sarah, it's Will. Don't be angry with me. I'm here for a reason."

He walked in the kitchen. Sarah was facing him, leaning against a work surface, her expression neutral. She was tall, pretty, with straight blonde hair.

She said nothing for a while, just stared at him, then, "I didn't reply to your letters for a reason. I'd have thought that lack of response was a clear message that I wanted nothing to do with you."

Will stood in the center of the kitchen, trying to hold back nausea. "I don't understand. I've never done anything wrong to you or James."

In the hallway, James was cursing. No doubt the shirt he was wearing was very expensive.

A trace of a smile emerged on Sarah's face. Her eyes flickered between the hallway and her brother. "Well, you have now."

Will waved a hand dismissively. "You've both got to come with me. Pack a bag, but we've got to be out of here in five minutes."

Sarah looked incredulous. "*You've* got to be joking!"

Will shook his head. "You're in danger. There are people waiting outside who can take you somewhere safe, just for a few days while I sort things out."

The incredulity turned to anger. "And who brought this danger onto me?"

Will was silent.

Sarah banged a fist against a cupboard. "You bastard!"

"Sarah, please . . ."

"Shut up." She looked confused. "Isn't it about time you told me what you did for a living?"

Will lowered his head. "I wish . . . I . . ."

"Yeah, you bloody wish." Her expression strengthened. "What happens if we don't leave?"

Sweet talk her, Will.

"You'll be killed."

Shock covered her face. Shaking her head wildly, tears now rolling down her cheeks, she shouted, "This is *why* I don't want you in our lives. You're trouble."

James stormed into the kitchen, anger vivid on his face.

But he turned and fled after both Sarah and Will barked at him in unison, "Get out!"

They returned their attention to each other.

Will's voice trembled as he said, "You don't know me, Sarah."

She hissed, "I *know* you. I saw how you changed on the day the men killed our mother and you killed them. The Will I knew had been *snapped* in half."

Will moved to her and placed his hands on her arms.

She shrugged them away, her voice now tearful, quieter, but still forceful. "Don't, just don't . . ."

But Will embraced her again, pulling her close to him as a tear ran down his face. "I'm so sorry. So very sorry."

She held her arms in midair, hesitated, then placed her hands on his back.

They stayed like this for one minute, silently holding each other.

Sarah asked in a near whisper, "The danger you've brought onto us—is it because you're doing something important?"

Will recalled Alistair's comment.

We don't know anything about the paper.

He felt wretched, lost for words, and now made no attempt to hold back the tears. "The danger is very real."

Sarah squeezed him tight, rested her face on his shoulder, and placed a hand delicately on his cheek. "Where have you gone, my little brother?" She gave one last squeeze, then said, "We'll do what you say on one condition."

Will sighed. "What?"

She took a step back, glanced at the hallway, then back at her brother. "He's weak, and is petrified of you. But when you're not around, he makes me laugh and takes care of me. I need that and he needs that." She held Will at arm's length. "We'll go with your people, so long as you promise me that you'll never contact me again."

Will dropped his gaze to the ground, felt dizzy and nauseous.

Nothing seemed real.

Except the hate he felt for himself as he quietly replied, "I promise."

As the vehicles drove off, one of Kurt Schreiber's men lowered his thermal night-vision binoculars, moved away from the window over-looking the street and Sarah Goldsmith's house, pressed numbers on his cell phone, and held the phone to his head. "They're on the move, sir. Cochrane's got two women and two men with him. All of them well past their prime, in their sixties, I'd say. They've taken both husband and wife. Our vehicles are moving into position."

"Don't let me down. They must remain under observation at all times."

The man smiled. "Don't worry, Mr. Schreiber. I've put some of our best on this. Wherever they go, we'll be on them day and night. Right up to the point you give us the order to kill her."

THIRTEEN

It was close to 3:00 A.M. as Will walked into the Auguststrasse apartment. The place was larger than he'd expected, sumptuous and airy, with light-colored art deco furniture, a modern kitchen visible through one of the archways, and a long hallway beyond another archway that led to bedrooms containing en suite bathrooms as well as a guest washroom.

Also unexpected was the fact that Suzy and Peter were still up. The CIA analyst was sitting at a twelve-seat dining table, taping keys on her laptop. She looked tired, but focused. Peter Rhodes was staring at a whiteboard containing handwritten words, arrows, and numerous question marks.

He was wearing a pink-striped shirt, no tie, slacks, and brown brogues. Spinning around as Will walked into the room, he grinned, clapped his hands, and said loudly in his upper-class accent, "The wanderer returns. Guess what? Since you've been away, I've managed to achieve the sum total of fuck-all."

Will dumped his travel bag onto the floor, kept hold of his duty-free shopping bag, and muttered, "I know how that feels."

Peter smiled even wider. "Glad you do! I'm cross with myself and am starting to get a little bit annoying to be around." He darted a look at Suzy. "Right, Suzy Sue?"

Suzy kept her eyes on her screen. "Damn right."

Peter jabbed a finger against the whiteboard. "Questions keep me going." The officer seemed totally energized despite the hour. "But I become a grumpy sod when I don't have answers."

Will walked up to Suzy, withdrew from the shopping bag a book he'd bought at the airport entitled *Work & Pregnancy: Have a Life, Have a Kid,* hesitated for a moment, held it out to her, and saw her frown as she took it from him. He asked Peter, "The questions?"

"Ones you've already asked yourself."

Will looked at the whiteboard.

Why did Yevtushenko steal the paper?
Where's "Mikhail"?
Why is his SVR team waiting in Berlin?
Why is the paper so important?
Why can't it be copied and its value therefore diluted?
Who is Number 1?

Will darted a look at Suzy. "Anything on the name 'Mikhail'?"

Keeping her eyes fixed on her screen, she replied, "Lots. Too much."

"Even by narrowing the parameters?"

She nodded. "I've gone through trace requests, our databases, NSA, Cheltenham Sigint"—she sighed as she slammed shut the laptop—"and even open source material. Thousands of Mikhails . . ."

"Mikhail is a popular name within the Russian mummy fraternity." Peter sat on the edge of the table. "You think he might pay Miss Petrova another visit? If so, might be worth briefing her so that she can try to get a surname."

Will shook his head. "He won't go back to her because he knows that she'd clam up. His agenda is to retrieve the paper and take Yev-tushenko back to Russia. He made that clear to her."

"Bit silly of him. Should have kept his powder dry and lied to her."

Will disagreed. "She's smart, and I think Mikhail knows that. No matter what he said to her, she'd have worked out that the Russians were going to punish her lover."

"So why did he visit her?"

"That question invites another."

Peter frowned, then jumped down from the table, strode up to the whiteboard, and wrote:

Why did he tell Alina that his name was Mikhail?

Will smiled. "Exactly."

Peter's mind was racing. Speaking more to himself, he said, "To put her at ease? Hope not, because that means the name's been plucked out of thin air. Maybe because the name could mean something to Yevtushenko? Possible, but that's only of value if Alina was privy to that information."

Suzy added, "We can't rule that last possibility out. If there's a connection between Yevtushenko and Mikhail, then Mikhail might have been hoping to use that connection to get her to work with the Russians."

"Quite." Peter studied the whiteboard. "But if that was the case, why didn't Mikhail hammer that connection home to her?"

Laith emerged from the hallway, wearing only a towel around his waist, his hair wet. The ex–Delta Force operative's expression looked thunderous, and as he walked to the kitchen while rubbing his face, he muttered, "Coffee."

Adam entered the room, fully dressed and yawning. "We're on in fifty minutes." The former SAS soldier also made for the kitchen, and said under his breath, "If it's another day of just sitting on our arses, I'm going to shoot someone just to liven things up."

Peter moved right up to the whiteboard and jabbed a finger against the latest question. "Why, why, why?"

Laith reentered the room holding a steaming mug, thought about sitting, decided it was too risky a movement with the towel he was wearing, and withdrew a thin white tube from his waistline. He puffed on it, and the tube emitted a tiny bit of odorless smoke.

Will frowned. "What on Earth is that?"

Laith gestured toward Suzy. "We got a child on the way. I only found out yesterday. In here, I stick to electronic cigarettes." As Adam joined him, Laith asked his colleague, "Lobby, or circuits of the exterior?"

Adam said irritably, "You can do the lobby today. I don't care how cold or wet it is outside. I need the exercise."

Laith shrugged. "Okay, I'll bring a good book."

"Here." Suzy tossed the CIA officer Will's purchase. In a sarcastic tone, she said, "Find out if 'having a life' means trawling databases for some guy called Mikhail."

Laith seemed unfazed as he turned the book over. "Sure. Anything else?"

"Yes. See if it says anything about why I'm so darn tired." She shook her head and said to herself, "I hate this feeling. I'm not normally like this."

As Laith and Adam left to go to their respective rooms and make final preparations for their shift at the Grand Hyatt, Will called to them, "I'm coming with you. I need to speak to Roger and Mark."

"Fine."

"You'll be the highlight of their night."

Will asked Suzy, "How long have you been up?"

Peter answered on her behalf. "Since this time yesterday. You're a tough girl, aren't you, Suzy. And bloody stubborn."

Will said quietly, "We're hitting a dead end on the name. Get some rest."

Suzy seemed unsure.

"Please."

She sighed. "Just a few hours' sleep, then I'll do some more searching. There're other leads to pursue, though I'm not hopeful." She stood, arched her back while rubbing her tummy, and began walking toward the bedrooms.

Will looked at the whiteboard. A thought suddenly occurred to him. "Suzy, what parameters are you using for the search?"

She stopped midway across the room. "Approximate age, obvious intelligence activities that we know about and reference someone called Mikhail, diplomatic listings of Mikhails who've been in posts that are known SVR covers, and I've managed to get some—not nearly enough, mind you—of the flight rosters of carriers that entered Germany during the forty-eight hours after the Gdansk operation. I've checked the handful of Mikhails that we know entered German airspace during that time. All are wrong."

Will remained motionless. Speaking quietly, he said, "I want you to narrow it down much more than that. When you wake up, you need to focus solely on our databases, and within that focus only on our Russian double agent files. In particular, I want you to see if a Mikhail crops up in any cases during the last five years where one of our agents has been compromised and captured or killed by the Russians."

Suzy grinned, turned, and started to walk back to the table. "*Now* you got me all revved up. Sleep can wait."

"No it can't, Suzy!" Will faced her and said in a more sympathetic tone, "This is so vital that the agent files can wait a few hours until my best analyst is fully reenergized."

Suzy looked unsure, then beamed. "You shouldn't be trying to charm a pregnant, married woman, Mr. Cochrane."

Will laughed softly. "Off to bed with you. *Both* of you." He frowned. "Boy or girl?"

"Too early to tell."

"Have you thought of names?"

"Not yet." Suzy paused, then smiled. "If it's a boy, I could call him Mikhail. Seems it's a good choice."

After she left the room, Peter moved close to him and asked quietly, "Why the double agent files?"

Will pointed at the whiteboard. "Let's assume that the SVR officer did give Alina the name 'Mikhail' for a specific reason. Perhaps there's a connection between the two Russians. Alina doesn't know what that connection is, but that doesn't matter."

Peter seemed to be following Will's train of thought. "Because Mikhail suspects she's in contact with Yevtushenko and will pass him the name?"

Will nodded.

"Doesn't get us anywhere nearer to understanding what the connection is, though."

Will considered this. "Yevtushenko's a conduit to, as you call him, Number 1."

William.

"SVR officer gives Alina the name 'Mikhail'; Alina passes the name to her lover; and lover boy passes it to Number 1. Exactly as the SVR officer hoped."

Peter frowned. "A message?"

"It could be."

"But the connection . . . ?"

"What if there is no connection beyond the fact that while Mikhail may not be known to Yevtushenko, the defector will certainly know *of* him."

"Mikhail's the big SVR officer's real name?"

"It's conjecture at present. But Suzy can help on that."

"But why would he want Yevtushenko to have his real name?"

"To unsettle him." He walked up to the board, and grabbed a marker pen. "Here's a thought: the crown jewel is stolen, Russians are going to do everything they can to get it back, so they send the one man who can achieve that objective." He momentarily glanced back at Peter. "A man who has identified and grabbed Russian double agents in the past." He looked at the board. "I think Mikhail knows who Number 1 is and needs Number 1 to understand who he's dealing with."

Peter stood next to him, his eyes also staring at the board. "Could be a pincer movement."

"Mikhail on the one side, his four-man team on the other?"

"It would explain why the team's remained static. Mikhail wants Number 1 to know that if keeps hold of the crown jewel, he'll hunt him down and put a bullet in his head."

Will considered this. "You're thinking that he's trying to force a sale? And the team is there to pay and take delivery?"

"Yes. Aggressive leverage. The team isn't a benign bunch of business-cover spooks." Peter folded his arms. "They're hard bastards, men who are waiting for Mikhail to drive Number 1 toward them so they can confront him with a bag of cash to buy back the paper, or failing that put a shitload of bullets into Number 1's body."

Will nodded. "It's a good theory, but wrong."

Peter frowned. "You're sure?"

Will said, "I think the team *are* shooters, but there's no pincer movement to be had."

"Look, we *are* conjecturing, but this has to make sense because . . ."

"No!" Will put a finger against one of Peter's questions.

Why can't it be copied and its value therefore diluted?

"Damn."

"Yes, damn." Will removed his finger. "There can't be a sale."

"Because a buyer would need to know that he or she's in possession of something unique."

"And anything on a piece of paper *can* be copied."

"None of this makes sense." Peter sounded exasperated. "How can this paper retain any value?"

"Its value is to the man who orchestrated its theft. He's not looking to sell it, and the Russians have no intention of trying to buy it back." He repeated, "There's no pincer movement."

"Then what?"

Will said quietly, "What if the Russians have sent a spycatcher? Their best. Mikhail is warning Number 1 that Mikhail's that man. And the team is there to support him while he does what he excels in."

"But if that's the case, why's the team still holed up in the hotel?"

"Perhaps because Number 1's hiding in a location that's known to Mikhail. No doubt it's an armed camp, too heavily defended for Mikhail and his men to go in there, but the moment Number 1 steps out then Mikhail will activate his team and go for him."

"A standoff?"

"It's possible."

"It would also suggest that Mikhail's got other assets in situ who are helping him watch Number 1's place."

Will agreed. Recalling what the injured Polish AW operative had said to him in Gdansk, he frowned. "Mikhail actively encouraged the Poles to stop Number 1's men leaving Poland, and by implication he wasn't concerned if the Poles took possession of the paper. Now we have a standoff between Number 1 and Mikhail, and that would suggest that the paper and Number 1 himself are no threat while they're locked down in their current location." He rubbed his face. "I suspect the Russians know that the paper's useless to anyone except Number 1; and that it's useless to Number 1 unless he has freedom of movement."

"But how does Mikhail know the location of Number 1?"

Will shrugged. "Someone close to Number 1 tipped him off, or maybe he's had him under observation for several weeks."

"Neither makes sense. An insider would have also tipped him off that the paper was about to be stolen. The Russians would have shot Yevtushenko the moment he tried to get near it."

"Maybe the insider wasn't privy to that information." Will shook his head. "No, you're right. An insider would have tipped off Mikhail about Number 1's location because that location had a precise value to the SVR. The value being that a highly valuable SVR paper was about to transit from Moscow to the location."

Peter nodded. "The same logic would apply to the need to have Number 1 under SVR observation prior to the theft."

"I agree." Will was deep in thought. Speaking to himself, he muttered, "Come on. Think, think."

Peter was silent.

Will frowned. Speaking slowly and deliberately, he said, "I think Mikhail already knew the location of Number 1, maybe had known for years, but had no specific concerns about him. But when the paper was stolen, Mikhail knew the only place it was headed was Number 1's hands. The Russian tried to stop that happening in Gdansk, but failed. So he then raced to Number 1's location and has been close to the place ever since."

"He should have the shooters with him."

"Yes, he should. Unless . . ." His voice trailed as new thoughts entered his mind. "Unless . . ." One thought stuck. "*Movement* remains the key. Suppose Mikhail knows that Number 1 has to take the paper to a place that crosses the path of the SVR team."

"Gives the Berlin boys a head start?"

"Yes, though before you ask, I haven't got a clue as to where that location is or why the paper needs to be moved."

"But you *do* have an idea as to what message Mikhail was relaying to Number 1."

Will moved right up to the board and drew a line between the last two questions:

Why did he tell Alina that his name was Mikhail?
Who is Number 1?

Will looked at Peter, then wrote three sentences alongside the line connecting these two questions:

My name is Mikhail. Your new Russian friend will tell you what I'm capable of. If you do anything with the paper, I'll kill you.

FOURTEEN

Will waited in a side alley close to the Grand Hyatt. He wondered how Adam was faring doing his circuits of the hotel, as it was cold *and* wet and still very dark.

Roger and Mark walked quickly toward him; Roger was dressed in an expensive suit and overcoat, meaning he'd done the lobby shift; Mark was wearing clothes that were designed to keep him dry and warm, and allow him to move quickly if need be.

They stopped, their faces barely visible in the poor light, and formed a circle with Will.

Will asked, "Is there any pattern to the team's activities in the hotel?"

Mark shook his head. "None, beyond that the team rarely shows itself."

"What's its setup?"

Roger answered, "The men have got four adjacent rooms on the fifth floor."

"Are the rooms cleaned daily?"

"Yeah, but the men stay in their rooms when that happens."

"Can we get a universal swipe key off one of the maids or another member of staff?"

"Should be easy, but it ain't going to be any use while the rooms are always occupied."

"Not always occupied."

"True, but the men have appeared in the lobby on their own for no more than sixty seconds before they've disappeared back to the elevator."

"Shit!"

"What would you hope to find in their rooms?"

"Anything that might tell us the whereabouts of their leader."

Roger shook his head. "We have to assume they're a professional unit. There just *might* be something on one of their cell phones, but I doubt it, and I doubt they'll have anything compromising in their rooms. Plus, when they leave their rooms, they'll have their cells with them."

Mark suggested, "We could grab one of the men. Try to make him talk."

Will looked in the direction of the hotel. "We can't afford to show our hand. Not yet. Plus, we might actually need the Russian team." He told them about Mikhail and the possibilities of what was happening.

Roger said, "If true, that means there's a lot riding on this Mikhail guy. It's all fine if he alerts his team that Number 1's on the move. Then we tool up and follow the team. But what happens if Number 1 slips the net before either team gets to him?"

"I think Mikhail knows exactly what he's doing." Will looked at both operatives. "If the Russians move at short notice, can you guarantee you can get everyone on them?"

"Without a doubt. Whichever of us is back at Auguststrasse can be with us in ten minutes max with all our kit. We've timed it during peak and off-peak hours. And we can do rolling pickups, on foot or public transport surveillance, plus if the Russian team's heading to the airport, we reckon we can get there twenty minutes quicker than a taxi driver."

"Good."

Mark said, "It'll all be fine, but we've got a lot of eggs in one basket. Mikhail may know what he's doing, but we're depending on his not being distracted or overstretched."

"He won't be . . ." Will's stomach suddenly knotted as a realization struck him. "Oh. Fuck!"

"Will?"

Will ignored his colleagues. His mind was racing and panicking. He cursed his stupidity.

If Will's theory was correct—that Mikhail had given his name to Alina in order to send a message to William and produce a standoff—William would do everything in his power to destabilize Mikhail.

Just as he'd done with Will.

He'd go after Mikhail's loved ones.

FIFTEEN

Will couldn't sleep during the flight. He was tired, but his mind was too active and his emotions confused. He tried not to think about Sarah, about the disgust he felt toward himself for putting her and her husband in danger, about the way she'd held him and asked, *Where have you gone, my little brother?*

But those thoughts remained. As did the worry that sometime over the coming days, a man with a gun could be walking toward a house in suburban Moscow, kicking the door in, and shooting Mikhail's family.

Until now, the right thing to do had been to allow the standoff between the SVR officer and William to continue until Will could establish William's location and the significance of the paper in his possession. But things had changed. He was totally reliant on Mikhail to keep William pinned down, and he was totally vulnerable to the possibility that Mikhail could lose his nerve, if he realized his family was under threat, and return to Moscow.

If no threat had yet presented itself to Mikhail's family, Will had one option available to him to accelerate matters. But that option would also place other people's lives in extreme danger.

That afternoon, Will stood outside a faculty building belonging to the Belarusian State University, Minsk. Students were leaving the building, carrying books and bags, some of them holding hands, all of them dressed in scarves and hats and coats. They all seemed carefree and full of joy, and as Will watched them he hoped that none of them would make the kind of choices he'd made toward the end of his degree program.

Alina exited the building, carrying Maria in one arm and a folded baby carriage in the other. She stopped and tried to open the carriage but appeared to be struggling.

Will walked quickly across the street. "Hello, Alina."

She barely glanced at him, looked annoyed with the carriage, and continued to try to release catches. "Damn thing. I think it really has broken this time. Here." She handed Maria to him. "Keep her warm."

Will took her, wondered what to do given he'd never held a baby before, then unbuttoned his thick overcoat, placed her inside, and drew the coat around her. "Thanks for meeting me at such short notice."

Alina was bent over the baby carriage, trying to yank bits of it apart, clearly on the verge of losing her temper. Something snapped close to her hand. She rose, holding a jagged piece of plastic tubing. "Shit!" She tossed the tubing away and kicked the carriage. "Another expense!"

"Come on." Will looked at the dark clouds above. "We need to get inside before the heavens open." He started opening his coat.

But Alina said, "She seems happy with you." She grabbed the carriage, walked up to a university security guard who was attempting to light a cigarette in the bitterly cold easterly wind, spoke to him, and left the useless carriage in his care. Returning to Will, she muttered, "I didn't bring Maria a waterproof coat because the carriage keeps her dry. If we walk quickly, we can be home in twenty minutes. But watch out for patches of ice."

She led the way, with Will anxiously scouring the ground for signs of anything that would cause him to slip with his precious burden.

They walked past shops and parkland before moving into residential streets. "I'm not sure I can be of any further help to you."

Will gingerly stepped onto a sidewalk and replied, "You may be right."

"Aren't you supposed to tell me that you know I'm hiding something from you?"

"I'd be relieved if you were; it would mean this trip hasn't been a waste of time."

"I'm going to disappoint you."

Maria seemed to be waking up. She was emitting small sounds and starting to move. Will held her close to his chest, hoping that his coat was keeping her warm and that she didn't try to wriggle out of her wrappings.

When they reached Alina's apartment building, snow was starting to fall. Will placed his big arms farther around his care. Alina tapped numbers into a security pad while cursing and shaking.

The warmth was immediate as they entered the building. Thirty seconds later, they were inside Alina's apartment. Alina took Maria, placed her in a high chair, and disappeared into the kitchen. As Will dumped his coat over the sofa, he could hear Alina putting a kettle on to boil and rummaging through cupboards. When she returned to the living room, she was holding a small plastic bowl containing a spoon and baby food. Placing the food in front of Maria, she looked at Will and frowned. "You've got Maria's dribble on your suit. Start feeding her; I'll get a sponge."

Will grabbed a chair and positioned it in front of the child. Sitting, he looked at Maria, saw the child bang her fists expectantly on the high chair's tray, and tentatively raised the spoon to her mouth. Maria swallowed the food, banged her fists again, and beamed.

Alina reentered the room holding two mugs of tea. After placing one of them next to Will, she crouched down beside him and smoothed a damp sponge over his jacket's lapel. "It should be fine."

"I don't mind." Will placed another spoonful into Maria's mouth.

"You have children?"

Will shook his head.

"Your wife is one of those busy career woman types?"

Will smiled. "I don't have one of them either. I live alone."

She stood and glanced at her baby. "Well, you're not doing a bad job. Sometimes it takes me an hour to get her to take her first mouthful. The cold must have built up her appetite." She sat on the sofa and took a gulp of her tea. Keeping her eyes fixed on him, she asked, "Have you come back because you're suspicious of me?"

Will laughed gently. "I have to be suspicious of people."

"Is that why you don't have a wife? You have trust issues?"

Will's smile faded.

"Must be an occupational hazard, I guess."

Will scooped the spoon through more baby food. "From what you've said, Lenka was different."

"Was?"

"Is."

She was silent for a moment before saying, "He's always been an academically intelligent man, but not smart. Does that make sense?"

"I know what you mean." He gave Maria more food.

"His flaw, and I've always loved him for it, is that he's *too* trusting of people. He should never have joined the SVR." She gripped her mug, allowing its warmth to soothe her cold hands. "You're obviously different."

Will held the spoon in midair, feeling a moment of sadness. "Yes." He placed the spoon into Maria's mouth.

"What suspicions do you have about me?"

Will scraped the last of the food onto a spoon and said, "I had to consider whether you were a Belarusian security service or SVR officer planted here to meet whoever came knocking on the door after Lenka disappeared, or a freelance agent for one of those services, maybe that you aren't Alina Petrova. So I checked up on you. While I can't discount the possibility that you're an agent, I do know for certain that your identity checks out and that you're not an intelligence officer." He placed the spoon into the empty bowl and turned toward her. "But I don't think you're an agent or have previously had any kind of relationship with intelligence services. The relationship that matters to you is the one you have with Lenka. I think that if anyone had approached you and asked you to spy on your lover, you'd have told them to go to hell."

Alina nodded.

"But I could be wrong."

She was motionless.

"Though I hope not."

Quietly, she said, "I'm not a spy."

"Many spies say that." Will grabbed his tea and nodded toward Maria. The girl was now playing with different-colored plastic shapes that were looped on a wire attached to her chair. "Has she had enough food?"

"Yes. Thank you, I . . ." Her voiced trailed and she lowered her head. "I too have to deal with possibilities right now." She looked at him. "You can't deny that it's possible Lenka's dead."

"Or that he's alive."

Alina shook her head. "He stole a piece of paper and delivered it to someone. What use is he to that person now?"

Will knew that she was right, but he could also see that she was becoming tearful. "Killing a man is not an easy thing to do." He pictured the armor-clad private contractors attempting to slaughter anything that moved in the Gdansk port. "We don't know if we're dealing with a killer."

Alina looked desperate. "Should I send him another message? Should *you* send him a message?"

"Saying what?"

"I don't know."

"Have you sent him any messages aside from the one about the contents of the note?"

She hesitated. "I sent him one right after Mikhail came here. But he didn't reply."

"What did you say?"

"The truth. That a Russian intelligence officer called Mikhail had been asking questions about him."

Will's heartbeat increased. "Any since?"

"No."

"Why not?"

"Because . . ." She drained the last of her tea. "Because I'm not sure the messages would be read by him. Maybe his phone is now with . . . them."

Will nodded.

Her expression changed, and she said quickly, "Couldn't you give me words to manipulate them? Anything that might keep him alive."

Will didn't answer her. Instead, he looked around the tiny but well-maintained home, then let his gaze rest on Maria. "If I can bring Lenka back to you, do you think he'll stay?"

"Of course. The only reason he hasn't lived with us was because he had a wage coming in. But whatever happens, there's no going back to the SVR." Alina smiled. "I think he'll be relieved that the decision's been made for him. Somehow, we'll make ends meet. He'll stay."

It was the answer Will had expected. "I did consider asking you to send Lenka another message, knowing it would be read by the man who's got him. Your message would have said that I'd visited you and advised you that I knew Lenka's location, that matters would be concluded tomorrow and that I would try to keep Lenka alive, but that it was imperative that you went somewhere safe until all of this was over in case there were repercussions. You would have added that you didn't believe that I was going to keep him alive, that Lenka should keep his phone safe and that you would contact him as soon as you were safe."

"What purpose would such a message have served?"

"It might have caused the men who are holding Lenka to panic and move."

And in turn to mobilize the SVR team, and to enable Will's team to follow them and gun down William and anyone working for him, all before William had time to threaten Mikhail's family and cause the SVR officer to back down from his vigil on William.

"But that's good! They'll abandon Lenka."

Will shook his head. "They'll put a bullet in his brain."

Alina looked uncertain. "If he's not dead yet, right now he's as good as dead. Isn't sending the message worth the risk?"

"Would you be willing to press Send on your phone, knowing you might actually be pulling a trigger?"

"I . . ."

"In any case, there are other risks."

Alina frowned.

Moving to the sofa, he sat next to Alina and held one of her hands between his. "I believe that the man who's leading Lenka's captors is *very* smart. There's every possibility that he will suspect your message was dictated by me. That would place you in danger." He glanced at Maria. "*Both* of you."

"We could move somewhere safe."

"Where?"

"My parents', or my aunts'."

"Does Lenka know their identities and locations?"

"Yes, he's . . . Oh, I see."

Lenka could be tortured to reveal their addresses.

"I'm sorry—we can't discount that possibility. Plus, I suspect you'd need to keep up your work at the university."

"I have to earn my salary."

"No doubt, but they could get you there."

Alina squeezed his hand. "There must be something we can do."

"Maybe, but sending a message would endanger far too many people."

Including his sister.

Alina stared at nothing and said quietly, "You said you'd try to bring him back to me. Did you mean what you said?"

"Yes."

Alina looked at him and smiled. A tear ran down her cheek.

Will said, "There is still hope."

"What hope?" She yanked her hand away from him. "You don't know where he is; you don't know who he's with; you know nothing about the paper he's stolen; and you don't know if he's alive or dead."

Will nodded. "All of that has to change. I need his home address in Russia. Can you give that to me?"

Alina frowned. "Sure, but . . . how can that be useful?"

"Have you been there before?"

"Three times. It's a rural cottage, outside Moscow."

"Did you notice whether he keeps a safe in the house?"

"I don't think so. . . . No, I'm sure I'd have seen one if it was there. The house is small."

"Does he have a private space—a locked cabinet, drawers, any-where that he'd use to keep things that only he could access?"

The confusion on Alina's face was evident. "No. I told you before: he didn't like to hide anything from me."

"That might be true, but he might have wished to hide something from you that he considered dangerous."

"Like what?"

"Information." Will stood and put on his overcoat. Maria was still playing with the shapes. Will grabbed one of them and moved it quickly back and forth on the wire while smiling at the child. Maria giggled and tried to get the shape, but Will moved it out of reach, then gave it to her. He thought for a moment before reaching into a pocket and withdrawing his wallet. It contained 1.6 million Belaru-sian rubles, the approximate equivalent of two hundred dollars. He pulled out all of the cash and held it toward Alina. "I don't know if it's enough to get a new baby carriage, but please accept it."

Alina looked offended. "We manage. I don't need your charity and I certainly don't need *spy* money."

Will tried to think what to say. He settled on honesty. "It's my own cash, and in any case if you get her a new carriage it will save me from being petrified that I'm going to slip while carrying her next time I come."

"Next time?" Alina's expression had changed.

"Just . . ." Will felt awkward. "Just to see you're both okay."

Alina's eyes narrowed. "Lenka may not be in my life right now, but as you say, I must have hope that he's alive and will come to me. I've no desire for another lover."

Will sighed. "That's not why I'm here."

The anger returned. "I agree. You're here because you have an agenda to get the stolen paper."

"*Please,* take the money."

"Are you attempting to cleanse your conscience?"

Will shook his head. "No, no." He gestured toward Maria. "I just want her to have a waterproof roof over her head. That's all. *Please.*"

Alina's expression became neutral. "No strings?"

"None."

She hesitated, then took the money. "I can't say it won't help. What do you hope to find at Lenka's house?"

"A secret."

"Won't the police have searched the place and be guarding it?"

"Probably."

"Then you mustn't go there."

Will saw that she was genuinely concerned. "You're right that I've got no idea what's going on. But I have to go there. It's my only chance of helping Lenka."

She kept her eyes on him, seemed deep in thought, and said quietly, "He told me before our first visit to his home that he'd made the place 'Maria-proof,' that he bought a gate for the stairs so that she couldn't hurt herself by climbing them, that the only dangerous place was the basement, though he kept that padlocked."

"Basement? Where?"

"In the hallway."

Will studied her. "What's in there?"

"I don't know."

"Yes you do! You have no secrets, remember?"

For a moment, Alina looked angry. Her expression changed. "Lenka told me once that if anything were to happen to him, I should go to the basement. One of the electricity sockets is false. Behind it is a hole. He keeps money and valuable documents in there."

"Thank you."

Alina shrugged and said in a matter-of-fact way, "I think we'd like it if you came back. Can you eat *kotleta pokrestyansky*?"

"Sure."

"Then I'll cook the dish next time you're in Minsk."

Very few women had cooked for Will. For the briefest of moments, he felt totally removed from the real reason he was here. "I'll trim the pork cutlets, if you like?"

Alina nodded. "That would be a help." She moved away from him. "I . . . I'll write down Lenka's address."

As she walked out of the room, Will placed one of his big scarred hands against Maria's cheek. She looked at him and smiled. Quietly, he sang her a children's song, one he remembered from his childhood, and when he finished he stared at her, feeling nothing but guilt. He was sure his decision not to send the message was the right one. It was probable that William would have seen through it and in turn would have killed Lenka and gone after Alina, Maria, and Sarah. But it was *possible* that the ruse would have worked. He wondered if Mikhail had a young daughter.

It seemed ever true that in order for him to save one person, at least one other had to die.

SIXTEEN

Tibor walked quickly along the corridors of CIA headquarters in Langley. He was in the part of the building that housed the National Clandestine Service and specifically was moving through the section belonging to the Office of Russian and European Analysis. Most of the doors in the corridor were closed; beyond them were intelligence officers who kept their doors shut to protect their secrets from others within the organization. Tibor smiled as he continued walking, because no number of closed doors could prevent Flintlock having access to the CIA's secrets.

As he moved along the corridor, he mentally ticked off the operations and investigations that he knew were ongoing within the rooms on either side of him—a four-person team was planning an attempt to sell a Brussels-based Russian FSB officer a vehicle which, unbeknown to him, contained a beacon tracking device; a case officer was pouring over one of his French agent's files because he was beginning to wonder if the agent's intelligence was too good to be true; a team leader was berating her staff after a countersurveillance operation in Copenhagen had gone badly wrong and resulted in a CIA operative being held in a Danish police cell for two days; a nervous officer was making preparations to up the ante after years of grooming a GRU major under business cover, and get on a plane to meet the major in Zurich and tell him that in truth he was not an arms dealer and that the major had instead been passing secrets to an officer of Serbia's Security Information Agency; an operations officer was at loggerheads with a paramilitary officer because one wanted a mission against a Chechen terrorist to continue to be invisible satellite surveillance and the other wanted to bring it to a head with a joint SOG–SEAL assault; and an intelligence officer was sitting at her desk doing nothing, racked with grief and guilt because one of her best Russian agents had taken his own life to end the constant fear that one day he'd be caught and exposed as a traitor.

One of the doors opened, and a field operative whose work focused on the Russian target emerged.

Tibor's smile broadened as he walked toward the man. *"Dobrý den,* Tim."

Tim frowned. He did not know who Tibor was, but reciprocated, "Good afternoon."

"If I were you, I'd come clean about the twenty thousand."

Tim's face paled.

Tibor chuckled as he walked past the man. Tim was unaware that CIA senior management knew that he'd stolen twenty thousand dollars that he was supposed to have paid to a Hungarian access agent, and had decided to give him two weeks to come forward and confess. If he did so and returned the money, they would accept his resignation and his pension rights would be protected. If not, they'd cut off his balls.

Tibor turned into a corridor belonging to the Office of Middle East and North Africa Analysis. Three men were standing outside a room, talking in hushed tones. One of them was Ed Baker, the head of the office.

Ed growled at Tibor, *"As-salâmu 'alaykum,* Tibor."

Tibor beamed. *"Wa 'alaykumu s-salâmu wa rahmatu l-lâhi wa barakâtuh.* Still grubbing around in the desert looking for crazies?"

Ed made no effort to hide his hostility. "I hope your star wanes someday soon."

As Tibor skipped past the senior officer, he replied, "If it does and wanes low enough, I'll apply for your job."

"Fuck you."

The insult heightened Tibor's good mood. He walked down more corridors until he reached the meeting room. After checking that his tie's knot hadn't slipped, he made three rapid knocks on the door and entered. Marcus, Damien, and Lawrence were seated at a table, looking at him. He shut the door, decided not to sit, and instead leaned against a wall and studied his Flintlock colleagues. "I've got some news."

"Of course you have."

"We wouldn't be here, otherwise."

"Though we're hoping the news is good."

Tibor considered how to respond. "It's bad news that could be transformed into excellent news."

Lawrence asked, "Yevtushenko related?"

Tibor nodded. "We've had a call from the golden source."

Marcus looked affronted, given that he was the prime point of contact with the agent. "Why did the source call you?"

Tibor waved his hand with a flourish. "Because I'm the good-looking one. Maybe the source has the hots for me."

Damien huffed. "Given the source's current family situation, I hardly think that's the case."

Tibor pretended to look hurt. "Really?"

Marcus shook his head. "When the call came in, you should have found me."

"Bit difficult given you were on a 747 this morning, flying back from that silly thing you're doing in Singapore."

"It's not *silly.* If my operation works, I'll get three governments to turn on each other and will change the landscape of Asia."

Lawrence was becoming impatient. "Any of us can take a call from the source. What's the news?"

Tibor looked at them, one by one. "Tomorrow, Mr. Will Cochrane is going to fly to Russia and attempt to break into Yevtushenko's home."

After a moment's silence, Damien asked, "You think he'll find something there that will tell him who's got Yevtushenko?"

"I don't think so. Whoever's clever enough to manipulate the Polish exfiltration route should also be astute enough to have briefed Yevtushenko not to leave anything behind that could lead men to him."

"Then, providing Yevtushenko remains off the radar, there is no *bad news*."

Marcus drummed his fingers on the table while staring at Tibor. "I guess that's not the issue, is it Tibor."

"Nope."

Marcus turned to his colleagues. "*We* never had the chance to brief Yevtushenko to cleanse his place of any evidence that he'd had contact with us. And my God, Yevtushenko's tradecraft's so poor that he would have needed that briefing."

Lawrence's mind was racing. "The FSB or SVR would have searched his home; maybe there's nothing to find or they took anything remotely interesting."

"Maybe, providing they knew what was *interesting*."

More silence.

Damien suggested, "We could send Miss Petrova another note saying that Cochrane's heading over to Yevtushenko's home. That should prompt the private boys to get him there."

Tibor shook his head. "The source says she's now cooperating with British Intelligence."

"Shit! That means he's seen our note to her."

"He has, and though he's got no knowledge of us he's smelled the whiff of our business cover operation against Yevtushenko."

Lawrence said angrily, "We can't allow Cochrane to get anywhere near us."

Tibor smiled. "Of course not."

With deliberation, Marcus asked, "So how can we turn this impending disaster into excellent news?"

Tibor folded his arms. "I've got an idea."

His colleagues were motionless.

"Yevtushenko's property is almost certainly going to have some kind of police presence, but I reckon it's going to be minimal . . . couple of cops, not much more. And they'll be there just to make sure the house isn't contaminated after the security services searched it when Yevtushenko disappeared."

"Cochrane will easily get past them."

Tibor held up his hand. "Thankfully, he will." He pointed at Marcus. "Have you still got Valerii and his men on your payroll?"

Marcus nodded.

"Good. So, I'm thinking you put a few of them around Yevtushenko's property—at distance and with long-range scopes, but in positions that ensure they've got every inch of the property's exterior covered."

"A hit? That could lead back to us."

"Let's make it a bit more subtle. Valerii spots Cochrane enter the property and then immediately makes an anonymous call to the cops saying he's a concerned passerby who's seen an armed man smash into the house."

Lawrence smiled, "Armed man? That's good. Suggests he's not a petty criminal who can be dealt with by the cops guarding the place. Instead, and given the significance of the property, it suggests he's an IO. The cops will take that break-in very seriously."

"And will immediately deploy in numbers to grab him."

"Though Cochrane will resist capture."

"And as a result, there will be a fight." Tibor drummed his hands against the wall. "We *do* need to be subtle, but we can't allow Cochrane to escape. If he gets out of range of the cops, he'll run into Valerii's ring of steel. And they'll use Russian police sidearms to gun him down."

SEVENTEEN

At 1330 hours the following day, Will was walking through the arrivals section of Moscow's Domodedovo Airport. Dressed in a business suit and overcoat, he'd entered Russia using a passport that was in the name of Christopher Jones and contained a multientry visa for business trips into the country. In his wallet and attaché case he had documentation to support his identity, including bank and business cards, a smart phone and laptop crammed with data showing he was a self-employed headhunter specializing in sourcing executives for the oil and gas industry, and a legitimate letter from a Moscow-based office-leasing agency saying that his meeting with them was confirmed for 3:30 P.M. this afternoon and that they'd be delighted if he decided to set up a subsidiary branch of his business in their premises.

Aside from his passport, so far none of this documentation had been needed, as he was not questioned by the airport's immigration or customs officers.

He moved to the Avis desk, gave his car reservation details to a female employee, and was supplied keys and instructions to locate his prebooked E-class Mercedes sedan. Ninety minutes later, he was heading northwest out of the center of Moscow. As he did so, he recalled that the last time he was in the city, he, Roger, Laith, and three Russian assets had been chasing an extremely dangerous man, culminating in the hostile escaping and most of the team being captured and tortured by soldiers. Then, Russia had been on the brink of war with the United States. Now the city looked busy, yet normal and peaceful.

Within one hour, he was on the outskirts of the city, driving through suburbia. Soon thereafter he was moving through countryside. He estimated it would take him forty minutes to reach the man who was going to give him the equipment he needed before going to Yevtushenko's house. Maybe today he could find out what was going on. Or maybe not. He hated the feeling of not being in control, though he was resolute that he would get to the truth.

The six Russian men were by the back of the SUV, finishing getting dressed in their white arctic clothing. They were in a deserted area of woodland sixty miles north of Moscow.

After donning his balaclava and pulling his jacket hood over it, Valerii looked at his colleagues. "Four miles on foot to the valley; then we split up and move to our positions. Understood?"

The men nodded.

Checking that his Bushnell PowerView 20x50 surveillance binoculars were firmly in place within his jacket, Valerii added, "Do it exactly as we planned."

Yesterday the men had reconnoitered the valley containing Yevtushenko's isolated house. They'd chosen three locations that collectively would give the team complete coverage of the property's exterior from distances ranging between four hundred and six hundred yards. And they'd chosen two backup locations for each angle of observation, in case they needed to move because Will Cochrane was approaching the house on a route that was too close to their positions. The men would be in two-man teams: one to watch the house, the other to watch their backs. All of them were armed with MP-443 handguns, the standard issue firearm carried by police officers in this part of Russia, though Valerii had instructed them that they were only to use them if it looked likely that Will would escape the police. But if it came to that, they'd know what to do. They were former Spetsnaz operatives—experts in concealment and surveillance, long-range marksmanship, endurance, and close-quarters combat. As their commanding officer, Valerii had led the men on numerous successful missions. Now he commanded them in far more dubious, illegal, and very profitable operations.

"It's crucial he's in the building before we call it in."

One of the men asked, "What should we do if the cops open fire on us?"

Valerii pulled out his handgun, checked its workings, and shrugged. "Don't do anything to them until Cochrane's dead. After that, you can do what you like."

Will stopped his vehicle in what was technically a farmstead, though it was rather more a junkyard. Around him were corrugated iron huts, three cars that were resting on bricks and had no wheels, a barn whose timber had completely rotted away down one side, a small house that retained sturdy walls but had no roof, bits of mangled and unrecognizable machinery, and a trailer. Beyond the farmstead was uninhabited forest. He got out of the car and stood on snow-covered ground.

A middle-aged man—medium height, ruffled jet black hair, a handlebar moustache, numerous old scars on his face—emerged from the trailer. He was wearing oil-stained blue overalls and was holding a double-barreled shotgun in one hand.

Will looked around before calling out in Russian, "Good to see you again, Arman."

"You're on your own?"

"I didn't bother to check"—Will grinned and nodded toward the gun—"because I knew you'd shoot anything that tried to creep up on me from behind."

"Nice car. Is it yours?"

"It's a rental."

"You're lucky. If it was yours I could have put both barrels into you and sold the Mercedes for parts."

Arman Shpalikov walked quickly toward him, despite the limp he'd had since serving as a Soviet captain in the war in Afghanistan. Shaking Will's hand with an iron grip, he replied, "Good to see you too, Philip. You want tea, coffee, vodka?"

From previous experience, Will knew that none of the options were preferable. "Black coffee."

"But vodka when you've done your work—right?"

"If I have time."

He led Will to his trailer. Inside were a tiny bed, a single-ring gas stove, a sink that was overflowing with dirty dishes and cups, a torn leather seat that ran flush against three sides of the trailer, and a two-foot-square table.

Will sat. "How've you been?"

Arman placed his gun on the table, put a pan of water onto the stove, struck a match, and lit the gas. "You know. Every day's a blessing."

It was. A piece of shrapnel was lodged inside Arman's body. One day it would reach his heart and kill him, but the stubborn old warrior refused to have an operation to remove it because he believed the shrapnel made him embrace every moment of being alive.

"How's business?"

The Russian grabbed two mugs and began rinsing them. "It shifts with the times."

Arman did many things: as a former tank commander, his forte was vehicle and machinery repair work, though when the work wasn't there he also made money by hunting wildlife and selling the catches at the local market, felling trees and turning them into logs and planks, buying and selling scrap metal, washing floors at a nearby restaurant, collecting refuse, and providing logistical support for MI6 operations in Russia.

Will had recruited him six years earlier because the Russian was an expert at sourcing things—guns, vehicles, communications equipment, fake documents, men who'd not think twice about killing someone for cash—and had a network of contacts who could help MI6 personnel move covertly across Russia in trains, boats, trucks, and other modes of transport. Though Will paid him for his service, Arman's motivation to work for him was grounded in his hatred for the Soviet Union and by extension his hatred for Russia, because in his view both countries had been run by the same set of psychopathic bastards.

That hatred had started when he was deployed with the Fortieth Army to Afghanistan to fight the mujahideen. He'd witnessed both sides commit numerous atrocities, but one in particular had left him mentally scarred. During a Soviet offensive into the Panjshir Valley, his tank became damaged and separated from the rest of his unit. He and the rest of his crew were captured by mujahideen guerillas who immediately used their knives to behead his soldiers. One of the guerrillas then plunged his knife into Arman's leg and kept twisting it while asking him in broken Russian how many Soviet tanks were heading along the valley. The torture continued for thirty minutes, during which time Arman told them nothing. He too would have almost certainly been decapitated, but Soviet soldiers who'd been looking for their missing tank attacked the group. The mujahideen fled into the hills and escaped, much to the fury of the officer commanding the Soviet rescue unit, a fury that was intensified when the major saw that one of the decapitated heads belonged to his younger brother.

Unable to walk, and in agony, Arman was placed on a stretcher, and the unit carried him three miles to the nearest village. He'd thought that he'd been brought there to receive medical help, but it transpired that the major had other intentions. After Arman was lowered onto the ground, the major ordered his men to round up every Afghan villager and point their guns at them. Further orders were issued. Five women were pulled out from the group, their legs and arms were bound with rope, and they were forced to lie down on top of each other until they formed a pile. Gasoline was poured over them. Holding a lighter in his hand and speaking to them through a translator, the major asked the rest of the villagers if they knew the whereabouts of the mujahideen who'd attacked Arman's tank crew. The villagers were terrified, screaming, and pleading with him that they knew nothing. Before Arman could say anything, the major ignited the lighter and tossed it onto the bound women. As the women burned to death, the major strode forward and grabbed a girl who looked about four years old. After tying her to a shovel, he stuck the barrels of two rifles deep into the ground either side of the burning corpses, got two of his soldiers to hold the shovel at each end so that both the tool and the girl attached to it were horizontal, ordered the men to hold the girl over the fire, and tied the shovel to the butt of each rifle. Watching helplessly as the girl roasted to death over the bodies, Arman screamed louder than he'd screamed when the mujahideen blade had been stuck in him.

That scream had stayed in his head ever since.

As Will watched the former tank commander open a can of instant coffee and spoon granules into cups, he wondered, not for the first time, if the real reason Arman had refused to have the shrapnel removed was because he was praying for it to reach his heart.

Arman pushed a mug toward Will. "I know it'll taste like piss." He smiled. "Good job you don't come here for my cuisine."

Will took a sip of his drink and tried not to wince. "Did you get everything I asked for?"

Arman nodded, opened a cupboard, and placed a Makarov handgun on the table.

Will stripped it down. Though old, the weapon was in immaculate condition, and there was not a speck of dust within its workings. "Perfect."

"Shame I can't keep my dishes as clean, eh?"

"One of the advantages of being bachelors is that we don't have to."

"You still unmarried?"

Will nodded.

Arman looked confused. "I've got every excuse for being single because I look like the wrong end of an artillery strike. You don't."

Will shrugged. "I've not met anyone who'll have me."

Arman looked mischievous. "You have problems in the man department? If so I can get you some pills, much better than Viagra."

"That's very kind of you, Arman, but I'm fine in that *department*." He thought about having another sip of coffee but decided not to. "Being unmarried suits me."

"You sure?"

"No."

"Thought not." Arman took a gulp of his drink, grimaced in pain as he stood, and said, "The other stuff you need's on the bed. I've got to prepare the vehicle. Help yourself to more coffee."

After he'd left, Will removed his business attire, carefully placing his shirt, suit, and overcoat onto a hanger, and dressed in the clothes that Arman had gotten him. Within minutes he was wearing a white Windbreaker jacket, waterproof trousers, and boots. He looked inside the small knapsack that Arman had prepared for him: a crowbar, mallet, pair of binoculars, set of screwdrivers, military knife, lockpick set, and two spare magazines for the pistol. After putting the bag on his back, he walked out of the trailer.

Arman was on the other side of a clearing, standing next to a large off-road motorcycle, revving its engine while listening to the noise it was making. He took his hand off the throttle as Will approached him. "It looks like a heap of crap, but I've checked it thoroughly and have given it a tune-up. You'll have no problems."

Will sat on the bike. "I should be three hours. Much longer than that means something's gone wrong." He smiled while looking at his rental car. "And that means you can do whatever you like to the Mercedes."

Will brought the bike to a halt on a deserted country lane and checked his map. He was four miles away from Yevtushenko's cottage. Deciding that he could get to within two miles of the property before leaving the bike, he revved the throttle, kept control of the machine as its back wheel slid on ice, and drove off the lane onto open farmland. The land around him was featureless and frozen under a few inches of snow. No doubt in the warmer months the land would be plowed and crops would be planted in it, but now it looked inhospitable and lifeless.

He increased the revs as he drove the bike uphill, gripping it firmly as it shuddered due to the uneven ground. Within ten minutes, he reached the crest of the hill, stopped, turned off the engine, lowered the bike to the ground, and looked around. He was on a large area of flatland; beyond it was a valley. Moving to the edge of the hilltop, he removed his sack, lay down, and extracted the binoculars. Based upon his careful study of maps prior to entering Russia, he knew the valley before him was five miles long and four hundred yards wide. Most of it was covered with forest, though a single-lane track was easily visible and stretched along the entire right-hand side of the valley. That would be the route that Yevtushenko would take when traveling to and from his cottage. The house was not visible, obscured by trees, though Will knew its approximate location. On either side of the valley were slopes that were three-quarters covered with trees and rose to the elevation where he stood.

After adjusting the binoculars, he examined the track and saw that there were vehicle markings in the snow—given that it had snowed heavily earlier in the day, they had to be only a few hours old.

Lowering his binoculars, he stared at the large valley. If the FSB or SVR had a long-range surveillance team hidden somewhere in there,

watching Yevtushenko's house, it would take him up to a day to find
them, and even then he'd only do so if he was lucky and the team was
amateur. He'd never find a professional team. But he thought it highly
unlikely that Russian intelligence would dedicate such resources.
Yevtushenko's house was low priority now that the Russian was out
of the country and would never return.

He placed his sack onto his back and began moving along the
ridge along one side of the valley.

Fifteen minutes later, he stopped, lowered himself to the ground,
and crawled to the edge of the slope. Using his binoculars, he looked into
the valley. The track was five hundred yards below him, and beyond it
he could now see Yevtushenko's cottage. Directly in front of the property was a police squad car; standing next to it were three uniformed
young police officers, smoking, chatting to each other, stamping their
feet to try to stay warm. Based on their location and disposition, it was
clear the police were there simply to deter an opportunistic criminal
from entering the empty house and stealing anything of value.

He moved back from the slope and ran along the ridge. After eight
minutes he stopped and looked into the valley again. He was now
three miles away from his bike and one mile from the house; below
him he could see nothing but forest. Running fast, he moved down
the valley slope and soon was traversing its base. All the time, he kept
moving his head, searching for signs of life. But he saw no one and
kept moving quickly as he started ascending the slope on the other
side of the valley. When he reached its crest, he kept running until he
was out of sight of the valley, then briefly stopped and bent forward
with his hands on his knees to try to catch his breath. After throwing
himself to the ground, he withdrew his pistol, crawled back to the top
of the slope, and used his binoculars to examine the route he'd just
taken. If there'd been police officers hidden in the forest, he hoped
that the action he'd just taken would have flushed them out and sent
them racing up the hill after him.

But he saw nothing.

He looked toward Yevtushenko's house. It was once again hidden from view behind trees, but he knew that the rear of the house was five hundred yards away.

He spent twenty minutes examining the land in front of and either side of the cottage, put the binoculars away, ensured that his pack was tight on his back, and moved cautiously down the slope toward the cottage, his gun in both hands.

Reaching the valley base, he kept his gun at eye level, twitching it left and right. Snow was deeper within the forest; with each footfall his boots sank to ankle height, and lumps of it were falling from the trees around him. He tried to keep his breathing calm so that he could turn and accurately shoot anything that made a sound louder than the impact of snow on snow.

He heard noise. Distant, distorted, artificial. It grew louder as he moved forward, and soon he recognized the sound as a man's voice speaking on a radio. The police. He wondered if they were patrolling around the house or whether the noise was coming from inside the property. Perhaps there were more cops guarding the place.

Switching his gun's safety catch off, he silently continued. Fresh snowflakes were now falling from the sky. In less than one hour, it would be dark.

He saw glimpses of stone wall. Yevtushenko's house was thirty yards away. Stopping, he crouched down and waited in case the armed police came into view. He stayed like this for fifteen minutes, but saw no one. Now leopard-crawling over the snow, he edged nearer to the house, stopping every few yards in case the police decided to make a walk around its perimeter. If they did and spotted him, he'd have no choice other than to put nonlethal shots into their bodies and smash their radio equipment save what was in the vehicle so that they would have a chance to crawl to it and seek help rather than freeze to death. By that time, he'd be long gone.

He reached the house, rose to a crouch, and stayed flush against its rear wall as he moved to the corner. Dropping low so that his head was against the snow, he peered around the corner for a fraction of a second. He saw nothing, though he could hear the police chatting over the sounds of their radios. Moving to the other corner, he repeated the same drill, but saw nothing except the road at the front of the house. The police were no doubt still standing outside the front of the building.

The rear wall contained two windows and a back door in the center. He tried the door—it was locked. Removing the lockpick set, he knelt before the keyhole, placed pins into the lock, and within seconds had it open. Gripping his gun in one hand, he slowly turned the handle, pushed the door open a few inches, waited, then moved inside.

At that moment, one of Valerii's men sent his boss an SMS: *Confirmed sighting. He's in. Make the call.*

Will was in the kitchen. It was tiny—barely seven feet by five feet—and its surfaces were clear of anything save a metal kettle, a jar of coffee, and some mugs that contained traces of coffee in the bottom. He touched the kettle; it was lukewarm. The police had recently made themselves a drink. He wondered how long it would be before they wanted another one.

His heart beating fast, he held his gun ready to shoot and moved out of the room into a hallway. Halfway down was a fully laden coat rack. To either side of it were oil paintings; one of them was of a baby girl, the other was of a beautiful woman lying on her side next to a river while reading a book. Alina. At the bottom of each painting was the inscription *My darlings*.

Will heard more police radio chatter, but none of it was coming from inside the house. He walked upstairs and entered the bedroom. It looked functional, had no woman's touch, and was clearly used by Yevtushenko only to sleep in. Ignoring the bathroom, he went back downstairs and approached the living room but stopped four feet from the entrance. When he'd last seen them, the cops had been facing away from the house, but if they'd adjusted position they would be able to see him easily if he entered the room with its three large windows. From where he was standing he only had a partial view into the living room. He saw a violin resting on a stand, more paintings, shelves that were crammed with books, a sofa, a small television, nothing else.

More police radio chatter. This time louder, though still from outside and incomprehensible.

He froze, wondering if the police were about to enter the house.

Ten seconds passed.

The police were no longer talking to each other, though their radios were still noisy.

Will moved back to the kitchen, his gun held high, expecting to see that the guards had moved to the rear of the house.

No one was there.

Back in the hallway, he stared at the floor. A thick rug ran along its length. He started rolling it up, then stopped as he heard the police car's ignition. Frowning, he wondered if the men were making preparations for a new shift to arrive. If that were the case, most likely one of the first things the new shift would do was come in to make themselves a hot drink. He quickly continued rolling up the rug, then stopped. A hatch cover was in the center of the floor; within indentations on either side of it were two small padlocks looped through fasteners that would normally be screwed into the floor but at some stage had been wrenched away from the wood.

When the property had been searched, they'd found the hatch.

Still, the cops were silent.

Beads of sweat ran down his back as he lifted the cover. Below, a set of steps descended into pitch black. For a moment, he wondered what to do. Go in there and be trapped? Or get out while he still had the chance to do so?

Perhaps the police were silent because they had nothing left to say to each other, their thoughts now only about getting home and having supper with their families. Or perhaps they were quiet because they knew something was wrong.

He made a decision and began climbing into the basement. When he reached the floor, he moved his hands around, searching for a light switch. One of them brushed against a cord. He gripped it and pulled downward. A single bulb illuminated the room. The place was no bigger than the kitchen. It was dank, smelled musty, and had pools of water on the floor. Shelves were on the walls and most of them contained tools. Urgently, he looked around.

There were three electrical outlets, positioned a few inches above the floor. Withdrawing his screwdrivers, he began unscrewing one of the metal plates. Wires were behind it. He did the same with the second plate, but it too was a functioning electricity supply. He crouched in front of the third plate and started removing each screw. As the last one came out, the plate dropped to the floor. Behind it was a ten-inch-deep hole. A plastic parcel was within the recess.

He removed the package and unwrapped the several layers of waterproof plastic. Inside there was no cash, only letters. More sweat poured down his back as he began scanning them. Most were correspondence from Alina—letters telling Yevtushenko that she dearly missed him since he'd left Belarus, that Maria was growing by the day, that their baby had just had her first full night's sleep without waking or needing to be fed, that the university was considering giving Alina a pay raise, that she was saving money to come and visit him again soon. Having placed the letters in a pile to one side, Will looked at the last two envelopes in the bag. They looked different from each other and different from Alina's letters.

He opened one of them. Inside was an SVR report marked TOP SECRET; beneath the header was the title *Director, First Deputy Director, Head Directorate S Only, Ref Deployment of Kronos*. The report was dated 1995 and stated that Colonel Nikolai Dmitriev had met Kurt Schreiber in Berlin as agreed, the papers had been signed, Kronos was the fail-safe.

The report said nothing else, though the name *Kurt Schreiber* had been circled in pencil.

Will stuffed the letter into his jacket, knowing that Yevtushenko would have breached security protocols by printing off the report and removing it from SVR headquarters.

He tore open the last letter. It was dated one month ago, addressed to Yevtushenko, and had been sent to a house in Minsk by a Brussels-based company called Gerlache.

Dear Mr. Yevtushenko,

Our business interests are taking us in new directions, away from the former Soviet Union states and toward Asia and parts of central Africa. Regrettably we therefore do not need to continue to retain your consultancy services.

However, we have some excellent news. One of our Israeli clients maintains a significant interest in setting up business ventures in Russia and needs to understand the political and economic risks before doing so. He would like to engage your services directly. We have charged him an introductory fee and he has agreed to pay you your standard rate of ten thousand euros per consultancy report. Your contract will now be with him and we will play no part in any business dealings you have with him.

He has been a trusted client of Gerlache for eight years and we can thoroughly vouch for his credentials and integrity. He will call you, outside of business hours, at some point during the next few days.

It has been a pleasure doing business with you and we are in no doubt that you will have a profitable relationship with our client.

His name is Simon Rübner.

Yours faithfully,
François Gilliams
Managing Partner

Will put the letter back into the envelope and placed it in a pocket. He wondered if there was anything else of interest within the room, or elsewhere in the house, but he knew that he had to get out of there. After turning off the light, he climbed the stairs, entered the hallway, and stopped.

Vehicle noise, different from the sound of the idling police car.

He ran to the kitchen, looked through the windows, saw no one, and opened the rear door. The vehicle noise was getting louder. Moving to the edge of the house, he glanced toward the track, and his stomach wrenched.

A truck was pulling up next to the house. Two hundred yards behind it, another had stopped; at least a dozen police with submachine guns and attack dogs were jumping out of it and heading into the forest. Will ran to the other rear corner of the house. A third truck was stationary, and more armed cops and dogs were moving toward the trees. Both ends of the valley were blocked off. Within minutes the property would be surrounded. His heart started racing as he realized that his only possible escape route was via the slope beyond the rear of the cottage and then along high ground to reach his bike.

He sprinted, knowing that he'd been wrong: the SVR or FSB must have put a team into the valley to watch the property. It was probable they were armed, and quite possible that he was running blindly toward them. But it made no sense that they were here.

In the distance, he heard dogs barking. Dodging trees, he tried to move faster, though the thick snow impeded his efforts.

A volley of automatic gunfire came from somewhere to his right, and bullets pounded the snow three feet in front of him. He dived left, a moment before a pistol shot sounded from somewhere ahead. Standing, he saw rapid movement ahead. A glimpse of a man in white arctic clothing. Then the man was gone. Will ran onward, zigzagging to try to make his body a difficult target, leaping over mounds of snow, racing between trees, his gun held high.

More movement—the man in white. Will twisted and slammed his body against a tree as the man raised his pistol and fired. The bullet missed him by inches.

Will fired two shots in rapid succession. Both hit the man in the chest, and he fell limp to the ground. Glancing over his shoulder, Will saw brief flashes of the cops' reflective jackets. They were about seventy yards behind him, moving through the forest. He looked ahead. The base of the valley slope was fifty yards away. He had to get to that higher ground.

The blow to his rib cage caused him to stagger back, his face screwed up in pain. A big man, identically dressed to the one he'd shot, was rushing toward him. The man swung his fist toward Will's head. Will sidestepped, slapped him in the throat with sufficient force to cause the man to fall to his knees while clutching his injury, punched him full force on the side of his head, and slammed the heel of his boot into the man's stomach. Dropping to the ground, Will wrapped an arm around the man's throat and squeezed until his thrashing legs became motionless.

As Will moved onward, the ground gradually became steeper, the forest more dense. More automatic gunfire came from somewhere behind him, and rounds ripped chunks off the trees around him. He changed angles again, pulling on tree trunks and branches to help him move faster through the thick snow.

A man ran through trees ahead of him. One of the surveillance team. He hadn't seen Will, but had a handgun held ready to shoot. Will stopped, held his breath, took aim a few inches in front of the man's moving head, partially exhaled, and fired. The bullet struck the man in the temple, and he fell sideways, dead. As he did so, a boot struck Will's kneecap, then his hip. Will dropped to the ground, his hand involuntarily releasing his gun. An operative was standing six feet away from him, silent, aiming his pistol at Will's head, his finger pulling back on the trigger.

Will braced himself, knowing he was about to die.

A German shepherd police dog leapt through the air and landed on the man, forcing him to the ground. The big dog was trying to pin the man down and tear out his throat. Will got to his feet and retrieved his gun. The dog yelped. Holding the dog's ear and jaw, the hostile had snapped its neck. Staring wide-eyed at Will, he pushed the dog off his body, grabbed his discarded handgun, and swung it toward Will. He dropped the weapon the moment Will's round struck him in the forehead.

More barking, accompanied by shouts. The cops were gaining on him and clearly knew his approximate location. Will moved, limping at first from the blow to his knee but soon able to jog, then run as the pain abated. He was now on the steep slope, heading out of the valley.

A pistol round sliced alongside one arm, cutting his jacket and his skin. Another struck his backpack. He dived for cover behind a tree, got into a crouch, readied himself, and swung out. In an instant, he saw a surveillance operative twenty yards away, pointing his handgun directly at Will. Will fired a fraction of a second before the man fired. The operative's bullet hit a part of the trunk two inches from Will's head. Will's bullet hit the man in the face. He ran to the prone body and fired two more shots into his head.

Ignoring scratches to his face and hands from the foliage around him, he frantically continued his ascent. His breathing was shallow, his body covered in sweat, but he dared not slow down. The edge of the forest was now visible. Beyond it he needed to cross forty yards of open ground before reaching the summit.

Two police officers rushed toward him from between trees to his left. Ahead of them was an unleashed dog, its teeth bared as it sprinted toward Will. Will spun to face them, in an instant decided the cops were trying to capture him alive, aimed his gun, shot the dog in the chest and the head, dashed toward the cops, who were now trying to raise their submachine guns, got between them, elbowed one in the eye, grabbed the other by the throat and slammed his body against a tree. Both men were writhing in pain on the ground.

Will left them there, turned, and was hit full force in the face by another surveillance operative. Staggering back, he saw a leg kick toward his stomach. He moved, trapped the leg between his forearms, gripped it tight and spun his whole body, causing the operative to flip onto his side. He stepped closer to the prone man, intending to stamp on the man's groin, but before he could do so the operative used his free leg to kick Will's chest and push him away.

After scrambling backward, the man got to his feet and charged toward Will. Will dropped low, moved left, and swung his fist upward at full force into the man's gut. The man crashed to the ground, moaning, and started crawling away from Will. He was badly hurt, but Will couldn't let him recover and get to a weapon. The two cops were still writhing on the ground, in pain. Will strode over to them and grabbed one of their discarded Vityaz submachine guns. He was about to use it on the surveillance operative, but five more police officers emerged out of the trees heading straight toward him. Will stood still, raised his gun, and sent a burst of fire into the ground in front of their feet. The cops froze. Will stayed still, pointing his weapon at them, then turned and sprinted farther up the slope.

Within seconds, he was out of the forest. Now he was exposed. And while he was sure the police had been trying to capture him alive, he wondered what orders they'd been given if it looked likely he was going to escape. Keeping his movements erratic, he pumped his legs as fast as he could, despite every intake of air causing pain in his lungs, his muscles screaming in agony from his exertions and the blows he'd received.

The summit was fifteen yards away. He changed direction again just before a burst of gunfire raced through the air where he'd been a split second before. Clearly, the cops were not going to risk him escaping and were now shooting to kill.

Spinning around, he saw three officers running out of the tree line. Using the Vityaz's telescopic sight, he took aim and put two rounds into one of the cop's legs. The man crumpled to the ground, screaming; his colleagues looked panicked and dived for cover. Will turned, ran, reached the summit, changed direction, and started moving along it faster. The ground was flat here and the snow much thinner and more compacted. He looked into the valley. One of the trucks was moving along the distant track in the same direction he was headed; those cops and dogs that he could see in the forest were also paralleling his route. Moving out of sight of the valley, his only thought now was to cover the two miles to his bike quicker than the men pursuing him.

One hundred yards ahead of him, two dogs clambered onto the summit, their breath steaming in the icy air as they looked around, trying to find their quarry. One of them barked; both locked eyes on Will and raced toward him. He barely slowed as he raised his gun and put four-round bursts into each of them. Within seconds, he was jumping over their dead bodies.

More snow started to fall, and the light was beginning to fade. Will knew the police would do everything they could to capture him before nightfall—he hadn't seen any of them carrying night-vision equipment, and German shepherd dogs were poor trackers in the dark.

He covered one mile, felt exhausted, and could feel that he was starting to slow down, though he thought that he was probably still moving more quickly than the cops in the valley basin. But the truck worried him. No doubt it was already at the end of the valley, stationary, waiting to receive updates on Will's location.

Deciding he had to risk another glance into the valley, he moved left while maintaining his speed. Now he was visible to anyone in the valley who was looking in his direction. At least three people were, because sustained bursts of gunfire came from three different locations in the valley below. Will darted right and out of sight. The rounds had been wide of their mark; he was beyond the submachine guns' accurate range. But he knew that he had to fight every physical instinct to further slow down, as his brief look into the valley had shown him that the police were still moving in force through the forest and that the truck was waiting ahead of him at the end of the track on the opposite side of the valley.

His head throbbing, he started counting each pace, reckoning that he'd reach his bike at the approximate count of fifteen hundred. Strong winds began to drive the snowfall toward him. He narrowed his eyes to try to avoid becoming disoriented by the white specks and had to work even harder to maintain his pace.

He reached a count of five hundred.

The taste of blood was in his mouth.

One thousand.

Every muscle in his body felt like it was being torn apart.

Twelve hundred.

He could see his bike on the high ground at the head of the valley.

Thirteen hundred.

He stumbled, nearly fell, knew that at any moment his legs would simply stop functioning.

Fourteen hundred.

He couldn't count anymore. Or run. His breathing loud, his hair matted with sweat and snow, his face screwed up in pain, he staggered forward until he was standing by the bike. Two hundred yards away, on lower ground and moving closer to him, was the truck. No doubt it was full of cops. In the forest, some of the police on foot had switched on the tactical flashlights attached to their submachine guns. Light was fading, but they were getting nearer. Tossing his gun away, he tried to lift the heavy bike. He got it off the ground a few inches before his oxygen-starved muscles gave up and the machine crashed back to the ground. Dogs barked. Someone in the forest shouted orders. Will knew that the police could see him; in a matter of seconds they would be in range to shoot him. He sucked in air, ignored the fact that his heart was pumping so fast he thought it could fail, gripped the handlebars, and moaned loudly as he tried again to haul the bike upright.

At least two dogs were now continuously barking and seemed to be drawing closer; no doubt they'd been unleashed. He leaned back, his teeth gritted, trying to use his body weight to raise the machine. The bike lifted a few more inches. His back was in agony, felt like it was burning. Gunfire. Most were off target, but one round struck the bike's seat and ricocheted through the air close to his head. He knew that if he dropped the bike now he'd have no chance of escape, so he screamed, pulled back with every remaining bit of strength, thought that he was going to lose consciousness, got the bike upright, immediately swung a leg over it, and sat on the machine, his breathing rapid. More shouting; the dogs had to be very close now.

He tried to kick-start the bike. Nothing happened.

He tried again; the engine still didn't engage.

Bullets struck the ground inches from the bike's front tire.

He raised his body, then thrust down to add weight to the kick-start.

Still nothing.

The truck stopped, just one hundred yards away. Men jumped out of the back.

He stood again. The act sent bolts of pain through his legs and arms. He breathed in and thrust down.

The engine engaged. He immediately revved the throttle, lurched forward as the bike's gears engaged, and pulled the throttle fully back. From the forest and the truck came multiple sustained bursts of gunfire.

But he was out of the cops' line of sight, speeding over rough ground away from the valley. He gripped the machine tightly as he drove it over mounds, jumped through air, thudded to the ground, and maintained its traction on the snow.

There was no more gunfire. The police would be running back to the truck to pursue him in the vehicle. And they'd be summoning quicker patrol cars to the area to block his escape. But he wouldn't be using the roads. For sixty minutes, he drove across farmland, along tracks and open fields, through woods and larger forests, only turning on his lights when he needed to.

He pulled into Arman's junkyard, turned off the ignition, and lowered the bike's stand. The trailer's interior was illuminated. Arman emerged holding a flashlight. Will got off the bike and staggered over to the Russian, then his knees buckled.

Arman grabbed him and held him upright. "Are you injured?"

Will couldn't answer. Couldn't think. Fatigue had overwhelmed him.

The former tank commander gripped him tightly, limping as he guided Will toward his home.

EIGHTEEN

Joanna lifted the instrument case out of the large packing box, placed it on Will's dining table, and called out, "Be a darling and put the kettle on."

"Right you are, my dear." Robert was in the kitchen, washing breakfast dishes. Next to him, leaning against a cupboard, was his shotgun.

Joanna opened the case. Inside was an old German lute. She whispered, "Beautiful," as she ran a finger along its strings. "Can't have you hidden away." She looked around, trying to decide where to put it, and settled on placing it on a shelf next to a framed photograph of a teenage Will playing viola in his school orchestra.

"Bloody rain's set in for the day." The former SAS captain poured boiling water into a teapot.

"Yes." Joanna was not really listening to her husband. Instead she was now staring at another framed photograph that she'd just removed from wrapping paper. It was of a young boy, unmistakably Will at approximately four or five years old; standing next to him was a tall man, wearing a suit. "Must be his father," she said to herself as she placed it on a mantelpiece. She moved to another packing case and withdrew a box. Inside it was a pristine *képi blanc*, the French Foreign Legion cap awarded to recruits upon completion of their arduous training. Underneath it was a worn baseball cap that would not have fit a child much older than ten years old. Joanna frowned and wondered, why did he hide one with the other?

Robert entered the living room holding two cups of tea with one hand and his Remington in the other. "How about lunchtime I leg it to the chippy and get some cod and chips?"

Joanna smiled. "That would be nice. Plenty of vinegar, but not too much salt. You know what the doctor told you."

Robert huffed. "Load of nonsense." Placing the mugs down, he asked, "You think you should buy Will some houseplants? All this boys' stuff isn't exactly going to charm the ladies."

"Which ladies?"

"How about some artificial plants?" Robert laughed. "At least they'd give the *impression* that there's life in here."

Joanna nodded, then turned sharply as she heard a noise in the hallway. Withdrawing her handgun from her belt, she said quietly, "Post's arrived. Usual drill."

They moved silently into the hallway. Robert got on one knee and pointed his shotgun at the center of the front door. Joanna walked down one side of the corridor, reached the entrance, glanced at her husband, who gave the tiniest of nods, swooped up the mail, and stepped back so she was flush against the wall.

Nothing happened.

Robert stayed in position as she carefully made her way back along the hallway. She leafed through the mail—junk, a couple of utility bills, a local council voter registration card, and a letter that was handwritten and addressed to Will Cochrane.

She opened the letter, read its contents, and said urgently, "We need to call Betty, then Will."

Dear Mr. Cochrane,

I wonder if you've heeded my advice to stay away from me and my business. I hope so, because matters are soon to be concluded and it would be a nuisance for me to have to deal with any interference. As it is, you've inconvenienced me enough to the extent that I've had to divert some valuable resources to the United Kingdom.

Those resources are dedicated to watching a person you care about. They will not back down unless I tell them to do so or I instruct them to kill the person. The decision I make will be based on the choice you make. I hope for your sake it is one that prioritizes the welfare of the person you care about over your desire to gain applause from your masters.

Are you a protector of the weak, Mr. Cochrane? If so, the decision you need to make is clear.

Time will tell.

And I will be there to listen.

Yours,
William

PART III

NINETEEN

Will felt tense and uneasy. He'd received a call from Joanna, who'd relayed the contents of William's latest letter to him and said that Betty and Alfie were immediately moving to a new location in the U.K. Now he was watching Suzy as she sat motionless at the Auguststrasse dining table with a cell phone against her head. Two hours ago he'd asked her to run the names Colonel Nikolai Dmitriev, Kurt Schreiber, Gerlache, François Gilliams, Simon Rübner, and Kronos through CIA databases. She'd telephoned Langley. Five minutes ago, someone had called her back.

Mark Oates handed him a mug of black coffee. "It's shift change in thirty minutes."

"How's the Russian team?"

"The same."

"Have they had any deliveries to the hotel?"

"Can't be certain, but we think not."

Will nodded. "And your team?"

Mark smiled. "We're either sitting on our arses or freezing our nuts off. Couldn't be better."

"That'll change soon." He wondered if the team's surveillance detail was taking its toll on them. But the paramilitary officer looked alert and energized. "It's imperative you're able to stick to the Russians the moment they move."

Mark took a swig of his coffee. "We know."

"How are your daughters?"

"What?"

"They're at university, right?"

Mark beamed. "Yeah. One's at Exeter, the other at Newcastle. They're loving it."

"Expensive these days."

"Damn right." Mark rubbed his face. "But they're the first in my family to do higher education. If it keeps them from having to do all-night laps of a hotel then it's worth every penny."

"Are you managing to find time to check they're okay?"

"Finding time's half the battle; getting them to answer my calls is just as hard. They want to be all grown up now, don't want Dad pestering them. Why do you ask?"

Will hesitated. "I'm the only one in the section who doesn't have any ties. I don't know how the rest of you cope."

Suzy held a finger in the air. "Peter."

Peter Rhodes moved to the whiteboard, a marker pen in his hand.

Keeping the phone to her ear, Suzy called out, "Nikolai Dmitriev. Confirmed that he was a colonel in the KGB and subsequently was the SVR's Head of Directorate S. Retired ten years ago and since then he's been running a vineyard in the south of France. The French kept their eyes on him for a while before concluding he was no threat."

Peter wrote down his name and the information Suzy had given him.

"Nothing on the Gerlache company, nothing on François Gilliams."

That didn't surprise Will. He was certain the company was a cover for an intelligence unit, the same team who'd supplied his name and home address to Alina, and that anyone allegedly working for the company would be using an alias.

"Nothing on Kronos."

Peter asked, "You've checked with DIA in case it's a weapons system?"

"I know how to do my job. I've told Langley to check in all the right places, including DIA. Kronos has no meaning to us."

"Except one." Will smiled. "In Greek mythology, Kronos was a Titan who carried a scythe that could slice open the sky. He defeated his father, the ruler of the universe, and devoured most of his sons when they were babies so that they couldn't grow up and depose him."

Peter asked, "How on Earth do you know that?"

Will shrugged. "Peter Paul Rubens did a painting of him eating his child, Poseidon. I've seen the painting and read about Kronos on the plaque underneath it."

Peter laughed. "It must be a blast hanging around you outside of work." He turned, looked mischievous, and wrote, *Kronos—the god who devoured his offspring.*

Suzy said, "Kurt Schreiber. Former Stasi colonel."

Peter spun around, his expression now serious. "Details of what he did in the Stasi?"

Suzy shook her head. "All we have is his rank. To have reached that level of seniority without his name appearing elsewhere means he must have kept his head down for most of his career."

Peter looked at Will. "Or his identity was protected."

Suzy frowned and said quietly to the caller, "You're sure?" She looked at Peter. "Six months ago, Interpol sent out a flag to London, Langley, and most European agencies—if the name Kurt Schreiber emerges in the course of our work, we're to alert Interpol immediately."

Will said, "We need to understand Interpol's interest in Schreiber."

"It's being followed up."

Will nodded. "What else have you got, Suzy?"

She didn't answer right away. Then she shut her cell phone, rubbed her tummy, and said, "Simon Rübner. Mossad intelligence officer. And for the last six months he's also been a CIA agent."

Will and Peter simultaneously exclaimed, "CIA!"

Suzy nodded.

Will's mind raced. "Give me the details. *Everything.*"

"I can't."

"Why?"

"I don't have the security clearance to read anything about Rübner."

Impatience surged through Will. "Patrick can get that clearance!"

Suzy was unflustered. "It was Patrick on the end of the phone. He tried to get clearance, but was then hauled into the Director of Intelligence's office and told to mind his own business. In fact, the director used far stronger language than that."

"Then Patrick needs to go over his head and speak to the president!"

Peter shook his head. "Come on, Will. It's a delicate time for us. Patrick and Alistair won't want to risk a fight at that level. The section could lose, or worse could happen."

Will banged a fist against the wall, recalling what Alistair had told him in London.

Things are changing. There are cries for transparency from the intelligence community, demands to do away with so-called shadowy task forces and the like. This is not just about you. If we get this wrong, some might grab this as an opportunity to shut us down.

Will asked Suzy, "Any reference to Mikhail in the double agent files?"

"I'm still searching. Nothing yet."

Roger entered the room, checking the workings of his handgun. "Have I missed something?"

"Not a thing. We've hit a fucking roadblock!" Peter walked up to Will and asked in a near whisper, "Did you get these names at Yevtushenko's house? How are they connected?"

"I found them among other stuff in Yevtushenko's basement. I've got no idea if they're connected and, given the *delicacy* of our situation, we'll never find out." Will looked at Roger and Mark. "Our only chance now is to follow the Russian team to the target."

He tried to understand what had happened in the valley. The surveillance team should have killed him; instead it seemed that they were trying to drive him back toward the police so that he could be arrested or killed by them. That was the only reason he got out of there alive. One thing he was certain about was that knowledge of his intended break-in of Yevtushenko's house was limited to the section, its coheads, and a handful of other senior officers in Langley and London. One of them had betrayed him, and that person had to be the same individual who'd leaked his name and address.

He wondered if that person was in the room with him.

TWENTY

Kurt Schreiber was sitting at his desk in the farmstead's study. In front of him were ledgers containing the accounts of his multiple companies, six files that he'd drawn up for potential new business associates, a folder containing a draft business plan to derail a major oil conglomerate's bid to establish drilling rights in the South Pacific and to then charge the conglomerate a small fortune to get the bid back on track, a list of men and women who needed to be killed, and a file that had the letter *K* on the front. That file had nothing in it—committing anything to paper would be far too dangerous—but he kept it in front of him to focus his mind. After all, none of his other projects were as significant as activating Kronos.

Simon Rübner entered the room and sat down opposite him. "You wanted to see me, Mr. Schreiber."

Kurt placed the cap over the nib of Will Cochrane's gold fountain pen and put it on top of the list of people he wanted dead. "What is the situation on our perimeter?"

"We think there's about fifteen of them on at any one time. At least double that number in total. All are armed, they've got sophisticated surveillance equipment, fast vehicles, and they look professional. They don't seem concerned that we know they've surrounded our place."

The old man waived a hand dismissively. "They want us to know they're watching us." He removed his glasses and polished the lenses. "Yevtushenko?"

Rübner ran fingers through his short beard. "We're trying to force food and water down his throat. It's not easy. His health's deteriorating; he's petrified."

The former Stasi officer smiled. "Of course he is." He became motionless, deep in thought. "Are matters progressing in Russia and the United Kingdom?"

Rübner nodded. "Cochrane's sister and her two guardians have moved location. We're watching them."

"The guardians?"

"A husband-and-wife team: Alfie and Betty Mayne."

"Their backgrounds?"

"Both ex-army, though they've been out for a very long time. God knows, Cochrane could have chosen better foot soldiers."

"They're not foot soldiers and that is precisely why he chose them. He trusts them more than anyone else to protect his sister. And that means they are very valuable to him."

"Do you want us to kill the target?"

Kurt thought for a moment. "Not yet. We don't know if Cochrane's still after us, so his loved one can still be used as leverage." His expression turned cold. "What about the SVR officer?"

Simon Rübner spoke quickly. "Mikhail Salkov's wife and children have been located and approached. We've explained to the wife the seriousness of her family's predicament. That happened twenty hours ago. Almost certainly she's communicated the approach to her husband."

"Of course she has." Kurt Schreiber glanced toward his study's window. "He's still out there?"

"On and off. But he always keeps men on the perimeter." Rübner walked to the window, looked out of it, and folded his arms. "The wife and children have moved locations. We've kept them under observation. What do you want us to do?"

"The tactic against Mikhail didn't work. Kill his family."

"Yes sir."

Kurt asked, "Is everyone ready?"

"Your men here and beyond the perimeter are primed. Mikhail's men will be taken completely by surprise."

"What time?"

"Three A.M."

"No survivors."

"Yes, Mr. Schreiber. I estimate that the convoy will be leaving here a few minutes later."

Kurt picked up the two sheets of paper containing the codes. "Good. Don't let me down, Simon."

Kurt placed the sheets alongside each other.

"What do you want us to do with Yevtushenko?"

"You're still keeping him in shackles?"

"He's chained up in the basement. But even if he wasn't, I think he'd be too weak to escape."

Kurt looked around. "This place has served us well, but after tonight it will be compromised. We'll change our base of operations to one of the other German locations." He smiled. "You'll kill our unwanted guards; we'll depart in convoy; Mikhail's reinforcements will arrive sometime thereafter, but by then we'll be long gone; they'll search the farmstead and they'll find Yevtushenko."

"Alive or dead?"

"Alive. But I wonder what the Russians will do to him, given that his theft of the paper has ultimately led to the massacre of their colleagues?"

Rübner felt a moment of unease. Though he was no stranger to death and violent acts, he took no pleasure in them. Kurt was very different. The former Stasi officer reveled in seeing others suffer. "They'll tear him apart."

"Precisely." Kurt looked sharply at the former Mossad officer. "All that matters is that you get me safely to the Black Forest tomorrow. In forty-eight hours, Kronos will be let loose. Then everything will be different."

TWENTY-ONE

Betty Mayne tried to imagine how Sarah Cochrane felt. During her service as an operative in Fourteenth Intelligence Company and her subsequent deployment by Will and others in MI6, she'd done a lot of protection work. It had taught her that the emotions felt by those in her care varied enormously depending on the circumstances of the threat against them, what types of person they were, how much freedom of movement they were given, what age they were, their gender, and, crucially, how long they'd been kept under protection. But over time, there were common patterns of behavior. If the duration of protection was longer than a week, the sequence was often absolute fear and confusion, open hostility toward the guardians, resignation to the situation, rebellion toward the protection detail, reckless behavior, confrontation, then resentment. The sequence was very different from patterns of behavior displayed by hostages. But sometimes the people Betty had protected had tried to hide their emotions by acting as if they were fine or resigned to their situation. Then they might try running away in the dead of night.

Fortunately, she'd been wise to their playacting and had stopped them from making an idiotic mistake. She'd quickly learned that for the sake of their safety, it was vital that she never trust the people she protected.

But Sarah was different. Since she'd been in Betty and Alfie's care, she'd gone deeper and deeper into her shell—barely speaking, getting out of bed only at her husband's insistence, struggling to eat, her appearance deteriorating. She wasn't pretending, Betty was sure of that. Instead it seemed that she was in some kind of trauma that was the result of something far bigger than her current circumstances.

They'd arrived in the Scottish Highlands three days ago, having left their previous location in the West Country's Dartmoor within thirty minutes of receiving a call from Joanna. Located on the shores of Loch Damph in the Northwest Highlands, the large four-bedroom hunting lodge would ordinarily have made a stunning holiday retreat. It was surrounded by mountains, had a stream that ran through a copse at the back of the property, was located at the end of a mile-long track beyond which it took twenty minutes to drive to the nearest residence, and had recently been renovated and extended to include a big dining room and conservatory, a gun room, and a double garage containing a walk-in freezer for hanging deer.

Betty had chosen it not only because it was isolated, provided an excellent view of anyone driving toward the house, and was very difficult to access on foot from other directions, but also because she thought the location would change Sarah's mood. It hadn't. If anything she'd grown even more withdrawn.

From the kitchen fridge, Betty withdrew bacon, venison sausages, eggs, mushrooms, and roasted potatoes left over from last night's meal. She doubted Sarah would eat much, but that wouldn't stop her cooking for everyone. At 1:00 P.M. exactly, they would all sit down around the kitchen table with food in front of them. And at 7:00 P.M. they would sit at the conservatory dining table to eat their dinner. When not on the move, routine was essential. It helped to normalize each day.

She walked out the kitchen door to fetch the men. Alfie was walking toward her, down one of the mountain slopes. The former SAS
sergeant looked much more at home in the wilds of Scotland than he
had when they'd collected Sarah and James from their elegant London home. Dressed in hiking gear, he was striding and leaping over
the uneven and frozen ground with the vigor of a man half his age.
He'd been checking his traps—primitive alarm systems made out of
wire and empty coke cans that if walked into would trigger sufficient
noise to be heard from within the house. They knew the alarms were
effective. It was the off-season of the tightly regulated deer-hunting
calendar; at this time of the year, deer would often come down from
the mountains to seek shelter in the valley and to eat food that was
left for them by the estates' gillies. Last night, Alfie had jumped out
of bed three times because of the noise of cans rattling against each
other, only to discover that each time his traps had been triggered by
large red deer.

James was visible between trees in the copse. Standing beside the
mountain brook, he was cursing loudly because his fishing line had
got caught in the trees. It was the third time today it had happened,
much to Alfie's amusement, though the ex–Special Forces man was
the one who'd had to clamber up trees and untangle the line. Betty
had disliked James on first meeting him—though no doubt highly
intelligent, he was also pedantic, fussy, weak, and foolish—but the
more time she spent in his company the more he'd endeared himself
to her. He always got up at 6:00 A.M., called in to his law firm and
lied to them that his wife was still ill and he needed to stay home to
care for her, played cards with Alfie until the early hours, and washed
dishes. And now he was hopelessly trying to catch their supper.

Betty looked around. Right now, the loch and its surrounding
mountains had four climates. In the north, it was raining; east, snow
was falling; west, the sky was clear and blue; and in the south, dark
clouds obscured mountain peaks. She lowered her gaze and looked at
the track. At the top of it was a stationary blue car.

Alfie reached her and said, "Second sighting I've had. What about you, petal?"

"The same." She kept her gaze fixed on the vehicle.

"Do we move locations on the third or fourth sighting?"

"Third sighting."

Alfie put one hand into his jacket pocket and placed a filterless cigarette into the corner of his mouth with the other. "I think you're right. Reckon they're just tourists who're back for a photo shoot." He lit his cigarette. "But third sighting means they're a bunch of bad 'uns."

Betty squeezed her husband's hand and said quietly, "I can't let Sarah see anything messy, angel. She's in a bad enough way as it is." She sat down on the frozen heath. "If anyone comes for us, we should try to minimize fuss."

Alfie passed his half-smoked cigarette to Betty, who took a drag on it and gave it back to him. "Where is she?"

"On the sofa, doing nothing."

"It's to do with her brother, isn't it?"

Betty nodded. "I think so."

Alfie flicked ash off the cigarette. "Can never get my head around the deep and meaningful stuff."

Betty kept her attention on the blue vehicle as it drove off. "That's one of the reasons why I love you. You're straightforward."

Alfie grinned. "Either that, or it's 'cos I ain't got the brain cells to know how to answer you back." An idea came to him. "After lunch how about I drive her to Lochcarron, make her useful, tell her she's got to buy some stuff for dinner, and by the way she's cooking?"

"It's worth a try." Betty held her hand out, and Alfie gripped it and pulled her to her feet. "I'll get lunch on. Be a love and help James with his tangled line. But don't call him a stupid plonker this time."

"Right you are." As Betty walked off to the lodge, Alfie placed his concealed handgun's safety catch on, withdrew his hand from his jacket, watched the stationary blue car, and muttered under his breath, "Best you don't come back."

. . .

One of Kurt Schreiber's men watched Alfie through his sniper rifle's telescopic sight. "He's looking in our direction, but there's no chance he can see into our car from this distance."

His colleague turned on the ignition. "Let him watch. The others are all in position to take over surveillance."

Four three-man teams, all secreted in the mountains around the lodge.

"Glad they're the ones who have to freeze their balls off today. And I'll be gladder still when Schreiber gives us the order to gun her down."

"Don't worry. Any day now." Keeping Alfie's head in the cross-hairs of his rifle, the sniper mimicked the sound of firing a silenced bullet.

TWENTY-TWO

G ot it!" Suzy beamed as she stared at her laptop screen. "Mikhail Salkov."

"You're certain?" Will placed a hand on the Auguststrasse dining table and leaned over her shoulder, looking at the computer.

The CIA analyst nodded. "It's taken me days to be certain. I'm damn sure he's the one."

"How did you get him?"

"Postings. I focused on the double agent files where we'd recruited agents being run by Russian officers posted overseas."

Wherein those Russian intelligence officers would be posted as diplomats and their real names declared to the host country.

"Had to trawl through over a thousand files to narrow it down to these four." She moved the cursor until the screen contained four scanned CIA contact reports. Pointing at the screen, she said, "These two Russian CIA agents were run out of the Russian embassy in Paris four years ago. Look." She tapped a finger. "Agent Folex informs his CIA handler that his SVR handler Trofim Vygotsky is leaving France in one week and is being replaced by Mikhail Salkov; that Salkov will be his new handler. And here," she moved her finger, "Agent Estler tells a different CIA handler the same thing. The second report is one day older than the first."

"That doesn't mean anything."

"Hold on." Suzy closed the reports, leaving two on her screen. "One year ago, two Russian CIA double agents are being run out of the Russian embassy in Oslo. Agent Adras and agent Shorm tell their CIA handlers that their SVR handler, a diplomat called Georgii Bordyuzha, is returning to a job in head office. He's being replaced by Salkov and a handover meeting's being arranged."

"Still doesn't mean that the SVR officer who's chasing the same paper as us is Mikhail Salkov." Will frowned as a thought came to him. "How long was Salkov posted to Paris and Oslo?"

Suzy smiled. "I knew you weren't just a pretty face. There are two reasons why Salkov's name jumps out at me, and your question relates to one of them."

"He was only posted to Paris and Oslo for brief periods?"

"Exactly. Paris: two months; Oslo: six weeks."

"Parachuted in to troubleshoot."

"That's what I'm thinking."

"And the second reason?"

Suzy closed her laptop and turned to Will. "Salkov meets Folex and Estler. One week later their bodies wash up on the shores of the river Seine, their necks broken. Salkov meets Adras and Shorm. Next day, Adras is hit by a speeding car; Shorm is robbed and stabbed to death in the backstreets of Oslo."

"SVR thinks they've got leaky agents in France and Norway, so it sends in a man to plug the holes." Will moved away from Suzy and stood next to Peter, who was staring at the whiteboard containing questions and possible answers.

Peter nodded. "You were right, Will." On the board, he wrote *Mikhail Salkov: Spycatcher.*

Suzy stretched her back. "I haven't analyzed MI6 double agent files because they won't release an encrypted stick for me to read their files out here. But I'm sure Mikhail's name will turn up alongside the deaths of some of their agents as well."

"So do I." Peter smiled, walked quickly to Suzy and to her surprise gave the American analyst a hug. "Excellent work, Suzy Sue!"

Suzy smiled, looked happy. "It is, isn't it?"

"Huggin's good." Laith yawned as he entered the room holding the book Will had bought Suzy. "Chapter Four says that embraces cause the release of endorphins that produce a feeling of contentment between mother and baby; it explains that you can get that release at work just as easily as at home or in a gym." He put an electronic cigarette in his mouth.

Adam Tark emerged from the kitchen and handed Suzy a mug. "German chamomile. I bought it this evening after my shift at the hotel. It's a calmative and digestive aid, perfectly safe once you're in the second trimester."

Suzy took the drink from the former SAS soldier. "Do you guys spend all your time in the Grand Hyatt thinking about what I should and shouldn't be doing while pregnant?"

Adam grinned, though his disfigured face made the expression look more like a grimace. "Most of the time, yeah." The Scotsman zipped up his fleece jacket. "Anyway, we've got vested interests. Me and Roger have bet two hundred dollars each that it's going to be a girl; Mark, Peter, and Laith have bet that it's going to be a boy." He glanced at Will. "Boss, you want in on the bet?"

"Sure, put me down for a girl." Will pulled on his jacket. "Providing that's okay with you, Suzy?"

"Why not?" The CIA analyst slapped both hands onto the dining room table and pushed herself up off the chair. "I'll decide who I want to win the bet, then pop a kid out who's got the right gender. Maybe the winners can cut me in for fifty percent of the takings."

Will smiled. "Any progress on Interpol's request for information on Kurt Schreiber?"

"Alistair and Patrick are still looking into it."

"Keep me posted." Will's cell phone rang. Roger was calling. He listened to the CIA officer speak for three seconds before snapping the phone shut and calling out, "Russians are on the move! Roger and Mark are in a vehicle, pursuing them. Adam, Laith: get the guns. We need to go now!"

Four minutes later, Will, Laith, and Adam were in an SUV. Adam was driving very fast, navigating his way through the city's midevening traffic. Laith was next to him, holding his military communications mic close to his throat. "We're mobile. Where we headed?"

In his earpiece, Will heard Mark's voice. "They're moving west. Two SUVs. Get your arses onto Unter Den Linden."

Will slammed a magazine into his SIG Sauer P226 handgun. "What's their speed?"

"Normal."

"Do you think they know you're on them?"

"No. Traffic's heavy. But if they're moving out of the city, we've got to hope they stay on a major highway."

Will unzipped a large canvas bag and withdrew three M4A1 assault rifles with grenade launcher attachments. He placed a rifle and an ammunition pouch containing spare magazines and grenades next to each of his colleagues, and kept the third for himself. "These mustn't be used unless absolutely necessary. And no dead Russians."

"No dead Russians?" Laith shook his head, patted his rifle, and smiled. "What has the world come to?"

Adam drove the vehicle onto a larger road. "We're on Unter Den Linden, heading toward Tiergarten district."

Roger responded, "You've got some catching up to do. Targets are moving through Westend, about five miles ahead of you."

Adam put his foot to the floor, expertly moving the SUV around slower vehicles. Will and Laith scrutinized the road ahead and occasionally looked behind, searching for signs of police cars. The last thing they needed was for a cop to attempt to pull them over for speeding.

"Target's moving through Pichelsdorf; has slowed to forty MPH."

Adam said, "Could be intending to turn off north, heading to Spandau. Or south on the Potsdamer Chaussee."

Silence for ten seconds.

Mark said, "They're taking the Potsdamer route. Still don't seem to be in any rush."

Will frowned. "Roger, what was their demeanor like when they checked out of the hotel?"

"They did it quickly, but didn't look like they were panicked."

Will nodded. "I think this road trip was planned in advance, and they're driving at speeds that will avoid the attention of the cops but still get them to their destination on time."

"Looks like it."

They drove onward for ten minutes before Adam said, "Okay, I've got a visual of you." They were exiting the city and entering countryside. "We're taking over point."

Mark answered, "Got it."

Roger and Mark's vehicle slowed, switched lanes, and moved behind another vehicle.

Adam drove past them and kept his SUV behind two other vehicles. Beyond them were the Russian cars. "Suggest we switch over every ten minutes. Nothing else we can do now except follow them."

Suzy saw that she'd received a message from Patrick telling her to call Alistair. Retrieving another cell phone, one of ten in her possession, she pressed the keyboard. Alistair answered on the fourth ring.

"You've got something for me?"

The senior MI6 officer answered, "Kurt Schreiber's name has been flagged by Interpol because any information relating to the man needs to be forwarded to the chief prosecutor of the International Criminal Court."

Located in The Hague, the court's remit was to investigate and prosecute individuals for genocide, crimes against humanity, and war crimes.

"What did Interpol say?"

"They've got no idea why the prosecutor's interested in Schreiber, though they did say that it's directly connected to a high-value witness."

"Who's the witness?"

"Interpol doesn't have a name, but does know the witness approached the court six months ago and ever since has been held in protective custody in Holland."

"He must be intending to give evidence on something Schreiber's done."

"That's my take."

"Have you spoken to the court?"

"I tried to speak to the chief prosecutor to find out what his interest was in Kurt Schreiber. He told me that I was to only liaise on this matter with Interpol, that if I tried to call him again, he'd complain to the president of the court and the UN Secretary-General that British Intelligence was attempting to pervert the course of justice."

Suzy huffed. "That was a bit strong."

"Clearly, he doesn't want our kind sniffing around him. Have you managed to get anything on Schreiber?"

"Nothing beyond his former status in the Stasi. Since then, the guy's vanished."

Two hours later, Will and his team were twenty miles outside of Hanover, driving in darkness on the main E30 highway.

Roger said, "Targets are pulling off the road, into a gas station."

Urgently, Will asked, "Any chance they've got either of our number plates?"

"Impossible in this light. Plus, we've always kept behind other vehicles, so their line of sight has been blocked."

"Okay. Roger, Mark: follow them in. We'll stop on the hard shoulder."

Three minutes later, Mark said, "They've fueled their vehicles, have moved them to parking bays, and are drinking coffee and eating. Hold." The line went quiet. "One man gets out of his vehicle; second gets out of the other. They move to the back of their cars. Withdraw large bags. Return to the passenger doors. Enter with the bags."

Roger spoke. "All are focused on what's in the bags."

Will asked, "What's happening?"

The CIA officer answered, "My guess is they're tooling up for direct action."

TWENTY-THREE

Mikhail Salkov drove his SUV across Lower Saxony's Lüneburg Heath. It was nearly 3:00 A.M., pitch dark, but he'd taken this route enough times to do it without the aid of maps or daylight. As ever, since being in Germany, he was dressed in jeans, boots, and a Windbreaker, clothes that would enable him to fight if need be. Tonight there *would* be a fight. He'd given instructions that at 5:00 A.M. the fifteen men on the perimeter of Kurt Schreiber's farmstead would be reinforced with the fifteen men on rest, and the combined force would assault Kurt's property. It was his last resort: he knew the farmstead was heavily defended, but time was now his enemy, as Kurt wouldn't tolerate being trapped in the complex for much longer.

He'd felt uneasy giving the task to the men who were watching the place. Most of them were eastern European assets, excellent at surveillance and other tradecraft drills, but less than half of them had any prior military training. Only Mikhail was ex–Special Forces, having spent five grueling years in Spetsnaz Vympel before transferring to the SVR, and he'd used his expertise to devise an assault plan to ensure that each man knew exactly what to do. Nevertheless, his men were amateurs. Last night he'd told his assets that there would be no shame if any one of them decided not to take part in the offensive. None of them had stepped down.

Over the last twenty-four hours, he'd considered many times whether he should move his four men to the farmstead perimeter. They were professionals, all Special Forces, and their presence here would easily be worth that of another thirty untrained but brave assets. But if anything went wrong tonight and Kurt escaped, he needed them to be ahead of Kurt, ready to block off his route to the Black Forest. For that reason, four hours ago he'd ordered them to leave their Berlin hotel, travel west, and wait on the outskirts of Hanover.

His thoughts turned to his family. His wife, Diana, had called him a day ago and told him that she'd been threatened by men representing the person he was seeking, that he was to send a messenger into the property he was watching with a note to say he was completely withdrawing from the place. His stomach had wrenched as he heard her speak, and when the call had ended he'd spent hours trying to decide what to do. Finally, he'd called her back and said that he was sending three trusted former police officers to their Moscow home. They would take her and their two daughters—Tatyana and Yana—somewhere safe. What he didn't tell her was that he'd arranged for a further four ex-FSB men to watch the safe place. He knew Kurt's men would follow his family and no doubt try to kill them when he realized Mikhail wasn't going to back down. If they did that, they'd be confronted by an unexpected force.

But the threat to his family had significantly enhanced Mikhail's desire to get his hands on Kurt Schreiber's throat. He wanted that just as much as he wanted to retrieve the paper. In just over two hours, he hoped to be holding a gun to Kurt's temple and a cell phone to his mouth, telling him to order his men to back away from his family. If the former Stasi officer didn't, Mikhail would have no hesitation in pulling the trigger.

He slowed the vehicle and turned off its headlights as he drew nearer to the place he always stopped to examine the perimeter and the farmstead before proceeding onward on foot. Driving the SUV off the road, he brought it to a halt and exited the car. During daylight, visible over the two thousand yards between this position and the farmstead would be undulated land containing heather, blueberry heath, streams, isolated trees, and the occasional herd of moorland sheep. Three hundred yards around the farmstead, the land was flatter and featureless. The perimeter where the SVR assets were stationed was close to the outskirts of that flatland.

Turning on his ISS T-iV HD Thermal Imaging Binoculars, he waited three seconds for the military-grade equipment to power up, then held it to his eyes. Though he was nearly one mile away, he could see the white images of four men, all positioned exactly where they should be. Moving the binoculars a few millimeters, he spotted three more of his men, all stationary and spread apart. The rest of his men were out of range and sight, beyond the farmstead's buildings. Checking that his powerful MK23 .45-caliber SOCOM handgun was secure under his jacket, he jogged forward.

Then he sprinted, leapt over a brook, and made for higher ground as he heard distant gunfire. Breathing fast, he placed his binoculars against his eyes and said, "Oh, no!"

One mile away, men were running out of the farmstead. From beyond the SVR perimeter, more men were moving toward the farmstead. His assets were stuck in between both forces. He stood still, knowing he couldn't get there in time, watching one of his men fall down, others emerging from behind the farmstead, three of them collapsing and staying still, flashes of light as some of them opened fire, more flashes of light from the hostiles as they returned fire. One by one, he saw his men being killed, standing no chance of escape, trapped in a pincer movement that had the sole purpose of massacring his men. He saw the last of them fall.

More light, but this was brighter. Vehicles emerged from outhouses in the farmstead. The men in the complex ran to them and entered. Those who had attacked the perimeter from outside the farmstead retreated; within seconds they were heading toward more vehicles that had been hidden out in the heath. Mikhail ignored them, focused on the multiple vehicles leaving the farmstead, and muttered, "Bastard!"

His reinforcements weren't due here for another two hours. If he called them now, it would take them at least twenty minutes to get here, probably longer. He watched the convoy. It was heading away from the farmstead on the road he'd driven in on. In approximately five minutes, it would be driving within one hundred yards of his hidden vehicle.

Mikhail decided the only thing he could do was wait for them to pass, get in his SUV, pursue the convoy, order his remaining assets to search the farmstead and dispose of their colleagues' bodies, and tell his four-man team of shooters that they needed to be ready to intercept the convoy. He reached for his cell phone and ran to his vehicle.

TWENTY-FOUR

"One of them is on the phone. Engines are running. Vehicles are rolling."

Adam turned on the ignition. "We'll take point." He kept his headlights off, watched the two Russian SUVs emerge back onto the highway, drove off the hard shoulder, moved behind a civilian vehicle, then turned his lights on. "Shit! They're driving at pace."

"Stay on them. I don't care if they see us." Will gripped his hand-gun, glanced over his shoulder, and saw Roger and Mark's vehicle race out of the gas station. "Something's wrong," he said into the phone.

"Yeah, I'm getting that feeling." Mark accelerated. "Don't think it was us that spooked them. There were nineteen other cars in the gas station."

Roger added, "It was the cell phone call that did it."

Will looked around. "Do you think they've got a countersurveil-lance team out? Maybe they spotted us; the call came from them."

"Nah. I've been looking since Berlin. There's no team."

"Then most likely the call came from Mikhail," Will said. Adam was now driving at nearly one hundred miles per hour. "But this isn't premeditated. There's been a change of plan."

Mark's SUV moved in behind Adam's. "They must know we're pursuing them. Let's just hope they think we're kids, looking for a race."

Will placed his pistol into his jacket and held his assault rifle with both hands. "Nice thought, but I doubt they're thinking that right now."

The Russians' vehicles were forty yards ahead of them, increasing speed, moving in between other cars.

"Exit's coming up. One hundred yards. They ain't slowing. Fuck!" Adam yanked the steering wheel down as the Russian team took the exit at speed. Taking the corner, he shouted, "They're trying to lose us."

Roger's vehicle was only feet behind, its tires screeching as it entered the bend. "They'd have been better off going into Hanover to do that."

"Exactly." Will wrapped the assault rifle's strap around his forearm. "They're heading to an assault. Standby. Most likely they think we're cops. They'll try to kill us if they think we're going to get in their way."

They were now on a minor road, straddled by countryside.

"Multiple oncoming headlights." Adam downshifted and braked hard as the Russian vehicles did the same. "Eight vehicles, all together. All look like SUVs."

Will stared at the approaching convoy, his mind racing. "That's their target, and that's our target!"

The convoy was now ninety yards away. One of the Russian vehicles sped alongside it, reached the end, turned and stopped so that it was blocking the road. The other did the same at the head of the convoy, which was now trapped between the two vehicles.

As Adam brought the car to a halt twenty yards away from the nearest Russian vehicle, the Russians leapt out of their cars and began opening fire with machine guns at the convoy. Immediately, men inside the vehicles returned fire.

Will jumped out of the car, took aim, and fired a grenade. One of the convoy vehicles exploded. As he reloaded the grenade launcher, he shouted in Russian, "Here to help! Here to help!"

The two Russians nearest to him were using their SUV as a shield, taking turns to break cover and fire rounds toward the convoy's fuel tanks. Those at the other end of the convoy were doing the same. Hundreds of rounds were striking their cars; the men in the convoy were firing through windows.

Will fired again, and a second vehicle exploded. Roger ran past him, his body low, heading straight toward the nearest Russians while shouting, "Friend. Friend." Adam, Mark, and Laith were either side of the road, firing controlled bursts into windshields.

Will saw movement. "Roger! Down! Grenade!"

As the CIA officer threw himself to the ground, the Russians' car lifted off the ground before crashing back down. Shards of metal tore through the two Russians, killing them instantly.

Roger crawled toward the Russians' destroyed vehicle and dived for cover as more rounds struck it. He shouted in English, "Hit them from their flanks," and repeated the instruction in Russian. He stood, exposing his upper body to the hostiles, and fired a sustained burst of rounds into the vehicles.

One of the Russian men at the end of the convoy broke cover and was shot in the head and chest.

Laith and Adam sprinted down one side of the convoy, Mark down the other. The last remaining member of the Russian team ran out from behind the car while firing his submachine gun. Bullets from the convoy smashed a large hole into his chest.

Will sprinted, jumped onto the hood of the first ruined vehicle, then leapt onto the roof of the second vehicle and began firing through the roofs, while the rest of Will's team attacked the line of cars from the sides. Will leapt to the next SUV, continued firing down into the vehicles' roofs, and moved onward, repeating the drill until he was standing on the last car in the convoy. After firing controlled bursts into the driver and passenger areas and the trunk, Will shouted, "Cease firing."

He jumped down and began searching each SUV with his colleagues.

Everyone in the convoy was dead.

Police sirens.

Will felt sick with frustration and failure as he called out, "We need to leave right now!"

Mikhail used his binoculars to watch Will and his team run to their vehicles and leave the scene. He waited a few seconds, then gunned his car and drove fast to the destroyed convoy. Exiting the vehicle, he ran along the convoy, glancing inside each SUV, ignoring the distant sound of police sirens. After he checked the last vehicle, he kicked it hard and shouted, "Bastard!"

Schreiber was not in any of the vehicles.

He'd tricked Mikhail by sending out a dummy convoy.

And that could only mean he was now loose, traveling toward the Black Forest. But Mikhail had no idea where in the vast region Schreiber was headed.

He ran back to his car, pressed hard on the accelerator, and chased after Will's team. Following the big MI6 officer was his last remaining hope. But he'd have no hesitation in killing the operative if he got in his way.

TWENTY-FIVE

An icy early-morning wind buffeted Simon Rübner as he knelt down and used a trowel to dig through the Black Forest mountaintop's soil. Momentarily, he wondered if he was in the right place, whether the code's numbers had been altered when in the SVR or CIA vaults. His tool struck metal, he wiped away soil, and he sighed with relief.

The metal box was in the hole.

He stared at it.

Many people had gone to enormous lengths to get him to this place, but none of them had sacrificed as much and worked as hard as he had to ascertain the location of the DLB. It had started six months before. He'd been toying with leaving Mossad to earn a more lucrative salary in the private sector and had made some discreet enquiries with prospective employers. He later learned that one of them was a cover company owned by Mr. Schreiber. Over the course of three weeks, he was interviewed by twelve men and women. They'd told him nothing about their backgrounds, but he could tell they were all former intelligence officers because they asked him precisely worded questions that were designed to not only define whether his responses were consistent but also to subtly elicit a portrait of his character. He could see what they were doing and they knew it. So he'd played it straight and told them that money was his prime motivator and that legalities had never been particularly interesting to him in his line of work. At the end of his twelfth interview, the female interviewer told him that she was recommending that he be advanced to the final interview and that if he was successful he would be hired. Two days later, on a Sunday morning, an elderly, diminutive gentleman knocked on the door to his home in the suburbs of Tel Aviv. He introduced himself as Colonel Kurt Schreiber and said that he was there to conduct the final interview.

Simon was totally unprepared for the interview and had to ask his wife and teenage daughter to go out for a few hours to give them privacy. He sat with Mr. Schreiber in the living room until midafternoon. At the end of the session, he was mentally exhausted. The German had barely spoken, instead had sat motionless, his eyes flickering behind his rimless glasses, with a slight smile on his face and an expression and demeanor that suggested immense intellect, focus, perception, and cruelty.

Simon had guided him to the front door, at which point Mr. Schreiber turned to him and said that he would pay him one million dollars per year with performance bonus on top and that he was to resign the next day. Simon had instantly accepted. The other jobs he was considering had salaries less than a fifth of what the German was offering.

After he'd given his notice with Mossad, he'd taken his wife and daughter to New York. Upon landing at JFK, he'd told the immigration officer that he was a private investor looking to set up a business in the States. The officer grilled him for fifteen minutes before telling him that he and his family needed to wait in a room until a decision had been made as to whether he could enter the country. Two hours later, another man entered the room and asked more questions before obtaining all of Simon's contact details and letting him go.

Of course, the delay of entry had allowed Immigration to contact other U.S. agencies and ultimately the CIA, who would have given U.S. Immigration assurances that they and the FBI would keep their eyes on the known Mossad officer and would use him for their own benefit.

He put his family in a Manhattan apartment and took possession of one of Mr. Schreiber's dormant but legal companies.

Four men from the CIA approached him ten days later, saying they were from a Belgium consultancy called Gerlache and were seeking to establish a partnership with a company that could provide information to U.S. companies seeking to set up operations in the Middle East. He'd accepted, and at first their requirements from him were unremarkable. He took their money, telling them that he needed the cash to support a wife and daughter who drove him crazy with their shopping sprees and that the daughter wanted them to stay in the States so that she could attend one of the fancy and expensive East Coast universities.

It was exactly what they wanted to hear.

And accelerated their decision to tell him that they had affiliations to U.S. political entities, knew that he was an Israeli intelligence officer, and wanted him to pass them Israeli secrets.

He'd pretended to be shocked and confused. He told them that what they were asking of him would make him a traitor, but that he'd become reliant on their money. They gave him assurances that no one would ever know about his secret work for them and that they would pay him double. He agreed. They had him hook, line, and sinker.

Or rather, he had them hook, line, and sinker.

They could barely contain their excitement when he started feeding them the names of Israeli agents operating in the West. But he did it slowly on the pretext that he had to discreetly get the information from Mossad files, whereas the truth was that Mr. Schreiber had told him to get all the information before he resigned.

He knew that the CIA officers were telling him the truth when they said that he'd become the Agency's top Israeli agent. And he was sure that his work for the officers had done wonders for their careers. It came as no surprise to them when he said that Mossad was likely to post him back to Israel unless he could convince his masters that he'd recruited a U.S. spy. They said they'd play the role of that spy and would give him U.S. secrets that should placate his employer. Everything they gave him was low-level crap that Mossad already knew. He played along with that for a while but one day said that he needed much more or Mossad was going to order him to find a better spy. He told them that he needed the identity of a Russian SVR officer who was on the Agency's books. This clearly unsettled them, but a day later they met and supplied him with the name of Lenka Yevtushenko. They said they'd set up an introduction to the Russian and that in return he'd better give them a whole lot more names and details of Israeli operations on American soil.

He was sure that the four CIA officers had given him the name of the SVR officer without authorization to do so.

He gave Yevtushenko's details to Mr. Schreiber, who approached the Russian and said that he had to steal the code or else Mr. Schreiber would tell the SVR that he was a CIA spy. Yevtushenko was petrified and said that his ability to travel was tightly restricted but that he would do the theft if Mr. Schreiber could help him get out of Russia. Mr. Schreiber agreed and told him that he was to use a highly effective Polish exfiltration route, but under no circumstances was he to go anywhere near the Polish embassy in Moscow as it would be under surveillance. He gave him precise instructions. Yevtushenko walked into the small Polish consulate in Saint Petersburg, said that he needed to speak in strict confidence to someone in the consulate who was familiar with intelligence matters, and was told that there was no one like that there but that he should liaise with their embassy in Moscow where there were professionals who could help him. He said he had to escape to Poland with a secret, that he couldn't go anywhere near the Moscow embassy, that time was running out. Some urgent calls were made to the embassy; everything was arranged for him. That afternoon, he stole half of the military grid reference from the SVR vaults and used the Polish exfiltration route to enter Gdansk.

At the same time, Simon and his family flew to Europe, having no further use for the CIA.

Mr. Schreiber had anticipated the possibility that Yevtushenko would be pursued by the SVR and had asked Simon to arrange for a deniable team of private contractors to confront not only the Polish ABW and AW officers who'd be waiting for the SVR defector in Gdansk, but also any Russians. Mr. Schreiber also put in place a team of his own men to take possession of Yevtushenko and the code.

Simon lifted the dead-letter box out of the soil, held it in front of him, smiled, and muttered, "All that effort to find you."

He opened the box, placed a folded piece of paper inside it, sealed the container, and returned it to the hole. After covering it with soil, he stood and looked at the Black Forest's magnificent vista. Tomorrow, Kronos would be standing on this spot.

Later that day, Kronos would meet Mr. Schreiber, who would give him the instruction to kill the treacherous bastard who was due to testify under oath in two weeks' time.

Men had ordered Mr. Schreiber to stop that from happening.

Because nobody could ever learn the secret behind Slingshot.

TWENTY-SIX

Betty Mayne sat at the kitchen table, watching Sarah attempt to peel and slice two cloves of garlic. It had taken Alfie two days to succeed in getting Sarah to accompany him to the nearest town to buy groceries. Today she'd reluctantly agreed, largely because her husband James had jokingly told her that if she didn't go he could finally tell all their friends that he'd become the dominant partner in their relationship. It was now evening, the blue sky darkening into dusk, and Alfie was making his usual rounds of the hunting lodge's grounds, setting his traps, watching and listening, having a smoke in the icy, fresh Highlands air, checking for anything that looked unusual, always keeping one hand close to his pistol.

Betty was wearing a thick tweed jacket, skirt, and hiking boots — clothes she'd worn to take James on a hike around the mountainous estate earlier in the day. James had cursed and wheezed and grumbled for most of the walk, but as they'd strolled alongside the loch toward the lodge one hour ago he told Betty that he'd had the best day he could remember, had decided that London life was no longer for him, recited the fauna and flora they'd seen on their route, and said that he was very worried about his wife.

He was now preparing a fire, and probably pouring himself a slug of single malt.

"Would you like me to help you, my dear?" Betty watched Sarah reach for shallots.

"You could get me a glass of wine." Sarah's hand shook as she held the knife. "Join me in one?"

"Not when I'm working." Betty stood, poured a glass of Shiraz, and handed Sarah the glass. "What are you cooking?"

"I don't know . . . yet."

"Keep it simple."

"Simple isn't good enough. I'm being judged by the men."

"Actually, you're being judged by me. The men will eat anything. They just want to see you moving."

Sarah held the knife still. "I know."

"What else do you know?"

"More than you!"

"I'm sure you do, my dear." Betty moved alongside her. "Maybe just put the chicken on top of what you've already chopped. Onions, garlic, celery, herbs. Bit of wine. Keep it simple. Blimey, Alfie will think he's in heaven."

"You're patronizing me."

"I'm talking to you." Betty put her hand on top of Sarah's knife-holding hand. "Shall we slice some potatoes, sauté them first, then add them to the mix?"

Sarah said between gritted teeth, "I don't normally play the domestic housewife."

Betty patted her hand. "Then what do you do?"

"I arbitrate corporate litigation. You wouldn't understand."

Betty nodded. "I wouldn't."

"Playing dumb?" Sarah grabbed the chicken and put it on top of the vegetables.

"Just being myself, my dear." Betty looked at Sarah, saw that her ordinarily beautiful face was greasy and swollen, full of anxiety, tortured. She picked up Sarah's glass of wine, took a sip, smiled, and placed the glass next to Sarah's fingers. "Rules are much more fun when they're broken."

"You're not breaking any rules. You know exactly what you're doing."

"Perhaps, but *you* wouldn't understand that, my dear."

"I . . ."

"I, what?"

Sarah said nothing.

Betty grabbed six potatoes, took the knife from Sarah, and sliced the potatoes into quarters. "When he came back from the Legion, he would barely speak at first. Four of us looked after him, the same four who helped you leave your home. We washed his clothes, ironed them, fed him, and made him attend the lectures for his degree at Cambridge. It was hard. He'd become someone he didn't like."

"Will?"

Betty placed the potato wedges into a pan and began frying them on the stovetop. "We were ordered to do it. The logistical help we gave him wasn't really necessary; I'd never met anyone so self-sufficient. What *was* necessary was that he needed to be integrated into society."

"Ordered by whom?"

"Will thought we were friends of your father before he was killed. We let him believe that. The truth was different."

Patrick and Alistair had been the ones who'd instructed the team.

"Why are you telling me this?" Tears ran down Sarah's face as she put the chicken in the oven.

"Because you need to realize how selfish you are." Betty tossed the potatoes in oil.

The comment shocked Sarah. "I'm not selfish. I just don't know what he does!"

Betty continued cooking. "When he wasn't studying, we'd spend time with him doing things. The four of us had a rule that none of us would talk about our prior military service, that it was essential we talk about normal life. We told him how to open a bank account, how to join the local library, how to eat in a restaurant." She drained the oil from the potatoes. "And how to cook. In the evenings, we'd play board games with him. He became rather good at Monopoly"—she smiled—"though he did try to cheat sometimes by stealing Monopoly money and hiding it under his side of the board."

Sarah wiped tears away and took a sip of wine. "He was like that when we were kids. Took me years to realize that he'd marked the cards we were playing with."

Betty chuckled. "Seems he hasn't changed." Opening the oven door, she sprinkled the potato wedges around the chicken. "After two weeks, I told him that we were leaving. He didn't want us to go, said that he liked us being around. I replied that he needed to start socializing with other students. So we left." Betty leaned against the work surface, staring at nothing. "Since then, I've often wondered if we should have stayed a bit longer."

"Maybe you should have done!" Sarah put her wine down. "Perhaps it would have stopped him getting involved in stuff that"—she swept an arm through the air—"screws up other people's lives."

Betty frowned and turned toward Sarah. "What do you think he does for a living?"

"I don't know. But I suspect that whatever it is, it's illegal."

"You think he's a criminal?"

Sarah nodded.

Betty considered this. "I suppose he is."

Sarah muttered, "I thought so!"

Betty knew that Will would be furious with her for what she was about to say. "After all, spying is a crime in most countries."

Sarah looked incredulous. "He's a spy? For whom?"

"For us, silly. Britain." Already, she regretted saying anything, though part of her knew it was the right thing to do. "He's an MI6 officer, has been since he graduated from university."

"Why . . . why didn't he tell me?"

"Because he's not allowed to. The Service uses him on very specific projects. There are only a few people in MI6 who know he's an officer." She wondered if she should stop talking. "They singled him out and put him on a very tough training course. Only him. Despite the odds against it, he passed, and for the last eight years he's been deployed almost continuously." She hesitated. "The other reason I suspect he didn't tell you is because you wouldn't let him do so."

The hostility was back in Sarah's face. "No. All the good you did for him after he left the Legion was undone. They made him become the person he didn't want to be. Probably much worse."

Betty said more to herself, "I don't think so." She frowned. "No . . . I don't think so, at all." She looked at Sarah. "There's no doubt he's exceptionally good at what he does. He's driven by guilt that he couldn't save your mother, and has been trying to make up for that by putting himself at great risk to protect others. But he knows there's another world out there. During the two weeks we spent with him, we gave him the tools to live within that world."

"Maybe, but he still chooses to do what he does."

Betty nodded. "He won't quit while there's a job to be done. But he's working hard to have a different side to his life. You can't see that because you've made no effort to get to know him during the last few years."

"Of course not! He's a dangerous man."

"Not to you. You're the only family he has left."

"I saw what he's capable of."

Betty was silent.

Fresh tears ran down Sarah's face. "The gang of criminals came in; they bound my mother with tape, some of it over her mouth; one of them threw me to the floor and put a boot on my head; then Will came in the room. He was . . . was only a boy."

"He was seventeen."

Sarah shook her head. "Only a boy, to me. They sent him out of the room to fetch cash. My mother died. He came back in holding a knife. I looked at him, he looked at me. The boy was gone. And he killed them."

"How do you think that made him feel?"

Sarah shrugged. "I don't know. I've never seen such explosive violence come from someone. Probably it made him realize how good he was at it."

"That's not what I meant. How do you think it made him feel, seeing you look at him with an expression that suggested you no longer knew him?"

Sarah didn't respond.

"He's been living with that ever since." Betty sighed. "And he's been trying to get you to understand that the *boy* you once knew is still inside him." Her tone became stern. "But you made a judgment about him, wouldn't see him, wouldn't reply to his letters, wouldn't do anything that could unbalance your perfect self-centered world. And as a result, he's felt totally disconnected from people around him because he's believed that if you can't see the good in him, then others must feel the same."

"He brings danger into people's lives!"

"No, he doesn't!"

A split second after Betty had uttered the words, a high-velocity round smashed through a window and struck the wall inches from Sarah's head.

Sarah screamed.

Betty shouted, "Get down!"

Alfie burst into the room, his handgun held high. "Direction of shot?"

Betty crouched by the kitchen table. "West, from one of the mountains."

Alfie moved to Sarah, put a hand on the back of her head, and pushed her roughly to the ground. "Stay down."

James called out in a terrified voice, "What's happening?"

"Get behind cover and stay there until I tell you to move!" Alfie stared at the broken window, waiting.

Nothing happened.

They stayed like this for twenty minutes, Sarah sobbing, Betty and Alfie motionless as they gripped their guns.

Alfie narrowed his eyes. "We've gotta get out of here."

The sniper got onto one knee on the mountainside and started stripping down his weapon. The man next to him continued staring through his binoculars toward the house. A third man was on his cell phone confirming to Kurt Schreiber that they had sufficiently unsettled the property's occupants to get them to move locations.

Just as Mr. Schreiber had wanted.

Because he couldn't allow Sarah's guardians to become too familiar with their surroundings and therefore further refine their security protocols.

They watched Alfie sprint to the car, start the engine, and stand next to the vehicle while training his handgun toward the darkness ahead. Betty rushed toward the vehicle, gripping Sarah and James. Five seconds later the car was speeding off down the track.

That didn't matter.

The rest of the surveillance team were all waiting in vehicles, ready to tail them to their next location.

And Mr. Schreiber had promised his men that if he gave the order to kill their target, it would happen there.

TWENTY-SEVEN

Kurt Schreiber glanced at Simon Rübner. "You've performed impeccably. After tonight, take a couple of weeks off."

"What about your other projects?"

"They're all in hand."

Rübner sighed. "I'm not going to say no. I could do with a rest."

"You're not going to say anything, and you'll do what you're told." Schreiber checked his watch. "Report back to me in fourteen days. I'll put you in charge of the Budapest initiative. It's time the prime minister knew who he was dealing with, and I want you to personally hand him the photographs while giving him a strongly worded verbal message."

"Certainly, Mr. Schreiber." He smiled, though he felt uneasy. "Good luck . . . tonight."

"Luck?" Schreiber laughed.

The old man opened the car door and stepped onto a cobbled street in the Bavarian capital of Munich. It was late evening, and a fine drizzle was descending over the dimly lit old town. Wearing a thick overcoat, suit, dark felt fedora hat, and rimless glasses, and carrying a stick to aide his journey, he walked into the Karlsplatz—a large square next to the Karlstor, which between the fourteenth century and 1791 was one of the main gates in the city wall. Now, its fountain had been transformed into a beautifully illuminated ice skating rink; adults and children were laughing and calling out to each other as they glided over it. Leaving the square, he walked alongside various streets, some that had remained unchanged since well before Adolf Hitler's creation of the Nazi Party in the city and others that had been rebuilt after the allies crippled Munich with bombs. When Schreiber was in the Stasi, the city had been part of West Germany—enemy territory. But he'd spent more time in places like this than he had in East Berlin, and knew every inch of the city.

He stopped opposite Michaelskirche, the sixteenth-century Jesuit church that was the largest Renaissance church north of the Alps. It was shut for the night. Over its closed doors was a gleaming bronze sculpture of Archangel Michael fighting a demon in human form.

His heart beat fast as he approached the entrance.

The plaza around him was deserted of people.

This was the moment.

He stood within twelve feet of the magnificent church's entrance and looked at the shadows within it. "Schreiber, looking for Kronos."

In the doorway, he saw a man's large boots.

"Colonel Schreiber. I arranged this meeting."

The man said nothing.

"You got my message. I'm here, as arranged."

Silence.

"Speak! I have little time."

Kronos stepped forward.

The church's lights shone down over his face. "I could have killed you ten times since exiting the Israeli's car and coming here. I'll speak when I wish to and your time is of no relevance to me. Where are the others?"

Though he had anticipated that Kronos would have followed him here, Schreiber had no idea how the assassin knew that the man who'd driven him to the city was Israeli. "Half of them are dead. The other half sent me."

"You have a traitor?"

"Exactly."

"Who?"

Schreiber gave him the name. "He intends to testify at a hearing in The Hague in two weeks' time. I can't let that happen. He's currently being held in a maximum-security facility in the southern Netherlands. My sources have confirmed that he's being moved from the facility ten days prior to the hearing and will be taken to another maximum-security complex. He'll be under significant protection at all times. Do you think you can do it?"

"Of course. What is he testifying?"

"All you need to know is that it relates to the Berlin meeting in 1995—a secret we shared at that meeting. I can't let that secret become public knowledge."

A secret that was omitted from the Slingshot protocols.

One that would kill hundreds of millions of people.

"You also need to know that I've been pursued by a British intelligence officer called Will Cochrane and an SVR operative called Mikhail Salkov. I don't know if they're still after me, but it's possible that Salkov knows about you." He supplied Kronos with the home addresses of both operatives.

Kronos shrugged. "They won't get in my way."

"Good. Once the job's completed, ten million dollars will be deposited into your account. Then, you must change identity and location. Are you married, have children?"

Kronos did not answer him.

"If you do have a family, you cannot stay with them. You must disappear."

"The deal was that I am permitted to lead my life until I'm

activated, that I must move locations after the job. There was never any mention of leaving my family."

"Things have changed! I can't afford for there to be any potential security leaks."

Kronos felt anger rise within him. "*You* can't afford any leaks?" He thought for a moment. "Are you sure you're representing everyone present at the Berlin meeting?"

Schreiber grew impatient. "Everyone's who's alive, yes. If you're doubting my authority to be here, then you'd better say so."

Kronos smiled. "I doubt everything that comes out of your mouth, you little shit. But the DLB was activated correctly." His expression grew cold. "You've changed the terms of the deal, so I'm forced to do the same. Five million will be paid in advance."

"What!"

"In advance. Changing identities and locations is an expensive business and requires preparation. Presumably, you want me to slip into that new life immediately after I've killed the witness. Aside from that, I need guaranteed compensation if I'm to walk away from my family."

"That's not . . ."

Kronos took three quick steps toward him. "What were you about to say?"

Schreiber stepped back, nearly tripped, fear coursed through him. "I was about to say, that's not a problem. You'll have half the money up front."

"I'm glad you made that decision." Kronos kept his cold stare fixed on Schreiber. "I'll take care of your target. In return, stick to your side of the bargain. If you don't, then you know what the outcome will be."

It was nearly midnight when Stefan got back to his home on the outskirts of the Black Forest. He entered the kitchen. Plates and pans had been washed up after his family's dinner. He knew they'd now be asleep. In the center of the table was a dinner plate, over which was foil and a note from his wife saying in German:

> *Three minutes in the microwave—don't forget to take off the foil first! I love you.*

He removed the packaging and smiled as he saw that his wife had prepared him *königsberger klopse*—veal meatballs in a white sauce containing lemon juice and capers—with roast potatoes and *schupfnudel.* After placing the dish in the microwave, he looked around and felt a twinge of sadness. He'd eaten thousands of meals in here, most of them with his family. It had been his rule that mealtimes were an important part of the day for the family to sit together, share the experience of eating his wife's wonderful cuisine, and swap stories. But the mealtimes were never a formal affair; instead they were usually filled with laughter and imaginary tales.

Removing the plate of food, he sat at the table, alone.

Fifteen minutes later, he rinsed his empty plate and placed it alongside the others to dry. His wife was a stickler for maintaining a clean and tidy household.

He arched his muscular back and yawned. Tomorrow would be a very busy day. He walked up the stairs and entered the twins' room. Mathias and Wendell were both lying asleep on their backs, their blond hair slightly ruffled, their faces looking angelic. He stood between their beds and brushed his big hands against their cheeks. "My darling boys."

He wished he'd been able to continue telling them his bedtime story about the forest gnomes' search for the legendary Timestop mushrooms. He wondered if he'd ever have the chance to finish the tale.

His thoughts turned to Schreiber. Tonight, the man had made a mistake by changing the deal so that Stefan had to abandon his family. One day, he'd make him suffer for that.

TWENTY-EIGHT

Will walked across the Auguststrasse apartment and stood opposite Peter. "I'm going to be away for a day or two, to see if Patrick really can't get access to the Rübner files. It's our last remaining lead. In my absence, you're in charge."

Peter said in a sympathetic tone, "This isn't your fault."

Will sighed. "It's a fact that most of my initiatives have just provided a handful of names and haven't got us anywhere nearer to the paper."

"Perhaps this guy Rübner's not linked to any of this."

"Maybe."

"You think you might be able to persuade Patrick to go over the director's head?"

Will shook his head. "I think you're right. He wouldn't win that battle. And that means I'm about to fail again." He stepped away from Peter, then paused. "The section's losing its teeth, and there's nothing we can do about it."

• • •

As Will exited the Auguststrasse apartment, Mikhail turned on his vehicle's ignition, engaged the gears, and slowly crawled forward. The MI6 operative was one hundred yards ahead of him. He'd keep him at that distance until the man hailed a taxi or got into a private vehicle.

His large handgun was tight against his beltline, ready for use the moment the British intelligence officer led him closer to the whereabouts of Schreiber.

Will walked quickly across the concourse of Berlin Hauptbahnhof, Germany's biggest train station. It was early evening, and the station was crowded with commuters. He found a pay phone, shoved twenty euros into it, and dialed an international cell phone number.

Patrick answered, "Yeah?"

"It's me. Can you talk?"

"Hold on." The line was silent for thirty seconds. "Can now."

"Okay. Are you able to cut through the bureaucracy to get to the files Suzy asked about?"

"Possibly, rather than probably. But either way, it's almost certainly a nasty one-way ticket for us if I try. Bureaucracy and self-interest's a pile of crap. What's this about?"

"I need you to get on a plane."

"When?"

"Now. Or as near to now as possible."

"Where am I going?"

"Israel."

Patrick said tersely, "That's a long flight."

"Please, Patrick."

"You're sure it's going to be worth my time?"

"No."

Silence. "It had better be worth my time."

"I'll meet you there."

"To do what?"

"We need to meet the in-country head from your organization."

"Okay. I'll get the meeting set up through the normal channels."

"No. It's imperative you set it up yourself. No one else must know."

Silence for seven seconds. "Give me a call back in thirty minutes and I'll give you details." He repeated, "What's this about?"

Will smiled. "It's about unblocking crap."

At four the next morning, Will was in a taxi heading toward the airport. He felt tired and knew that he'd have to get some sleep on the flight, but right now his mind was too active to allow him to rest.

Understanding Rübner's role was key. Will suspected that once Rübner had been given Lenka Yevtushenko's name, he had been involved in coercing the Russian to steal the paper from the SVR. But Langley was blocking Will accessing information on Rübner, so his plan was now to approach someone who almost certainly would have been a customer of Rübner's CIA intelligence reports, intelligence that could indicate whether Will's suspicion that Rübner had been manipulating his CIA handlers for his own ends was correct.

And one of the biggest customers of all would have been the CIA Head of Tel Aviv Station.

Mikhail watched Will check in at the El Al desk. He frowned, having no idea why the MI6 officer was travelling to Israel, as it was highly unlikely that Schreiber was in the Middle East. In any case, this presented him with a problem. If the MI6 officer obtained information in Israel that could pinpoint Schreiber, he'd relay that information to his men in the Auguststrasse safe house, who'd then immediately deploy. Stuck in Israel, Mikhail would have no chance to follow them. But he would also be taking a huge gamble if he let the officer out of his sight.

He made a decision.

TWENTY-NINE

Kronos sat in a café in the arrivals section of the Frankfurt air-port, studying the people who were exiting passport control as well as those who were moving across the concourse. He ignored most individuals, instead focusing only on those who were dressed in the uniforms of pilots. He'd discounted all of the thirty-two pilots he'd seen during the last five hours, as only four of them had been wearing the insignia of the Dutch carrier KLM, and they'd been no good to him as it was clear they were about to fly out of the airport. He needed a Dutch pilot who'd landed and was about to go off duty.

He took a sip of his coffee, checked his watch, and casually flicked through the pages of *Die Welt* while occasionally glancing over the top of the newspaper. Wearing an expensive suit and overcoat, and with an attaché case by his feet, he looked like every other business-man who was traveling through the place. If challenged by airport security, he would explain that he was waiting for a colleague whose flight had been delayed. Every thirty minutes, he'd checked the arriv-als board to update his knowledge of flight arrival times. Currently, there were seven flights that weren't running on schedule. He also knew exactly what time every KLM carrier was due to arrive.

One of them had landed thirty minutes ago from Amsterdam Schiphol. Its pilots would soon be walking into view.

He'd thought through every possibility. The pilots could use private vehicles to exit the airport before he had a chance to follow them, could use taxis but not declare their destination until out of earshot within the vehicle, could be met by loved ones or KLM limousine drivers who'd whisk them away without declaring where they were going, or could get changed into civilian clothes in a secure part of the airport and then use a hidden exit. That didn't matter, because he was prepared to wait here all day and night until a Dutch pilot walked up to the external taxi rank and announced his destination to the driver. When that happened, Kronos would be standing right behind the man and would hail the next available taxi to take him to the same location.

Most likely it would be a hotel. He hoped so, because hotel rooms were easy to break in to.

But it didn't matter if it was somewhere else.

Among many talents, Kronos was adept at burgling the most secure complexes.

Four men walked into view.

Kronos kept his paper motionless as he fixed his gaze on them.

All were wearing KLM pilot uniforms.

They walked across the concourse, past a group of teenage girls who gave them admiring glances while giggling and nudging each other, then stopped and shook hands. Three of them walked off but not in the direction of the main exit.

They were no good to him.

The fourth pulled his trolley suitcase behind him as he moved toward the exit. The blond man looked to be in his early thirties, and the slight smile on his face suggested he was happy to be in Germany.

The assassin folded up his newspaper, placed cash on the table to pay for his coffee, grabbed his attaché case, and followed the pilot toward the taxi rank.

THIRTY

Will drove his hired Jeep south, away from Israel's Ben Gurion airport. Soon he was on Highway 6, heading toward the Negev Desert. Around him were lush fields of grass, and the temperature was in the mid-seventies; it was nothing like the harsh winter he was used to in Europe.

Ninety minutes later he was circumventing the functional-looking city of Beersheba. Ahead of him was the stunning desert. He stopped the car in a small Bedouin village, directly outside a café that contained a couple of men smoking hookahs. Sitting at one of the outside tables, he ordered tea from a waiter and looked around. On the opposite side of the dusty street, two young girls who'd been playing were now watching him, fiddling with their long black hair. The men in the café were also staring at him while they smoked. Even though Will was dressed in jeans, boots, and an open-neck shirt, he knew he looked out of place.

That didn't matter.

What did was the location of the village.

The Arab waiter brought his drink and placed it on the table, next to Will's car keys. In Hebrew, he asked, "You lost?"

Will smiled, pretended to look embarrassed. "English."

The waiter repeated the question in English.

Will shook his head and replied, "Tourist." He nodded toward the desert. "Desert trekking. Thirsty work."

A woman came out of a house and ushered the two girls inside. The waiter said, "They think you're an Israeli cop. They're frightened."

As the waiter returned to the inside of the café, Will took a sip of the sweet tea and tried to relax. The aromatic smell of the hookah tobacco wafted across his table and prompted brief memories. He recalled walking through a vibrant and bustling Moroccan souk one evening, following one of his Syrian agents, who was unaware of his presence and was heading to a covert meeting with an Iranian intelligence officer; sitting in a café similar to this one, in Cairo, scouring the buildings opposite to spot the man who'd planted a bomb in the café and was waiting for the right moment to blow it apart and kill the men who were sitting three tables away from him; drinking tea in a Bedouin tent with a Jordanian tribal leader who believed he could help Will negotiate the release of an American aid worker who'd been captured by a gang of criminals with affiliations to an Al Qaeda cell; and eating dates and baklava with a stunning Lebanese woman who told him that she was falling for him, when in fact Will knew she wanted to put a bullet in his head.

He lifted the tea to his mouth, then froze. A sedan car was driving along the street, two men inside. The car slowed down and stopped forty yards away. The driver remained in the vehicle; the passenger got out and walked quickly along the street toward the café. He was dressed like Will, looked European or Israeli, and was wearing shades. The car turned in the street and drove off in the direction it had come from. By the time it had disappeared from view, the passenger was only a few yards from Will's table. Will stayed still as the man walked right alongside his table, scooped up his car keys, kept walking, entered Will's Jeep, and drove off. Two seconds later, an SUV entered the street, driving fast. Will placed cash on the table to pay for his tea, watched the vehicle draw closer, waited, then stood and jogged to the street. The SUV slowed to walking pace, a door opened, the vehicle came alongside Will, and he grabbed the open door and jumped inside. Immediately the vehicle accelerated fast, causing Will to lurch backward into the seat.

Three men were in the speeding vehicle. As Will slammed the door shut, one of them said in an American accent, "Get your head down."

Will did as he was told, lying sideways so that he was not visible to anyone outside of the SUV.

The man in the front passenger seat said, "First turning on the left, thirty yards."

"Got it." The driver changed gears.

The man next to Will looked at him. "Ninety percent certain we weren't followed. But we're going to have to take a fairly complex antisurveillance route back to the embassy. The Israelis are superb at this stuff, so we can't afford to take any risks. Just keep out of sight. Okay?"

Will nodded. He didn't know if the Americans were paramilitary operatives, intelligence officers, or Special Forces. But he did know that they were under CIA orders to get him into the U.S. embassy in Tel Aviv without him being seen by the Israeli security services.

The CIA Head of Tel Aviv Station closed the thick steel door to the embassy's safe room, locked the handle in place, and sat opposite Will and Patrick. Middle-aged, chubby, wearing an ill-fitting brown suit and circular spectacles, and with a grin on his face, Geoffrey Pepper looked more like an accountant than a senior intelligence operative. He said in a southern accent, "All that effort just to get you into a soundproof room."

The place rather more resembled a small cell. It contained three chairs and a small table with two secure telephone units.

Patrick had been picked up on the outskirts of the northern city of Haifa and had arrived at the embassy thirty minutes before Will. He wouldn't have liked the journey—he'd been out of the field too long and these days was more used to being driven in limousines—though he would have far more hated the idea of being covertly photographed by the Israelis if he'd turned up at the embassy by more luxurious means.

Geoffrey fixed his attention on Will. "Who are you?"

Patrick held up a hand. "He works for me. That should be all you need to know."

"Should be, but I'm kinda the inquisitive type."

Patrick was about to respond, but Will interrupted. "I'm an MI6 officer."

His grin still in place, Geoffrey said, "MI6? Oh dear. If I'd known, I'd have told my Station to burn all our files and hide the family jewelry before you got here." He turned to Patrick. "What do you want?"

Patrick shrugged. "I've got no idea."

For a brief moment Geoffrey's smile vanished, then it returned. "You have every right to be here . . ."

"Damn right."

"Though it would be a discourtesy to waste my time." Geoffrey looked at Will. "Presumably MI6 has an *idea* as to what you want."

"No. MI6 doesn't know I'm here, let alone why."

"Oh, this just gets better and better, doesn't it, gentlemen?" Geoffrey's eyes flickered. "So, shall I conclude this is all very *off the record*?"

"If you like." Will wondered how the head of station was going to react to what he was about to say. "We're here to talk about the CIA asset Simon Rübner."

Geoffrey was motionless, silent.

"Given that he's a Mossad officer, I'm certain your station would be a customer for Rübner's intelligence."

Geoffrey said nothing.

"Rübner's name has popped up in a major operation I'm running. It's crucial I understand Rübner's value to the CIA."

The station head darted a look at Patrick. His smile had now vanished. "You got locked out of Langley, so thought you'd come knocking on my door?"

Will continued, "That was my idea, not Patrick's. I think Rübner's not all that he seems. But we have been . . . locked out. We need your help."

Geoffrey leaned back in his chair, rested one leg over the other, and drummed his fingers. "If Langley's keeping its mouth shut, then so will I."

Patrick said quickly, "Not *Langley*, self-interested unknown persons *within* Langley."

"Have you spoken to one of the directors?"

Patrick nodded. "I spoke to the Director of Intelligence. He won't tell me anything."

"Then it *is* Langley that's keeping its mouth shut."

Will asked, "Do the names Gerlache and François Gilliams mean anything to you?"

"Should they?"

"I think Gerlache is the front company used by the CIA intelligence officer running Rübner, and François Gilliams is his alias." He recalled the note that had been handed to Alina. "It's possible Rübner is being run by more than one officer."

Geoffrey stopped drumming his fingers, seemed deep in thought, and said, "I'm not betraying any confidences by saying that you're right we've been receiving Rübner's intelligence, though we're not the prime customer."

"Who is?"

Geoffrey shrugged. "Langley and the FBI."

"Why the FBI?"

The station chief's smile was back on his face. "To answer that would be imprudent. Make your own deductions."

Will said, "Rübner was feeding you details about Mossad operations on U.S. soil. The feds were the prime customer because they were the ones authorized to shut down the operations."

"Maybe." Geoffrey looked at Patrick and said quietly, "I'm afraid you've made a wasted trip. You can't expect me to give you information that the director himself has refused to divulge to you."

Will repeated, "Gerlache, François Gilliams?"

Geoffrey sighed. "I don't know the identity of Rübner's case officer. It's quite possible he's been using a French or Belgian front to meet Rübner, but on that point I know as much as you do."

Patrick turned toward Will. "Geoffrey's right to say nothing."

Geoffrey frowned as he switched his attention to Will. "You'd have known that, young man. So, why drag someone as senior as Patrick halfway around the world to hear that I'm not going to breach security, lose my job, and possibly end up with a prison sentence?"

Will spoke quickly and in a hushed tone. "I needed Patrick to set this meeting up without others knowing." He looked around. "I had to talk to you without fear that we were being watched or overheard."

"Makes no difference to the result." The station head began tapping his fingers again. After a few seconds he asked, "Why do you think there's something wrong with the Rübner intelligence?"

Will ignored the question. "Does Rübner's work for the CIA benefit you?"

Geoffrey seemed surprised, then smiled. "Good question." He thought for a moment. "Not really. In fact, it's been a bit of a pain in the ass."

Will could understand why. If Rübner was selling out Mossad operations on U.S. soil, this would place the CIA Head of Tel Aviv Station in a delicate situation given that part of his work involved liaising with Mossad, Shin Bet, and other Israeli intelligence agencies on issues of mutual concern. He asked, "Were you involved in the targeting and recruitment of Rübner?"

Geoffrey shook his head. "Nope, beyond telling Langley that Simon Rübner was a Mossad officer. I've no idea how they got him after that."

"So, you have no personal vested interest in the Rübner case?"

Geoffrey beamed. "I'm not going to blab to you just because my career might not benefit from Rübner."

"Of course." Will leaned forward, clasping his big hands, his expression now cold. "But before I answer your question about what's wrong with Rübner, I need to know if you're in cahoots with the *bastards* who leaked my identity and home address to cover up an act that, if they knew about it, would have the president and every senator wishing to string them up by their throats."

Patrick turned sharply toward him. "What!"

Geoffrey's eyes narrowed. "I think you have some explaining to do, young man."

"Like you, I'll explain what I damn well like."

"Sure." The station head looked unsettled, glanced at Patrick, then back at Will. "We're not your enemies."

"I hope you're not. Because I'm giving you due warning that I'm going to find out who betrayed me, and I'm going to drag them over the body of the director and dump their fucking asses at the feet of the president. And if the director's involved as well, I'll squeeze his balls until he screams. Nobody's going to keep their mouth shut."

"You'd tear apart the CIA because someone pissed you off?"

"No! But I'll do it to find the scum who've put several innocent men, women, and children's lives at severe risk." Will leaned back. "The people who're keeping their mouths shut are going to suffer, and they'll do so with complete presidential and judicial backing once the truth comes out. You might not be involved, but I'm telling you now that it's not in your interest to ally yourself in any way to these people."

A bead of sweat ran down Geoffrey's face. Facing Patrick, he said, "I'm not involved in the Rübner case. Nobody in my station is. We get the intel, but other than that we're out of the loop."

Patrick responded in a stern voice. "But you know what the intel is. That might help us."

Geoffrey looked confused. "If I make the wrong call, I'm screwed."

Will pointed at him. "If you make no call, I guarantee you those innocent people will die."

The station chief kept his eyes on Will's boss. "There is no 'off the record' at our level. If I tell you anything without clearance to do so, you've got to assure me that you have my back."

Patrick pulled out a pen and notepad, wrote for a few seconds, then tore off a sheet and handed it to Geoffrey. "That's my handwriting, my signature, today's date, and confirmation that I've given you authority to speak openly about the Rübner case with impunity."

The station head looked at the note. "You still have that level of power, Patrick?"

"If I don't, then it's my neck on the line, not yours."

Geoffrey breathed deeply. "What's wrong with Rübner?"

Will answered, "I think that Rübner's CIA case officer gave him the name of a low-level SVR officer who also happened to be a CIA asset. One of our own was sold out. That agent is now either dead, or on the brink of death. I'm trying to find him. And I think the case officer's trying to stop me before I uncover the truth."

The station head seemed to be composing himself, though his mind was racing, "Do you know when the SVR officer's identity was supplied to Rubner?"

"I can't be specific." Will recalled the contents of the Gerlache letter. "But it could be approximately one month ago."

"Interesting."

"Why?"

Geoffrey lowered his head and muttered to himself, "Jeez, this is some call." He looked up. "Rübner's intel dried up one month ago."

Will said, "That doesn't surprise me."

Geoffrey frowned.

Will elaborated. "I think Rübner vanished soon after he got the SVR officer's name."

Lenka Yevtushenko.

"Where to?"

"To the organization he's working with."

"It was Mossad all along?"

Will shrugged. "I can't answer that until you speak openly. What was Rübner's intelligence?"

The station head ran a hand over his face. "The identity of Mossad agents operating on U.S. soil. It's been gold dust and has enabled us to round them up and put them in prison."

Will laughed.

"What's so funny?"

Patrick added, "Yeah, I'd like to know the answer to that as well."

Will's expression changed. He felt that things were starting to make sense. "When did you supply confirmation that Rübner was a Mossad officer?"

Geoffrey answered, "Approximately six months ago. He must have been recruited within days of us supplying that information, because that's when we got the first stream of intelligence."

"How did you know he was an Israeli operative?"

"Because seven years ago he'd been posted to Brussels; the slot he took is a known Mossad cover. Plus his name was attached to a joint operation we did with the Israelis four years ago. He was billed as a political liaison officer, but we could smell he was an operative." He sighed. "The U.S. wasn't the only customer for Rübner intel. We shared it with the Brits as well. And they had independent confirmation of Rübner's Mossad credentials."

"He was selling out U.K.-based Israeli agents?"

"Correct. Via MI6, Rübner's intelligence reports were supplied to MI5."

Will shook his head. "What a cock-up."

The two senior CIA officers stared at him, expectant.

Will rubbed his eyes. "You need to call your counterpart in Mossad and tell him that Simon Rübner is a CIA asset."

"No way."

"Yeah, no way." Patrick placed a hand on Will's forearm and gripped it tight. "No fucking way!"

Will ignored the fact that Patrick was pressing his fingers deep into his arm. "Do it. And I think you'll find out something quite surprising."

Geoffrey's eyes were wide. "No. We can't betray a CIA agent!"

Patrick released his grip on Will's arm and thrust a finger against his chest. "And even if we did something as crazy as that, we could be playing right into their hands by telling them that we know this was a Mossad operation."

Will shook his head. "Rübner's no longer a CIA agent. And whatever he was doing for the CIA, I'm certain it wasn't set up by Mossad. Even if they had a requirement to get hold of an SVR officer, they would never have floated Rübner in front of the CIA with the remit to reveal the identities of their U.S. and U.K. agents."

Patrick lowered his finger. "I agree with that."

Geoffrey mopped his brow with a handkerchief. "So do I. In the United States, Rübner's intel has enabled the arrest of fifteen Mossad spies; twice as many are under FBI surveillance. The Brits have got their claws into a similar number." He pocketed his handkerchief. "But even though we might be able to rule out that this was an Israeli operation, we most certainly know for a *fact* that Rübner was working for us. And that fact cannot be disclosed to Mossad."

"It's going to have to be, in order for us to get closer to the truth." Will looked at Patrick. "*Please*. Back me on this."

"I can't!"

"Please. It's the right thing to do."

"God damn you. You can't ask me to do this."

"I already have."

Patrick stared at him. After a long silence, he muttered, "You're taking one *hell* of a risk."

"I know."

Patrick was motionless for twenty seconds. While looking at the ceiling, he said in a loud, authoritative voice, "As the most senior officer in this room, I'm making the decision that Mossad should be made aware that Simon Rübner has been a CIA agent. If that decision is the wrong one, then I fully accept that I and I alone should suffer the consequences." He lowered his head, looked straight at Geoffrey. "I'm instructing you to make the call."

Geoffrey appeared taken aback, and spoke imploringly. "Patrick, this is wrong. You could be—"

"Do it!"

Geoffrey picked up the handset of one of the phones, held his fingers over the keypad, and glanced at Will. "Patrick clearly has a huge amount of faith in your judgment. I hope you respect that."

He pressed numbers, held the phone to his head, waited, spoke fluent Hebrew to whoever was on the end of the line, and was silent for thirty seconds. No doubt the person he needed to speak to in Mossad was being summoned to the phone. He spoke again, his tone hushed, his words quick and urgent. The call lasted ten minutes. By the time the Head of Tel Aviv Station placed the handset down, his face was covered with perspiration.

"Indeed the Rübner case has been an *almighty* cock-up." Geoffrey looked at Will. "Simon Rübner moved to New York six months ago with his wife and teenage daughter, one week after he'd resigned from Mossad."

Patrick exclaimed, "He's no longer Mossad? You're sure?"

Geoffrey nodded. "Since then, the Israelis have been trying to ascertain who's been compromising its U.S. and U.K. agents. Rübner's been at the top of its list of suspects, given the timings of his departure and the first round of arrests, and the fact that the identity of every compromised agent was known to Rübner. Mossad's been trying to track him down so that it can have a very blunt chat with him. A month ago it found out that Rübner had been in the States, but by then it was too late because he'd done his disappearing act. Mossad's got no idea where he is now."

Patrick looked at Will. "You suspected this to be the case?"

Will nodded. "That's why I needed the call to be made." He stared at nothing. "It was a clever setup. Simon Rübner moved to New York immediately after he left Mossad. Somehow, he deliberately made himself visible to the CIA, who then asked Geoffrey's station to do a trace on him. The result suggested he was still a serving officer. CIA thinks for whatever reason that Rübner might be able to be recruited, and that cash is the best carrot. It approaches him using a deniable cover company called Gerlache. Almost immediately, it gets him to pass them secrets, then it declares that in truth it's CIA. He agrees to continue working for them but only on one condition—that he can pretend to Mossad that *he's* recruited a CIA officer. After all, he tells them, that's what he's in America to do. Terms are struck. The CIA gives Rübner chickenfeed U.S. intelligence . . ."

"Congress would need to approve every piece of intelligence supplied to Rübner."

Specifically, that approval would come from the Senate Select Committee on Intelligence—an organization created in 1976 after Congress had investigated CIA operations on U.S. soil and established that some had been illegal. The SSCI comprised fifteen senators who were drawn from the two major political parties and whose remit included oversight of U.S. intelligence activities and ensuring transparency between the intelligence community and Congress.

Will agreed with Patrick. "And in return, Rübner continues giving them gold dust secrets—the identities of the Israeli agents. But he does it drip feed." He looked sharply at Geoffrey. "Correct?"

"Correct. The agents were being sold out one by one, over a five-month time frame."

"And *that's* what's so funny." Will frowned. "And smart, for that matter. You'd have expected the CIA to be getting intelligence from Rübner on ongoing Mossad operations. But Rübner couldn't give them that, because he was out of the loop, though his knowledge of U.S. and U.K. Mossad agents was still very relevant. He used that knowledge as a smoke screen to hide the fact that he simply didn't know stuff that an officer in his position should. Drip-feeding it to them was crucial, because he had to get the CIA to the point where it would break rules to keep him on their books." Will placed the tips of his fingers together. "That moment came around one month ago, at which point he ups the ante and says he knows the CIA has got a huge team of analysts covering Russia, that Mossad is struggling on the Russian target, that he needs to know the identity of an SVR officer who the CIA is certain would betray secrets. Maybe the CIA's reluctant to help at first. Maybe Rübner threatens them that if they don't give him what he wants, he'll clam up. Careers and reputations are now resting on the Rübner intel. Knowing that the SSCI would never approve the sacrifice of a Russian CIA agent, Rübner's case officer and his colleagues secretly give Rübner the name of the SVR officer I'm now looking for."

Patrick shook his head, his expression somber. "And Rübner takes that name and runs, his objective complete. You think Simon Rübner is the man behind everything you're working on?"

"Possibly, though my feeling is that I'm dealing with someone at a much higher level. And I'm wondering if it was *that* person who approached the SVR officer and told him that he had to do a job for him or else he would tell the SVR that he'd been working for the CIA. That man gave the Russian his name, a covert communications drill for them to be in contact, and some very specific instructions." He was now thinking aloud. "Shortly thereafter, the SVR officer does what he's told by stealing an extremely valuable piece of paper and escaping to Poland. But a day or two before then, he decides to find out who he's dealing with. He trawls through SVR databases and stumbles across one report. It's brief, and contains purely logistical detail pertaining to a meeting that happened in 1995. He prints it off, smuggles it out of SVR HQ, and hides it in his home." He nodded. "One of the names on that report is the name of the man who approached him, the man who paid Rübner a lot of cash to leave Mossad and set himself up in New York, the individual who orchestrated everything."

He recalled the two names referenced in the SVR document he'd found in Yevtushenko's house.

Colonel Nikolai Dmitriev.

Kurt Schreiber.

He was now certain that one of them was the man who called himself William.

He sighed. "It's a real pity you don't know the identity of Rübner's CIA case handlers."

Geoffrey shrugged. "Even if I did, sounds like they'd have no idea where Rübner's at right now." He frowned. "There is one guy who'll know their identity."

Will leaned forward, expectant.

"He's one of yours—MI6. Up until recently, he was based in the British embassy in Washington, acting under first-secretary cover though he was fully declared to us, operating as liaison to my side of the fence. Specifically, he was the only Brit who was allowed to handle the Rübner intelligence."

"How do you know his identity?"

"He's always been listed on the intelligence reports' distribution lists, together with the instruction that any inquiries related to U.K. actions resulting from Rübner's intel should be directed to him."

Will's mind raced. Such an individual would have made it his business to ensure that the Rübner intelligence was accurate, and that meant he would certainly have interacted with his CIA handlers. "What's his name?"

Geoffrey drummed his fingers, clearly trying to remember. "Got it. Like the Greek island—Rhodes. Peter Rhodes."

"Rhodes!" Patrick's face flushed red with anger.

Will's heart sank. "You're sure?"

Geoffrey nodded. "Of course. What's wrong?"

Will didn't answer.

Nor did Patrick.

Both were in shock.

Rhodes had never mentioned his involvement in the Rübner case.

And such involvement could only mean one thing.

Peter Rhodes was the traitor who'd supplied the CIA unit with his name and address.

THIRTY-ONE

Dark clouds hung over Frankfurt as Kronos walked along Tönges-gasse carrying a canvas overnight bag. He entered an Internet café, ordered a coffee, and purchased thirty minutes of Web use. Choosing a terminal at the far end of the establishment, he ensured that his screen could not be seen by any of the café's other occupants, then logged on.

Within seconds, he was staring at Holland's AIS air traffic control website. He clicked Online Flight Plan, then filled in the user name and password—information he'd stolen from the KLM pilot he'd followed from the Frankfurt airport to the city's Westin Grand hotel. The man had been sleeping while Kronos had sat on the other side of the room and used the pilot's BlackBerry to load the AIS website, click on the Forgot Password button, read the subsequent AIS e-mail reminding him of his password details, and then delete the mail.

He'd been certain that the pilot would be registered with the site, a portal that was only available to Dutch nationals who were involved in Holland's aviation industry. But if it'd turned out that the pilot wasn't an existing member, Kronos would have used his name, passport number, and aviation ID to register. There'd been no need—the man had been a member since he'd earned his wings five years ago.

Kronos took a swig of his coffee as he was directed to a new page. After entering a date, he stared at the information before him. One entry told him exactly what he needed to know.

After logging out of the site and deleting his Internet browsing history, he exited the café. Forty minutes later, he was standing in a pay phone in Frankfurt Hauptwache train station. He called a number in Holland, gave the man who answered six letters followed by the number he was calling from, then hung up. Five seconds later the pay phone rang.

He answered and spoke to the man for two minutes before concluding, "I may have to fire a lot of rounds, so you'll need to make large custom magazines. But it's crucial the magazine doesn't unbalance the weapon."

He called another Dutch number, repeated the same security routine with six different letters, and when the man called him back he gave him precise instructions, ending with "No bigger than a lighter. And I'll need spares to test their effect."

Replacing the handset, he walked briskly across the concourse and boarded a train headed to Stuttgart. As the train pulled out, a couple and their two young children paused by the empty seats in front of him. The mother said to Kronos, "Everywhere back there's full. Do you mind?"

"Not at all."

"I must warn you though—my kids are on a high because we took them to the zoo today. I'd understand if you'd prefer quieter companions."

Kronos laughed. "I've got twins. I can sleep through anything. Please, take the seats."

He closed his eyes. Soon he'd be back in the Black Forest and home with *his* children. And no doubt *they'd* be on a high when they saw him. After he cuddled his sons, he'd pretend to be stern with them and say that they needed to finish their homework before their bath time. If they were good, his reward would be the two nineteenth-century German wooden soldier toys he'd bought them.

He imagined their faces lighting up as they unwrapped the brown paper packaging and looked at the Prussian guards.

The soldiers' faces were stoic, noble, with integrity. They looked like they had a job to do.

Just as he did.

He thought about some of the most challenging assassinations he'd conducted. None of them had been as complex as the one he was now planning.

But that didn't matter, because he knew exactly what he was doing and was in no doubt that he'd be able to get close enough to his target to smell the man's fear.

THIRTY-TWO

Will walked slowly along the banks of the river Spree, adjacent to several hundred yards of the remains of the Berlin Wall. A fine rain started to descend, and he pulled up the collar of his overcoat and put his hands in his pockets. He wasn't moving toward any destination, just needed time to think—aside from traveling back to Germany, he'd done little else since his conversation with Geoffrey Pepper.

Part of him felt anger. He was certain that Peter Rhodes had given Rübner's CIA case officer Will's identity and home address, had wittingly or unwittingly set in motion a sequence of events that had led to his sister needing to go into hiding, and had betrayed knowledge of Will's intention to break into Yevtushenko's house.

But he also felt confused and sad. Peter was naturally likable, smart, irreverent, yet thoroughly professional. And he was courageous. Despite immense danger to himself, his service as a NOC had required him to play the part of an advisor to a murderous business-man with a nerveless performance. He was a natural actor, and Will now wondered if he used that skill to hide a less pleasant aspect of his personality. He decided that wasn't the case. Peter could be a chameleon when in the field, but when he was surrounded by MI6 officers he was himself.

He leaned against the remains of the Berlin Wall, trying to decide what to do. If he involved Alistair, the Controller would send men to grab Peter, take him back to the United Kingdom, and put him on secret trial. That would almost certainly result in the officer being given life imprisonment. Will could put two bullets in his head. When the truth came out, nobody would question his action. But even though Peter deserved both, neither decision seemed right.

He stayed still for fifteen minutes, allowing rainwater to wash over his face as he stared at the river. Most of the time he rigorously protected his independence and ability to make decisions on his own. But occasionally there were moments when he wished he could walk away and let others go through the anguish of trying to decide the solutions to situations like these. Now was one of those moments.

But he had to make a decision.

He reached for his cell phone, hesitated, then called Roger.

Laith grabbed an empty mug and headed toward the safe-house kitchen. "I've just had a call from Roger. Will's on his way back."

Peter asked, "Did he get access to the Rübner files?"

Laith shrugged. "Didn't say." He called out, "Oh, and Peter. Will wants to meet you in one hour in the lobby of the Steigenberger Hotel. Alone."

Laith called Will. "He's on the move, on foot at the moment but looks like he might be trying to hail a taxi. Adam's mobile. If he does get a cab, we'll stick to him."

• • •

Sixty minutes later, Will was in the departures section of Berlin Brandenburg Airport. The newly constructed international airport was bustling with travelers. Standing in the center of the concourse was Peter Rhodes, oblivious to the presence of Will, Adam, and Laith. He was motionless, staring at the flight departures board.

Will looked at his paramilitary colleagues. They were apart, fifty yards beyond Peter. He nodded at Laith, sighed, and navigated his way through the crowds. "Hello, Peter."

The MI6 officer turned quickly, shock on his face. But then he smiled. "So many destinations to choose from."

"I don't envy you."

Peter returned his gaze to the board. "I've got a passport, a credit card, and have no idea what I'm doing. But I did know that I didn't fancy meeting you at the Steigenberger Hotel."

Will was silent.

Peter muttered, "I suppose the choice of destination will be made for me. Saves me a lot of hassle."

Will moved in front of him. "Why did you do it?"

Peter's eyes flickered mischievously. "Because I'm a bastard."

"No, you're not."

Peter lowered his head, seemed to be considering Will's response. "I got a lot of brownie points for distributing the Rübner intelligence. It got me promoted, an increase in salary." He looked up. "I'm getting married in a few months. My fiancée and I need every penny we can get."

"So you decided that you couldn't let anyone know that Rübner had tricked us and that your career had been accelerated on the basis of a lie?"

"That pretty much sums it all up."

Will shook his head. "Peter, you could have just been honest. You've had a great career. You'd have been promoted anyway."

"Maybe." Peter's smile faded. "Trouble is, one little lie follows another little lie and soon you suddenly realize you've created one big lie and there's no way back. I should have distanced myself from *them*. But they were insistent. We gave Rübner the identity of Yevtushenko and the means to contact him, hoping that Yevtushenko would disappear and no one would be the wiser. We should have done so with SSCI approval, but we knew the Senate would never have given it to us. So my CIA friends made their own decision. I'd love to tell you that they did so without my knowledge, but that would be untrue."

"You thought that if I got to Yevtushenko, he'd tell me that he'd been set up by the CIA team running Rübner, and that I'd quickly then link that person to you?"

Peter did not reply.

Will took a step closer. "Your treachery has put my sister's life at risk."

"What?"

"You gave the CIA team my name and home address. They gave that to the man who's now in possession of the paper. He's threatened to kill Sarah unless I back down."

Peter looked confused. "They weren't supposed to do that! They were just supposed to send you a message to your home, telling you to mind your own business."

"Well, they decided to do much worse. And after you told them I was going to break into Yevtushenko's house, they put a team in place to stop me escaping and to get me shot by the Russian cops."

Peter shook his head. "No, no. That wasn't supposed to happen. I told them in case there was stuff in there that you shouldn't see—to give them the chance to get there first and sanitize the place."

Will said between gritted teeth, "You played right into their hands. Who are they?"

Peter huffed. "I might have been played for a fool, but my mouth's shut on that. You're going to put me in a cell and throw away the key." He looked around, his eyes locking on Adam, then Laith. Nodding, he looked back at Will. "It appears that you might do worse. I've no reason to speak to you."

Will pointed at the flight departures board. "You can get on one of those flights . . ."

Peter frowned.

". . . if you tell me who was running Rübner, the identity of the people you were working with to stop me getting closer to Yevtushenko."

"You'd just let me walk away? I doubt that."

"Where's your fiancée?"

"England." Peter rubbed a hand over his face. "Today she's getting measured for her wedding dress."

"You can never see her again."

Peter lowered his hand. His face was now pale.

"You'll be arrested if you try to set foot in the U.K.; you'll be arrested if anyone spots you in Europe; the States aren't an option; nor are any of the Commonwealth countries." Will raised his voice to be heard over the din coming from the crowds around them. "It won't be a case of just walking away. You'll be on the run, by all accounts with very limited funds. What I'm offering you is a life of looking over your shoulder, of poverty, of living in some hellhole, petrified that at any moment your front door is going to be kicked in. But maybe that's a better option than solitary confinement in a maximum security prison, or"—he glanced toward Laith and Adam—"a more absolute solution."

Peter looked confused. "Why would you do that for me?"

"That question's been plaguing me for the last twenty-four hours." He pictured Luke's head ripping open when he shot him in Gdansk. "Maybe I'm just sick of doing the dirty work."

Peter opened his mouth to speak but said nothing.

"You need to make a decision!"

The crowds were getting thicker, and though travelers brushed against the two MI6 officers, they stayed still.

"Decision, Peter."

Beads of sweat ran down Peter's face, and he screwed his eyes up as if he were in pain.

"Time is running out!"

"Okay!" Peter's breathing was fast. More quietly, he repeated, "Okay."

"Who was running Rübner?"

Peter stared directly at Will, his expression imploring. "Somehow, can you get a message to my fiancée? Tell her I'm truly sorry."

Will nodded.

"Thank you." Peter looked at the flight schedules. "Can't go anywhere West, nowhere first world, nowhere with a U.K. extradition treaty in place." He smiled bitterly. "You're right; it has to be a hellhole." His breathing slowed. "Look after the section. They need you."

"That's not your concern anymore. You keep your mouth shut about everything you know. And if you warn off Rübner's CIA handlers, I'll personally come after you."

Peter nodded. With resignation, he said, "I've no reason to speak to them now. After all, keeping their secret has got me to this place. There's four of them. All are very senior Agency case officers, with a lot of power and autonomy." He held out his hand.

Will hesitated, then shook it. "If ever you see me again, run." He lowered his voice and said with genuine concern, "Look after yourself."

Peter smiled. "I'll try my best." Glancing around, he laughed. "I don't think the arrivals section of the country I'm headed to is going to look anything like this." He looked at Will one last time. "Rübner's CIA handlers have the code name Flintlock."

PART IV

THIRTY-THREE

Kurt Schreiber walked along the corridor toward the door, which was flanked by two armed bodyguards. He entered a vast, sumptuous room containing leather sofas and armchairs, original paintings by Leopold Bode, Hans Dürer, and Matthias Grünewald, a large log-burning fire that had been prepared by one of the twelve-bedroom property's housekeepers, and walls clad in oak panels that had been taken from a nineteenth-century Prussian man-of-war. Extending down one side of the room was a forty-yard balcony where, during the summer months, he would frequently spend time eating or drinking with his numerous shady business associates while admiring southeast Germany's Bavarian Alps and overlooking the valley two thousand yards beneath them. But today, the sliding glass doors were shut to prevent the icy mountain air and snow from entering the warm residence.

On the border with Austria, the isolated mountaintop property was Schreiber's favorite retreat. Because it was extremely difficult to access and was at all times guarded by at least twenty armed men, it was also his most secure.

The old man sat in his usual armchair by the fire, poured a glass of Camus Cognac Cuvée, took a sip of the liquor, and rested his glass on the coffee table, next to a plate of Abendessen bread and a file. The room had an air of serenity, Heinrich Schütz's *Zwölf geistliche Gesänge* played softly in the background.

He tore off a chunk of bread, raised it to his mouth, and paused midair. He imagined over one hundred million men, women, and children eating their last mouthful of food before spewing blood-drenched vomit and dying.

That's what would happen if Slingshot was enacted.

Schreiber chuckled and tossed the bread into his mouth.

He leaned forward and opened the file. Six sheets of paper were inside. He placed them next to each other and stared at the men's profiles and their attached photos.

General Leon Michurin, Russian, deceased. Seven years ago, his alcohol-abused body took its final gulp of vodka.

General Alexander Tatlin, Russian, deceased. The chain-smoker had died last year in agony from lung cancer.

Colonel Nikolai Dmitriev, Russian. The former senior SVR officer had moved to southern France ten years ago to grow wine, while keeping his mouth firmly shut about his previous life in espionage.

General Joe Ballinger, American. The retired four-star general, who'd previously spent all of his adult life on a war footing, now spent most of his days analyzing his vast investment portfolio from his New York mansion.

CIA officer Thomas Scott, American. A man who'd wanted to be head of the CIA, got passed over for promotion, and resigned from the Agency in disgust. Since then, the Yale-educated former operative divided his time between teaching at Harvard, sitting as a trustee on the boards of several charities, and participating in political think tanks.

Admiral Jack Dugan, American. After retirement from the military, Dugan had used his military connections to carve out a lucrative career in the arms industry. His wealth had not only enabled him to buy a three-million-dollar home in Potomac, Maryland, it had also funded his successful U.S. senatorial campaign.

The six men who'd attended the Berlin meeting in 1995.

He put a finger on the photo of one of the four surviving members.

The treacherous bastard who intended to give evidence about Slingshot to The Hague.

He recalled Dugan's comment to him.

We're the kind of men who like to have impenetrable security wherever we go.

Lifting Dugan's profile, he placed his rimless reading glasses on and muttered, "Your security has caused me a lot of trouble."

THIRTY-FOUR

At midmorning, Will, Roger, and his men watched the Jeep stop at the side of the deserted country lane on the outskirts of Berlin. The land around them was featureless, flat, and made more dreary by a persistent rain that was turning to hail. Suzy got out of the car, pulled up her jacket's hood, and approached their stationary vehicles. Despite the weather, all of the men were standing on the side of the road.

Will asked quietly, "What have you got for me?"

She told him about Interpol's request for any information on Kurt Schreiber, the location of an unknown high-value witness in the Netherlands, and the impending hearing in The Hague.

Will lowered his head, deep in thought. He felt weary, had only managed to snatch a few hours' sleep each day since the paper escaped his clutches in Gdansk. "You think Schreiber's the witness?"

"Impossible to know."

"Still nothing on the word *Kronos*?"

"Nothing."

Will thought about Sarah. Every six hours he received SMSs from Betty to update him on her safety. "We need to go after Rübner's wife and daughter. Rübner himself will most likely be invisible. But children need schools; wives like to socialize. Find them, we'll find Rübner. And when we get him, we'll make him talk."

Laith spoke angrily. "We're not in the business of harming women and kids."

"My sentiments exactly." Will ignored the hailstones hitting his face. "There'll be no harm; we'll just put the fear of God into them. We have no other choice."

Mark rubbed his stubbly face. "I'm not comfortable with this."

Nor was Will, though he couldn't show that doubt to his team. "Could you sell out your country's agents and do that simply for money?"

The former SBS commando shook his head. "Fuck, no."

"I doubt any of us could." Will nodded. "Rübner will stick close to Yevtushenko and the paper. That means his family's in Europe, possibly Germany itself." He walked away and stood with his back to the others in the center of the deserted road. He stayed like this for one minute as the others watched him, then turned and looked at Suzy. "Scour Europe, find Rübner's family." He turned to Roger. "I need you to do something for me today. After it's done, rejoin your team and use your men as a hunter-killer unit. Once Rübner's family has been located, get him, make him talk."

"You're not joining us?"

Will shook his head. "Tonight I'm going to visit The Hague."

Mikhail stayed motionless, prone on the ground. He watched the officer and his men move back toward their vehicles. The paramilitary team and American analyst drove away from him; the MI6 operative came right toward his hidden location.

Who should he follow?

He made a decision.

This time he would not let the MI6 officer out of his sight.

THIRTY-FIVE

Alina removed Maria from the new baby carriage Will had bought her, put the child into a high chair supplied by the shabby Minsk café, and placed her daughter's food on the table between them. The place was a third full. Outside it was snowing, and the road adjacent to the eatery was a mix of white snow and muddy slush.

A waitress came to her table and snootily asked, "Are you going to buy anything?" She pointed at a sign. In Belarusian, it read ONLY FOOD PURCHASED IN THESE PREMISES MAY BE CONSUMED HERE.

Alina felt angry, unzipped her purse, and saw that it contained barely enough rubles to buy her a mug of coffee. She ordered a drink, and added, "I doubt this shit hole sells baby food, and if it did I wouldn't poison my child with it."

The waitress stormed off.

Alina unscrewed a jar of homemade turnip and carrot puree, sat down, and began spooning the meal into Maria's mouth. "Daddy's going to come home soon."

Maria swallowed some of the food as bits of it dribbled over her chin. She grinned and made a chortling sound.

"We have to believe that, don't we?" She scrapped the mess off Maria's face, trying to keep her tone light and happy, even though she felt exhausted with worry and over the last few weeks had burst out crying at the most random of moments. "Maybe Daddy could take us out for a picnic. Would you like that?"

The waitress slammed a mug of black coffee on the table and stood expectantly by Alina's side. Alina sighed, withdrew all her money, and placed it next to the mug.

After the waitress was gone, Alina put her cold hands around the mug, letting the warmth soothe her fingers. "The trouble is, Daddy did something very silly and we won't be able to do the picnic until he says sorry to a lot of people."

Maria moved her arm to push away the next spoonful and started speaking unintelligible words.

"Come on, little lady. Just five more spoonfuls." She tried to put the spoon into her mouth again, but Maria repeated the movement, her face became angry, and she banged a fist on the high chair. "I wish the Englishman were here. You'd eat from him, wouldn't you?"

She placed the spoon into the jar and took a sip of the coffee. It was weak and acrid. Probably the waitress had deliberately made it that way. She didn't care and took another sip, glad of its heat. She'd completed the last of the day's university lectures. Today she'd asked her students to challenge Aleksandr Solzhenitsyn's view that poetry was born from the torment of the soul with her own view that it was rather an encounter with truth.

Alina sighed. She still had other chores to do, including going to the jewelers to see if anyone had bought the necklaces she'd left with the shopkeeper a week ago. The deal was, she'd only get cash for them if they were sold, and even then it would only be 60 percent of the retail price. A mental image entered her head of Will Cochrane trimming pork cutlets in her tiny home while she prepared their promised meal of *kotleta pokrestyansky*. She wondered why.

Perhaps because increasingly she realized that her future was either being alone with Maria, or one day being with a man who could help her with broken baby carriages, could make Maria smile and eat her food, and wanted what she wanted: a break from loneliness.

As she stared out of the window at passersby struggling through the driving snowfall, she knew in her heart that whatever happened, Lenka was never coming back.

THIRTY-SIX

Peter Rhodes watched the fire begin to die and shivered as the icy Asian wind came through cracks in the mountain shack. Momentarily, he considered putting the remainder of the logs onto the embers before they were extinguished. He decided there was no point.

His oil lamp flickered, casting shadows over a roll-mat bed, a bench and chair, a horse saddle and luggage, and a portable single-ring gas cooker that was positioned on the soil and straw floor. He got off his bed, opened the front door, and was nearly knocked off his feet by a gust of snow-carrying wind. After steadying himself, he looked around in case there were men on horseback coming for him. The endless mountain range would look beautiful on a postcard, but in person it looked desolate, terrifying, and barren of life.

He'd arrived here last night. Tomorrow his intention was to head farther east along the mountains. He estimated he could be clear of the range in ten days, at which point he would move south toward warmer climes.

As arduous as the journey was, he believed it was essential that he travel this way, that he had to avoid easier modes of transport and routes in case he was challenged while using them. It was vital that he remain alone and go places where no one in their right mind would wish to try to track him.

But being here had made him realize that this type of life was not for him.

He kept his head low as he forced his body through the high-altitude wind to reach the shack's adjacent stable. Opening the door, he moved to the pony he'd bought yesterday from a tribesman in a lowland village. Though the pony's head was bowed and her demeanor miserable, he knew that she was considerably more used to the mountain elements than he was. She gave a welcoming snort as he brushed his hand against her neck. "Good girl. Good girl."

He put a rope onto the pony and guided her out of the stable. Removing the leash, he clapped his hands and shouted, "Go on, now!"

She neighed, remained still.

Peter slapped her on her hind leg and repeated, "Go!"

The pony looked at him, then began walking down the mountain slope, carefully picking a trail between boulders. He didn't know if she'd survive the thirty-mile route to the village, or if she'd even remember the way there, but he did know that she'd die if he left her here.

He returned to the shack, forced the door shut, and rubbed snow off his stubbly and grimy face. Sitting down at the table, he removed his cell phone from his luggage and saw that it had one bar of signal. He sighed with relief—one bar was all he needed. He rubbed his numb hands to aid circulation and get his fingers working. They throbbed with pain as he slowly typed an SMS.

Cochrane found nothing of interest at Lenka's house. We've all been recalled to London. Operation deemed a failure and has been terminated. Cochrane deployed on other matters. Our secret is safe.

He pressed Send and smiled as he saw his phone flash red, meaning its battery was about to die. He had no way of charging it, but that didn't matter, as this was the last time he'd use it. The message successfully transmitted, he tossed the phone to one side.

It was the only way he could think of to try to make amends for his treachery. One of the Flintlock operatives would receive the message and advise his colleagues that Will was no longer hunting Yevtushenko. They'd believe that their sacrifice of Yevtushenko, to get more of Rübner's stream of intelligence, remained a secret.

But Will knew all about Flintlock and their role in trying to kill him. Peter wondered what he was going to do to them.

He thought about his fiancée, Helen. He didn't think she'd be unduly worried that she'd not heard from him. Helen knew he was an MI6 officer and was used to the fact that he was frequently away on missions and sometimes not contactable. No doubt she was busying herself with further preparations for their marriage. He wondered what wedding dress she'd choose, and pictured the beautiful woman walking up the church aisle toward him. They hadn't yet drawn up a list of people they wanted to invite to their wedding—most of them would be family and friends, a handful would be colleagues. Perhaps Alistair would be in the audience, maybe Will too.

The image faded.

As he looked around, he couldn't imagine being farther away from that day.

His actions had ruined his career, his honor, and his love of a decent woman.

There was nothing else for him now.

He removed his hemp jacket. All he now had on was a cotton shirt, trousers, and boots. After stamping out the remains of the fire and turning off the oil lamp, he exited the shack and scrambled down two hundred yards of the mountain slope. That was far enough; within minutes he would not have the strength or will to climb back up. He sat down on snow-covered ground, facing the full blast of the subzero-temperature wind. Closing his eyes, he wondered how long it would take and whether he'd feel pain. He'd read that Napoleonic troops who'd suffered severe hypothermia while retreating through Russia had felt a moment of warmth just before it happened. He hoped that was true.

Within fifteen minutes, he was violently shivering, confused, and light-headed.

His body started to freeze.

Within thirty minutes, he was dead.

THIRTY-SEVEN

Kronos walked into the smoky bar and sat at an empty plastic table. In the style of an American diner, the place had rows of tables and benches alongside windows that faced the edge of Rotterdam's vast seaport. Aside from the female attendant who was standing behind the bar washing glasses with a bored expression on her face, the only other people in the establishment were a group of five males; they were all wearing blue overalls, looked like tough sailors or dockworkers, and were seated at the far end of the diner, laughing, singing, and drinking Flemish gin. Outside, heavy rain descended from the night sky, noticeable through the multitude of neon lights that lit up the security gates leading to the dock and the ships and freight containers beyond them. Kronos looked at the attendant. Clearly she had no intention of waiting tables. He ordered a coffee from the bar and took the drink back to his table.

Staring at the security gates, he wondered if tonight the ship's captain would suffer bad luck and be searched as he tried to exit the port. He wasn't unduly worried about this, for he had backup options, though it would be a waste of valuable time.

Cars and trucks were entering and exiting the port. There were too many of them, and they were indistinguishable in the night-time conditions, so it was fruitless trying to ascertain which vehicle belonged to the captain. He removed his attention from the security gates and gripped his coffee mug. Mathias and Wendell would now be tucked up in bed, and his wife would be reading to them. This was the second night that he'd missed their evening routine, and he hated that. His wife had been understanding when he'd told her that he'd been asked at very short notice to stand in for a sick colleague who'd had to pull out of a teachers' conference in Amsterdam. And thank goodness his school was shut for the winter vacation, meaning he hadn't had to make excuses for a sudden absence from work. It would have galled him to let his pupils down at a time when they were gearing up for their summer history exams. Even so, if felt wrong to be away from his family. He supposed he'd better get used to it.

A large, rough hand slapped Kronos's shoulder. "Ernst, how the devil are you?"

The German assassin turned and looked at Jack Vogels. In German, he said, "You're late."

The Dutch captain replied in the same language. "Of course I am." He grinned and pointed at the docks. "I can sail my ship across the world and arrive within a minute of when I'm supposed to arrive. It's only when we have to deal with the idiots on land that it all goes to rat shit." He sat at the table, placing a small canvas bag on the seat next to him. "You want a proper drink?"

"No."

"Come on. Won't hurt." He clapped his hands while glancing at the bar attendant.

She rolled her eyes and sauntered over. In Dutch she muttered, "Spent too long on water and lost the use of your legs?"

Jack's grin widened as he put his muscular arm around her waist and pulled her close. "Don't be like that, Marijne. You *know* that all of me is in perfect working order." He winked at Kronos. "Get us two large *brandewijns*."

After she left, he switched back into German. "You staying the night? Want me to get you some girls?"

"No thanks. I'm heading back to Germany this evening."

Jack's smile vanished as he patted the canvas bag. "Not with this."

"Of course not. It'll be left somewhere safe in Holland."

"Good." His jovial expression returned. "For a moment, I thought you'd lost your touch."

"You have the spares I asked for?"

"Yes. Plus the tools you need to adjust their impact." He smoothed a hand over the canvas bag. "Be very gentle with these babies. They're nasty."

"I hope they are." Kronos could see that the group of men was looking at them. They'd stopped singing and had grown quiet, looked hostile. "Best we lower our voices. I think the men behind you object to the German language."

Jack was dismissive. "I know them. Dockers on the wrong end of a postwork knees-up. Rum bunch, but they know they'll lose their jobs if they touch me." He nodded toward the canvas bag. "Important job?"

"All my jobs are important. If you want to know more about this one, please proceed and ask. You'll die after I finish speaking."

For a moment, Jack looked unsettled. "I . . . I don't want to know anything about it."

"And that's how it must always be."

Marijne brought the liquor to their table, leaned toward Jack, and whispered, "I finish at midnight."

The captain patted her behind. "I'll see you then, my beauty."

As she returned to the bar, Jack downed the drink, wiped his mouth with the back of his hand, and said, "It's a shame you're heading home. I'm sailing tomorrow afternoon, so I'm going to make the most of tonight. You could have joined me."

"Indeed."

Jack stood. Quietly, he added, "Don't hang around here." He shook Kronos's hand and walked out of the bar.

Kronos placed cash next to his untouched drink. Reaching across the table, he gripped the canvas bag and stood to leave. The men were still staring at him.

One of them called out in slurred words, "German pig?"

From behind the bar, Marijne slammed a glass down and looked angrily at the man. "Stop it, Theo!"

The dockworker ignored her, got to his feet, and took two steps toward Kronos. "German pig."

The other men stood. All of them were big.

Kronos was motionless, keeping his eyes fixed on the men.

"This isn't a place for pigs!"

The assassin stared at them. He could see that they'd reached a stage in their drinking where joviality had passed, that they now needed a fight. No doubt it would make their evening if they could all stand around his prone body, kicking his head until it became a bloody pulp. He glanced at Marijne and saw uncertainty and fear on her face. Clearly, she knew what these men were capable of.

He reached for his glass of *brandewijn*, clicked his heels together, raised the glass, and began singing "Wilhelmus van Nassouwe," the national anthem of the Netherlands.

The men frowned, though the hostility remained on their faces.

Kronos sang louder, his voice note perfect, no hint of an accent as he recited the peaceful Dutch song.

One of the men smiled, then laughed. The others looked puzzled before joining their colleague in laughter. They grabbed their glasses, lifted them high, and accompanied Kronos in the song. The café was filled with the sound of the anthem.

When the song finished, Kronos downed his drink, placed a fifty-euro note on the bar, and said commandingly in Dutch, "Gentlemen. That was excellent. You all deserve a drink." He clicked his heels again, turned, and walked out to the sounds of more laughter and singing.

As the assassin stepped into the driving rain, he smiled. A moment ago, he could have snapped all five men's necks in under thirty seconds. But they were just simple-minded thugs whose dumb brains had become addled with booze. They probably had families to go home to. Just like him.

But he wasn't going back to Germany and his family.

He wouldn't be leaving the Netherlands until he'd conducted an assassination that would be his masterpiece.

THIRTY-EIGHT

It was early evening as Will strode through a fine rain and winter chill in De Wallen, the red-light district in Amsterdam's old city. Divided down the center by a canal, the district's labyrinth of streets and side alleys was filled with tourists and locals gazing at the multitude of cabins containing scantily clad prostitutes; entering and exiting the neon-lit sex shops, theaters, and peep shows; drinking in bars; or smoking marijuana in the coffee shops.

He barely registered his surroundings, instead wondering if tonight he was about to make a big mistake.

Moving east away from the district, he crossed canals, past street vendors selling warm *stroopwafels, pannekoeken, poffertjes,* and *Vlaamse frites,* and dodged buses and trams and mopeds being driven at speed. One mile later, he was walking along Zeeburgerpad, a strip of land straddled by canals. Pleasure cruisers chugged along the waterways, with more tourists inside them being given waterborne tours of the city. Other boats were moored along the riverbanks, beside cobbled streets containing residential houses and a windmill that had been transformed into a microbrewery.

He stopped by a houseboat, clambered on board, and knocked on a window. A young woman appeared on the other side of the window, then briefly disappeared before opening the door. Will entered.

The interior was open plan and contained a double bed, a kitchenette, and a living room. Two suitcases were adjacent to the bed, brightly colored clothes spewing out of them. The air was thick with the smell of cannabis, cigarette smoke, and petunia oil.

The attractive Dutch brunette moved to the kitchen, wearing only a short negligee. "You want wine?"

"No thanks." He sat on a red sofa in the shape of a heart. "I've got to work later."

"So have I, and I've got to look the part." Katharyne van Broekhuizen poured herself a glass of rioja and sat opposite a vanity mirror. While applying makeup, she asked, "How've you been, Anthony?"

"Busy."

"You look tired. Are you eating okay?"

"When I have time." He watched her pat foundation over crow's-feet that hadn't been there last time he'd seen her. "What about you? Do you get to do . . . other stuff?"

"A bit of sleep. That's about it."

"When will it end?"

She used a blusher brush on her cheeks. "Two months, three months, six months . . . who knows?"

"You won't be able to keep this up much longer."

"I've got no choice." She sprayed perfume onto her throat, took a sip of wine, and turned to face him. "Next time you're in town, will you buy me dinner?"

Will answered quietly, "I'll treat you to a nice meal when you get out of this game."

Katharyne seemed to consider this, then smiled. "Okay, deal." She stood, removed her negligee, and started rummaging through one of the suitcases. Finding a pair of matching panties and bra, she put them on, together with a pair of velvet heels, and frowned as she stared at a rail containing dozens of dresses.

"You look stunning in black."

"Do I?"

Will nodded.

She picked a black silk cocktail dress and slipped into it. "Can you zip me up?"

Will walked to her, placed his hands on her hips, gently spun her around, and fastened the dress.

She turned to him, wafted the hem of her outfit, and asked, "What do you think?"

He smiled. "I think you're gorgeous."

She briefly kissed him on the lips, pretended to look angry, and wagged her finger. "But you never make a pass at me. That's very naughty of you."

"I can't, because you're . . ."

"Working?"

He hesitated. "Yes."

She took another sip of her wine and lit a cigarette. "You said that last time you came here."

"And yet you're *still* here."

She laughed, then her voice trailed as her expression grew sad. "I feel secure, I guess . . . comfortable in front of you."

"I feel the same way about you."

"Why is that?"

Will stayed silent.

She shrugged. "I got what you asked for."

"Is your back covered?"

"Yes. I made sure of that." She opened a clutch handbag and withdrew a leather parcel and a folded piece of paper. After handing Will the parcel, she stared at the paper, was about to give it to Will, then pressed it against her lips so that her lipstick mark was on it. "For you." She held it at arm's length toward him.

Will took it, looked at the mark of her lips, and smiled.

His smile faded as he gazed at the woman who called herself Katharyne but was really Johanna Kaps, a Dutch AIVD intelligence officer who'd infiltrated a brutal Turkish gang of human traffickers who were using underage eastern European girls as prostitutes in Holland. Eight months ago, she'd posed as an ex-prostitute turned madam who knew how to bribe local officials and thereby navigate local licensing laws for prostitutes. She'd lived deep cover ever since, risking execution every day if she were discovered. It was an incredible act of bravery, and one that was taking its toll on her.

"I *will* buy you that meal when you finish this job."

"MI6 money?"

Will said softly, "My money." He stroked the back of her hair. "MI6 doesn't know about your work for me."

Johanna's eyes watered. "Good, because I never wanted to work for them, only you."

Will kissed her on the cheek.

Her hand clutched his. "It's a shame things weren't different."

"Even if they were, it wouldn't . . ."

"I know."

They both knew. Johanna was too similar to him. They lived in a world where they had little in common with the people around them, and though they did extraordinary things, they recognized that their isolation from normality made them flawed individuals. Though it was highly unlikely they'd ever find them, they needed partners who could help them connect with ordinary people. If Johanna and Will had a relationship, neither would be able to help the other with that monumental task.

Two hours later, Will was standing under a streetlamp in the Wassenaar diplomatic district of The Hague. Wearing a stylish raincoat and expensive suit, he hoped he looked like an ambassador's bodyguard to any observers. But aside from the occasional passing car, the area was deserted.

He withdrew from his overcoat the small leather parcel, unwrapped it, and took out a Benelli handgun, which he secreted in his pocket. Next to him was one of the district's large residences. He jogged alongside the property's ten-foot-high exterior wall. The side street he was on was empty and mostly dark, with rainwater running down the gutter. He stopped, jumped, grabbed the top of the wall, scanned the property, dropped back to the street, and ran to the north and east sides of the house where he repeated the drill. Silently, he cursed. There was CCTV on every side of the house. The cameras had been carefully positioned—no blind spots.

He'd also seen one bodyguard outside the front of the house and an older man inside, in the living room. He was silent, trying to establish what to do. The cameras would be working, so he'd be spotted the moment he entered the grounds. He pulled out a scarf and covered his face, deciding his only option was to go over the wall and do it fast.

He heard a noise, moved flush against the wall, and looked toward the end of the side street. A slow-moving limousine. It stopped by the electronic gates; a chauffeur got out and spoke into the intercom. The gates began to open as the chauffeur returned to his vehicle. Will moved along the wall, withdrew his handgun, and sprinted as the car moved forward.

He ducked low and moved at walking pace behind the car as it crawled up the driveway toward the front of the big house. He waited as doors opened, feet crunched over gravel, and a doorbell rang.

Voices.

Will instantly stood and raised his weapon.

The bodyguard and chauffeur were standing close to the vehicle. Will shouted, "Don't!" as they reached toward their concealed handguns. They froze, and he took two steps toward the guards while keeping his gun trained on them. "Hands outstretched!"

As the men slowly extended their arms, Will glanced beyond

them at the two older men who were standing close to the front door. Both had expressions of shock. "You two. Facedown on the ground."

The men's mouths were wide open, but they made no noise as they did what they were told.

Will walked cautiously toward the guards. "You both understand English?"

The men nodded.

"I'm not here to kill anyone, remove anyone, or steal anything. If you do exactly as I say, you'll have protected your boss far better than if you try to resist me." He trained his gun on one of the men. "You—remove your weapon with your thumb and forefinger and throw it away."

The man hesitated, then moved his hand toward his gun.

"If you put three fingers on there, I'll pull the trigger!"

The guard gripped the weapon's handle as instructed, eased it out of its holster, and tossed it onto the driveway. His expression was angry.

"Hands out!" Will pointed his pistol at the other guard. "Now you."

The man did the same, while saying in heavily accented English, "You're making a big mistake." He threw his gun away.

"Turn around."

The men turned so that their backs were to Will, side by side.

Will took a step toward them. "On your knees."

One of the men did as he was told.

"On your fucking knees!" He took another step, and as he did so, the man who was standing spun around and punched a fist through the air toward Will's rib cage. Will stepped back, and the fist missed. He slammed the butt of his handgun into the guard's throat, then shoulder blade, and as the man slumped down onto his knees, the back of his head. The guard crashed facedown onto the ground, unconscious. He pointed his gun at the other guard. "You want to try something similar?"

"No. No." The fear in his voice was evident.

Will removed two short lengths of cord from his overcoat and tossed one of them in front of the guard. "Tie him up—facedown, throat to wrists to ankles. Do a very good job, or I'll put bullets in the back of your knees."

The guard set to work, sweat pouring down his face. He clearly knew what he was doing, as the cord was expertly knotted, and within twenty seconds the unconscious guard was tied up.

"Your turn."

"Please, don't . . ."

"Get in position!"

The guard lay facedown and arched his back so that his hands and feet were touching.

Will jabbed his foot against the man's genitals, warning him that he'd kick him there if he did anything reckless, yanked his head back, and used the second cord to truss him up. Will knew from experience that the position was agonizing—attempts to escape would cause the binds to choke the throat.

"You'll be cut free in about fifteen minutes." He ignored the guard's moans as he picked up the guns and stuffed them in his coat.

Will strode up to the two older men. "Which one of you is Eric van Acker?"

Nobody answered.

"Van Acker!"

One of the men answered, "It's me."

"Stand."

The chief prosecutor of the International Criminal Court got to his feet.

The portly man looked to be in his late fifties, and was wearing a suit and no tie. When he spoke, fear was evident in his voice, though also a degree of defiance. "My wife and children are due back from the ballet shortly. If you're going to do anything, make sure it happens before they arrive."

"I'll keep that in mind." Will walked up to him and put the nozzle of his pistol against the prosecutor's temple. "Why are you interested in Kurt Schreiber? What's his link to an impending testimony at the ICC?"

Van Acker's expression changed. "You're not the first British man to ask me those questions. Two days ago, I received a call from someone who introduced himself as Alistair McCulloch, a senior member of the Secret Intelligence Service. Do you work for him? Has he sent you here to bully me?"

"He doesn't know I'm here. But it's in your interest that you answer my questions."

"It's in *your* interest that you leave right now, before the police arrive and shoot you."

"If they arrive, you'll be dead." Will pulled back the hammer on his gun. "I'm not here to negotiate with you. It's simple: You speak, you live. If not, I pull the trigger. And then I'll pay the president of the court a visit and ask him the same question."

"There's no need." The man who was lying alongside the chief prosecutor began getting to his feet.

"Down!" Will swung his weapon at the elderly man.

But the man waved a hand through the air and stood. "I am Albert Metz."

The president of the International Criminal Court.

The tall, thin, well-dressed man pointed a finger at Will. "You threaten my chief prosecutor and me, and you attempt to pervert the course of justice. To your face, and in the presence of witnesses, I can tell you that both are very grave crimes."

Will smiled. "I've broken bigger laws than this." His smile vanished. "You're standing in the way of a Western intelligence operation that I believe may be linked to your high-value witness's presence in The Hague. That pisses me off. To *your* face, I'm telling you that if your obstructive behavior results in my operation failing, then I'll make sure that every state signatory to the Rome Statute knows that the ICC is run by a group of pencil-pushing bureaucrats who've no interest in justice. Your careers and reputations will be fucked."

The court's president took a step toward him. "I doubt you have that authority, young man."

Will kept his gun planted against van Acker's head. "Oh, I most certainly do." He stared at the prosecutor. "Why are you interested in Kurt Schreiber?"

"None of your damn business."

"Wrong!"

Between gritted teeth, van Acker said, "I'm not at liberty to divulge that information."

Will walked up to him, pointed his gun at his head, and muttered, "Are you telling me that this has been a waste of time? That I should just get this over with?"

"I think you should." A Russian man's voice.

From behind Will.

Will froze.

Footsteps crunching over gravel.

The lawyers were now looking over Will's shoulder toward the sounds.

Mikhail came alongside Will and put his handgun against the MI6 operative's head. The big SVR officer smiled, though he looked menacing and focused. "And after you've pulled your trigger, maybe I should pull mine, because following you here was my last *fucking* lead."

Will remained motionless, his gun still flush against the president's head. "Lower your weapon, Mikhail."

The Russian frowned. "How do you know my name?"

"Mikhail Salkov, I know all about you. We got you on your overseas postings."

"Very clever," he huffed. "Still, makes no difference given where you're now standing."

"You think so?"

"I know so. Make these men talk, or you're of no further use to me."

Will smiled. "You followed me after my team and your men attacked the convoy. You watched me leave the Auguststrasse apartment and tailed me to the airport. And this morning, you observed me briefing my team on the outskirts of Berlin."

"An informed guess. You never spotted me."

"If that's true, then I wouldn't have needed to cover my back tonight. Would I?"

Mikhail frowned again.

Will called out, "Have you got him?"

Roger jumped down from the wall, his pistol aimed at the center of Mikhail's head. "Yeah, he ain't going anywhere."

Will nodded at Mikhail. "I've been looking out for you since we attacked the convoy. I spotted you three times. And I suspected you might break cover this evening."

"You want me to drop him?" Roger was very still, his finger poised to pull back the trigger.

"Gentlemen!" Albert Metz placed a frail hand over Will's forearm. "Who are you?"

Speaking quickly, Will answered, "I'm an MI6 officer. The Russian is an SVR operative. We've been working the same operation, from different angles. Is Schreiber the high-value witness?"

"I can't answer that!"

"What's this about?" Mikhail nudged his muzzle against Will's temple.

At first, Will didn't respond, his mind racing. He was in no doubt that Mikhail would pull the trigger if it helped him get closer to the missing paper. But if the Russian shot him now, he'd achieve nothing. Moreover, Will had witnessed him risk his life to protect others in Gdansk. The man wasn't a cold-blooded murderer. He made a decision and told Mikhail about the ICC's interest in Schreiber and the witness being protected in the Netherlands. "Do you know who the witness is?"

"No. But he won't be Kurt Schreiber."

"Why not?"

Mikhail was silent.

"What's on the missing paper?"

More silence.

"You told the Pole you saved in Gdansk that we must all try to get the paper, that it's lethal. Even though my superiors think I'm crazy for doing so, I've been trying to help you."

"This is a *Russian* operation to retrieve *Russian* property."

"This *was* a Russian operation that failed."

Anger flashed across Mikhail's face. "You've no idea who you're dealing with."

"From where you're standing, do you really think you have the upper hand?"

"I'm not talking about me, you idiot! Schreiber sent out a dummy convoy. That means he's now loose."

Roger called out, "We're running out of time!"

But Will remained still, keeping his eyes on Mikhail. "Kurt Schreiber orchestrated the theft of the paper?"

Mikhail nodded. "He's behind all of this. He's gone to the Black Forest, but I don't know where."

"The paper?"

Mikhail hesitated.

"What's on it?"

Mikhail muttered, "You're right—this has been a fucking failure. And there's nothing more we can do."

"The paper!"

Mikhail stared at him. "It's one-half of a military grid reference. Schreiber's theft of it must mean he's got the other half of the paper. It pinpoints a DLB in the forest. He'll have used it to activate an assassin."

A realization struck Will. "An assassin, code name Kronos."

"How do you know that?"

"Am I right?"

Mikhail sighed. "I don't know his identity, but that most certainly is his code name. He's Russia's most deadly assassin and it appears that he's been activated to . . ."

"Stop a high-value witness from opening his mouth in The Hague." Will looked directly at Metz. "Correct?"

"Lower your weapons." Metz spoke with a commanding voice. "If we're to talk, we can't do so like this."

Will hesitated, then pointed his gun at the ground.

But the SVR officer kept his weapon in place against Will's head.

"Gun down. Let's hear what they have to say."

"Not while your American friend's still aiming at me."

Will shouted to Roger. "Lower your weapon. For now."

Roger did so.

Van Acker's eyes were wide, and sweat and rainwater were dripping down his face.

Mikhail smiled, then flicked his gun's safety catch on and took a step back. "Let's hope you both have something of value to say to us."

The president of the court slowly exhaled. "The witness came to us six months ago and said that he needed to testify under oath to his knowledge of a secret pact between Russia and the United States. He gave us the names of everyone who was directly involved in the pact."

"What pact?"

Metz shrugged. "We don't know. Despite our numerous attempts to get him to tell us more, the witness has consistently refused to say anything further until he is under oath in a televised courtroom. He's said that he's only got one chance to tell the world about this pact, that in doing so he's probably signed his own death warrant, but that he has to keep his mouth shut before then because he trusts no one, including"—he nodded toward van Acker—" 'pencil-pushing bureaucrats' like us."

The prosecutor added, "We agreed to his terms, set up a date for a hearing, and have kept him under high security ever since."

"Where?"

"None of your damn business. He made it very clear to us that powerful men would do everything they could to stop him from speaking at the hearing." Van Acker's expression was now hostile. "The most powerful and ruthless of them all is Kurt Schreiber. We alerted Interpol so that they could search for him. But our witness never mentioned this assassin, Kronos. How much of a threat is he?"

Mikhail answered, "He's the most dangerous threat there can be."

Will turned to the lawyers. "What kind of security have you got around the witness?"

"World class!" Van Acker pointed at Will. "We're very used to protecting high-value targets."

Will frowned. "What are the points of vulnerability?"

Van Acker was about to reply, but Metz interjected. "Long-range sniper rifles, surface-to-surface missiles, airborne assaults, covert infiltration, overt land attacks using dozens of men—our specialists have considered every possible means of attack against people in our care. The witness is in a very safe place."

Will muttered, "There must be a way Kronos can get to him. You need to let me speak to the witness's security team."

Metz glanced at van Acker, looked confused, then returned his attention to the intelligence officers. "If what you say is true, this places us in a very grave situation. We've given the witness our word that we will protect him."

"Let me make an independent security assessment." Will spoke imploringly. "Bring me in on this."

Metz bowed his head.

"Please!"

The court's president eventually looked up. "Providing you can supply me with letters of authority from your premiers, I'm willing to bring *both* of you in to help stop Kronos."

Will and Mikhail answered simultaneously, "No!"

"It's both, or nothing. Neutralizing the Kronos threat must be coordinated. I can't have one of you running around doing things that could compromise the witness's security."

Will felt overwhelming uncertainty, and he knew Mikhail would be feeling the same way. "Men with our respective backgrounds don't like working together."

"Then grow up and overcome your differences."

Will glanced at Mikhail; the man was staring back at him. He turned back to the lawyers. "Our hands can't be tied."

"I'm afraid they'll have to be. You can't interfere with the protection of our witness."

Will shook his head. "I don't intend to. Kronos's objective is to kill your witness. Our objective will be to kill the assassin before he does so."

THIRTY-NINE

Sixty minutes later, Will and Mikhail were standing facing each other in Alexanderkazerne. Roger had left them a few minutes earlier after Will had instructed him to rejoin his colleagues in their hunt for Rübner's family.

A fine rain continued to wash over Will's face as he stared at the SVR officer. "Every instinct I have says we shouldn't be working together."

"I feel the same way."

Will pointed at him. "If you do anything that could compromise my work, I won't hesitate to deal with you."

Mikhail patted the part of his overcoat concealing his gun. "Likewise, if you fuck up, I'll *deal* with you."

The two officers were silent for thirty seconds.

Then Will asked, "If Kronos was employed by the Russians, why did you try to stop his activation?"

Mikhail shrugged. "We don't know why Kronos was deployed. But I knew that we didn't want the activation code to get into Schreiber's hands without authority from the Russian premier, because there was a note to that effect on the paper. That was my only lead. I had Schreiber's location, so I tried to intercept the paper before it got to him."

"How did you know where he was?"

"We've been tracking him for years. He moves around a lot, but so do we."

"Where was he?"

"In a farmstead in Lower Saxony. I have assets there in case any of his men return, though I'm doubtful they'll do so." He thought about the men who'd died there and of his four-man team of professionals who been slaughtered by the convoy. He wished he could write to their families, explain how brave they'd been, but that would be impossible.

"Does he have a base of operations in the Black Forest?"

"No. But he does have five other bases in Germany. As soon as the paper was stolen, I got assets to watch all six properties. When he was spotted in Saxony, I diverted resources to that location."

"He must now be at one of his other locations."

Mikhail felt frustrated. "He's not, and that means he has another base that I don't know about."

Will moved right in front of him. "Is Lenka Yevtushenko alive?"

"That information's none of your concern."

"He did something stupid. But he doesn't need to be hurt because of what he did."

Mikhail wondered why the British man cared. "He breached the SVR's trust in him. He'll be taken back to Moscow and disciplined."

"So he's alive?"

Mikhail stared at him for ten seconds. "Yes. He's in bad shape, but I've ordered my men to patch him up. They wanted to kill him, because they lost friends and brothers at the farmstead." He sighed and looked away from Will. "He *was* very foolish and he'll have to account for what he did. But that will be done in the proper way."

"Let him go. He's got a woman and child to look after."

Mikhail laughed. "He should have thought of that before he stole the paper."

"I believe he did think of that. Schreiber blackmailed him and no doubt would have also given him a financial incentive to do the job. Yevtushenko was faced with the choice of imprisonment in Russia, or stealing the paper and setting up life with Alina and Maria."

"Blackmailed him?"

Will hesitated, didn't know if he should give Mikhail information that could either persuade the SVR spycatcher to his way of thinking or make matters worse for the defector. "Yevtushenko had been working for the CIA. Schreiber found out and used that information to get him to steal the paper."

Mikhail's expression darkened. "In that case, I'll take him back to Russia not only to face the charge of stealing secret intelligence. He'll also stand trial for being a CIA agent."

Disappointment hit Will. Telling Mikhail the truth had been the wrong decision. "To what end?"

Mikhail moved closer to him, his eyes cold. "Against my better judgment, I'll get the authority from my premier to work with you and the Dutch. But Yevtushenko is a Russian matter. We will severely punish him and nothing you can say or do will stop that from happening."

FORTY

Alfie Mayne unloaded the last of the cases from the car's trunk and carried it toward the vacation home. Located on the Isle of Wight's stunning and rugged southwest coast, and overlooked by a down named after the poet Alfred, Lord Tennyson, whose magnificent mansion turned hotel was toward the top of the hills, Alfie had chosen the place because it was not only remote but had been the place his cash-strapped mum and dad had brought him on vacation from their south London council apartment when he was a kid. He remembered building sand castles on the beach, tossing crab lines into rock pools, eating cheese sandwiches that had been contaminated with sand, breathing the farmland smell around the trailer site they'd always stayed at, and drinking tea out of a flask with his mother while his father had tried to repair their worn-out old Morris Minor car on the side of a country road.

The ex-SAS sergeant wished his parents had been able to afford to stay in the large house he was headed toward; not for his benefit—he loved the excitement of sharing a trailer with his parents and waking up to the smell of wild mushrooms and bacon being cooked in the kitchenette—but for his parents, who'd never stayed anywhere more plush than places that called themselves bed and breakfasts but were really cheap rooming houses.

He placed the case down in the hallway and turned to face the cliffs and the beach beyond them. At age seven he'd run along the same beach, laughing so much his stomach hurt, as his father chased him wearing rolled-up trousers and a knotted handkerchief on his head while pretending to be the ghost of an ancient pirate.

It was a lifetime ago.

He walked into the four-bedroom home, past one room containing Betty, who was singing to herself while she unpacked clothes, and another where James was on the phone to his law firm, coaching someone on the wording of a legal report. In the living room, Sarah was sitting on the sofa, her knees bunched under her chin as she stared out of the window. She'd barely spoken during the drive down from Scotland, aside from telling Alfie that she wished he wouldn't smoke in the car and could he please wind up his window.

He sat next to her. "Going to drive into Ventnor this afternoon. There's a lovely fishmongers on the harbor there. Everything they sell is fresh off the boat, same-day catch. Fancy joining me for a spin?"

"No thanks."

"Got something better to do?"

Sarah did not answer.

Alfie followed her gaze toward the window. Outside, waves were crashing over a beach that looked considerably less appealing during winter than it did during his summer vacations here. "My old man died out there when I was fourteen. Heart attack. Think all that rationing stodge he grew up on finally took its toll on the poor bugger. My mother never got over it, but she hung on in there until the day I joined up with the army. Then she let go. Funny, isn't it? When they're around, we think everything will be like that forever. Then they're gone and you're left with silly regrets."

"Regrets?"

Alfie shrugged. "Few hours before he collapsed, me dad asked me to go fishing with him, just like we used to do when I was younger. I said no 'cos I was more interested in watching the pretty girls on the beach."

Sarah looked at him. "Is this another of your little pep talks?"

Alfie kept his attention on the beach. "Dunno, petal. I guess being here just reminds me of stuff." He glanced at her. "Given what he does for a living, it's only a matter of time before your brother's killed." He returned his attention to the beach and quietly said to himself, "Yeah, should've gone fishing with you, Dad."

FORTY-ONE

Tibor entered the windowless room in CIA headquarters, sat down, and spoke to his Flintlock colleagues. "It's over. Cochrane's given up trying to find Yevtushenko."

Damien slapped a hand onto the table. "Excellent!"

"Did the source say anything else?" Lawrence made no effort to hide his feelings of relief and joy.

"Only that Cochrane's been deployed on another mission; that his attempts to locate Yevtushenko were deemed a failure." Tibor smiled. "But reading between the lines, I think Cochrane's superiors have given him an almighty kicking."

Marcus chuckled. "Oh well. We didn't get him killed, but hopefully we've screwed his career."

The operatives were silent for a while. All of them felt as if a weight had been lifted off them.

Lawrence was the first to break the silence. "Gentlemen, we must be more careful in the future."

"No shit." Tibor straightened his silk tie. "Yesterday I bumped into the Director of Intelligence. He said that Patrick had been sniffing around the Rübner case. He'd sent him packing, but he asked me if there was anything about the Rübner case that he should know about. I told the DI that Rübner had probably lost his nerve and had done a runner, that there was nothing more to it than that. I added that Patrick was an interfering busybody who was probably trying to dig up old cases because he had fuck-all else to do right now. The DI seemed happy with that. Plus, when I got him talking about our North Korean destabilization operation, it was clear that Rübner was completely off his mind."

The mention of Patrick unsettled Tibor's colleagues. Though Flintlock was privy to most of the CIA's secrets, they'd never been told what Patrick's place was within the organization. Tibor was right to describe him in the way he'd done, because that was exactly how Patrick would be perceived by others in the Agency. But it was only recently that they'd learned from Peter Rhodes that Patrick was the cohead of the task force that Cochrane and Rhodes belonged to.

Lawrence asked, "You're sure the director got him to back off?"

"Yep. Thank God the DI's a rulebook guy. Patrick doesn't have clearance to the Rübner case and his intelligence, so the DI tells him to mind his own business."

Lawrence was reassured by this. Because they were the DI's chosen ones, they all knew that he would crucify them if he ever found out the truth about Yevtushenko and Rübner.

Tibor stated, "Our priorities now are our other operations: North Korea, getting the bomb into the delegation's building in Dar es Salaam, turning the Asian cells against each other, feeding more disinformation to the Saudis, and further positioning France against Germany."

Damien frowned. "It would've been good to know who got Yevtushenko out of Russia and why."

Tibor disagreed. "It will be for some low-level, chickenshit reason. Fuck Yevtushenko, fuck Rübner, fuck Cochrane. We've got big boys' stuff to get on with."

FORTY-TWO

Kronos cupped his hand under the center of the rifle, lifted the weapon a few inches, and nodded approvingly. "Perfect balance."

Leaning against a bench, a bespectacled gunsmith used a cloth to rub oil from his hands. Around him, the basement workshop contained more benches on all sides containing anvils, tools, manuals, electronic scales, spot lamps, magnifying glasses, a blowtorch, and gun parts. The middle-aged Dutchman pointed at the gun. "I modified parts from a German DSR-50 sniper rifle. It was a devil of a job. The customized magazine added an extra three pounds to the rear end."

Kronos removed the clip and looked at the large bullets. "How many?"

"Twenty per clip, as you requested."

Kronos slammed the magazine back into the weapon and raised it to eye level. "You're sure it won't need zeroing on site?"

"Absolutely. Once you've zeroed it at a range, the weapon can be transported and will be accurate when you need it to be. The case will help protect it, but even so you'd need to give the gun a fairly hard knock to put it out of alignment with the scope. I've spent hours ensuring the assembled parts are perfectly married."

"Excellent. Faults?"

The gunsmith frowned. "What do you mean?"

"What faults does it have?"

"I can assure you that there are none."

Kronos smiled. "Every make of weapon has its own idiosyncrasies. Including"—he glanced at the man—"those made by specialists."

The Dutchman sighed. "I've tried to minimize recoil as much as I could, but you'll need a firm grip, because it still kicks like a mule. Plus, I can't suppress the sound any further without reducing projectile velocity. You'll be heard from over fifty yards away. Other than that"—he ran a finger along the full length of the barrel—"this is the best rifle I've ever made."

"Good. Neither fault presents me with a problem." Kronos rested the weapon on a table and expertly stripped it down, placing the parts into foam inlets within a rectangular case. He withdrew an envelope containing fifty thousand euros and thrust it toward the gunsmith.

The man hesitated. "I'll need another ten thousand. It took me much longer than I thought to complete the work."

Kronos slowly shook his head. "There was no deal to pay you by the hour."

"Nevertheless, I think I deserve . . ."

Kronos slammed the case shut and turned to face the gunsmith, towering over the man. "Consider this: I know your name, your place of work, your home address, your favorite restaurant, the pub where you like to have an occasional glass of Grolsch, your children's school, and a hundred other facts about you and your family. A further ten thousand euros will severely antagonize me. Do you think the extra hours you worked are worth that situation?"

The Dutchman's face paled and his eyes widened. "I . . ." He grabbed the envelope. "Please . . . please, forget what I said."

Kronos smiled, slid the case inside a canvas bag, and held out his hand. "Good. And now you can forget what *I* said."

With a sweaty palm, the gunsmith shook his hand. "Thank you."

"And thank you for making such an excellent weapon." Kronos's expression turned cold and he gripped the gunsmith's hand very tightly, causing him to wince. "A man in your delicate line of work needs his fingers. Never give me cause to come back here"—he nodded toward the blowtorch and anvils—"to remove them."

FORTY-THREE

Will called Patrick and updated him on recent developments. "The court's lawyers are adamant that their security around the witness is watertight. They're keeping him in a military installation in the south of the Netherlands. In two days' time, he's going to be flown north to another secure facility in The Hague. At all times, he's going to have a ring of steel around him."

"You threatened the court's president and chief prosecutor?"

"I had to. Time's running out."

"It'll run out for you if you keep behaving this way."

Will ignored the comment. "Once I persuaded them that their witness is under severe threat, they began to cooperate with me to some extent. But they won't give me access to the witness unless they have written authorization from your president and my prime minister, confirming my credentials and that I am acting with their backing."

"Shit. That's a big ask, since I'm not entirely sure you have their backing."

"Can you arrange the authorization?"

The CIA officer was silent for a few seconds before answering, "I can try."

"Also, they've asked the Russian premier to gain identical authorities for SVR officer Mikhail Salkov." He told him about the court president's terms.

When he spoke, Patrick's tone was deliberate and incredulous. "Cooperating with the Russians? This could turn into a cluster fuck."

"I know!" Will felt frustration. "Right now, the last thing I need is to work alongside an SVR spycatcher."

"Sounds like you've got no choice. In any case, from what you've said, there's no way the assassin can get to the target."

Will agreed. The Dutch security teams that protected witnesses appearing at The Hague were second to none. "I can't work it out. No matter how good the assassin is, by all accounts he'll fail. But I need to make my own security assessment by analyzing the setup around the witness."

Patrick sighed. "Okay." He paused. "How's your loved one?"

Mention of Sarah made Will feel even more anxious. "She's had to move locations. There was a severe threat at the previous site. I'm getting regular updates."

"Are you holding up?"

Will wondered how the cohead would react if he told him the truth—that he was mentally and physically exhausted, was living in constant fear that he'd receive a call from Betty saying that they'd failed, didn't know if it was the right decision to ally with the Russian spycatcher, had no idea how he was going to look Alina in the eye and tell her that he'd broken his promise to bring Lenka home, and so far had failed to get closer to Schreiber and Kronos.

"I'm fine."

FORTY-FOUR

Kronos hauled the long canvas bag onto his shoulder, slammed the car trunk shut, and strode over the grass-covered undulating ground that ran along the Dutch coastline. The land around him was deserted, and light was fading, though easily visible ahead of him was the North Sea—dark and agitated, waves pounding against the sandy shore.

Wind and rain buffeted Kronos as he moved along the coast, walking for thirty minutes until he reached an area where the ground was flatter. He placed the canvas bag on the ground, unzipped it, and removed a hammer, a nail, and a wooden board, over which was stapled a paper target. Walking to one end of the flatland, he hammered the target onto a tree, retreated twenty-five paces, and used the heel of his boot to scuff a line in the ground. Returning to the bag, he withdrew a shopping bag containing food scraps and the rectangular case containing the components of the hand-built rifle. He assembled the weapon, attached the sound suppressor, and inserted a magazine containing twenty NATO rounds. Moving to the place where he'd scuffed the ground, he lowered the gun's bipod, lay down, and glanced around to ensure there were no passersby. Taking aim at the center of the target, he fired three bullets. All struck a half-inch-square area of the target, a fraction to the right of the bull's-eye. He made adjustments to the scope and fired three more times. Each bullet hit the center of the target.

Satisfied the weapon was zeroed, he got to his feet and scattered the contents of the shopping bag onto the ground. Holding the rifle with one hand and grabbing the canvas sack with the other, he walked out of the flat area and began jogging over rougher ground. It took him seven minutes to reach an elevated position, one mile away from the flat area. He lowered himself to prone position, looked through the rifle's sight, and located the piles of food scraps. Nothing was there yet, but he knew it wouldn't take long—in winter, there was little to eat out here.

He waited, motionless, his finger on the trigger.

Just as he'd done in Budapest, Helsinki, Prague, Tehran, Ankara, Casablanca, Nicosia, Lagos, Phnom Penh, Kuching, and in a desert during the First Gulf War when the dying Soviet Union couldn't be seen to support its Iraqi ally but secretly had vested interests to ensure the United States didn't push into Baghdad. Then, he'd had a U.S. general in his sites, waiting to pull the trigger if his tank battalion moved a few feet nearer to the Iraqi city. But under orders to withdraw, the general turned around and in doing so unwittingly saved his life.

Movement.

A seagull flew into the flat area and walked toward the food. Then another. Then five more. The birds stopped by the scraps, looked around, and lowered their heads to feed. Kronos moved the sight's crosshairs so that they were over the center of the body of one of the birds.

He fired seven rounds in three seconds. All of the birds exploded.

FORTY-FIVE

Mark Oates stared down the empty street on the outskirts of Germany's eastern city of Leipzig and wondered what it would be like to live in one of the five-bedroom detached houses that lined the tastefully landscaped, tree-lined street or drive one of the Porsches or Mercedes that littered the driveways. When she was alive, his wife would have loved the opportunity to raise their two daughters in houses with this much space; instead she'd had to do the job in a two-bedroom row house close to the SBS base. Lowering the car window to let in some of the icy early-morning air, he glanced at Laith and said, "When my first daughter was born, the Royal Marines very *kindly* gave me four weeks' leave so that I could bond with her and *cherish* every moment of her first days in the world. Fuckin' hell—selection into the SBS was a walk in the park compared to what I had to do. No sleep, constant fear and paranoia, shit and piss everywhere, more kit in the house than a squadron would take to war, a wife who was in a state of either ecstasy or deepest depression, sterilizing everything, feeding, clearing up vomit, burping the baby, praying for her to sleep, and, when not doing any of all that, shuffling around the house while heavily hallucinating. The marines offered me the same amount of leave when my second was born. Instead, I volunteered for deployment behind enemy lines in Iraq."

Roger's voice came over his earpiece. "I've got twins. You should have seen me in my place during the first few weeks of them being born."

Laith was flicking through the book on pregnancy that Will had bought Suzy. "My ex was in labor for ten hours. I don't think she could've been in more pain if someone put red hot pokers in her eyes for that length of time." He snapped the book shut. "Tell you what: all that resistance to torture stuff they teach us—reckon we'd be better off talking to women who've given birth, find out how they do it."

Suzy's voice came over the air. "Guys, I can hear all this crap."

Mark smiled. "Sorry, love."

Laith added, "Yeah, sorry."

"Damn!" Roger sounded irritated. "None of us thought about a twin situation for the sweepstakes."

"I did." Suzy was speaking from her hotel room. "If it's twins, I scoop all the cash."

"I think you'll need it if that's the case." Mark kept his eyes on the road, and his smile vanished. "Let's hope today's third time lucky."

During the last forty-eight hours, they'd pursued leads in Bremen and Cologne, both of which had proven fruitless. Suzy had been working nonstop to find Rübner's wife and daughter. Using the approximate dates she suspected Rübner left America and moved to Europe, she'd ascertained from Germany's BfV that the Rübner family had legally entered Germany, though they couldn't be sure if the family was still in the country. She'd gained access to and analyzed a vast amount of data, including school enrollment records, new car owner registrations, car rentals, gym and library memberships, cell phone purchases, and rented and purchased property agreements.

Mark said, "Getting locals coming out to play on the street. It's rise-and-shine time."

Roger instantly responded. "Same in our location." Roger and Adam were stationary in a van in an adjacent road.

"Still a bit early for a school run."

"Give it another hour."

"Still not comfortable doing this."

"Ain't that the truth."

Will and Mikhail strode through southern Holland's Eindhoven Airport. Three seconds after powering up his cell phone, Will saw that he had four messages: one welcoming him to use of a Dutch roaming phone service, another from Betty saying that they were now by the coast and that Sarah was cooking them sea bass for dinner and seemed to be coming out of her shell, a third from Patrick asking him to call, and the last from Roger saying that his team were about to do a take down on a woman and daughter who they were 80 percent sure were Rübner's family.

He called Patrick. "Yeah?"

"The written authorizations have been faxed to The Hague. Alistair and I had to pull some almighty strings and favors to get it done. Our premiers are very twitchy about the Russian angle."

"So am I." He glanced at Mikhail, felt uneasy being alongside the Russian. "Moscow's faxed its authority."

"I was kinda hoping they wouldn't."

"What are we supposed to do now?"

"Wait at the airport."

"Wait?"

"Yep. They'll find you and take you to the base where the witness is being held."

Will snapped the phone shut and looked around. He repeated to himself, "Wait."

. . .

Roger spoke. "Woman and teenage female exit the house. Woman's holding car keys. SUV's lights flash. They're thirty yards from vehicle. No one else around. Intercept now, now, now!"

Mark gunned his vehicle and drove it at high speed down the street, steered it right onto a smaller road, then right again onto the residential street containing the targets. Laith opened his passenger door, yanked on the seat belt to lock it in place, and gripped it as he stood half out of the speeding car. Ahead of them were the woman and teenager. Beyond the couple Roger and Adam's black van was reversing fast toward them. Laith braced himself and shouted to Mark, "Stop!"

Mark slammed on the brakes, and as the vehicle slowed Laith jumped onto the road and raced toward the targets. Simultaneously, Adam jumped out of the back of the van, grabbed the woman, and dragged her fast into the vehicle. The teenager was about to scream, but Laith approached her from behind, placed his big hand over her mouth, muttered, "Best not to," and forced her ahead, pushing her next to her mother. Laith shut the van's rear doors, then jogged back down the road as Roger drove off in the van.

Mark overtook them, driving along several streets before coming to a halt and jumping out. He began walking toward the mother and daughter's home. Under his jacket, he had a handgun, two spare magazines, and a military knife.

As Roger drove the van through the suburbs of the city, Adam sat cross-legged in the rear and stared at the mother and daughter. They were hugging each other, sobbing, looking terrified. The Scotsman asked in German, "You speak English, French, or Russian?"

The mother nodded. "English."

The former SAS operative smiled. "Good. My German's pretty rusty and I don't speak Hebrew. Mind you, quite a few Englishmen tell me they can't understand me when I speak English."

"What do you want?"

Adam clasped his hands together. Like his colleagues, he had weapons concealed on him, though he wasn't going to withdraw them unless it was absolutely necessary to do so. "We're not going to kill you or rape you. And providing you cooperate with us, we're going to release you as soon as we can." He held out his hand. "One or both of you will have a cell phone containing Simon's number."

The mother responded angrily, "I left my phone at home."

Adam was unflustered. "Did you now?" He moved his hand toward the girl. "Let's hope you didn't."

Tears were running down the teenager's face, and she was shaking. "I don't have any money. Not here." She glanced imploringly at her mother. "Have you got money for them?"

"I don't want your money!" Adam kept his arm outstretched. "Just your phone."

With a trembling hand, the girl reached into her school blazer pocket and withdrew a pink cell. She quickly passed it to him, then grabbed her mother with both arms and pulled her close.

The mother spat, "If you do anything to her, I'll kill you!"

"That's fair enough." Adam flicked open the phone, scrolled through its address book, and found a number under the name *Papa*. He pointed the screen at the girl. "Simon Rübner? Your father?"

The mother interjected, "What do you want with him?"

"Just a word. We need to find his boss."

"He works alone."

"No, he doesn't. He works for a guy called Kurt Schreiber. You know him?"

The mother looked venomous, said nothing.

"Aye, I think you do. He pays for yer fancy lifestyle. Bet you've got a lot of vested interests in Schreiber keeping yer old man on his payroll."

"Go to hell!"

"One day I will. When did you last see your husband?"

The mother looked hesitant, then opened her mouth to speak.

But Adam spoke first. "If you lie to me, it'll go bad for all of you."

Fresh tears emerged onto the mother's face. "He's not at home. He's been away for a few weeks. Work."

Adam returned his attention to the daughter, moving the cell phone screen to within inches of her face. "Rübner. Yes, or no?"

"Yes . . . yes. What . . ." The girl started crying loudly. "What . . . what are you going to do to Papa?"

"That depends on him. Do you SMS him?"

The daughter nodded.

"Good. Hebrew or German?"

"German. Papa insists on it, so I improve my language skills."

Adam looked at the phone, scrolled through a couple of messages she'd sent to her father, and saw that she was telling the truth. "How do you refer to your mother when talking to him?"

The girl looked confused.

Adam barked over the sound of the van's engine, "What do you call her? Mummy? Mum? Mother?"

"Mumie."

Adam leaned forward. "You sure? 'Cos if you're trying to warn off your papa by speaking to him in the wrong way, then"—he gestured around him—"this'll be your home for a long time."

The daughter whimpered, "Muma."

"That's better." He tossed the phone onto the daughter's lap. "Write him a message. But don't send it until I've read it. Message will read: *Emergency. Muma ill. Heading home now. Phone running out of battery.*"

The girl steadied herself as the van took a corner, then began typing the message. She held the phone out.

Adam took it and read out the message.

Roger, a fluent German speaker, called out, "That'll do."

Adam pressed Send, pulled the phone apart, and removed its battery. Discarding the pieces, he said, "Now, you ladies need to sit tight until Papa gets home."

. . .

A pretty woman, holding a clipboard and wearing a matching blue suit with the words EINDHOVEN AIRPORT STAFF on the jacket, approached Will and Mikhail at the airport café. With a smile on her face, she asked in English, "Mr. Cope and Mr. Klyuev?"

Mikhail answered, "Yes."

"I've been told to collect you. May I see your passports?"

They presented them to her.

Her smile broadened. "Please bring your bags and come with me."

She led them past restaurants and throngs of commuters, through a door marked AIRPORT STAFF ONLY, down corridors, out a door, along the edge of a taxiing runway, and into an aircraft hanger. There were no planes in the building. Instead it contained eight men all wearing jeans, boots, bomber jackets, and baseball caps, and beyond them two SUVs.

The woman's smile vanished as she turned to Will and Mikhail. "I'm Superintendent Engert, police." She pointed at one of the men. "My second in command is Kapitein Derksen, Unit Interventie Mariniers. We're from DSI."

The Dienst Speciale Interventies, or Special Intervention Service, was an elite law enforcement unit formed in 2006 to protect Dutch society from the threats of terrorism. Experts in dealing with complex situations such as hostage taking and aircraft hijacking, the unit comprised superbly trained police snipers and Special Forces personnel from the UIM, a force comparable to DEVGRU and U.K. SBS.

"We'll take you to the base where the witness is being held." Engert turned to Derksen. "Do it exactly as I ordered it to be done." She returned her attention to the two intelligence officers. "You're on Dutch territory, are answerable to Dutch laws, and right now are under Dutch command. My men are going to place hoods over you and they won't come off until you're inside the base. Don't bother trying to use time to calculate the approximate distance between here and there, because they're going to take a messy route to confuse you. If you try anything silly, they have my authority to knock you unconscious." All trace of the welcoming expression was gone; instead she stared at them with an icy and professional air of command. "In short, don't try to fuck with us."

Laith had been lying in the same position for six hours, hidden in a cluster of trees within a small stretch of parkland, using binoculars to watch the street containing Rübner's family home. Though he couldn't see him, he knew that Mark was 165 yards away, scrutinizing every inch of the quiet residential street from a different angle.

The big operative kept his breathing slow and tried to ignore the biting winter air that was penetrating his jacket, jeans, and boots. During his service in the Airborne Rangers, Delta Force, and SOG, he'd learned that the cold became your enemy at unexpected times. When deployed to the Arctic, Antarctic, or mountain ranges, operatives were typically equipped with clothing that acted as a total barrier to the extreme weather in those locations; problems usually only occurred if an operative made a mistake or became injured. But it was in situations like this that he'd seen operatives struggle and sometimes go down with hypothermia. If nothing happened in the next hour, he'd suggest to Mark that they swap positions, just so both men could briefly move their aching bodies.

He thought about Will Cochrane. This was his third mission with the MI6 officer. At first, he hadn't taken to the man. Cochrane had appeared cold, aloof, reckless, and insubordinate, and at times he seemed to have a death wish. Perhaps some of those observations were still partly accurate. But over time, he'd seen glimpses of another man altogether—a man who had moments of utter compassion that counterbalanced his ruthlessness; an individual who displayed unwavering loyalty to those who helped him; a man who put on a metaphorical suit of armor not only to shield him from the horrors he had to deal with, but also to imprison the demons inside him. Not for the first time, he wondered how he'd cope with Will's level of responsibility. Not well, he decided.

His body tensed as he saw a sedan drive slowly down the road. One man was in the driver's seat. He spoke into his throat mic. "You getting this?"

"Yep." In a quiet, controlled voice, Mark read out the number plate so that Suzy could note it in her hotel room. "He's cautious. Traveling approx fifteen MPH."

"Heard." Suzy asked, "How far is the vehicle from the house?"

"About eighty yards."

"Not enough time for me to ID the vehicle owner."

Laith edged a few inches nearer to the road and slightly adjusted position. He started flexing his toes to aid circulation.

"Slowing down again. Approx ten MPH." Mark paused. "Now he's stopped, fifty yards from house . . . just waiting, engine still on. Driver's middle-aged, Caucasian, blond hair, close-cropped beard."

Laith withdrew his handgun and flicked off the safety catch. If the man drove fast out of the street, they'd have to let him go. He might not be Rübner, in which case if they forced the car to stop by shooting its engine block and tires, the wrecked car would be an almighty warning sign to the Israeli if he did subsequently turn up. Equally, if the driver was Rübner, he could bolt just to see who was flushed out by the action. They had to make him feel safe to approach the house on foot. But when that happened, there'd be no hesitation: Laith and Mark would explode into action, grab him, haul him back into his car, and drive fast away from the city.

Holding his gun in one hand and his binoculars with his other, he stared at the driver. The man was motionless, looking straight down the street in the direction of Rübner's home. He stayed like this for ten minutes, just waiting.

Laith pressed the tips of his boots into the hard ground, readying himself to get to his feet and sprint.

"Driver opens his door . . ." Mark's voice was now tense. "But he still ain't moving."

Laith muttered, "Come on," between gritted teeth. He inhaled deeply, then held his breath as he saw the driver put one foot onto the pavement, then the other. The man got out of the sedan, quietly shut the door, glanced around, and began walking down the deserted street.

"Athletic build, roll-neck jumper, windcheater trousers, canvas boots. Looks like he can do a runner."

"Yeah." Laith moved his binoculars to keep the driver in his sights. The man was walking slowly and had one hand positioned over his stomach. "He might be carrying a weapon close to belt buckle."

"Okay." Mark was breathing fast. "I'm moving nearer to you. You've got point."

The driver stopped, withdrew a cell phone, and held it to his ear. Two seconds later he replaced the cell into his pocket. In all probability, he'd just tried to call his daughter or wife. He continued walking, was now thirty yards from Rübner's house.

Mark whispered. "I'm in position, fifteen yards to your east."

Laith secreted his binoculars. The driver was easily visible to the naked eye and was walking on the other side of the road, across his line of sight. He reached the bottom of the driveway leading to Rübner's property and looked around.

Laith and Mark would break cover when he was halfway up the drive.

The driver turned so that he had his back to the intelligence officers.

Laith raised his upper body onto his elbows and brought his knees under his chest.

The man took two steps along the drive.

And another.

Laith gripped his pistol tight.

The driver took a fourth step.

Any moment now.

Engine noise.

Loud.

The driver stopped, half turned.

Laith froze.

A rush of movement from the west side of the street.

Men. Four of them. All carrying handguns.

A car raced past them and screeched to a halt near the driveway.

The target ducked low, spun, pulled out a gun.

One man shouted, "Rübner," a fraction of a second before he and the others opened fire.

The force of the volley caused Rübner to flip backward, release his gun, and fall awkwardly onto the driveway with bullets in his head and chest.

Two of the men rushed to the body and quickly examined it. One of them nodded, and called out in Hebrew, "It's done. Go, go!"

The men piled into the car, and it sped away.

Laith shook his head with disbelief. A Mossad hit team had finally caught up with Simon Rübner and expertly punished him for betraying their agents. But in doing so, they had unwittingly killed the last lead to Kurt Schreiber and Kronos.

FORTY-SIX

Kronos lit tobacco in his old briar pipe, opened a metal container, and delicately removed one of the cigarette-lighter-sized devices supplied to him by the Dutch merchant captain in Rotterdam. He examined all sides of the device, unscrewed the bottom cap, and eased out a section containing a circuit board and timer. After making adjustments to the timer, he quickly slotted it back into the device and jogged across the large, empty warehouse. In the center of the building were drums crammed with scrap metal. He placed the device into the center of a drum and ran back to the other side of the warehouse. Checking his watch, he waited.

Ten seconds later, there was an explosion.

The device had torn apart the barrel.

He examined the debris, deciding that the explosion had caused too much damage. Retrieving another spare device, he unscrewed the top cap and removed the PE4 plastic explosive. Tearing it in half, he placed one piece of the explosive back into the device, sealed it, set the timer, and placed it into another barrel.

This time the explosion didn't penetrate the barrel.

Kronos looked inside. The bomb had done exactly the right level of damage; he would adjust the quantity of PE4 in the two devices he'd shortly be using so that they would do the same amount of destruction.

It was time to go. He had one last task.

FORTY-SEVEN

The hood was removed, and Will blinked fast and for a moment felt disoriented. He'd been blindfolded for at least four hours, maybe much longer. Beside him, Mikhail rubbed fingers against his eyes, cursed, and looked around. They were in a brightly illuminated room that was furnished with a functional metal table and chairs and nothing else. Kapitein Derksen was sitting on a chair, one leg resting over the other, smoking a cigarette while keeping his gaze fixed on the intelligence officers. Two of his men were standing close by, their expressions hostile and suspicious.

In English, Derksen said, "Long journey." He took a drag on his cigarette and blew out a stream of smoke. "Bet you feel like shit."

"I've done worse." Will's eyes ached as they gradually adjusted to the light. "We're here?"

"We're here." The black-haired Special Forces commander stood and stubbed out his cigarette. He was of average height but had a physique that some might conclude derived from bodybuilding, though Will suspected it came from the rope-climbing and other skills required of hostage rescuers—skills that produced strength and stamina well beyond those of an Olympian gymnast. "You want water, tea, coffee? We can't offer you anything better than that because we don't keep liquor on the base."

Mikhail answered, "Black coffee."

Will smiled and put on his most gentlemanly voice. "I'd like a cup of tea, please, but could you make sure it's made with leaves, that the pot is prewarmed before the boiling water's added, the tea is infused for three minutes, and it's served without milk or sugar?"

Derksen looked at him with a stern expression, though he had a twinkle in his eye. "This isn't fucking Claridge's Hotel. A tea bag, warm water, and that'll be it. Good enough?"

Will pretended to look disappointed. "Never mind." His expression changed. "Forget the tea, let's get to work. I'll need to have a complete tour of the base, its perimeter, and any land beyond it that overlooks the base, need to study maps of the area, look at the airstrip where the aircraft will take off with the witness, a complete breakdown of the flight plan, and will also need every detail you have about the secure facility in The Hague. Oh, and of course I'll need to speak to the witness."

The twinkle in Derksen's eyes vanished. "The boss—she's a clever lady and keeps us on our toes. Her office has a safe containing ten thousand euros. Every week, we play a game of guards versus intruders. We take turns so that we know what it's like to be on both sides. The guards never know when or how the intruders will strike. In one of our barracks there's a life-size dummy of a man. If an intruder can reach him, or knock his head off from a distance, or blow up the building he's in, then that man gets Superintendent Engert's jackpot. Trust me—we could all do with that cash. But so far, no one's succeeded." Derksen sat on the edge of the desk. "The base covers one square mile. It was designed from scratch to protect men who entire countries wish dead. At any one time, we have a minimum of three hundred specialists on duty here, and twice as many can be on duty within one minute of an alert. If your assassin had managed to grow wings and had superpowers that made him invisible, he might be able to penetrate the perimeter of the base. But he'd never be able to reach his target." The Special Forces officer slapped his hand on the table. "Regardless, I'll give you want you want, with the exceptions that the maps won't show this base's location in Holland and you're not going to meet the witness."

"You have to let me see him . . ."

"I don't *have to* do anything you ask of me! There are extremely strict rules about who can access people under our protection. We never deviate from those rules because we know how to keep people alive."

Will felt exasperated. "Anything the witness can tell us about the assassin must be of value to us."

Derksen shook his head. "No. It would be a hindrance. The witness's potential knowledge about Kronos's past assassinations will naturally skew our thinking toward believing he'll do something similar to those previous hits. It's safer if we have a blank canvas and believe that he's capable of anything."

Will was about to respond but stopped. What Derksen was saying made sense. "Who is the witness?"

"Nice try, but I know you're not permitted to know that information until we move him from here." The Dutchman's expression softened. "No doubt, I'd be a complete amateur trying to do the things you do in the field. At the same time, I suspect you've never spent every waking second of months on end trying to establish how someone"—he waved his hand around—"could break into one of the world's highest-security facilities."

Will nodded. He'd never spent months on end in one place, let alone somewhere like this. He lowered his head, deep in thought. More to himself, he asked, "What the hell is Kronos going to try to do?"

"When protecting a high-value target, the greatest point of vulnerability is if he's being transferred from one place to another."

Will looked up. "You think he'll attack him during the trip north?"

Derksen shrugged. "Maybe, if he's got access to a jet fighter or a sophisticated long-range heat-seeking military surface-to-air missile system." He smiled. "But on the basis that he hasn't got those things, I believe that we're safe. Most of the flight will be at twenty thousand feet. It will take off and land in our secure facilities. We can't be reached."

Will glanced at Mikhail, then the Dutch commander. "The only remaining possibility is that the assassination attempt will be made at the hearing itself."

Derksen nodded slowly. "Yes."

"Are you worried about that?"

"No. It is impossible to kill a man there. Every inch of land, air space, and subterranean space around the courts is protected."

Frustration coursed through Will. Though he would analyze all the security around the witness, he could tell that Kapitein Derksen was a no-nonsense professional who knew exactly what he was talking about. Part of him wished that weren't the case. Kronos would attack a crack in Derksen's security and that's where they'd get him. But Will was convinced that there were no cracks. His phone bleeped; he had a message from Mark.

> *No chance for chit-chat with Rübner. Israelis got to him first,*
> *right under our noses. We've released mother and daughter.*
> *Rübner's dead.*

Will kicked one of the metal chairs and spat, "What the fuck is happening?"

FORTY-EIGHT

Kronos was motionless as he stared at the complex through night-vision binoculars. He'd been observing the place for two hours, watching vehicles move back and forth, men and women at work, establishing patterns of behavior. Dressed in blue overalls and boots, he looked like many of the people he could see, though he hadn't really needed to adopt the disguise. He'd easily infiltrate the low-security base and reach his goal without being seen.

But he couldn't take any chances.

He'd wait in his hidden location for at least another two hours, while observing everything beyond the high-wire fence that separated him and the complex. Then he'd complete his final task.

Five hours later, Kronos stripped out of his clothes and tossed them onto the bed. The big German stretched his muscular and scarred frame, and sighed as he heard the headboard in the adjacent hotel room begin to bang against his wall, just as it had done an hour earlier.

He supposed he couldn't complain—the seedy Amsterdam hotel was a favorite venue for prostitutes and their customers. That's why he'd chosen it; the hotel employees turned a blind eye to everything.

He started running a bath and opened the case containing the stripped-down sniper rifle. After his bath, he'd spend two hours checking the weapon and making preparations. Then he'd leave the hotel and hit the road. There was still a lot of work to do before sunrise.

He felt calm and in control of matters, and knew that this was because he'd spent nearly two decades planning the potential assassination of one of the men who'd attended the disused barracks in Berlin. Every possibility had been considered—an assault in the States, Russia, Europe, elsewhere; urban, rural, mobile, or static. He'd cultivated assets who could get him things at short notice and thereby allow him to enter and exit countries with nothing compromising on his person. He walked to the window and stared at the city. The Hague was less than two hours away.

Kronos smiled.

He'd considered and planned for *every* possibility, including killing a man in a maximum-security courtroom.

FORTY-NINE

Will called Roger. "They're flying the package north tomorrow at fifteen hundred hours. I've conducted an independent security assessment. There's *no way* into the base, *no way* the hostile can get to him."

Roger was silent for five seconds. "There's always a way."

"I know, but we cannot identify what it could be. Trust me—I've never seen a more secure facility that's run by experts as good as these people. There's no bullshit with these guys; they're as desperate as I am to find out how their security could be breached."

"What do you want us to do?"

"I need you and the rest of the men here. Tell Suzy to head back to Langley to speak to Patrick about Rhodes and the F-word boys in the Agency. Patrick and Suzy mustn't do anything yet, though. I want to deal with those bastards in person."

"Damn right. But just make sure I'm there with you when it happens. Are the Dutch happy for us to join you?"

Will glanced along the barracks. Mikhail and Derksen were the only other people in the long barracks; they were talking to each other and out of earshot of Will's call. "Not really. But they've agreed we can accompany them on the flight providing we stick to their protocols in the event of an attack—they protect the target, we engage the hostile."

"They'll provide hardware?"

"I've got that sorted. They've got an armory here that I think would make even your old unit blush with envy."

"Okay. We can land this evening. How do we get to you?"

Will smiled. "Just wait at the airport. They'll take care of everything else. But a word of warning—don't fall for the pretty woman's charms."

Sarah stopped on the Isle of Wight coastal footpath and looked down the cliff toward the sea. She was wearing corduroy trousers, mountain boots, and a thick Aran sweater underneath an oilskin coat.

As she turned to Betty, a sea breeze blew her hair away from her face. "James and I have decided to move out of London. Our law firm has been very good about things. They think my illness and absence from work has been related to the stress of London life. For the last twelve months, they've been considering opening a branch in Edinburgh, and they've just asked us to be partners of the office."

Betty thrust her hands into her tweed jacket and nodded approvingly. "It'll do you both a world of good. Will you live in the city?"

"No. The great thing about Edinburgh is that it's surrounded by countryside. We'll get a place there, commute in." She lowered her head. "A new life."

"You'll have to tell Will. He'll miss you."

"He never saw us in London," Sarah huffed. "Alfie said my brother might die soon."

"Sometimes my husband talks nonsense. Just ignore him."

"It's true though, isn't it?"

"Your brother is one of Churchill's rough men. People like that are hard to kill."

Sarah frowned.

"Winston Churchill's quote: 'People sleep peaceably in their beds at night only because rough men stand ready to visit violence on those who would harm us.' "

"Well, you can add my father into that category of men. A knife killed him."

Betty wondered how to respond, because she knew that Alfie and Sarah were right. She breathed in deeply and said with a strident voice, "Come on, petal. We'd better get back to the men before they start killing each other again."

Roger, Mark, Laith, and Adam looked mad as hell. They'd just been brought to the base and were now standing in one of the barracks. Will and Mikhail were with them, as were some members of the DSI. Like all parts of the base, the long rectangular room had been stripped of all but the most essential of furnishings.

"Five hours to get here!" Laith shook his head, his deep southern voice booming. "I didn't know Holland was big enough for *anywhere* to be five hours away."

Kapitein Derksen laughed. "I think you're mistaking Holland for Luxembourg."

"Well, there's no mistaking the pain behind my eyes." The ex-Delta operative took a step toward Derksen, and for a moment it looked like he might swing a punch at the man. "Next time you're in the States, make sure you look me up so I can stick a bag over your head and take you for a nice spin in the trunk of my old Chevy."

"William." Superintendent Engert was leaning over a large table covered with maps and other paperwork.

Will moved to her side.

Pointing at a map, she said in a clipped tone, "At thirteen hundred hours, the witness will be moved to this holding pen here. At thirteen thirty hours, the aircraft will land here. It will taxi to this hangar, where it will be searched thoroughly. At the same time, the whole base will be on alert. My men will be in predetermined positions."

Will stared at the map. "What kind of plane are you using?"

"G-IV-SP."

"Civilian carrier?"

Engert nodded. "They're capable of transatlantic flights, but we need it because we want high altitude for part of the flight, plus it can carry fourteen passengers."

"Threat during takeoff?"

The police commander checked her watch. "Some of my men are already in position." She prodded her finger against several locations around the base runway and outside the perimeter. "Snipers, assault teams, dogs, plus we've got thermal imagery in all the right places, backed up by Claymores and other land mines. The teams will be there until the plane's high enough to be out of range of a land-based attack. And before you ask, we've refined this type of exfiltration over a thousand drills to the point it's impossible for anyone to get close enough to put a SAM lock on the craft."

"I presume it'll be the same for landing in The Hague?"

"Yes, we're taking no chances."

Will's team and Mikhail were now standing around the table, listening to Engert's briefing.

Roger asked, "Where's the witness being held now?"

Engert didn't look up. "In his villa."

"Villa?"

She smiled. "It's what we call it, though in reality it's a fortress within a fortress within a fortress. But he hasn't been complaining. The rooms are more luxurious than a five-star hotel." She drummed her fingers and stood upright. "When you land in The Hague, I'll be there to take over security of the northern base."

Mikhail asked, "You won't be traveling with us?"

Engert shook her head and pointed at Derksen. "We take turns escorting high-value targets, but we never travel together. If we both got wiped out in an attack, it would leave too big a hole in the team." She grinned. "We're a bit like a royal family in that respect." Her smile vanished. "Understand this: if an attack is made at any point before the witness takes the stand, my men will use maximum force to fend off the attack. Their sole priority will be protecting the witness. Don't get in our way."

FIFTY

Will and his men had been given rooms in the base and had been told by Engert that they should get their heads down as there was nothing they could do now until morning. But as he sat on the edge of his military camp bed, Will had no thoughts of sleep. He was tense and felt that everything was out of his control. Ordinarily, he'd take a walk through the base and get some night air to try to clear his head, but the base was on lockdown and in any case Will and his team were highly restricted as to where they were allowed to go. He banged a fist against the bed, frustrated and helpless.

Roger knocked on his open door and leaned against the frame. The CIA officer looked irritated. "Laith's driving me nuts. Guy's pacing up and down the corridor like a caged animal."

"I know how he feels."

"Yeah, we all do." The American rubbed a hand over his face. "When I was looking to leave the SEALs, I got approached by the Secret Service, who said they'd be very interested in having someone with my skill set on board. I turned 'em down in a flash, said there was no way I could spend a career protecting folk and just waiting for something unexpected to happen. I opted for SOG instead because they're the ones who go out and do stuff."

Will completely understood. In the field, people like him were the hunters, the ones who had power and autonomy, who could define the unexpected. But now that role belonged to Kronos—Will and his team were in reactive mode. He didn't know how Engert, Derksen, and the rest of DSI coped with the stress of this existence. "What happens if we fail?"

Roger shrugged. "We go home, grab a beer, then wait for the next mission."

Will was silent.

The CIA officer smiled. "You can't comprehend that, can you?"

"What?"

"Failure."

"I can easily comprehend it; everything I've done so far has been a failure."

Roger frowned, shook his head. "This all started with a single sheet of paper going missing. Most people thought you were crazy to pursue this operation, given we had no idea what was on the paper and had zero leads. Look what you've achieved to bring us this far."

Will smiled. "I've brought us to a situation of going stir crazy in a Dutch high-security military base."

Roger burst out laughing. "Yeah, you've done just that." His laugh receded. "We're keeping well away from Mikhail."

"Good. Don't speak to him without me being present."

"You don't trust him?"

"What do you think?"

"Yeah, dumb question."

"I'm the one who feels dumb right now." Will stood. "Come on. Let's get the team together. Texas Hold'em poker. Fifteen dollars big blind. If nothing else, it means one of us will fly out of this base tomorrow with something to show for being here."

FIFTY-ONE

Joanna surveyed Will's London home with pride and satisfaction. All of the boxes had been unpacked and removed; the West Square apartment was perfect. She looked at the dining room table and tried to picture Will sitting there, eating a meal with a woman, laughing with her. To her surprise, the image came naturally and the event seemed possible. She imagined them retiring to the other end of the living room, Will placing one of his Segovia records on the Garrard turntable, lighting a fire, pouring her a calvados, and sitting next to her on the Edwardian sofa. What would they talk about? Perhaps music, if they had that in common. Or maybe Will would try to impress her with his past exploits in MI6 and the Legion. No, he would never share those memories with someone he liked. He could capture her interest with his knowledge of London and its secrets, knowledge gained from his many walks through the capital's streets and alleys, though he'd need to omit telling her all the dark secrets. And he could enthrall her by describing the beauty that he'd seen during his overseas travels: Indian mists revealing glimpses of palaces and placid lakes in Rajasthan; shooting stars racing through a blue diamond-encrusted night sky above southern Chile's archipelago; fishermen and their trained cormorants drifting in tiny boats in the azure lakes of the Jiuzhaigou Valley; and candles being lit across Myanmar's plain of a thousand pagodas. He'd taken time to see these and a multitude of other stunning places, even though he'd been there to kill men.

Joanna rubbed her arthritic hips as she walked into the kitchen. Robert was in there, frying bacon. "Darling, the post will be here in a minute."

Her husband was wearing a chef's apron that Joanna had bought for Will's return home. On it were the words WILLY THE KITCHEN WIZARD. "Right you are, old girl. You want ketchup in your sandwich?"

"No. And I don't want you putting any in yours, either."

Robert huffed. "Bloody doctor's orders are going to see me die early of boredom."

They heard whistling in the stairwell outside the front door. The postman. Robert turned off the pan, grabbed his pump-action shotgun, and nodded at Joanna.

Two minutes later, Joanna's hand was shaking as she held the letter and reread it to make sure that her eyes hadn't deceived her.

Dear Joanna and Robert,

Have you enjoyed your stay at Will Cochrane's house? I'm sure he'll be very grateful that you've spent so much time unpacking his items and making his home look tasteful. I particularly like how you've combined the Louis XV lacquer and ormolu commode with the set of Venetian trespoli and the pair of eighteenth-century Guangzhou imperial dress swords. Like me, Mr. Cochrane has a good eye for antiquities, though his tastes are too eclectic. I commend you for achieving the near-impossible task of arranging his collection within one home.

I'm writing to let you know that you don't need to remain in his house any longer. This will be the last letter I send. I'd be grateful if you could let him know that Mrs. Rübner has contacted me in what can only be described as a state of hysteria. To my disgust, I learned that British and American men kidnapped her and her daughter in order to try to get to me. I had wondered if Mr. Cochrane had given up chasing me; it appears that has not been the case. There is no excuse for what he did to Mrs. Rübner and her daughter, though I'm grateful he released them unharmed. But I cannot forgive him for killing Mrs. Rübner's husband, a man who was also a trusted and valuable employee of mine. That action was deplorable.

I've been left with no choice other than to address that.

Every morning, you've been extremely meticulous with the way you've collected mail delivered to Mr. Cochrane's house. I estimate you'll be reading these words at 0704 hours.

Exactly four minutes after Will Cochrane's loved one was shot in the head.

Yours sincerely,
William

FIFTY-TWO

Alfie snapped his cell phone shut and ran as fast as he could along the Isle of Wight's Compton Bay beach. While Betty was preparing sausages and eggs and waiting for Sarah and James to come downstairs, the retiree had been taking an early-morning walk along the empty beach in order to rejoin the coastal road and then watch the holiday home and its surroundings from a distance. But Joanna had called him before he got to that location. It still left the sixty-five-year-old ex-SAS sergeant half a mile of coastline to reach the house.

The same words raced through his mind as he tried to force his aging legs to move faster and his lungs to give him more oxygen.

Bloody hell, no! Bloody hell, no!

He wheezed, his stiff limbs and back throbbed, and his temples ached from the exertion and the icy winter air. Why did he have to be this old, this far away from the house? He could see it now, tiny, at least eight hundred paces away. His heart was pounding. Maybe it would give out on him and he'd die here, just as his old man had done. A pointless death.

Each footfall made his boots sink inches into the wet sand. Bleedin' sand—loved it as a kid; hated it in the army. All those runs along it carrying a rifle and webbing. But at least he'd been in his twenties then. What was he thinking about sand for? Because he didn't want to think about anything else, that's why.

Taste of blood in his mouth. That was normal. Get that regardless of age. Spat out more blood in his time than he could remember. Got plenty more of it inside. Just need to remember that yer body can do five times more than yer mind wants it to do. That's what got him through the freezing sleet and wind in the final stage of SAS selection: a hellish mountain trek with sixty pounds of gear on his back, while carrying a rifle with no sling. Shit, that was tough, and had come on the back of four weeks of endless marches and runs, most of 'em on your own, just a basic compass for navigation, back breaking from the weight, up and down mountains, shivering all the time, every inch of yer feet pissing gunk from blisters. Long time ago. Since then, he'd gotten old. Running along this small bit of beach was every bit as tough as final selection.

As his legs slowed, he felt his handgun rub against his hip. Probably had taken the skin off by now. Didn't matter, skin would grow back. Soon he'd take the gun out. Not yet. Had to be close. Must remember the house entry drills. Watch the angles; speed crucial; chest shots first. Christ! Speed? What a joke.

He reached the base of a set of wooden steps leading up the cliff to the road. His breathing was shallow, legs like lead, head gettin' dizzy. Control that. Get yer mind in shape. Might have shooting to do.

Who you kidding? You're not in the Regiment's Special Projects Team now. Just a knackered ol' codger. Yeah, but you can still shoot, remember? The years ain't touched that. Bless 'em.

Using one hand on a rail to aid him, he hauled his body up the steps, used the back of his other arm to wipe sweat from his brow. Can't have that shit in your eyes. He reached the top. House one seven three yards away. Cross the road, follow edge of the open heathland, keep low, gun out when within pistol kill range. Fuck what the passengers of any passing cars thought. Nothing on the road, though— two miles visibility along it to the southeast, one mile northwest.

He walked across the road, wincing as his whole body felt like it was being torn apart. Wish Cochrane was here. Get a grip. He ain't here, dickhead; you are.

Okay. Small-arms kill range now. Gun out. Two hands. Drop low.

Sixty yards from house. Top windows, east wall—one, two, three, four: all clear. Bottom windows: no sightings. Still leaves four rooms unaccounted for. Front or back entrance? Neither has element of surprise if a professional team's in there. Reckon front's best. Gives better angles, plus sight of two more rooms on approach.

Priority: kill bastards, secure target zone.

No bastards?

Hunt bastards down. Kill bastards.

Got to remove emotion. Done it before, remember? Yer pal Geordie's team in Borneo; knew they were all cut up before you went in to get the bodies and give a bit of payback to their killers. Aden, Northern Ireland, Falklands. More dead mates. Couldn't think about them while doin' yer job. Thinking and stuff comes after.

Different now though, ain't it? You've let Cochrane down. Sarah's dead.

And all you can do now is rescue Betty and James.

Betty. Standing next to her all those years ago. Poky south London church. Him in his cheap but neatly pressed suit and shiny shoes. Confetti in his Brylcreemed hair. Her in the dress her mum and sisters had made for the day. Goodness, his missus looked lovely. Proud day that. Best day. She sorted him right out, she did. Made him grow up and get values. Made him more of a man than all them marches.

Biggest test of yer manhood coming up. Need to be able to step over Sarah's body, keep your gun high, angles, body shots, room clearance, don't think, don't feel. Yet.

He reached the edge of the house.

Movement behind one of the windows.

Then nothing.

Shit!

Looks like we're in for a firefight.

Body's feeling a bit better. Hands? Arms? They ain't shaking. Eyes? Brain? Good enough.

Right, lads.

Who dares wins.

Get it done.

He crawled alongside the front of the house, rose to a crouch beside the front door, held his gun with one hand, used the other to grip the door handle, and eased the door open a few inches.

Silence.

Now.

He stood, kicked the door fully open, and rushed forward with his gun held high.

He froze.

Sarah was slumped on the floor.

Covered in blood.

FIFTY-THREE

The military base was a hive of activity, with DSI and other Dutch law enforcement personnel moving quickly on foot and in vehicles to other parts of the establishment, some of them standing guard around the runway and adjacent hangars, and a small cadre of DSI professionals checking weapons and communications equipment in the long, rectangular barracks where Will and his team were. The six Dutchmen were the protection unit who'd be escorting the witness north to The Hague. Kapitein Derksen was one of them. Like his men, he was wearing a blue jacket, jeans, combat belt, canvas boots, balaclava, and bulletproof vest with the word POLITIE on the front and back.

After stripping down his FN P90 submachine gun and his Glock 17 pistol, Derksen walked over to Will and Mikhail. "The witness has been moved to the holding facility; the plane landed an hour ago and has been searched; we'll be green light in thirty minutes. Do it as I told you—very fast." Within the small area of balaclava that exposed his eyes, there were no signs of any emotion. "You have everything you need?"

Mikhail patted his overcoat. Underneath it was a holster containing a Glock handgun. "We could have done with clothes like yours and"—he nodded toward the officer's P90—"more firepower."

"You have to be distinguishable from my men, so we know who're the professionals and who're the amateurs," Derksen snapped. "Fifteen minutes before takeoff." He turned and walked back to his men.

The MI6 and SVR officers approached Roger, Laith, Mark, and Adam. Like Will and Mikhail, they were all dressed as if they were about to attend a winter business conference in a five-star hotel.

Will said, "When we get to The Hague, I'm going to try to keep us in play. We'll have ten more days of sitting on our asses in another secure facility before the hearing." He glanced at Laith. "Gives the rest of us a chance to win back our cash."

Laith smiled. "You'll lose again if you think poker's a game of chance."

"Okay." Kapitein Derksen's voice filled the barracks. "Let's go!"

The DSI unit and Will's team jogged out of the building, then sprinted past other barracks and into a large aircraft hangar. In the center was the G-IV-SP aircraft. Its engines were running, and the pilots were visible in the cockpit, clearly making their preparations. Machine-gun-carrying police officers were standing around the craft; others were kneeling by the open hangar doors, pointing their weapons toward the runway.

In Dutch, Derksen barked into his throat mic, "Sierra 1. We're in position at Zulu."

Four of his men rushed into the plane as Derksen and another knelt by the plane's steps and raised their guns. Looking at Will, Derksen snapped, "Get in."

Will, Roger, Laith, Mark, Adam, and Mikhail entered the plane. It was quite small but luxurious. Two uniformed officers were at the head of the passenger area. One of them had a sniffer dog on a leash;

the other, holding a clipboard, approached a DSI officer. The two spoke for a few seconds before the DSI operative took the clipboard, carefully examined the papers on it, and signed at the bottom. The paperwork showed that every space within the plane's interior had been searched three times on the secure base by three separate police units. The two police officers left the plane, and the dog's tail wagged quickly as the animal moved past the men.

Sumptuous leather seats lined each side of the plane, facing each other and separated halfway along by a bar and cupboards containing food. No doubt, ordinarily this type of carrier would be used for VIP businessmen and perhaps senior politicians. Will and the rest of the team moved to the front seats, sat, and waited. Five seconds later, Derksen and his colleague entered the craft.

Between them was an old man.

The witness.

The plane started taxiing as the old man was shown to a seat between two large DSI operatives. The remaining four Dutchmen took up positions close to him. One of the officers started talking quickly on his mic, relaying instructions and updates.

The silver-haired witness was wearing a gray suit, a necktie, and a somber overcoat. His etched, serious expression suggested that he had no appreciation for the craft's luxurious interior.

The plane's engine noise grew louder.

Will darted a look at Kapitein Derksen as the plane began increasing in speed. "Who is he?"

Derksen remained silent, motionless, gripping his submachine gun, just like the rest of his men.

"Who is he?"

The plane accelerated and took off.

"Kapitein Derksen . . . !"

Derksen answered, "Now that we're airborne, I'm permitted to give you his identity. His name is Nikolai Dmitriev, former colonel with the KGB and SVR."

Dmitriev. The name Will had seen in the papers he'd discovered in Yevtushenko's house.

The officer who'd attended the secret meeting in Berlin in 1995.

The man who'd approached The Hague six months ago in order to give evidence about a secret pact.

Will stared at Dmitriev, then glanced out of the window, bracing himself in case the plane was hit by a missile.

Nothing happened.

"Now that you know my identity"—Dmitriev pointed a frail finger toward Will—"it would be appropriate to know who you are."

Will answered in Russian, "We're part of the protection detail."

"Really?" Dmitriev stared at each man before returning his attention to Will and stating in English, "None of you look like Dutch cops."

Derksen leaned toward the Russian while fastening his seat belt. "They're along for the ride because they've got information which will enable us to further keep you safe. Other than that, nothing's changed. I'm in charge on the flight; you do exactly as I say."

"Information?" Dmitriev kept his gaze fixed on Will. "What *information*?"

Derksen motioned to Will to stay silent.

But Will answered, "We're intelligence officers, multi-agency, though all of us have been working together to neutralize a specific threat to you."

The old man briefly closed his eyes. "A threat that has a code name beginning with the letter K?"

At first, Will didn't know if he should answer. If a person was going to kill him, he'd often wondered if he'd want to know that person's identity just before it happened. It made no difference to the outcome, though perhaps it could give it some kind of meaning. "Yes. You know exactly who he is."

Dmitriev opened his eyes and stared at nothing. "Then everything has gone according to plan."

Will frowned. "What plan?"

Dmitriev said nothing.

Adam rubbed his disfigured face, wincing slightly.

Mikhail asked, "Does it hurt?"

The Scotsman looked at the spycatcher with an expression of suspicion, then smiled. "Aye. Cabin pressure during takeoffs and landings. Keeps me sharp."

Mark leaned forward and gently punched Adam's knee. "Just as well there ain't any air hostesses on the flight, matey. Your ugly boat race would send 'em packing."

"Nah. I'd play the wounded war hero sympathy card. Works every time. It's almost made it worthwhile having ma face blown off."

The plane was ascending fast. Engert had told Will that the pilots had been carefully selected due to their prior military experience and ability to get planes up and down quicker than most commercial pilots.

Will eased back into his seat while keeping his attention fixed on Dmitriev. So much had been done to try to kill the Russian; in equal measure, a vast effort and number of resources had been deployed to protect him. All because of what was in his head. What was the secret, and why were things going according to plan? They'd find out when Dmitriev took the stand. But as Will looked at the retired intelligence officer's haunted expression, he wondered if that would happen.

Derksen moved along the aisle and entered the cockpit. Twenty seconds later, he reemerged and said, "We're high enough now. Next thirty minutes should be fine. Pilot will let us know when he starts his descent."

Everyone removed his seat belt. Laith stretched out his legs. "Time for some shut-eye. Hey, Derksen—you got one of them hoods you like putting on people? Might actually be useful this time round, help me get some sleep."

The DSI officer ignored the comment. Instead he patted a hand on Dmitriev's forearm and retook his seat. "We're safe for the time being."

They all heard the sound of two near-simultaneous dull thuds. One second later, the plane started violently shuddering.

"Damn turbulence."

The shuddering got worse; men were lifted a few inches out of their seats; there was a moment of weightlessness, more shuddering; the plane seemed to be descending, rolled left; all of the men on one side of the plane were hurled into the aisle.

"What the fuck's happening!"

Will tried to get to his feet, was thrown forward into Roger and Mark, gripped the overhead lockers to get himself upright, then lurched into the opposite seats as the plane banked right, his shoulder banging into more luggage compartments. Wincing in pain, he pulled his body along the floor toward the cockpit. Behind him men were shouting, their bodies crashing into each other and the sides of the plane.

The copilot was sending out urgent distress calls, sweat pouring down his face, his body shaking but held in place by his belt. Next to him, the pilot was gripping the wheel, desperately trying to retain control of the craft.

Will got to one knee, using both arms to grip the back of the copilot's seat. "What's happened?"

Between gritted teeth, the pilot answered, "Both engines taken out. Immediate failure."

"Explosions, fire, electrical fault?"

"I don't know! Just stopped working."

"What can we do?"

"*You* can't do anything. Get back in there. We're going to have to see if we can glide the bird down." The pilot glanced at his colleague. "Any coordinates yet?"

The copilot nodded. "Just got them. Only one strip in the area, but it's long enough. Tiny commercial airport. I'm speaking to its traffic controller."

"Okay." The pilot's whole body was shaking. "Tell him to get emergency services to the airport."

Will crawled back into the passenger compartment. Inside was chaos. Some men were still being tossed around; others had managed to get their seat belts on and were grimacing as the straps bit into their stomachs with every movement of the plane. "Engine failure! Crash landing!"

Derksen grabbed Dmitriev, pulled him down next to him, and quickly fixed the seat belt onto the old man. "An attack?"

"We don't know." Will rose to his feet and was immediately thrown backward as the plane went into another dive. After tumbling down the aisle, he slammed into the cockpit door. Two cupboards at the end of the aisle opened, and china plates and cups smashed their way down the plane toward him. A Dutch operative's head smacked against the door, inches from his own, and the man immediately lost consciousness. Another flew across the aisle with sufficient force to knock out not only himself, but also the DSI operative he hit.

The plane was now shaking so badly that everything in Will's vision was a blur of constant movement.

The pilot's strained voice came over the speakers. "Brace for impact!"

Held in place by the angle of descent and an unconscious operative, Will looked out of a window. Land was visible, getting nearer, rushing past them. He glanced at his team. All of them had managed to get their belts on and were holding onto anything to try to keep themselves still.

Derksen shouted at Will, "Has to have been a bomb. Must have been a malfunction; only part of it went off."

Will agreed. "At stop, get Dmitriev as far away from the plane as possible."

"No shit!"

Will's heart was racing, his body covered in perspiration and aching from the impacts. Was this how it was going to end? Most of the Spartan Section wiped out in a plane crash? He forced himself to think about other matters: fire, smoke, evacuating the plane, fuel leak-age, keeping Dmitriev alive.

The plane was bouncing through the air, so quickly Will won-dered if it would just tear apart before it hit the ground.

The land was rushing faster past them, was closer, closer. One hundred yards away.

Fifty.

Will looked at Roger and his men. Might be the last time he'd see them.

Roger stuck his thumb up and smiled at Will.

It's been fun working together.

That's what the gesture meant. Or something similar.

Twenty yards.

Derksen thrust Dmitriev's head down and held it firm while silently mouthing words.

Maybe a prayer.

Ten yards.

All of the men were silent now. Preparing for death.

Thoughts raced through Will's mind. What would it be like? As quick as a bullet? Or body lacerated by shards of metal? Did he regret anything? Yeah, every damn fucking thing.

Five yards.

I'll soon be with you, Dad. Finally get a chance to grab that beer together. Is Mum with you? Do they have beer where you are?

Two yards, runway racing beneath them.

One yard.

Good-bye, Sarah. I'm sorry about James's shirt. Don't join me and the parents anytime soon.

Bang.

The noise was deafening. Movement everywhere. Men shaken in their seats; the unconscious ones being flipped up and down. Sparks streaming alongside the outside of the windows. Metal screeching, bits of it falling off. Glass smashing. Wind rushing through the cabin. Men shouting. Screaming. The plane twisting and shuddering.

It was like this for fifteen seconds.

The plane tilted. Half of a wing was ripped off, the remainder dug into the runway, sparks spewing out of the trail. The plane spun, lifted off the ground, walloped back down, spun again.

Blood in Will's mouth. Brain banging against the inside of his skull. Pain everywhere. And confusion.

Plane still spinning, heading off the runway toward grassland. Good or bad thing? Will had no idea. Off the runway, mud and grass flying up the sides of the craft, some of it entering the plane and covering faces and bodies.

Different noise now. Rough ground. Slowing down. Tail snapped off. Shit! Back end of plane upending. Two bodies flying your way. Cover your head. No idea which way's up or down.

Thwack.

Will lay still, men on top of him. Movement? No, everything seemed to have stopped. No sound. No sight. Does that mean death?

Then shouting. Familiar voices.

Roger. "Fucking move!"

Derksen. "Fire in the rear! Get that door open!"

Mark. "Shit! Shit!"

Mikhail. "Will?"

Weight being lifted off him. Breathing easier. Light, but acrid. Mikhail over him. Arms grabbing him. "Come on, Will."

On his feet. Going to collapse. No, being held firm by the Russian. Carnage everywhere. Laith and Adam yanking on the emergency exit's handles, faces covered in crap, clothes ripped. Derksen barking orders.

"Come on, Will."

You're alive. Think. Action.

Will rushed to the door and grabbed a piece of the handle. "One, two, three. Now!"

They turned the handles, Will and Laith simultaneously kicked the door, and it fell away.

"We've got an exit!" Will glanced at the three unconscious Dutch operatives, piled by the cockpit door. "One each, fifty yards from plane." He hauled one of the men onto his shoulder, clambered out of the wreckage, and ran as fast as he could before lowering the man onto grass and sprinting back to the plane. Laith and Adam passed him in the opposite direction, carrying the other injured men. Inside the plane, Derksen and the remaining two DSI operatives were moving up the aisle while holding guns in one hand and Dmitriev with the other. The old man had cuts on his face, looked ashen and in shock, but otherwise seemed unharmed. Roger and Mark were in the cockpit checking the pilots. Blood was pouring down the copilot's face; his colleague had his head tilted back, eyes screwed tight, and was moaning.

"What's their condition?"

Roger's answered, "Copilot's out of it but alive; pilot's conscious."

"Broken neck or back?"

"Don't know."

Will cursed and looked toward the rear of the plane. Black smoke was billowing in the rear compartment, and he could see flames. If they moved the pilots and they had broken necks or backs, they could kill them. "Fuck it! Plane could go up any second. We've got to get them out of here."

Roger and Mark began unstrapping the pilots as Derksen and his men guided Dmitriev out of the craft.

Will called out to Derksen, "There are aircraft buildings about three hundred yards away, forest beyond that; couldn't see any other cover apart from the control tower, which is four hundred yards in the opposite direction."

"Okay. We'll take him to the buildings."

Will looked at Mikhail. "Go with them." He helped his colleagues one by one carry the pilots and lay them on the ground adjacent to the plane. Removing his thick overcoat, he laid it flat. With Roger, they rested the pilot on top of the coat, grabbed corners of the coat, and ran the makeshift stretcher to the part of the field containing the unconscious DSI men. He glanced at Roger and said, "Stay on Dmitriev," grabbed the coat, and rushed back to Mark and the copilot. They repeated the drill, placing the injured man in the coat, and began carrying the copilot away from the plane.

They were thirty yards from the wreckage when the plane exploded and sent them crashing to the ground. Will covered his head as shards and chunks of metal flew through the air, waiting helplessly for a bit of the craft to smash through his skull. He breathed deeply; nothing had hit him. Rolling onto his side, his stomach wrenched as he looked at Mark. A jagged piece of metal was protruding from his thigh; his shredded trousers were covered in blood.

Mark said between gritted teeth, "I can make it to the others . . . but can't help you with the copilot anymore. Sorry."

"Shit!" Will dashed to him, saw that the metal had gone right through Mark's leg, and prayed that it hadn't severed a major artery. Removing his belt, he said, "Got to get a tourniquet on there before—"

"I know what to do." Mark grabbed the belt and began wrapping it around his thigh. "Help the others." After fixing the strap in place, he crawled past Will, beads of sweat on his grubby face, while trying to ignore his agonizing injury.

Will lifted the copilot and used a fireman's carry to get him to the other injured men. Roger, Derksen, Mikhail, and the two other Dutch operatives were one hundred yards away, taking Dmitriev toward three white buildings and two stationary Islander planes. Laith and Adam were examining each man, trying to ascertain their injuries and make them as comfortable as possible. "Where the hell are the damn emergency services?" He glanced toward the distant control tower. "The air traffic controller called them at least ten minutes ago."

Laith shrugged. "Appears we're in the middle of frickin' nowhere."

Will looked around the airport. Aside from the three buildings, the tower, the strip of runway and open grassland on either side of it, there was nothing else here save forest on all sides of the complex.

Something felt wrong.

A tiny, isolated airport.

Hidden away.

Zero security.

Fuck!

This was meant to happen.

Laith screamed, crumpled to the ground. Adam yelped, flipped sideways.

Will dived forward, just before a third bullet struck ground where his feet had been. "Sniper! Sniper!" He glanced at his colleagues, saw both had been shot in their calves, sprinted, zigzagged, dived again, and rolled. Sprinting ahead to Roger and the others, he screamed, "Get to cover!"

Derksen turned to face him, 150 yards away, then collapsed. Three seconds later, his two colleagues were lying next to him, all of them writhing in pain from the leg shots. Roger and Mikhail grabbed Dmitriev and tried to move the old man as fast as they could, but they only managed a few paces before Roger shouted, "Fuck!" He released Dmitriev, staggered, and collapsed while holding his hand over the gun wound to his knee. A moment later, Mikhail was knocked off his feet and fell on top of him, the back of his knee a bloody mess.

"Get to the buildings! Keep moving!"

Dmitriev walked as fast as he could, though he was an easy target. Will dashed right, as a bullet grazed his thigh. Wincing in pain, he kept sprinting, changed direction again, wondering why the sniper was incapacitating the team but not killing them.

He raced past Roger and Mikhail, both alive but unable to move due to their injuries.

Another shot.

Jesus, what was that?

A burning sensation behind one leg.

Severe pain.

Will fell forward, pulled out his handgun, used his elbows to crawl onward.

Couldn't stand.

Not with a high-velocity bullet having passed through his leg.

Dmitriev was eighty yards from the buildings. Why wasn't he shot?

Fifty yards behind him, Will crawled inch by inch, his face screwed up, his breathing rapid.

Kronos placed the sniper rifle down, withdrew his pistol and military knife, walked past the bound and gagged air traffic controller, and made his way down the control tower. So far, everything had gone according to plan. With the login info he'd stolen from the Dutch pilot in Frankfurt, he'd logged on to Holland's AIS air traffic control website and obtained information about general aviation commercial carriers that had lodged their flight plans in Dutch airspace for the day that Dmitriev was being transported. Only one plane was logged to fly between the southern military base and The Hague, and he established that it was currently being serviced and kept in a civilian airport. He'd infiltrated the place and inserted two cigarette-lighter-sized explosive devices into the carrier's engines. Both were timed to go off at a moment during the flight when the only nearby airstrip was this one. As extra insurance, he'd taken over the air traffic control tower and used its communications system to guide the captain of the plane to this place. The captain had no idea that he was talking to an assassin who had no intention of calling emergency services.

It would have all been so much easier if his plan had been to kill Dmitriev without speaking to him first.

He still had to be careful. By now, Dmitriev would have reached the buildings, and might have decided to continue onward into the forest. That didn't matter, because he'd easily catch up with the old man. What did matter was that, though injured, the Russian's security team could still shoot him from a distance. He'd had to keep them alive, because it was possible he needed their help. Moreover, he was a professional, and his orders were to kill Dmitriev; he'd received no instructions to kill anyone else.

Exiting the building, he ran into the forest and sprinted close to its edge. He caught glimpses of the three white buildings. He'd reach them in one minute. Then everything would be concluded.

Fighting every instinct in his body to stop, roll over, and wait for help, Will kept crawling toward the buildings. He was forty yards away, but might as well have been four miles away at the speed he was moving. Dmitriev was there, waiting by one of the walls, looking left and right, no doubt trying to decide what to do. Will attempted to call to him, but blood entered his mouth and made him choke. Dmitriev moved.

No! Stay in sight and within handgun range.

But Dmitriev edged along the wall and then disappeared from view behind the building.

There you are.

Kronos darted between trees as he saw the old man hobbling into the forest while looking wildly around. The Russian hadn't seen him yet. It wouldn't matter if he did; he had no chance of escape. Silently, Kronos leapt over broken tree limbs and foliage, then slowed to walking pace. "Nikolai Dmitriev!"

The Russian spun around, terror on his face.

Kronos raised his gun and walked quickly toward the man. "You know who I am and you know why I'm here."

Dmitriev opened his mouth to speak, but no words came out.

"Stand still."

The Russian did as he was told. "Why . . . why didn't you shoot me?"

Kronos moved behind Dmitriev, placed the muzzle of his hand-gun onto the crown of Dmitriev's head and the tip of his knife under his throat. "I may still shoot you, or stab you, or both."

Dmitriev closed his eyes. "I won't . . . won't beg for my life."

Kronos moved his mouth close to the Russian's ear. "I'd be disappointed if you did."

Dmitriev opened his eyes, fear and confusion coursing through him. "Then what are you doing? You want to savor the moment before you do it?"

The assassin smiled. "You know that's never been my style." His smile vanished. "I want answers, but make sure you take great care to give me the truth. Lie to me, and I'll kill you without hesitation. First—was my activation authorized at state level? Second—what is the secret that I've been deployed to protect?"

Dmitriev frowned. "They . . . they didn't tell you?"

"Just answer me!"

Sweat streamed down the old man's face. "The surviving individuals present at the Berlin meeting are no longer in office, though that may change soon. That's why I need to testify in ten days. I can't let them assume power."

"Was it authorized at state level? Testify to what?"

"No . . . no. They're acting in a private capacity to stop me from telling the world about Slingshot."

Kronos moved his finger over the trigger. "Slingshot?"

"That's the secret. It refers to genocide."

In a flash, Kronos pulled Dmitriev closer to him so that the old man's body was completely in front of his. "Lower your weapon!"

Will stopped crawling, his breathing labored, his shaking arms pointing his weapon toward the men. "Can't do that."

"Englishman?"

Will spat blood, didn't answer.

"Will Cochrane?"

Mention of his name didn't surprise Will. Schreiber would have supplied it to Kronos. "Let him go!"

"A silly suggestion."

"Let him go. Otherwise I'll put a bullet through Dmitriev's head to get to you."

"You'd have done that already if you wanted to."

Will tried to keep his gun still, felt light-headed, wished he could see even an inch of Kronos's face, had no idea what to do.

But Kronos did. "I kept you, your men, and Dmitriev alive for a reason. Be grateful for that, and try to establish why I did it. Goodbye, Mr. Cochrane."

Kronos edged away from him, keeping Dmitriev firmly in his grip.

Will blinked fast. Make a nonlethal shot into Dmitriev to get the man to drop to the ground? Given his age, it could still kill him. Kronos could easily kill him.

The men moved farther away from him, into the forest.

Will's mind raced. Why didn't Kronos put kill shots into the team? Why didn't he just destroy the plane midflight? There had to be a reason.

Answers.

That was it.

Kronos needed answers.

He watched the men disappear from view, lowered his gun, felt his head spinning, then lost consciousness.

Kronos guided Dmitriev deeper into the forest, stopped, took three steps away from him, and pointed his gun at the Russian's head. "Turn around."

Dmitriev faced him, a look of resignation on his face. "I thought it would end somewhere like this."

The assassin was motionless. "Genocide?"

Dmitriev nodded. "Sometime after you pull the trigger, it will happen."

Kronos narrowed his eyes. "I never trusted Schreiber. When he met me recently, I suspected that he wasn't there with official authorization. Also, he gave me an instruction that I could never act upon."

Leaving his family.

"I want to know every detail about the planned genocide. Based on that, I'll decide whether to pull the trigger."

Will felt cold hands hitting his face, a voice, something trying to shake him. What was happening? Where was he? Something felt really bad on him. God, it felt awful! Oh yes, gunshot wound. He opened his eyes. A man was leaning over him, talking. Couldn't make sense of the words. Who was he?

Everything came back to him.

Colonel Nikolai Dmitriev stared at him. "He's gone."

"Gone?"

The old man nodded. "He said that he made the right decision keeping you and your men alive, that I needed all the protection I could get before appearing at The Hague."

Dmitriev extended a hand and helped Will get to his feet. Wincing, and keeping his injured leg off the ground, Will placed a hand on the Russian's shoulder and hoped the old man could take the weight. "You're still under threat?"

"No. To Kronos's knowledge, not from anyone else. And he made it clear that I need never fear him. He swore that he won't come for me again."

Will stared at the airport, at the distant wreckage of the airplane, and at the injured men that littered the place. He shivered, felt exhausted, every inch of his body in agony. He reflected on Kronos's promise to Dmitriev. "Thank God."

FIFTY-FOUR

James was crouched beside Sarah in the Isle of Wight house, his arms around her, rocking her back and forth.

Alfie shouted, "What's happened?"

James was in shock. "Sarah's okay. We're not . . . not hurt. Kitchen . . . kitchen . . ."

Alfie's heart pumped fast as he walked past the couple, his gun still held high, eyes narrow, sweat pouring over his entire body. Pausing to one side of the kitchen entrance, he ducked low and swung into the room. Bacon and sausages were burning in a frying pan.

So was something else.

Betty's head.

Bullets had torn chunks out of it and had forced her dead body to collapse over the stove.

"Betty!" Alfie looked around urgently. No one else here. The fucking bastards had long since gone. His arms involuntarily swung down, and he dropped his gun and staggered toward his beloved wife. Tears running down his face, he started shaking. "Not my Betty. My dear, dear Betty."

. . .

Kurt Schreiber lifted the ornate telephone handset and held it against his face.

"It's done, Mr. Schreiber."

"As I instructed?"

"Exactly. We did it in front of the sister."

"Excellent. You and your men are to return back here."

"You don't want us to keep watching the others?" The man laughed. "Or give them a bit more of a shock?"

"No. Maximum damage has been done. The others are of no use to me now."

Schreiber replaced the handset and interlinked his fingers, deep in thought. By killing Betty Mayne, he'd sent a powerful warning to Will Cochrane. In similar situations, most men would back down from pursuing him. He wondered if Cochrane was such a man.

FIFTY-FIVE

The young Dutch police officer looked nervous as he entered Will's hospital room in Eindhoven's Catharina Ziekenhuis hospital. He extended his arm. In his hand was a cell phone. "Sir, you have a call. Urgent."

Will grimaced in pain as he sat up in bed. In rooms close to him were Roger, Laith, Adam, Mark, and Mikhail. No one else was allowed into the ward except nurses, doctors, and armed Dutch cops. "Who is it?"

"I'm not permitted to know. My commanding officer ordered me to bring the phone to you."

Will nodded. "I need some privacy."

The cop hesitated, seemed unsure what to do, then left the room.

Will held the phone to his face. "Yes?"

He listened to Alistair speak for ten minutes, though it felt like only ten seconds. When the call ended, his head was spinning, images racing through his mind. He felt disbelief, nausea, anger, and overwhelming grief.

Unable to get hold of Will, Alfie had called his Controller to relay devastating news.

Betty was dead.

Will stared at the hospital equipment by his bed, though nothing registered. He was motionless, felt as if he'd been stunned by an almighty sucker punch.

A punch that had been delivered with brilliant precision by Colonel Kurt Schreiber.

Schreiber had known how Will had reacted to the perceived threat to his sister. The former Stasi officer had watched him eschew bringing in hired guns to protect Sarah, in favor of entrusting her safety to people who were considerably older and had wisdom and a wealth of experience, meaning they meant something to him. Schreiber had ascertained their identities and had singled out Betty as the perfect target, knowing that her death would cause Will to be debilitated with overwhelming guilt. He'd also ensured that she was murdered in front of his sister, whom Schreiber could easily have killed but instead kept alive so that she could understand that Will's line of work caused those around him to be sacrificed.

Schreiber had killed Betty, and no doubt he had also killed Will's relationship with his last remaining family.

Kurt Schreiber had completely outsmarted Will Cochrane.

FIFTY-SIX

"Y ou both need to get back to the military hospital as soon as this is done." Though his tone was stern, Patrick's expression held concern and compassion as he looked at Will and Roger. They'd been flown to the States on a medical flight. The rest of the team was still recuperating in Holland.

Roger was in a wheelchair. The doctors had advised him that it would be weeks before he could get out of it, and even then he'd need several months of further treatment. Will's injury had done less damage, though he was on crutches and would subsequently need a walking stick for a month or two. But nothing was going to stop them from being here.

The CIA Director of Intelligence moved around the boardroom within CIA headquarters, picked up a phone, and glanced at Patrick. "You guys ready?"

Patrick smiled as he looked at his men. "You bet we are."

The director pressed numbers, held the handset to his mouth, and muttered, "Grab the bastards from their offices. Do it fast. Make sure we have a minimum of eight guards outside the boardroom to take them away after it's done." He replaced the handset. "They're on their way."

Five minutes later, Tibor, Damien, Lawrence, and Marcus were escorted into the room by burly security men. The Flintlock officers' expensive suits were ruffled, their faces flushed. Tibor looked angrily at the director. "What the hell's going on?"

"Sit down and shut up!"

The men were forced into seats, facing Will and Roger across the table. The director and Patrick sat next to the Spartan Section operatives.

Like Roger, Will was wearing an expensive suit. It had been agonizing to get into it, but he wanted to look the part. He lifted one of his crutches and slammed it down on the table with sufficient force to make the Flintlock officers flinch. "My name is Will Cochrane. It doesn't bother me to share that information with you, because where you're going you're not going to have a soul to talk to for the rest of your lives. What does bother me is that your actions killed a loved one, and that you tried to have me killed in order to cover up the fact that you sold out Yevtushenko's work for the CIA to Rübner just so you could keep getting his intelligence."

Tibor interjected, "Now, wait a minute . . ."

"Keep your fucking mouth shut, you little shit!" Will stared at each man. "Your treachery has given you life imprisonment with zero chance for parole. Every second you have in the facility will be hell. And it's going to be made worse by something I'm about to tell you that you don't know. Rübner was deliberately planted in New York so that people like you could approach him. But he was no longer working for Mossad. Instead he was working for a private individual who desperately wanted to identify a serving SVR who was on the payroll of the CIA. You played right into his hands."

The director pointed at them. "We can forgive you for being taken for fools by Rübner and his boss, but handing over Yevtushenko's identity without SSCI approval is automatic big jail time." He glanced at Will before returning his stare to the Flintlock officers. "And jeopardizing the life and the family of our best intelligence officer means you're going to die in there."

The Flintlock officers looked ashen, petrified, and confused. Tibor said, "We . . . we can make amends. Make a public apology . . . Just let us go quietly."

Will lifted the crutch off the table and placed the end of it against Tibor's chest. "Your best hope is that one of the prison guards takes pity on you and slips you a length of rope."

FIFTY-SEVEN

Mikhail's face screwed up in pain as he put his feet onto the floor, grabbed his crutches, and forced his body out of the hospital bed. Though they would be distraught that he was injured, he hoped his wife, Diana, and their two girls, Tatyana and Yana, would laugh if they could see him now—wearing pajamas and slippers, his hair ruffled. He put some coins into a pocket and hobbled out of his room. A sweat broke out over his body as he tried to ignore the pain that was searing up his leg into the base of his spine.

He moved along the corridor, past rooms containing Mark, Laith, and Adam. Aside from medical staff and armed Dutch police officers, no one else was allowed in the hospital wing. The injured DSI operatives had been taken to another facility, where they were not only receiving treatment but also being questioned as to what had happened during the flight.

A nurse approached him, her expression quizzical and angry. In English, she said, "You shouldn't be walking. What are you doing?"

Mikhail stopped. "I need to call my family."

"You know what the police told you. No calls to . . ."

"The police," Mikhail said softly, his breathing labored, "are uncertain what to make of this situation and have put in place procedures that make no sense." He patted a hand against his leg. "We're hardly a threat to anyone."

"It's for your own protection."

Mikhail sighed, felt weary. "Please. I need to speak to my daughters."

The nurse looked unsure.

"I just want to tell them I'm okay."

She glanced over her shoulder toward the pay phone. The nearest cops were in the adjacent wing, out of sight of the phone. "Just your family?"

"Yes. I'll be quick."

The nurse smiled and nodded toward his crutches. "Not with those, you won't." Her smile vanished, was replaced by a look of authority. "Okay. But if anyone asks me, I'll deny we ever had this conversation."

She walked away, heading to the other men's rooms to check up on them.

Mikhail stood in front of the phone, tried to catch his breath. Glancing left and right, he saw the corridor was empty and inserted some coins into the unit. A man answered. Mikhail spoke a few words to him in Russian and waited. Diana came onto the line; his wife spoke to him for two minutes, her comments and tone ranging from anger, to fear, to delight. She passed the phone to Tatyana, who was cross and combative—it didn't bother Mikhail because these days the teenager was frequently like that. He told her he loved and missed her and that she was to help her mother as much as she could. The phone was handed to Yana.

His youngest daughter shouted, "Daddy, Daddy, Daddy!" and gushed her adoration for him. Then she adopted a stern voice and concluded, "It's wrong that you're not here."

After saying good-bye, he ended the call and stared at the key-pad. Though his family were used to the fact that he was frequently away from them while conducting overseas missions, under these cir-cumstances it *was* wrong that he wasn't there to look after them. His thoughts turned to Lenka Yevtushenko. Three days ago, he'd ordered his men to vacate the Saxony farmstead and move the Russian defec-tor to another location in Germany. He recalled Will's comment.

Let him go. He's got a woman and child to look after.

And his riposte.

I'll take him back to Russia to face not only the charge of stealing secret intelligence. He'll also stand trial for being a CIA agent.

He placed more coins into the machine, and his finger hovered over the keypad. What was he thinking? At first he wasn't sure. A gut instinct? If he was about to break SVR rules, he had to do so with something more concrete than a hunch. He thought for a moment, nodded, and began pressing numbers.

Why?

Because if he punished Yevtushenko, he'd also be punishing his family. Cochrane had known from the outset that even if everything else in the mission was a failure, reuniting a foolish but decent man with his partner and daughter would be a good outcome. Mikhail now understood that.

He spoke to one of his assets, heard the man try to argue with him, told him to shut up, and gave him very precise instructions to transport Yevtushenko to Belarus within the next few days. "Keep him in hiding, away from Minsk for a month or two. I'm going to tell my superiors that we found him dead at the farmstead, but they may still check his lover's address during the next few weeks. But they'll soon get bored and move on to other matters."

His last call would be to Will Cochrane.

FIFTY-EIGHT

Stefan looked at the food his wife had laid out on the kitchen table and beamed. *Kartoffelsuppe, kalbsrouladen, spargel,* and *kartoffel*—one of his favorite meals. He poured his wife a glass of spätburgunder red wine and looked at Wendell and Mathias. "Tuck in, boys, before Daddy eats it all."

The twins piled food onto their plates and began eating with smiles on their faces.

His wife gently squeezed Stefan's hand and began serving him. "How was the conference, my dear?"

Stefan laughed. "It was as riveting as watching paint dry." He swallowed soup and exclaimed, "Ooh, that's good!"

Wendell asked, "What story are you going to tell us today?"

Stefan ate more food and thought for a moment. "You remember I told you about the giant earthworm that lives in the Black Forest?"

"Yes! *Lumbricus badensis.*"

Stefan nodded. "It's cruel and smart. But it has a weakness."

"What is it?"

"The worm has no honor."

"But that doesn't matter, Daddy, because it's the most dangerous creature in the forest."

Stefan sliced into his veal. "Honor matters enormously. There is one creature in the forest that's much more dangerous than the worm *and* has honor. Would you like me to tell you the story of when the worm met this creature?"

His boys nodded eagerly while filling their mouths with more delicious food.

Stefan smiled. "Once upon a time, there were three bad woodsmen who gathered in the Black Forest to discuss their desire to gain wealth and power. They decided the best way to achieve this was to cut down all of the forest's most ancient and valuable trees and sell the wood. All of them agreed that it had to be done in secret; that they would be severely punished if anyone found out what they were doing. But a songbird overheard them and flew away to tell good woodsmen about the plot. The bad woodsmen tried to shoot the bird, but they missed. Determined not to let the bird ruin their plans, they went deeper into the forest, lit torches, and entered one of the vast tunnels that led to the giant earthworm's lair. They were terrified of the worm but knew that it was the only creature that could help them. Upon entering the lair, they saw the worm feasting on dead cattle. Its red eyes were staring at the woodsmen. The eldest woodsman stepped forward and told the worm that they would give it ten dead cows if it could kill the songbird before he spoke to the other woodsmen. The worm laughed, slithered close to them, and bared its enormous blood-stained fangs. The smell of its rancid breath filled the cavern as it told the men that it could only kill things on land. At first, the men didn't know what to do. Then one of them had an idea and told the worm that they would pay it twenty dead cows if it could find a creature that could kill the bird. The worm considered this. The dead cows would make its body even bigger and stronger. It agreed and told the men to leave before it changed its mind and bit off their heads."

Mathias popped the end of a piece of asparagus into his mouth, bit it in half, held the stem out, and grinned. "Like this."

"Use your knife and fork please, Mathias." Stefan took a sip of his wine. "Now, the worm knew that it would have to find a very special creature to hunt down and kill the songbird. Only one such creature lived in the forest. Do you know what it was?"

The boys shook their heads, wide eyed.

"Most of the forest's inhabitants thought the creature didn't exist, that he was a myth. But the worm knew different. That night, it used its tunnels to slither to the base of the Feldberg, which as you know is the Black Forest's highest mountain. It broke through the soil and took all night to reach the mountain summit. Standing there, watching the entire forest, was the eagle king."

"You've never told us about the eagle king, Daddy!"

"That's because he's a secret. And both of you must swear to me that you'll never tell anyone about his existence."

The boys nodded quickly, desperate to hear more of the story.

Stefan pretended to look serious. "Very well. The eagle king was *the* most deadly creature in not only the Black Forest, but also all the lands around it. He loathed the giant earthworm and wondered if he should rip its body in half. The worm could see that the eagle had anger in his eyes, so spoke quickly, telling the king that it would pay him ten cows if he could kill the songbird. The eagle placed one of his huge talons close to the worm's eyes, and told it that he would do the job only if he was given five cows in advance. The worm agreed and slithered away quickly, knowing that the eagle was the only creature that had the power to kill him."

Stefan stuck his fork through a potato. "After the cows were delivered to him, the eagle flew down from the mountain summit and scoured the vast forest. It took him three days to spot the songbird flying north toward the edge of the forest. But to his surprise, as he approached it he was attacked by a younger eagle. It turned out that the good woodsmen had received news that the songbird was coming to them with important information and had sent out their best eagle to protect the songbird. They fought, but the younger eagle was no match for the king. He fell to the ground, injured, and the eagle king swooped on the songbird, gripping his neck between his razor-sharp claws. The songbird thought he was going to kill him, but instead the eagle asked him why the worm wanted him dead. The songbird told him about the bad woodsmen's intention to cut down a large part of the forest and that he was trying to warn others about it." Stefan paused, looking at each son. "You see, the eagle king was cleverer than the worm. He knew it was evil and would have bad reasons for wanting the songbird dead. That's why he'd demanded that he be given five cows in advance. And unlike the worm, the eagle king was wise and honorable and only killed other creatures if it was absolutely necessary to do so. He could never kill a creature who was trying to protect his beloved forest. So he released the songbird and told him to fly fast to the good woodsmen. The songbird reached them and told them what he'd overheard. Hundreds of men picked up their axes and entered the forest to kill the bad woodsmen." Stefan smiled as he finished his meal. "And that is the end of our story."

Wendell frowned. "That can't be the end."

"Why not?"

Mathias shook his head, knowing his twin brother's thoughts. "The young eagle wouldn't be injured if the giant earthworm hadn't been so bad."

Wendell wasn't happy. "And the eagle king needs to say sorry for hurting the younger eagle." An idea came to him. "The best way he can do that is to find the worm and allow the younger eagle to kill it."

Stefan held his knife in midair and stared at nothing.

Speaking more to himself while nodding slowly, Kronos whispered, "You're right."

FIFTY-NINE

Patrick rang the doorbell of the London safe house and glanced at Will. "You been here before?"

Will nodded. It was the Pimlico property he'd visited after the fiasco in Gdansk. The elderly housekeeper opened the door, looked at Will's crutches, and said in a haughty voice, "Try not to damage the carpet with those things."

They entered the Regency house and moved into the tastefully decorated living room. Alistair was there, flicking through TV channels, wearing his favorite three-piece suit and Royal Navy tie. The MI6 controller frowned. "How long are you going to be on those things?"

Will awkwardly removed the crutches from his armpits and slumped into an armchair. "The doctors want me to switch to a walking stick tomorrow."

Alistair continued flicking through channels, checked his watch, and muttered, "I can't afford for you to be idle for too long. There's plenty more work out there."

"Thanks for your concern. You think the Spartan Section's got a future?"

"We'll see." He found a news channel filming a reporter standing outside the International Criminal Court in The Hague. "Here we go."

Nikolai Dmitriev tried to control his breathing and force his body to relax. He'd waited a long time for this moment. The last thing the old man needed was a bout of nerves. After uncrossing his legs, he adjusted the knot on his tie and smoothed his frail hands over his suit. Armed police were all around him in the court's secure waiting area. No one else was allowed in here, not even court officials. He stayed motionless, his back ramrod straight, staring at nothing as he mentally recited the statement he was to make.

Dutch cops started shouting in an orderly fashion. One of them placed a hand on his shoulder and said, "It's time."

Dmitriev stood and followed officers out of the room, down bare corridors, and then into a large room containing men, women, tables, chairs, microphones, and cameras.

The courtroom.

All eyes were on him as he was guided to a stand to take the oath. Upon completion, he sat at a table that held a microphone and a glass of water. Facing him on the other side of the room were nine officials, including the court's president and chief prosecutor.

The prosecutor leaned toward his microphone. "Mr. Dmitriev. Do you understand that this is a hearing, a chance for you to supply us with your statement? It is not a trial."

Dmitriev nodded. "Yes, I understand."

"Good. If your statement warrants subsequent criminal proceedings, those trials will be held either here or in other relevant jurisdictions." The prosecutor glanced at the president, who nodded at him. He returned his attention to Dmitriev. "Please proceed."

The former KGB colonel withdrew a sheet of paper, placed reading spectacles on, and momentarily stared at the cameras, knowing that his statement would be aired live to the world's media. It seemed to him ironic that a life lived in the shadows would lead to this. Holding the paper with a shaking hand, he cleared his throat, inhaled deeply, and read the statement.

"In 1995, I was a senior officer in Russia's foreign intelligence service, the Sluzhba Vneshney Razvedki. In December of that year, I was ordered to attend a secret meeting in Berlin. The others present at that meeting were Russian generals Leon Michurin and Alexander Tatlin, former East German Stasi colonel Kurt Schreiber, United States admiral Jack Dugan, CIA officer Thomas Scott, and American army general Joe Ballinger. The meeting was initiated by Kurt Schreiber and was authorized by the presidents of the United States and Russia.

"Our objective was to establish a set of military protocols for joint U.S.–Russian action against China, should the need ever arise to take action against the emerging superpower. These protocols would be stored in the relevant military headquarters in Russia and America, ready for use at a moment's notice."

Dmitriev took a sip of water, his heart beating fast.

"The American president believed that the joint military action would entail deployment of Russian conventional missiles from submarines located in the Philippine Sea and that their targets would be Chinese land-based missile sites. These strikes would be a warning to China, nothing more. American involvement would be deployment of its sophisticated interceptor missiles, sent from warships also located in the Philippine Sea, in order to stop Russia's missiles from being shot down before they reached their targets.

"However, Kurt Schreiber believed that China would never stop flexing its muscles simply as a result of strategic missile strikes. At the secret meeting, he argued that China needed to be shocked into submission. The others present at the meeting agreed with him. Various options were considered before it was decided that the best solution was a massive assault on China's civilian population. The Russian

missiles would not be conventional, instead they'd be carrying biological warheads. The American missiles would protect an act of
genocide."

The prosecutor interrupted him. "On what scale?"

Dmitriev felt sick. "The Russians would be targeting cities,
densely populated civilian areas. In one wave of strikes, we estimated
we could kill over one hundred million people."

"For the benefit of the court, repeat that number."

"One hundred million, probably much more."

The prosecutor looked unsettled and glanced at his colleagues.
"We've never judged a case like this. That amount of death is
unimaginable."

Dmitriev shook his head. "History shows that it is *very* imaginable."

The prosecutor wrote down notes. "Please clarify how the protocols can be enacted."

Dmitriev looked at each court official and saw fear and confusion
in their eyes. "If China becomes a threat, the Russian and American
premiers speak. They instruct their generals to dust off the protocols.
Within four days of that, Russian submarines will be in the Philippine Sea. Above them will be U.S. destroyers. Russian biological warheads will be deployed to Beijing, Shanghai, Hong Kong, and other
cities. American interceptor missiles will shoot down any Chinese
resistance. Simple." Dmitriev read the end of his statement. "For the
record, and to be absolutely clear on this, the American president had
no knowledge of the agreement to use biological weapons. There is no
reference to them in the protocols, they merely state that Russia will
use conventional weapons. Subsequent U.S. presidents and generals
who picked up the protocols would assume the same: America would
be helping Russia to conduct a surgical, conventional strike against
select military targets, not collude in genocide."

The prosecutor was writing notes. He stopped and looked up.
"What about the Russian president of the day? Did he know that
secretly Russia would be deploying biological warheads?"

Dmitriev nodded. "Yes, but you have to understand that this was our final solution, one that we all hoped would never be used. And the only reason he never mentioned it to his American counterpart is that we told him that if he did so, the Americans would tear up their copy of the protocols. But . . ."—Dmitriev rubbed his wet eyes—". . . things have changed. Dugan is now a senator, has the ear of the president, and has been put in charge of a political think tank—independent of Congress, the military, and other agencies—with the remit to analyze current strategic threats to the United States and provide creative solutions to combat those threats. He's employed his former colleagues Joe Ballinger and Thomas Scott. The three of them will persuade the U.S. president that China is our biggest long-term threat and propose the protocols drawn up at the Berlin meeting should be enacted."

"Do the protocols have a name?"

Dmitriev nodded, feeling like a weight had been lifted from his shoulders. "The protocols are called Slingshot."

Alistair clapped his hands, turned off the television, and spun around to face Will. "Excellent! Your starting point was merely a scrap of paper and you pursued it to this. Bloody brilliant." He pulled out his cell phone. "The prime minister will have watched the hearing, and I'm getting you in front of him. You'll get a knighthood."

Will shook his head, pushed himself off the seat, and put the crutches in place. "If it's okay with you, I'd rather not."

"You have better things to do with your time?"

"Actually, yes."

Alistair looked furious. "God, you're an obstinate so-and-so." The MI6 Controller suddenly burst out laughing and pointed a finger toward Will. "But you've given the section a future. No one's going to dare to touch us now."

Will hobbled away from the coheads, then stopped and turned. "What will happen to Dugan and the others?"

Patrick answered, "Could be life imprisonment, but I'm guessing this will be a death penalty situation." The CIA officer looked solemn. "They've duped numerous American presidents and could have sucked us into a world war."

"It would have been war, and China would have had the moral high ground." Will tried to imagine the devastation caused by the biological attack against China, and the hundreds of millions of innocent people who would have suffered agonizing deaths. "China's a problem, but not on this scale. Idiots keep trying to identify the bad guys and start wars. It undoes everything we do." He lifted one of his crutches and pointed it at his coheads. "Are you making progress on locating Schreiber?"

"He's a marked man now. Every Western intelligence agency and law enforcement unit is on alert."

"Are you closing in on him?"

Alistair sighed. "He's vanished. Any leads we had to him are now dead."

Will lowered his crutch, shook his head, and felt like shit. "Schreiber's got to be found." He thought about everything Schreiber had done, his cold and brilliant brutality, his threats against Will's people, his success. "Every fucking Western intelligence and law enforcement agency is out of its depth."

"Without you we . . ."

"Without me you should be better."

"William, don't take that tone with your superiors."

"My superiors?" Will thought about Betty. "Fuck you. Fuck it." He turned, hobbled away, and said, "Why is it always up to me?"

SIXTY

Suzy sat at her desk in Langley and switched on her computer. Around her were hundreds of other CIA analysts; the place resembled the trading floor of a large investment bank rather than the brains of the Agency. She felt tired, knew that it was merely due to a stage in her pregnancy, and wondered if the boy or girl in her womb felt the same way. Boy or girl? It mattered to the section's men, because money was resting on the outcome. Damn fools. She picked up the book Will had bought her: *Work & Pregnancy: Have a Life, Have a Kid.*

For the first time, she opened it and started flicking through the pages. She frowned as she saw that most of the pages had pencil notes in the margins; passages of text were underlined or circled.

She recognized Adam's handwriting. *Herbal teas with antioxidant properties are great in the second trimester.*

And Roger's. *Iron-rich foods can be found in unexpected places like kids' cereals.*

In one section, Mark had written, *Check this out—good exercise routine for Suzy.*

And at the back of the book, Laith had written a shopping list of baby items, each exactly priced. The total cost was twelve hundred dollars, the value of the sweepstakes.

She closed the book, deep in thought. Why did her pregnancy matter so much to the operatives? They were killers, not gentle men. She turned to her screen and began trawling through the titles of dozens of telegrams, many from the Agency's overseas stations. She stopped on one and opened it up.

**MI6 OFFICER FOUND FROZEN TO DEATH,
CAUSE OF DEATH NOT SUSPICIOUS**

Oh dear God. Peter Rhodes. Should she tell Will? She supposed he'd find out soon enough. But she didn't need to be the one to tell him that his act of kindness had turned out to be a death sentence. Anyway, she didn't know if she'd be able to break the news to him without shedding a tear, and she made it a personal rule to *never* cry in front of colleagues, especially men. They always misunderstood what it meant.

She placed a hand over the book and sighed. The team didn't mind if her baby was a boy or a girl. What did matter to them was that a new life was coming into the world, and they had to support her with that process.

Maybe because the men believed that in some small way they were giving something back to humanity.

SIXTY-ONE

That evening, Will entered the ground-floor communal entrance to his West Square home, looked at the stairs, and wondered how he'd manage the two flights to reach his third-floor apartment. The crutches were severely pissing him off; he hadn't even been able to buy groceries for his dinner, as he had no way to carry them.

The door to the ground-floor apartment opened. Retired major Dickie Mountjoy stepped into the corridor. The former Coldstream Guards officer was about to make a brisk walk to the Army & Navy Club in central London's Pall Mall. He did so at precisely the same time every weekday evening, and once at the club would socialize with other ex-guardsmen. Never former infantry officers, and heaven forbid anyone who'd spent their career at sea. It was Wednesday, so this evening he'd partake in a drop of sherry, then lamb hotpot with vegetables, followed by a glass of port. Then he'd march home so that he was back in time for the ten o'clock news and a cup of cocoa while completing the *Telegraph* crossword.

Sporting a pencil mustache and wearing a camel overcoat, immaculately pressed trousers, and Church's shoes that had been polished to the standard required of parade grounds, the old soldier looked at Will with disdain. In the same tone he no doubt would have used when dressing down a new recruit, he asked, "How'd you do that then?"

Will tried to appear embarrassed. "I went for a jog along the Thames; broke my ankle stepping off the curb."

Major Mountjoy jabbed the tip of his rolled umbrella against the wooden flooring. "You've spent too long behind a desk. Civvies like you become a liability when it suddenly occurs to them to get some exercise under their belt."

Will smiled. "Maybe you could give me a military exercise regime. It might knock some shape into me."

Mountjoy huffed. "Bit late for that. Best you get back to flogging more of that dodgy life insurance to upright people like me."

"It's not dodgy."

"It damn right is, Sunny Jim. My Agnes saved every spare penny to set us up for retirement. During her last weeks, you bastards didn't pay out a thing and we had to use all of our savings to make her comfortable before the end."

The widower swept his umbrella up, so that it was perpendicular under his armpit, and strode out of the property.

"Shit, shit, shit!" David the mortician was running down the stairs as fast as his flabby body would allow. Food stains and loose cigarette tobacco were on his sweater. "Another bloody call-out." The divorcé ran past Will, glancing at his injury. "Don't let it get infected; otherwise you could be visiting my mortuary."

As the front door slammed behind David, Will began the painful and slow ascent of the stairs. It took him two minutes to make the first flight. Breathing fast, he reached out to grab a handrail, and when he did so one of his crutches crashed to the floor. Cursing, he picked it up and fixed it back into position.

Phoebe opened her door and looked at him with concern. "Poor darling."

Will gave her the story about the jogging accident.

The thirty-something art dealer was dressed to kill, which usually meant she'd be going out to watch a middleweight boxing match somewhere in town. She took a sip of her champagne. "You want me to help you up the stairs?"

Will looked at her six-inch heels and smiled. "I think we *both* might struggle with that."

Phoebe wagged a finger. "Us girls are used to it, darling."

"It's okay, I'll manage. Are you picking up a Chinese takeout tonight?"

"Of course, but not until after the fight. You want me to get you some?"

"That would be very kind."

Phoebe placed a hand on her hip, striking a sexy pose. "You suggesting we make a night of it?"

Will laughed. "I think you'd be picking the wrong guy for that. It's been an exhausting few weeks, I'll probably be asleep by nine. If you could leave the takeout outside my door, I'll settle up with you in the morning."

"Nonsense. You can return the favor and cook me a meal one evening."

Will lied, "My cooking's dreadful. Tell you what, though— David's a great cook, and he's in need of some company. I bet he'd be delighted if you knocked on his door one evening."

Phoebe considered this. "He's not my normal type, although . . . that might not be a bad thing. But what about you? When you're here, you always seem to be on your own."

Will blew her a kiss. "I'm used to it." As he continued hobbling up the stairs, he called out, "Szechuan chicken with noodles, if they have it."

He entered his apartment and was immediately struck by the changes to the place. He limped through the hallway, past the bedrooms that now contained new lamps, Egyptian cotton bedding, framed drawings, and new paint on the wardrobes and chests of drawers. He smiled as he stared at the living room. Joanna had done an incredible job. Everything had been unpacked and carefully positioned to add contours, depth, and different dimensions to the room. His antiquities were prominent but cleverly located to match the different styles and colors within the place.

It looked like a real home.

He picked up his German lute, sat on the sofa's arm, and rested the instrument on his injured leg. Quietly, he began playing Bach's Lute Suite No. 1 in E minor, while continuing to take in his surroundings.

His front door buzzed, meaning someone was outside the communal downstairs entrance. Probably David had suddenly realized he'd left without his keys, a usual occurrence. Will placed his instrument down, picked up the intercom handset. "Yes?"

A woman answered. Will hesitated, then buzzed her in.

One minute later, Sarah was standing before him in his living room. "What happened?"

"I got shot, doesn't matter."

Sarah recalled Alfie's comment about Will's line of work. "One day, a bullet's going to hit you in a place where it *does* matter."

"Probably." He looked at her. "Why are you here?"

"James and I are moving to Edinburgh in two days' time. Our law firm's secured us a fully furnished house in the country."

Will's heart skipped a beat. "That's great." He smiled. "When can I come and visit?"

Sarah broke his gaze, looked uncomfortable. "Betty told me what you do for a living."

"Did she, now?" Will sighed. "Perhaps she was right to do so."

"Maybe." Her lower lip trembled, face flushed, trying to hold back tears. "I thought about it, told myself that maybe it changed things knowing that your job required you to do something . . ." She frowned, trying to think of the right word. "*Noble*." She wiped her face with the back of her hand, now looked angry. "But there's nothing *noble* about seeing three men burst into a house and put bullets into a woman's head!"

"Sarah, that wasn't my—"

"Fault?" She pointed at him. "Then whose fault was it?"

Will was silent, felt wretched.

"Whose bloody fault?"

He opened his mouth, but no words came out.

"I was right next to her when it happened. Her blood was all over . . ." She looked at the palms of her hands and rubbed them against her skirt. "You've made your choices, Will, just as I've made mine. James and I don't want you in Scotland. We don't want you anywhere near us!"

As Will watched her storm out of his home while crying loudly, tears rolled down his own cheeks. As he'd predicted in the Dutch hospital, Schreiber had killed his relationship with the last remaining member of his family.

SIXTY-TWO

Six weeks later, Will stripped out of his sweat-drenched tracksuit, turned on the shower, and walked quickly to his front door as he heard the mail drop onto the mat. He'd been checking his mail every day in the vain hope that Sarah had written to him, changing her mind about him coming to visit. In his heart, he knew that it was false hope, but the notion had kept him going during the preceding weeks of recuperation and physiotherapy. His leg was now fully healed, and a week ago he'd been able to start going for daily early-morning runs.

He leafed through the mail, then froze. An envelope that had no stamp or address on it, merely his full name written in ink.

Another letter from Kurt Schreiber?

The psychopath was still loose; no agency had been able to trace his whereabouts.

He tore open the envelope and withdrew a sheet of paper.

It's taken me some time, but I've found him. Are you fully fit? You'd better be, because I'm gifting you the opportunity to

obtain justice. Timings must be precise. 1200 hrs GMT on the day
after tomorrow. But be very careful. His place is heavily guarded.
I'll be watching over you and will help where I can. Address
overleaf. Do not approach from the north side or I will not be
able to see you.

Will turned the sheet over. A location and grid reference for an
isolated mountain residence on the German-Austrian border, and a
cell phone number. His heart beat fast as he pulled out his phone and
called Alfie Mayne. "Please, can you meet me?"

After he ended the call, he stared at the letter again. He wondered
if it was another of Schreiber's tricks—to lure him to a place where
he could easily be killed. No. There were easier places for Schreiber's
men to attack him, and he certainly wouldn't give Will a date and a
time for such an assault.

The man who'd written this note had meant what he said.

Will knew exactly who he was.

Kronos.

Two hours later, Will was in Highgate Cemetery. He was very familiar with the famous nineteenth-century graveyard, having been here
often, and walked confidently through the eerie place of the dead,
along narrow twisting paths, between gnarled trees, past gravestones
wrapped in vines and covered in moss, through the tunnel of the
Egyptian Avenue and past the Circle of Lebanon and the grave of
Karl Marx.

He looked at the sky and saw that dark rain clouds were beginning
to take over. Spots of rain began to hit him as he continued onward,
pulling up the collar of his overcoat, moving toward a section of the
cemetery that held no residents of any particular interest or notoriety.
The rain became heavy.

He walked onward for twenty yards and stopped in front of a

small headstone. Alfie was standing next to it, dressed in the same ill-fitting suit he'd worn when he'd helped Will collect Sarah from her home, one hand clutching flowers wrapped in sodden paper. He'd shaved his face an hour ago with his favorite cutthroat razor; bits of tissue were stuck to areas he'd accidentally cut. The former soldier nodded toward the grave. "You did me proud, son, getting my missus a place in here."

Will looked at Betty's grave. "I don't think I have any pride left."

Alfie momentarily glanced at the MI6 officer. "Can't think that way."

Will crouched down and smoothed fingers over the inscription on the brand-new headstone.

MY BETTY. FINALLY GRABBING A BIT OF REST.

Quietly, he muttered, "Too many die because of me."

Alfie placed a hand on Will's shoulder. "Betty wasn't one of 'em. She was doing a job. Always loved workin', she did. Always loved . . ."

Will stood and looked at Alfie, who was fighting his emotions. "Why didn't you have a service?"

"Letters, matey. Would've had to write bleedin' letters to the family and the like. Hate writing. Plus"—he awkwardly bowed down and placed the flowers on Betty's grave—"well, you know, I just wanted a bit of quiet with her. On my own. Just her and me, like it was when we were on honeymoon in Blackpool in the seventies."

"I'm sorry. I shouldn't have met you here. I'm intruding."

Alfie gestured to the grave next to Betty's. "You've as much right to be here as I do." He smiled, though the look was bitter. "I wonder what they'd think of us, standing over them."

Rainwater ran over Will's face. "Maybe they'd want us to join them sometime soon."

"You want that?"

"They'd make sure we kept on the straight and narrow."

"And cook us a nice meal." Alfie nodded slowly. "Yeah. Reckon we should both join 'em soon. We'll fuck up if we stay here."

The two men were silent for a minute.

"What are you going to do now?"

"Keep workin'. Can't stop and think." Alfie placed a filterless cigarette in the corner of his mouth, struck a match, and lit it. "Trouble is, I'm retired." He removed the cigarette, covered its embers with his hand to stop the rain from extinguishing it, and placed it alongside the flowers. "There we go, my petal. You always liked a couple of cheeky drags on my cigarettes."

Smoke wafted up from the grave for a few seconds before the cigarette became saturated and dead.

Alfie turned away from the grave. "Betty would probably say something like, 'Revenge will give you indigestion—get on with other stuff.' Bet she'd be right, but trouble is I can't think of anything else. I want the bastard who did this."

Will stared at the old SAS warrior, now retiree. He hesitated, then sighed. "I know where he is."

Alfie's eyes narrowed.

"I'm going to try to kill him."

Alfie took a step toward Will. "And I'm going to help you."

Will lowered his head. Alfie's predictable response had prompted overwhelming sadness within him. "It's going to be hard."

Between gritted teeth, Alfie spat, "You think, *sunshine,* these old bones ain't up for the task?"

Will was silent. Though Alfie was a foot shorter than Will, the MI6 officer knew that the broad ex-soldier still had enough power to punch him off his feet.

"Do you reckon Betty would like me to sit around watchin' bloody daytime TV while you're going after the bastard? After . . . after . . ." His lips trembled. ". . . after what they did to her . . . her face . . . cookin' and the like?" Tears rolled down his face. "Cookin' like her lovely breakfasts. Oh, Jesus!"

Will placed two hands on Alfie's arms.

Alfie shook his head wildly, more tears running down the tough man's face. "Get yer hands off me, you poofter."

But Will held him firm. "It's okay, Alfie. Okay."

Alfie shrugged his arms away, his voice quavering as he said, "No, it ain't okay, son. It's bleedin' nothing like okay."

"I know. That's why I told you."

Alfie exhaled slowly and reengaged eye contact with Will. "You want me to come with you?"

"Yes."

"And that's why you told me?"

"Yes."

"Testing me? Just like selection?"

"Of course. A test to see how you reacted. Just like your old SAS selection interrogation exercises." Will had no idea if what he was saying was the right thing, he was taking his lead from Alfie, though he knew in his heart one absolute truth: Alfie deserved to be there when he had Schreiber in his sights.

"Did I pass?"

Will smiled, felt utter compassion for his comrade-in-arms. "I know your bones still have what it takes. But there's no going back. We'll be walking into an armed fortress."

Alfie asked, "You bringing other men?"

Will shook his head. "If I tell Alistair and Patrick what I know, they'll instruct me to bring the bastard in for a trial, though privately both section heads would prefer me to put a bullet in his head. But this has escalated; the premiers of America, the U.K., and Russia want this dealt with through a judicial process. A show trial. Alistair and Patrick will lose their jobs if I tell them I'm on a kill job. I can't put them in that position."

"You must have men you trust who'll keep their mouths shut."

Will thought about Roger, Laith, Mark, and Adam. "Yes, but they were badly injured by Kronos. Worse than me. They're still recuperating. There's no one else, apart from you, Joanna, and Robert, but I can't involve those two because . . ."

"Yeah. They definitely ain't got the bones for it." Alfie's voice strengthened. "This chap, Kronos—you going to try to take him on too?"

"No. I doubt I'd win. Plus, he's the one who's helping us."

Alfie glanced at Betty's grave and the grave next to it. "Then we keep this . . . private. In any case, don't need help from other blokes. Never have." He smiled. "Sorry, ladies, and please excuse my language: we're about to fuck up again."

Will looked at the grave next to Betty's.

His mother's grave.

What *would* she think if she could see him now? Would she be angry, sad, proud, all of those things? He didn't know. She'd died at a time when he was still a carefree boy who'd never given her any cause to worry about him—he'd excelled at school, had been a committed member of its orchestra, was in those days always smiling, was sometimes awkward in adult company but no more than most teenagers, liked to cook for her, and was never spiteful to his sister. His mother hadn't been given the chance to know how she'd fare with a more troublesome Will Cochrane.

"In forty-eight hours we need to be in Germany. I'll get the weapons. At midday, we need to make the assault. After that," Will said, nodding, "maybe Mum and Betty will cook us that nice meal."

SIXTY-THREE

Two days later, Kronos clambered up the ever-steepening mountainside. Deep snow covered the Bavarian mountain and the rest of the Alps; the sky was clear and blue, making the surroundings visually stunning. But the German assassin had no care for the mountain range's beauty; instead he was totally focused on reaching the place where he could observe from a distance Kurt Schreiber's mountaintop residence.

Strapped to his back was a case containing a Barrett M82 .50-caliber antimateriel sniper rifle. As a highly proficient mountaineer, Kronos could have taken a shorter route by ascending one of the range's more severe mountain faces, but he couldn't take the risk of making such an ascent and potentially damaging the weapon in the process. He'd therefore selected a path that for the most part enabled him to walk rather than climb. But that meant his journey was much longer. So far he'd covered twelve miles on foot. He had another mile to go.

He thought about his regular walks up one of the Black Forest's mountains with his twin sons. They loved their outings with their father, though they frequently complained of fatigue as they neared the summit. Now that the DLB had been used, he'd choose another mountain in the forest for them to climb each week. Maybe a higher one. His boys were ready for a new challenge, and though he would never push them too hard, he would continue to ensure that they received regular, healthy exercise—even if they whined about it. He wondered what they'd be saying to him if they were by his side right now. Smiling, he pictured having to carry them in his arms until they could find a nice spot to have one of their mother's delicious picnics.

His smile faded.

Forget what they would *say* to him.

What would they *think* if they could see him now, moving purposefully toward a place where he intended to kill many men?

To them, he was a strict but loving and fun father who did nothing more exciting than teaching history at their local school. And that was all they wanted from him. His mundane life made them feel secure and loved, and his dinnertime stories were more than enough adventure for their little minds. They wouldn't want him to be going out and actually enacting dangerous situations similar to those presented in his tales.

They'd be horrified if they could see him now, and rightly so.

That thought made him feel terribly guilty.

For the sake of his family, he made a pledge that today would be his last adventure.

Will drove the car off the deserted track and into a forest clearing, stopped the vehicle at the base of one of the Bavarian Alps, and looked at Alfie. "This is as far as we can drive before we're spotted on the mountain road."

Alfie withdrew a map from the glove compartment, opened it, and studied it for the fifth time that day. "Five miles up the single-track road, route snakes like crazy so we're gonna get a bit of cover, but

elevation moves from zero to two thousand yards, so there's gonna be
a lot of times we're exposed."

Will pulled out a single sheet from his jacket and handed it to
Alfie. "Hardly tells us anything, but for what it's worth, that's an aerial shot of the place."

Alfie unfolded the paper and stared at the photo of Schreiber's
residence. "Big property, only one road in and out, fuck-off big drop
on three sides of the property, so Schreiber's got nowhere to run. You
get this from NSA or GCHQ?"

Will shook his head. "Google Earth."

"What the bleedin' 'ell is that?"

"Never mind." He exited the vehicle, strode to the trunk, and
opened it. Alfie joined him. Both men were dressed in white ski jackets, trousers, and hiking boots—clothes that would give them some
degree of concealment as well as protection from the subzero temperature. He unzipped a bag and withdrew two Heckler & Koch MP5
submachine guns, two USP .45 Tactical pistols and thigh holsters, and
body harnesses containing spare magazines.

"Flash bangs?"

Will shook his head. "I couldn't get any stun grenades at such
short notice."

"Shit! We ain't gonna get anywhere near Schreiber without 'em."

Will looked away toward the mountains. "Kronos knows that his
best use to us is as a long-range sniper. He'll be out there somewhere.
With him, we stand a chance of getting close."

"Maybe, but you're forgetting one thing, son."

"What?"

Alfie pointed at the aerial shot of Schreiber's residence. "To get
through the walls and still stand a chance of taking off a target's head,
he'll be using high-velocity rounds—I reckon fifty caliber. We'll be on
our arses if one of those things even scratches us."

"Kronos is an expert shot. He won't miss his targets and accidentally hit us."

Alfie strapped the holster to his thigh, inserted the pistol, donned the magazine harness over his jacket, and gripped his submachine gun. "When we're in the building, and it all goes to rat shit, there's every chance he'll mistake us for two of Schreiber's men. It's the fact that he's an expert shot that worries me."

Kronos walked fast over the plateau at the mountain summit, ducked low as he neared the top of the valley, unstrapped his rifle case, went prone, and crawled forward over the snow. He rolled onto one side, opened the case, and assembled the working parts of the devastatingly powerful rifle. Extending the barrel's bipod, he positioned the weapon so that it was facing the valley, stuck five spare ten-round magazines in the snow next to the gun, rolled back onto his stomach, gripped the rifle, and looked though its X26-XLR long-range thermal scope. Eighteen hundred yards away from him, on the other side of the two-thousand-yard-deep valley, was Schreiber's residence. Built at the beginning of the eighteenth century, the Romanesque-style house had two towers positioned over a white asymmetrical building containing gables, numerous windows, a slate roof, and mock archery slots. The place resembled a small castle, though it had only ever been a private residence for wealthy businessmen, politicians, and artists.

Now, it was home to an evil man.

On the north, south, and west sides of the residence were sheer limestone drops that extended to the base of the undulating forested valley and its glistening lake. To the east, a single-track road snaked down a gradually descending ridge. That was the only way to reach Schreiber's place by vehicle. But Cochrane would be crazy to approach the residence from that direction. Too exposed. Instead, he'd be making a commando assault by scaling one of the two-thousand-yard-high vertical rock faces. Kronos wondered how many men would be accompanying him. At least ten, he decided. Probably more.

• • •

Will slammed the vehicle's trunk shut, glanced at his watch, checked that his harness and leg holster were firmly in place, and held his submachine gun in one hand. "It's time."

Alfie took a last drag on his cigarette, flicked it away, took a step toward the mountain path, then stopped. "Thank you."

"What for?"

"For bringing me along."

Will smiled. "I needed all the help I could get."

"Maybe. But another thing struck me about that Google Earth thingy. If you were on yer own, or with blokes half my age, you'd be scaling the mountain to get to the bastard rather than"—he pointed at the five-mile road leading to Schreiber's mountain residence— "making this suicide run."

"Alfie, I . . ."

"It's alright, sunshine." Alfie grinned, his eyes moist. "You don't need to say anything." He thrust out his hand.

Will gripped it firmly.

They nodded at each other.

Both knowing that there truly was nothing more to be said.

They put the butts of their guns into their shoulders.

And moved up the mountain road.

Kronos kept scouring the rock inclines for signs of men in white arctic-warfare clothing, using ropes and other equipment to scale the mountain. But he saw nothing. He wondered if Cochrane had ignored his instruction not to use the north face. Perhaps the MI6 officer wanted to assault the castle without being seen by Kronos, for fear that Kronos had other motives for luring him here and would easily pick off him and his men. But that didn't make any sense.

He returned his attention to Schreiber's residence. Since 1995, he'd monitored the movement of all of the men present at the Berlin meeting. Schreiber was the canniest of them all: constantly changing locations within Europe, buying new properties to live in, sometimes purchasing properties with no intention of staying there. None of his bases were listed under his own name; instead they'd been bought using one of his numerous aliases or one of his cover companies. But the manifold layers of subterfuge hadn't prevented Kronos from establishing Schreiber's various locations. Some of those places were still under observation by SVR operatives who worked for Mikhail Salkov. But they didn't know about this place. No one did, apart from him and Will Cochrane.

He checked his watch. 1210 hours. Was Cochrane late? Not coming at all?

He checked his cell phone. It was the number he'd given Cochrane. No missed calls or messages.

He squinted through the thermal scope and moved the gun inch by inch to the right.

He froze.

Two men.

Halfway up the mountain road.

On foot.

Carrying guns.

The big man was Cochrane.

The other man was . . .

Twice his age.

Urgently he moved his scope right and left, searching for other men. Nothing.

Between gritted teeth, the German assassin muttered, "You mad, mad men."

Anger flashed across Kurt Schreiber's face as one of his guards burst into his vast living room. "You're supposed to knock!"

The man shook his head, was breathless, looked agitated. "Mr. Schreiber. Two men, halfway up the mountain path, both carrying guns."

"Game hunters with rifles?"

"No. Men dressed in white, carrying submachine guns. One of them is Alfie Mayne."

Schreiber chuckled. "And the other is a big man in his thirties."

"Correct, sir."

"Will Cochrane and Mayne are coming here to have a chat with me about what I did to Betty." He smiled, removed his rimless glasses, and polished them with a silk handkerchief. "How many men do we have?"

"Now that the others have returned from the U.K., twenty-six."

He placed his glasses back on, and his smile vanished as he stared at his employee. "I would have thought that was more than enough to deal with this trivial matter. Kill Cochrane and Mayne; bring their bodies to me."

"Yes, sir."

The man was about to dash out of the room, but stopped when Schreiber jabbed a finger against the coffee table. "And if you *ever* come in here again without knocking, I'll ensure that *your* dead body is laid alongside those of the men you're about to kill."

After the guard left, Schreiber lifted two files. One of them contained the profiles of the men who'd been present at the Berlin meeting in 1995. Now that Dugan, Scott, and Ballinger had been sentenced and executed, Nikolai Dmitriev and Kurt Schreiber were the only surviving attendees of that meeting. One day that would change—he'd issue orders for Dmitriev to be located and killed. But for now, Dmitriev remained in protective custody, and in any case Schreiber needed to lay low. He didn't mind. Dugan had paid him fifty million dollars to oversee the activation of Kronos. And that meant he could stay off the radar for a long time.

He tossed the file into the fire and turned his attention to the second file. A file that was empty, and had only the letter *K* on its front. Kronos's failure to kill Dmitriev had utterly shocked Schreiber. If only he'd known the assassin had lost his touch, he'd have used one of the others for the job. But between Kronos's failure and Dmitriev's testimony, there was no time to do so. He sighed, thought about the fifty million, then smiled and threw the file into the fire. "Once, you were our finest. It appears that's no longer the case. Good luck living with that realization."

Will moved slowly up the narrow mountain road, Alfie right behind him. Both men held their machine guns high, ready to fire. All along the right of the twisting road was a thirty-yard-high vertical rock escarpment; to their left was the drop to the tranquil valley. They'd been walking for four miles. One mile ahead and high above them was their destination, appearing and disappearing with every bend in the road.

The icy air caused their breath to steam; their bodies were tense. They knew that at any moment they could be struck by a hail of gunfire.

Will glanced to his left. On the far side of the valley were more mountains. The closest was approximately eighteen hundred yards away. He wondered if that was where Kronos was waiting. It would give him perfect sight of Schreiber's residence, of the long road leading to it, and of Will and Alfie. What would the professional assassin be thinking as he looked at the two men cautiously making their way up the track? No doubt, he'd believe they were idiots. Or had a death wish.

Right now Will didn't care about death. Or life. All that mattered to him was getting Alfie in front of Schreiber. Sarah was right. It *was* his fault that Betty had died. He had to make amends for that, regardless of the consequences.

Alfie was breathing fast, but at no point had he slowed or complained. Instead, the ex-SAS soldier had kept silent, expertly covering the angles with his gun, working with Will so that both men could open fire with maximum impact when assaulted. Sheer determination and a desire to get his hands on Schreiber's throat were enough to keep the retiree moving along the steep road.

Will gestured for them to stop, and crouched down. "Around the next bend, we've got five hundred yards to reach the house. There's only one small bend to give us cover, but aside from that it's a kill zone."

Alfie's aching limbs throbbed as he crouched next to Will. "Okay, just give me a few seconds." He breathed in deeply several times, winced as he stood, patted one of his legs, and muttered to himself, "Five hundred yards and the house. That's all I need from you, old boys. After that, you can both fall off for all I care." He sucked in a big lungful of air, lifted his gun, and nodded. "Let's get it over with."

Kronos saw Cochrane and Alfie run from cover toward the house, their guns held high.

This was it.

Assault.

He swung his sniper rifle toward Schreiber's house. Men emerged from the castle, sprinting, all of them carrying assault rifles. He counted six, then eight, then fifteen. They were expertly moving down the road, taking turns covering each other while others advanced.

They opened fire.

Five hundred yards away, Cochrane and Alfie dived to the ground and returned fire.

Kronos placed his finger on the trigger.

"Move!" Will rolled sideways. Bullets ricocheted off the road, inches from their bodies, as Alfie and Will went right. They got to their feet and slammed their bodies flush against the escarpment. From across the valley, a heavy-caliber shot boomed. Then another, followed by a third. "That's it! We've got to get to the last bend while he's taking them down. Go!"

Will sprinted forward, firing his submachine gun, knowing that he was easily in range of the men's assault rifles and that his shorter-range bullets stood little chance of hitting them. Twelve men were spread out, four hundred yards ahead of him. One of them collapsed to the ground after a .50-caliber sniper round ripped half his head off his body. Will stopped, aimed, and sent controlled bursts toward the others.

Alfie ran past him as fast as he could, wheezing heavily, shooting as he continued onward, before stopping, throwing himself to the ground, and continuing to shoot at the hostiles. "Move!"

Will sprinted, just as Kronos fired two more shots and dropped two more men. The sound of gunfire was now deafening and almost continuous. Will raced past Alfie, reached the bend, and dived for cover as more bullets raced through the air where he'd just been. He glanced at Alfie, broke cover, and sent a sustained volley of machine gun fire at the remaining nine men. His bullets struck two men, who twisted and fell off the road down the mile-long drop into the valley. "Come on, Alfie! Now! Now!"

Alfie ran, his back screaming in pain from his exertions, toward the bend while Will continued firing long bursts toward their assailants from his exposed position.

Another boom from across the valley. Then two more.

Three men fell to the ground with holes the size of fists in their chests.

Alfie zigzagged toward Will. Just like he'd been taught to do by the regiment, though then he'd been able to move four times quicker. He reached the MI6 officer, who spun around, grabbed his jacket, and pulled them both to the cover of the bend's escarpment. Bullets slammed into chunks of rock and sent debris flying through the air two feet from their position.

Will swapped magazines, waited a few seconds, then swung out of the bend and fired five-round bursts at the four men, one hundred yards away. One of them flipped backward with a line of machine gun rounds across his upper body. Will sidestepped back into cover as the men returned fire, and glanced at Alfie. "Hundred and fifty yards to the house, three men left out there, let's wait."

. . .

Kronos inserted a new magazine, breathed in, exhaled half a lungful, held his breath, and squeezed the trigger. One mile away, his bullet ripped through a hostile's shoulder and exited through his face. He moved the rifle as the last two men started sprinting back toward the house, kept his sight's crosshairs two feet in front of one of the men, and fired. The round smashed the man's hipbone and ripped out half of his gut. His colleague was frantically trying to reach the house, moving erratically, keeping low. Kronos pulled the trigger. The .50-caliber projectile removed the lower half of one leg. The man fell prone, his screams audible from this distance, amplified by the valley and echoing over its contours. Kronos watched the man vainly trying to crawl over the remaining fifty yards of road in front of Schreiber's residence. He ignored him for the moment, focused on the front door, fired twice, and saw his antimateriel rounds knock the entrance partially off its hinges. After putting in a fresh clip, he returned his attention to the injured man, took aim, and turned his brain into pulp.

Will and Alfie stepped away from the bend. One hundred and fifty yards ahead of them was the imposing grand entrance to Schreiber's mountain residence. For the first few yards, they walked, their guns trained on the broken door, waiting for more men to spew out onto the road. Despite the icy mountain air, Will's body was covered in sweat. He could barely imagine what state Alfie's body was in.

"Gotta hope the German's got that door covered, 'cos we're screwed if he ain't."

Will's eyes were narrow as he kept the foresight of his MP5 trained on the entrance. Another .50-caliber bullet knocked the broken door flat onto the ground. Will moved his gun. "That's his answer. Watch the windows. Go, now!"

They jogged forward, gun sights searching for anyone who might fire at them from one of the ten windows on this side of the house.

Fifty yards.

No movement

Hundred yards.

Silence.

One hundred and twenty yards.

The top left window smashed. A man. Rifle. Will and Alfie fired. The hostile tumbled out of the window and thudded onto the ground.

They reached the entrance, Will moved flush against the wall to one side of it, Alfie the other.

Alfie slammed in a new magazine. "There'll be as many inside. Wish we 'ad them flash bangs, sunshine."

"Me too. If he wasn't using it before, Kronos will be switching to thermal now. We've got to keep some distance between us and the hostiles so he knows who we are. Take it slow."

Will spun into the doorway, his MP5 held at eye level. Alfie moved behind him. They entered Schreiber's residence.

"Mr. Schreiber! They've reached the house. Get to the back of the living room. I've got men outside the room. But for God's sake, stay down. Somewhere out there is a sniper. He's clearing a path for Cochrane and Mayne so that they can get here and kill you."

Schreiber smiled. "Make sure your men stay on the north side of the house, out of sight of the sniper. That way, it should be impossible for my two visitors to reach this room. But if they do, I'll talk to them and watch them walk away after leaving me untouched."

Will and Alfie kept low as they moved along the corridor, taking long strides and placing their feet flat on the red-carpeted floor in order not to bounce and move their weapons from their steady horizontal level.

The house had been tastefully decorated, with paintings and oil lamps covering the oak-paneled walls, and it was big—the corridor ran for seventy yards. Closed doors lined both sides. As they reached the first door, Alfie rotated and walked backward, ready to shoot anyone who burst out of the rooms. All was silent, though they knew that somewhere in the house would be armed men.

They reached the end of the corridor. Will lay on his front and quickly glanced around the corner. Getting to his feet, he cupped a hand around Alfie's ear. "Another corridor. Forty yards long. Two closed doors on the left. Big staircase halfway along on the right. No sight of any hostiles."

They turned the corner. Immediately, the door to the closest room opened and they caught a brief sight of an arm. It threw something toward them—a small object that was now rolling along the carpet.

Grenade.

Will sprinted forward, dropped low, scooped up the grenade, and tossed it back toward the open door. The explosive detonated as it reached the doorway, and shrapnel and blood smashed against the opposite wall.

Will moved forward, checked the room, saw two men's smashed bodies, and gestured for Alfie to follow him onward. They reached the second door. Will pointed at it and his weapon. Alfie understood the meaning of the gesture. Will raised three fingers, then two, then one. Both men stepped in front of the door and fired a sustained burst of machine gun fire through the wooden entrance. Will kicked the door open. One man was lying over a table with bullet holes in his throat and an eye socket. Another was slumped against a wall, his handgun discarded to one side, clutching his shoulder, his face screwed up in agony. Without hesitating, Will shot him in the chest and head.

They exited the room. Search the rest of this floor or move upstairs? Will took a step forward a split second before a shot rang out and grazed his shoulder. It had come from somewhere up the staircase. Though it could have killed him had he not moved, the shot had given him his answer. More armed men were upstairs to protect Schreiber. Momentarily wincing from the injury, Will raised his weapon and took slow steps toward the base of the stairwell. Alfie moved to his left and aimed his weapon to one side of the stairs. Will focused on the other side. They took another step. Three men appeared at the top of the stairs.

Will shot one of them.

Alfie another.

The third was knocked off his feet and slammed against a wall by a high-velocity sniper round.

Keeping their guns trained on the top of the stairs, they took one step at a time, paused, then another step.

Kronos watched Will and Alfie move cautiously up the stairs. His thermal imagery showed them as white figures; if they got too close to other men, he'd have difficulty distinguishing them. He scanned the top two floors. Previously, he'd seen momentary flashes of white on both floors—men moving quickly—but now there was nothing. Schreiber's guards had retreated to the rear of the building, putting too many walls between him and them to be spotted. His only hope was for Will and the older man to stay this side of the house and lure out the guards. He trained the crosshairs ahead of their steps and focused.

Halfway up the staircase, a corridor ran off down the center of the second floor. It was narrower than the first-floor corridor, though similarly contained closed rooms on either side. At the far end was a tall window giving a view of the Alps. Alfie got to his knee, aiming his weapon down the corridor. Will kept his gun pointing toward the top floor. They stayed like this for two minutes and saw no one.

Will whispered, "Think they're all on the third floor, rear of the house, out of sight of Kronos."

Alfie got to his feet. "Best we go and say hello, then."

There were twelve steps up to the third floor, covered by a luxurious carpet. At the top of the stairs, they could see a ceiling and the entrance to another corridor. They took two steps, waited in case armed men appeared or grenades were tossed down, and continued. Two more steps. Stop. Keep the guns trained ahead. Listen for any noise. Be ready to spin around in case they attack from below. Fingers on triggers at all times. Three steps. Keep breathing calmly even though hearts are pounding. Step, step, stop. The landing now fully visible and a few feet of the corridor. Step. Remember, they'll have the element of surprise. Step. And we don't know a fucking thing about the layout of the top floor. Step, step.

The corridor.

Different design from the others.

Wider.

Double oak doors seventy yards away at the other end.

Only two doors on the left of the corridor, both big, and one on the right.

To avoid detection by Kronos, the armed guards would either be behind the door at the end or in the room on the right.

Or they'd be in both of those places.

Alfie moved forward a few paces, keeping low, his MP5 at eye level, then stopped.

Will moved past him and stopped after a few paces.

They both got to their knees.

And waited.

Sweat dripped down Will's face as he kept his gun pointing at the door on the right. Alfie would have the end door covered.

Nothing happened.

Will frowned. Had they killed all the guards? Perhaps there was no longer any danger.

Chunks of brick and plasterboard raced across the corridor as hundreds of bullets ripped through the end of the right hand wall.

Will and Alfie dived to the ground as bullets came closer to their position. Within three seconds, the entire length of the corridor was being shot up by guards on the other side of the wall. Alfie crawled to Will, squinting to shield his eyes from dust. The noise was incredible, causing their ears to ring. As bullets raced inches above their prone bodies, both men were braced for death.

The firing stopped.

A second later, the door on the right swung open.

Stun grenades.

Shit, no!

Will and Alfie pulled their triggers as white light and deafening noise engulfed them.

Disorientation.

Can't see anything.

No idea what our bullets are hitting.

Kronos shot the first man who appeared in the entrance to the room. Two more tried to step over the body. He shot them both. Quickly, he changed magazines. The flashes of light he'd seen had almost certainly come from stun grenades, and that meant Cochrane and Alfie were blind for at least ten seconds. A shotgun-carrying guard forward-rolled into the corridor, expertly got to his knee, and took aim. Kronos fired, and the man's neck snapped. The assassin moved his crosshairs back over the entrance. Only one thought was in his mind.

You know I'm here, and I'll kill anyone who shows himself to me.

Will breathed deeply, nearly collapsed as he got to his knees, shook his head wildly, and grabbed Alfie. "Can you move? Think?"

"I . . ." Alfie blinked fast. His breathing was shallow. "Been . . . been a while since that's happened to me."

Will stood and helped his colleague to his feet. "Cover the end of the corridor. I've got to clear the room containing the hostiles."

Alfie shook his head. "Two-man job."

"No, Alfie. I . . ."

"Two-man job, and you know it!"

Will was about to respond, but Alfie walked ahead, his gun aiming at the first doorway.

Damn it, Alfie, don't!

He silently cursed as he moved quickly alongside Alfie. They stopped next to the entrance. Will thumped his chest and sliced a hand through the air to indicate that he'd be covering the center and right side of the room, that Alfie should cover the left and center of the room. They inserted fresh clips, Will looked at Alfie, both nodded, and they ran into the room.

Big room. Furniture. Target ahead. Fire. He's down. Change angles. Three more targets. They're firing. Stand still. One burst. Move. Two bursts. Targets down. Sector clear. Spin around. Alfie's sector. Two tangos left upright. Alfie drops one of them. Fire. Will drops the other. Move. Sweep room. Check behind cover. Tables, chairs, sofa, desks. Nothing.

Room clear.

Smoke and the smell of cordite hung in the air. Will ran to Alfie. "You okay?"

The retiree smiled. Close to his feet were four men, three of them killed by Alfie. Behind him were the bodies of the other three men killed by Will. "Told you. Two-man job."

Will was about to walk out of the room, then froze. How would Kronos know they weren't hostiles who'd killed their assailants? They could be shot the moment they stepped into the doorway. He looked at Alfie, who was motionless, staring at the entrance. Clearly he'd had exactly the same thought.

"This is a big call, son."

"A bloody big call." Will desperately tried to decide what to do.

. . .

Kronos tensed as he saw one man walk out of the room holding his gun with two hands high over his head. A shorter man followed him, also holding his weapon above his head. Clearly, both knew he was watching them through his rifle's sight. Their size matched that of Will and the old man, but he had no way of discerning their features. They could be Schreiber's men, trying to trick him.

He moved his finger over the trigger.

What to do?

If only he'd been able to keep Cochrane and his colleague in his sights.

Though only they could have killed the men in the room.

If he pulled the trigger, would he be rewarding them with death?

Or would he be avenging their deaths in the room?

What to do?

He kept the crosshairs in the center of the taller man, moving his rifle as the men walked slowly down the hallway. If the men in his sights were Cochrane and the older man, they now stood a good chance of killing Schreiber. But if the men were Schreiber's guards, they would protect their boss while summoning reinforcements. Almost certainly, they'd try to locate and assault Kronos while others got Schreiber to a car. Kronos would kill the guards, but by then Schreiber would be long gone. If that happened, and given today's assault on his life, Schreiber would almost certainly eschew all of his European safe houses in favor of relocating to a place that even Kronos didn't know about. He'd disappear for good.

The solution was clear.

As uncomfortable as it made him.

He had to kill the men in his sights.

He squeezed back on the trigger.

One more millimeter before a .50-caliber round was fired.

The big man and his older colleague still had their guns held up with outstretched arms, moving closer to the end of the corridor and the room containing Kurt Schreiber.

So easy to kill them.

Just one millimeter.

So easy.

Kronos thought about his story to his sons and their response after he finished the tale.

That can't be the end. The young eagle wouldn't be injured if the giant earthworm hadn't been so bad. And the eagle king needs to say sorry for hurting the younger eagle. The best way he can do that is to find the worm and allow the younger eagle to kill it.

Could he go home to his family and finish the story in the way he was now contemplating?

Kronos's finger was motionless.

Could he?

No.

Stefan eased off the trigger.

Had to have faith that the man in his crosshairs was Cochrane.

Had to give Mathias and Wendell an ending they deserved.

Even if that ending enabled the giant earthworm to escape forever.

Will stopped. The door at the end of the corridor was a few yards away. It was the only place Schreiber could be. Slowly, he lowered his arms and placed the butt of his submachine gun into his shoulder. He knew Kronos should have killed him; it was the logical thing to do. He wondered why the deadly assassin hadn't done so.

"This is for my Betty." Alfie pointed his gun at the oak doors.

"It is." Will walked forward, gripped the door handle, twisted it and pushed. Locked. He fired at the door hinges and lock, kicked the door away, then immediately slammed his body against the adjacent wall, expecting a hail of gunfire to come through the entrance.

All was silent.

He entered the room.

It was a big living room—floor-to-ceiling windows on two sides, leather sofas, armchairs, and coffee tables, a roaring fire, oak-paneled walls, paintings by German artists, and a bookshelf that segmented the room and ran down its entire length. At the far end of the room were glass sliding doors, beyond them a long balcony that overlooked the Alps and valley. In front of it was a large mahogany writing desk. A diminutive old man was sitting at the desk, wearing a suit and rimless spectacles.

Kurt Schreiber was still, looking calm. The bookshelf and walls shielded him from Kronos's sight.

He was looking directly toward Will and Alfie as they moved closer, their guns trained on him.

"Kurt Schreiber?" Will took three paces toward the man.

Schreiber smiled, his hands flat on the desk.

"Schreiber?"

Schreiber's eyes twinkled. "You know who I am and I know who you are."

Alfie ran forward, anger coursing through him.

"I wouldn't do that if I were you! Not unless you wish for more . . . death."

Alfie stopped. "You killed my wife."

Schreiber retained his smile. "Not me. She was executed by men who were acting on my precise instructions."

"You fucking . . ."

"If you kill me, someone else you both know will die."

"Shut up, you bastard!" Alfie made ready to fire.

But Will placed a hand over Alfie's gun. "Wait." He stared at Schreiber. "What do you mean?"

Schreiber glanced out of the window. "Do you like the view? It's so beautiful and tranquil." He returned his attention to Will and Alfie. "If you kill me, Sarah will be killed."

Will's stomach muscles tightened.

"Did you think I'd leave her alone while she started her idyllic new life in Edinburgh?" Schreiber shook his head. "That would have been a mistake, particularly as I anticipated that you'd come for me. She's being watched by men who won't hesitate to carry out my orders. I called them as soon as I heard you were approaching and told them that unless I phoned them back within an hour and told them I was safe, they were to use knives on her. And"—his smile broadened—"I told them that they could take their time with the task."

Will removed his hand from Alfie's gun. "Make that call!"

"That's a silly request. If I make the call, I'm dead."

"If you don't, you're dead!"

"You'd kill your own sister? Because that's what you'll be doing if you shoot me."

Will was motionless.

"He's bluffing." Alfie's face was full of anger.

Will slowly lowered his gun. "I don't think so."

Schreiber rubbed his hands. "Correct, Mr. Cochrane. I never bluff. Instead I calculate and strategize accordingly. I've lived my entire life that way." He stood. "If you let me walk out of here, nothing will happen to her."

"Liar! You've no interest in keeping Sarah alive."

Schreiber clicked his tongue. "You're smarter than that. If I kill her, I have no leverage over you. It's very much in my *interest* to keep her alive in order to keep you away."

"Someone else will get you. Your power's dwindling. Soon you'll have nowhere to hide."

Schreiber frowned. "Dwindling? On the contrary, my business is flourishing and expanding." His expression turned cold. "However, I concede that I can't hide from old age. Rübner's death was a bit of a setback, as I was grooming him to take over my projects. But it doesn't matter now, as I've found a replacement, a woman who's perhaps even more talented."

"Who?"

"None of your business." He glanced away. "Call off your sniper. Let me walk away. Sarah will live. It's as simple as that."

"Still think he's bluffing. We can't let him go, Will."

"I'm afraid you've no choice, Mr. Mayne. And Will Cochrane knows that." He moved around the desk. "Don't you?"

Will nodded.

"Bleedin' 'ell, Will. This can't be happening!"

Schreiber took two paces toward them. "Call off your sniper."

"Don't listen to him!"

"Call him off."

"Will?"

Will withdrew his cell phone and tapped numbers on the keypad.

"Don't do it, Will!"

He held the phone to his face and spoke. "If I touch him, Schreiber will kill my sister. We've lost. Get right away from here. Don't touch Schreiber." He closed the phone.

"Jesus!"

Will glanced at Alfie. "Trust me, I'm sure he's not bluffing."

Schreiber pointed a frail finger at him. "If that was a dummy call, my men will follow my orders."

"I made the call, he listened, and he will follow *my* orders." Will nodded. "You're free to go."

Schreiber nodded. "Very well." He picked up his walking stick, moved across the room, passed Will and Alfie, and turned to face them when he reached the door. "Gentlemen, I do hope we never meet again."

"We won't." Will sighed. "What does it feel like?"

"What?"

"Being someone capable of orchestrating genocide."

Schreiber shrugged. "It feels just fine. But the bigger question you should be asking yourself is, how does it make *you* feel letting someone like me go?" He laughed and walked out of the room.

Will and Alfie stood still, silent.

They stayed like this for one minute.

Alfie shook his head, felt utter disbelief. "You're certain he wasn't bluffing about Sarah?"

"Yes."

"In that case, you made the right call, son. *Bloody hell*—we had him bang to rights, but the devious bastard was one step ahead of us."

Will moved to the large window and looked at the mountain road winding down the ridge toward the valley. Alfie joined him. Will smiled. "He's not the only devious bastard."

Kurt Schreiber exited the mountain residence, walking down the road toward the garages. As he passed the bodies of his men, his thoughts turned to his business empire. He'd need a new base of operations and more men, and would need to spend time with his new deputy so that he could groom her to take on day-to-day responsibilities for his activities while he kept a low profile.

He grinned. So many people involved in the Slingshot project had failed.

Dugan and the other conspirators.

Dmitriev, who was now living in fear that one day Schreiber would order his assassination.

Kronos.

And Will Cochrane and his colleagues.

The only man to walk away with anything to show for his involvement was Kurt Schreiber.

He pulled out car keys and hobbled down the road, ensuring that he took in all of his beautiful surroundings. This was the last time he'd come here. He'd miss this place.

Still, he'd never been a man to look back. Instead, he'd always embraced fresh beginnings.

The .50-caliber bullet smashed through his upper torso. After he collapsed to the ground, another removed his head.

. . .

Kronos stripped the sniper rifle down to its working parts, quickly slotted them into their compartments, shut the case, and walked back down the mountain. He wondered why Cochrane had let Schreiber walk out of the house. One explanation was that the two men he'd had in his sights were not Cochrane and the older man, rather were Schreiber's guards. But if that was the case, why would they have let Schreiber expose himself to Kronos's thermal imagery? No, the men in Schreiber's room had to have been Cochrane and the older man. For some reason they couldn't pull the trigger, so they did the next best thing and persuaded Schreiber that the sniper would not harm him when he left. Goodness knows how Cochrane had done that.

He could have shot the former Stasi colonel as soon as he spotted him leaving the living room. Instead he'd waited until Schreiber had exited the house, so that he could switch off his thermal imagery. He'd wanted to see Schreiber's face clearly through his sights. One last time. Before he shot the man who'd inspired Slingshot, ordered him to kill Dmitriev, and insisted that he leave his family after the assassination in Holland.

Stefan smiled. Thanks to Schreiber, his family was five million dollars richer. But that wasn't why he was smiling. Tonight he'd be back home, sitting around the kitchen table with his twin sons and his wife. He cherished every moment he had with his beloved family. And tonight would be special, because he'd be able to tell them the rest of the story.

Hidden from view outside the property, Mikhail Salkov watched Sarah and James unpacking boxes within their new Scottish home. They were moving back and forth between the rooms, completely oblivious to the danger that had been surrounding them.

He looked at the countryside around him. The house was isolated, though Edinburgh was only five miles away. His family home was similar. Located a few miles outside of Moscow, it gave his wife and daughters the chance to get their fixes of both city and country living. He hoped Sarah and James gained happiness living here.

He looked at the dead man by his feet, then lifted and threw him on top of the three other bodies in the trunk of his SUV. Thank goodness he hadn't needed to be here two weeks ago. Then, he'd still needed a walking stick to aid his injured leg. Fully fit, he was able to observe Schreiber's surveillance team for hours before receiving the call from Cochrane.

The MI6 officer had anticipated Schreiber's ploy to use Sarah as leverage if Will succeeded in infiltrating his Bavarian residence and came face-to-face with the man. For weeks, he'd had other men watching Sarah and Schreiber's team. The British Special Forces men were under orders to act if Sarah was threatened, but Will knew that they'd never agree to a cold-blooded hit on U.K. soil. He needed a ruthless, deniable expert for that. So today he'd ordered his men to leave and had asked Mikhail to take care of matters if required to do so. The call would be the trigger, the wording precise and intended to mislead Schreiber.

If I touch him, Schreiber will kill my sister. We've lost. Get right away from here. Don't touch Schreiber.

It meant, kill the men watching my sister.

He'd been surprised that Cochrane had given him the task, though he had quickly concluded that it was Cochrane's way of saying that he trusted the SVR spycatcher because he'd broken rules by not taking Lenka Yevtushenko back to Russia. If he ever met Cochrane again, he hoped it would be in circumstances that allowed them to remain allies. One never knew in this line of work.

He slammed the trunk shut and got into the vehicle. He had a long drive ahead of him to reach the deserted woodland where the bodies would be buried. After that, he could finally go home.

SIXTY-FOUR

The taxi stopped on the long residential street in Minsk. Will told the driver to wait and turned to the man sitting next to him in the rear of the vehicle. "I promised her that I'd bring you home. In return, I want you to give me your word that you'll have nothing more to do with intelligence work, will get a job in one of the local universities or schools, will never return to Russia, will stay with Alina and Maria for the rest of your life."

Lenka Yevtushenko nodded slowly. "I give you my word, but it's not a difficult thing to do because I want all of those things more than anything else."

Will handed Lenka a grocery bag. Inside were the ingredients to make *kotleta pokrestyansky*, the meal that Alina had promised to one day make for Will. "You've been apart for quite some time. There's nothing like cooking a meal together to break the ice." He smiled. "You caused a lot of trouble by stealing that piece of paper."

Lenka opened the door. "You mean pieces of paper."

"What?"

"Pieces of paper. Schreiber instructed me to steal twenty of them. Only one had a partial grid reference on it. The other nineteen were full codes. When I was held at the farmstead, the guards spoke openly about it. I guess they believed I was a dead man so didn't care what I heard. Schreiber needed backup options in case Kronos had died during the last twenty years, or was no longer fit to conduct the assassination."

"He had the ability to activate nineteen other sleeper assassins?"

Lenka nodded. "Kronos was his preferred choice for the assassination of Dmitriev, because he was the very best. In any case, Schreiber was of the view that the other assassins would still be of value to him because he could use them to kill anyone who tried to go after him at some point in the future." He bowed his head. "If only I'd known the true value of what I'd stolen."

He exited the vehicle, shut the door, and walked to the front entrance of Alina's apartment building. Within one minute, Alina and baby Maria were there. Alina threw one arm around Lenka and pulled him close to her. She was shaking with sobs. They stayed in their embrace for minutes before speaking inaudible words. Alina looked at Will. She gave the slightest smile, kept her eyes on him, then turned and took her partner and her child into their home.

Will sat motionless.

Staring at other people's happy lives, with no idea how to become like them.

No hope of becoming like them.

He told the driver that he'd decided to walk back to the city center, thrust cash at him, and got out of the car. Tomorrow he'd be in London. He'd report to Alistair that Schreiber's anonymous female successor had nineteen other sleeper assassins who could be activated if Will or others tried to destroy Schreiber's empire.

That wouldn't stop Will Cochrane.

He'd never stop.

Until he was killed.

Snow began to fall.

Spartan buttoned up his overcoat and walked along the empty street.

Alone.

GLOSSARY

ABW—Agencja Bezpieczeństwa Wewnetrznego. Poland's domestic security agency. It is responsible for preventing threats to Poland from terrorism, organized crime, and foreign espionage.

AIVD—The General Intelligence and Security Service. Holland's secret service, with responsibility for combating nonmilitary domestic threats.

AW—Agencja Wywiadu. Poland's intelligence agency, tasked with gathering secret intelligence from abroad.

Barrett M82 point fifty caliber antimateriel sniper rifle—A semiautomatic antimateriel rifle, developed by the American Barrett Firearms Manufacturing Company. The rifle has an effective range of up to two thousand yards.

BfV—Bundesamt für Verfassungsschutz. Germany's domestic intelligence and security agency, equivalent to Britain's MI5 and the United States' FBI.

Browning Hi-Power 9 mm handgun—One of the most widely used military pistols of all time, having been used by the armed forces of over fifty countries. The magazine holds thirteen rounds and is an excellent close-quarter weapon. However, it is heavy and has a strong recoil, making it less effective compared to the lighter and more accurate models made by Glock, Sig Sauer, and Heckler & Koch, for example.

CIA—Central Intelligence Agency. The United States' overseas intelligence agency, tasked primarily with gathering intelligence from foreign human sources as well as conducting special operations.

Coldstream Guards—Part of the Guards Division, it is one of the elite Foot Guards regiment of the British Army.

DA—Defense attaché. Typically, a high-ranking serving military officer who is attached to one of his or her country's overseas embassies. DAs are tasked with interacting with the embassy's host country on a range of military matters, including military procurement.

Delta Force—Alongside DEVGRU, the United States' primary antiterrorist special operations unit, though, like DEVGRU, it is deployable in all covert and overt theaters of war and operating environments.

DEVGRU—U.S. Naval Special Warfare Development Group, popularly known by its previous name, SEAL Team 6. It is one of the United States' premier multifunctional special operations units and draws its recruits from other SEAL units.

DGSE—Direction Générale de la Sécurité Extérieure. France's overseas intelligence agency, tasked primarily with gathering intelligence from foreign human sources as well as conducting special operations.

DIA—Defense Intelligence Agency. A member of the U.S. Intelligence Community, DIA is the primary agency tasked with producing military intelligence for the United States Department of Defense.

DLB—Dead-letter box. A method of espionage tradecraft that allows one spy to pass an item, using a secret location, to another spy without their having to meet.

DSI—Dienst Speciale Interventies, or Special Intervention Service, is an elite law enforcement unit formed in 2006 to protect Dutch society from the threats of terrorism. Experts in dealing with complex situations, such as hostage taking and aircraft hijacking, the unit comprises superbly trained police snipers and Special Forces personnel from the UIM.

DSR-50 sniper rifle—A bolt-action antimateriel rifle, developed and marketed by DSR-precision GmbH of Germany. The weapon fires .50 rounds.

FN P90 submachine gun—A selective fire personal defense weapon (PDW) designed and manufactured by FN Herstal in Belgium. It was designed as a compact yet powerful weapon for law enforcement and military personnel operating in confined environments, such as vehicles and ships, as well as special forces and counterterrorism units.

FSB—Federal Security Service of the Russian Federation. The main domestic security agency of Russia, comparable to the FBI and MI5.

GCHQ—Government Communications Headquarters. The British intelligence agency responsible for providing signals intelligence (SIGINT) to the U.K. government and armed forces. Comparable to the United States' National Security Agency (NSA).

GCP—Groupement des Commandos Parachutistes. A highly trained reconnaissance unit of the French Foreign Legion's Parachute Regiment (2ème Régiment Étranger de Parachutistes).

Glock 17 pistol—A semiautomatic handgun, designed and produced in Austria.

GRU—Glavnoye Razvedyvatel'noye Upravleniye. The foreign military intelligence directorate of the general staff of the Armed Forces of the Russian Federation.

Head of Station—The most senior member of an intelligence organization's overseas station. Typically, but not exclusively, operating out of the country's embassies, stations can contain as few as one intelligence officer or as many as twenty or thirty personnel.

Heckler & Koch MK23 handgun—One of the favored handguns of special operations units in the United States' Special Operations Command. It is a semiautomatic pistol and fires .45 ACP rounds.

Heckler & Koch MP5 submachine gun—A 9 mm German automatic weapon, and one of the most widely used submachine guns in the world. Very popular with military, law enforcement, intelligence, and security organizations.

HMG—Her Majesty's Government of the United Kingdom of Great Britain and Northern Ireland.

ICC—International Criminal Court. A permanent tribunal established to prosecute individuals for genocide, crimes against humanity, and crimes of aggression. The court's official seat is in The Hague, Netherlands, though it can conduct legal proceedings elsewhere.

ISA—Intelligence Support Activity. One of the United States' four tier-1 Special Missions Units, alongside Delta Force, DEVGRU, and the air force's 24th Special Tactics Squadron. Its primary role is to obtain actionable intelligence in advance of missions conducted by Delta or DEVGRU, for example.

14th Intelligence Company—Also known as "The Det," the highly classified British military unit was expert at surveillance in hostile locations. Used extensively from the 1970s onward, it targeted Irish Republican and Loyalist paramilitary groups. The unit has since been disbanded and its duties have been taken over by the newly established and globally deployable Special Reconnaissance Regiment.

IO—Intelligence Officer.

KGB—Komitet Gosudarstvennoy Bezopasnosti, or Committee for State Security. It was the national security agency of the Soviet Union from 1954 until 1991 and was the premier internal security, intelligence, and secret police organization during that time.

Life Guards Regiment—The senior regiment of the British Army and part of the Household Cavalry.

M4A1 assault rifle—A fully automatic variant of the standard M4 carbine, the M4A1 is favored by most U.S. special operations units. Due to its compactness and firepower, the rifle is an excellent close-quarter counterterrorist weapon.

MACV-SOG—Military Assistance Command, Vietnam/Studies and Observations Group. A highly classified U.S. special operations unit that conducted covert unconventional warfare prior to and during the Vietnam War.

MI5—The British domestic intelligence agency, equivalent to the United States' FBI, though MI5 officers have no powers of arrest.

MI6—Secret Intelligence Service (SIS). Britain's overseas intelligence agency, tasked primarily with gathering intelligence from foreign human sources as well as conducting special operations.

Mossad—Institute for Intelligence and Special Operations. Israel's overseas intelligence agency, tasked primarily with gathering intelligence from foreign human sources as well as conducting special operations.

MP-443 handgun—A Russian military- and police-issue pistol. It is a semiautomatic gun with a magazine containing seventeen 9 mm rounds.

National Clandestine Service (NCS)—The clandestine arm of the CIA, it has responsibility for the collection of intelligence from primarily foreign human assets based overseas and special operations.

NOC—Non-Official Cover. The cover used by intelligence officers who cannot be seen to have any official links to their government. Unlike officers who pose as diplomats and therefore can receive diplomatic immunity if they are caught spying in a country, NOCs have no such safety net and, if caught, face imprisonment or execution. Because of this threat, NOCs are handpicked for recruitment and given extensive further training. [Note author's biography.]

NSA—National Security Agency. The United States' agency responsible for providing signals intelligence (SIGINT) to the U.S. government and armed forces.

PB 6P9 handgun—A Russian silenced pistol, developed for Spetsnaz and intelligence agencies.

PE4—A plastic explosive used by the British military. Like C4, it is a cream-colored solid, can be molded into any shape, is very stable, and can only be detonated by a combination of extreme heat and a shockwave, such as a detonator. PE4 has a greater velocity of detonation compared to C4.

Q Departments—Various paramilitary, surveillance, technical, and logistical departments within MI6 that support the activities of intelligence officers.

Remington 870 shotgun—A U.S. manufactured pump-action shotgun, widely used by law enforcement and military organizations throughout the world.

Rome Statute—The Rome Statute of the International Criminal Court was the treaty that established the court. Adopted at a diplomatic conference in Rome in 1998, the statute established the court's functions, jurisdiction, and structure. The court entered into force in 2002. At time of print, 121 countries are State Parties to the Rome Statute.

Royal Marines—The primary commando force of the United Kingdom. Formed in 1755, the force was initially solely an amphibious infantry unit. Though it is still under the command of the Royal Navy, it is now recognized as one of the world's leading combat units in all other combat spheres including air, desert, arctic, and jungle.

Safe House—Residential or commercial properties owned or rented by intelligence agencies and used for covert meetings, surveillance, interrogations, and other matters.

SAM—Surface to Air Missile.

SAR—Search & Rescue vessels belonging to Poland's coastal fleets.

SAS—Special Air Service. The world's oldest, most experienced, and arguably most effective special operations unit, the British SAS is regarded as the benchmark for all tier-1 units and special forces around the world.

SBS—Special Boat Service. A U.K. special forces unit, directly comparable to the United States' DEVGRU (SEAL Team 6), though the SBS is older and more experienced. Recruitment and selection into the SBS are considered even tougher than entry into the renowned SAS.

SEALs—Sea, Air, Land teams. U.S. special operations personnel who can operate in any combat environment. Highly trained and very effective.

Sig Sauer P226 handgun—In service with numerous military and law enforcement units worldwide, the Swiss-designed and German-manufactured weapon has many variants. Due to its superb resistance to extreme conditions and excellent accuracy, it has become the preferred handgun for SEALs personnel.

SOG—Special Operations Group. The paramilitary wing of the CIA's Special Activities Division. Many members are drawn from Delta Force and DEVGRU.

Spartan Program—The twelve-month-long selection program for premier MI6 officers in which they attempt to attain the code name "Spartan." Only one officer at a time is allowed to endure the program, and only one successful trainee is allowed to carry the code name until his death or retirement.

Spartan Section—The highly secretive joint MI6/CIA unit that supports the Spartan MI6 officer.

Spetsnaz—The generic term for Russian special forces. The Russian army, navy, GRU, and SVR all have Spetsnaz units attached to them and under their command. They are wholly separate units. For example, Spetsnaz Alpha (SVR) is a completely different unit from Spetsnaz Vympel (GRU), and recruitment, selection, and training follow different paths.

SSCI—Senate Select Committee on Intelligence. An organization created in 1976 after Congress had investigated CIA operations on U.S. soil and established that some had been illegal. The SSCI comprises fifteen senators who are drawn from the major political parties and whose remit includes oversight of U.S. intelligence activities and ensuring transparency between the intelligence community and Congress.

Stasi—The Ministry for State Security was East Germany's official state security service. Headquartered in East Berlin, the Stasi was one of the world's most effective and ruthless intelligence and security agencies.

SVR—Sluzhba Vneshney Razvedki. Russia's primary overseas intelligence agency, comparable to Britain's MI6 and the United States' CIA.

UIM—Unit Interventie Mariniers. A Dutch special forces unit that specializes in counterterrorism missions. Able to operate inside and outside the Netherlands, the unit is expert at direct action, surveillance, and maritime operations.

USP .45 Tactical pistol—A semiautomatic handgun designed and manufactured by Heckler & Koch in Germany. Incorporating an excellent recoil reduction mechanical system, the weapon is able to fire the powerful .45 rounds with superb accuracy. Given this, and its resilience to harsh conditions, the handgun and other USP variants are very popular with special forces and elite law enforcement units.

Vauxhall Cross—An area of south London, adjacent to the river Thames and home to the headquarters of MI6.

ACKNOWLEDGMENTS

To Jon Wood and the team at Orion (U.K.), David Highfill and the team at William Morrow/HarperCollins (U.S.), Luigi Bonomi and Alison and the rest of the team at LBA, Judith, and the Secret Intelligence Service (MI6).